MAFIA LUST

L. STEELE

FOR THOSE WHO LOVE POSSESSIVE, MORALLY GRAY, ALPHAHOLES

1

"For where thou art, there is the world itself, And where thou art not,
desolation"
(Henry VI Part 2 – Act 3, Scene 2)

JJ

"You motherfucker." Sinclair Sterling, my host for the evening—though
he doesn't know it yet— draws himself up to his full height. Anger
thrums off of him. "The fuck are you doing in my house?" The muscles
of his neck tighten. He draws back his arm, and his fist connects with
the face of the man standing opposite him.

The man who's as tall, as broad, and is dressed in a dark black suit which could be the twin to Sinclair's camel-colored one. The man who's as powerful as Sinclair in every way, for he's the leader of the *Cosa Nostra*. The man who barely flinches as he absorbs the blow, then shakes his head.

A collective gasp runs through the assembled crowd. Michael's shoulders bunch. Tension leaps off of him. The hair on the back of my neck rises.

"Oh, fuck." I take a step back. Not that I'm a coward, but any moment now I expect the Don to pull out his gun and empty it into Sinclair's head. Instead, Michael Sovrano raises his hands.

What the—? I've never seen the most powerful man of the underground crime scene in Europe make a conciliatory gesture, especially when he was provoked. Sure, Michael is going legit but he's still the leader of a lethal Mafia clan. Their reach extends to corners that Sinclair's never could. Sinclair plays on the right side of the law, but you don't become number one on the Rich List in Europe without cutting more than a few corners.

Of course, since Michael and his brothers have gotten married, the mindset of the *Cosa Nostra* has changed. From being focused on growing their prowess in the underworld, they have transitioned to moving their businesses into legitimate entities. Something I whole-heartedly support. Turns out, making money by legal means involves jumping through as many hoops and cutting corners as you'd do leading an organized crime syndicate. I should know.

For the past few years, not only have I run the Kane company, the foremost crime organization in the UK, but I've also moved many of its dealings to the Kane Corporation, the lawful business I incorporated. A thriving business for which I am the CEO. The position by any other name is the same. You're the leader, the visionary, the person who sees the big picture. The one who connects the dots, forges alliances, and on occasion, brokers peace. Where I get my cut, of course. Which is why I'm here. Not that either of these men know it yet. All the better. The situation plays in my favor, putting me in a position of strength. I couldn't have planned it better.

"Get off my property—" Sinclair reaches for his inside pocket.

I step forward. "I wouldn't do that if I were you."

Sinclair jerks his chin in my direction. "JJ Kane." His frown deepens. "The fuck do you want?"

"I know you didn't invite me. However, I do think you'll be happy that I stepped in."

"You with this bastard?" Sinclair nods in Michael's direction.

"I'm not with either of you, ol' chap. I'm like Switzerland. Bloody neutral and all that."

Sinclair frowns.

Next to me, Michael glowers.

"Sinclair." The petite woman with pink threaded through her hair standing next to Sterling tugs on his sleeve. "Sin, stop. He's my sister's husband."

Sinclair's shoulders bunch. His features still wear that expression of fury. Then he turns his head in his wife's direction and his gaze softens. "Summer—" He frowns. "This man… He's responsible for everything that happened to me and the rest of the Seven."

Of course, he's referring to the rest of his friends with whom he runs 7A Investments, the leading financial services company on this side of the pond.

Summer's eyelids flicker. She looks past Sinclair to where Michael's wife—her sister—stands with her hands over her belly. Summer's gaze widens. She steps around her husband, who moves with her to block her approach. It's a stance of extreme protectiveness. Interesting. In the little time I've known Sterling as a business associate, I've only seen his work face. This is Sterling as a husband. A protective husband. It's also an angry, pissed-off man who's trying to come to terms with his past. A past I have details to because… I never do business with a person unless I have investigated him thoroughly.

"Sin, please." Summer tugs on his sleeve. "I haven't seen my sister in months. Please, I need to go to her now."

Sinclair hesitates, then steps aside. Summer moves at the same time as Michael's wife, her sister. The two women embrace.

"Karma," Summer breathes. "I missed you so much."

Karma sniffs. "Me, too. I'm so sorry I didn't stay in touch properly all these months."

"I was worried sick about you. One cryptic message from you that you had a new boyfriend and you were going to Sicily with him, and I don't see you for months. Months, Karma. How could you do that?" She steps back and searches her sister's features. "You are okay, though. Aren't you? You're safe. Not hurt or anything?"

Next to Karma, Michael shuffles his feet. His arms are loose at his sides, but his fingers are poised in readiness. Opposite him, Sterling's stance, too, is one of alertness. The two men glare at each other. The air between them thrums with tension.

Behind Sterling, his friends—I count five more of the Seven—are poised to jump to his defense at the first sign of trouble. Considering we're on the lawn of his house, where his friend has just gotten married, it's fair to say we're in his territory. A dangerous place for his enemy to be, and without backup. Which is the situation Sovrano is in. Although, knowing him, his brothers can't be far off. Which makes this situation worse than a football stadium packed with hooligans where the visitors won.

"I'm fine." Karma once more places her hands over her stomach. Summer glances down at her gesture, then back at Karma's face. "Karma." She swallows. "Are you—?"

Karma nods.

Summer's features break into a big smile. "Oh, wow." She squeezes her sister's hand. "So am I," she whispers.

"No way." Karma gapes, then her features crumple, and her voice cracks. "I'm so... so very sorry I didn't keep in touch. It's my fault we lost so much time."

"We have so much to catch up on." Summer sniffles. She turns to Michael and holds out her hand. "I'm Summer Sinclair, Karma's sister. Welcome to the family."

Sinclair makes a choking sound.

A ripple of something seems to run through the rest of the crowd. If the tension had crackled before, now it seems to press down on all gathered. A cold fog of fury gathers speed and coils in on itself. The blood thuds at my pulse points, and all of my senses go on alert. I need to step in before someone takes a wrong step, and it starts a shit storm of tsunami proportions. Not that it'd matter to me. If the Seven and the Sovrano brothers—who also happen to be seven in total—is that a coincidence? —engage in an all-out war, the winner would be... You guessed it; yours truly.

It would work neatly to my benefit. Except I'm here at Sovrano's request. Also, because Karma personally asked me to help broker a deal with the Seven. It's the only way for her to be reunited with her sister. And apparently, chivalry isn't dead. At least, where I'm concerned.

Michael glances down at Summer's proffered hand. Sinclair tenses. The tendons on his throat stand out.

Behind Sinclair, his friends tense further. The apprehension in the space ratchets up. My nerves stretch to their breaking point, but I don't move. Neither do the men. Not even Michael. Everyone seems to be holding their collective breath when the sound of barking cuts through the tense atmosphere. The thud of paws on grass reaches us, then a small bundle of dogginess shoots out from behind Sinclair. The puppy brushes past Summer and comes to a halt in front of Michael. It glances up at the big man and pants. The animal wags its tail so hard, it threatens to fall off. It woofs again, then leaps up to plant its paws on Michael's pant leg. Every muscle in Michael's body seems to go rock hard. His gaze narrows on the puppy. Sinclair steps forward. Summer draws in a sharp breath. Then the Don bends and rubs the puppy above his nose.

The little fella closes his eyes in ecstasy and pushes into his hand. Michael scratches the dog behind his ears, and the dog pants loudly. Then begins to hump Michael's leg.

Michael freezes, a look of shock on his face.

Karma chuckles.

Summer snorts.

Sinclair's face reddens. "Down boy. Here Max. What's wrong with you?"

"Umm..." Summer chortles, then seems to get a hold of herself. "Darling, I did say it was time to get him neutered."

Both Michael and Sinclair wince at the same time. A look of comical horror is mirrored on their features. They exchange glances. Then Sinclair grabs the puppy and lifts him. Max turns his attention to Sinclair and licks his mouth.

"Enough." Sinclair moves his face to the side, and Max licks his cheek, his ear. Sterling finally manages to pry the puppy off of himself and places him on the ground. Max barks again, then sits his butt on the ground and whines.

A slightly frazzled Sinclair pulls out his handkerchief and wipes his face.

Meanwhile, Michael finally clasps Summer's still extended hand. He lowers his head and kisses her knuckles. "My wife's sister is my own sister. I pledge the loyalty of the *Cosa Nostra* to you, and by extension" —he glances at Sinclair— "to your family."

2

JJ

"Well, isn't this civilized?" I pour 24-year-old Macallan into three tumblers, then slide two across the counter.

Neither Sinclair nor Michael—now sporting a black eye—make a move to reach for theirs.

After the puppy successfully defused the tension outside, the women hugged each other again. Summer insisted that Michael and Karma come inside their house. Sterling didn't look happy, but he didn't protest, either. He glanced over his shoulder, and his friends nodded, a palpable air of relief running through the crowd. Muscles relaxed. Jaws unclenched. The men didn't take their gazes off of Michael but they also didn't seem like they were going to throw up their fists at the least provocation. The reception was being held at the Sterling's home in honor of the newlyweds. Everyone followed Summer and Karma into the house. The sisters decided to catch up while the others partook of refreshments of the liquid kind from Sterling's substantial bar. I suggested to the two men that we adjourn to a more suitable location, like Sterling's study, for instance, where we could address the elephant in the room, i.e., Michael's connection to Sinclair's past.

They agreed.

Sinclair didn't seem happy about the fact that I asked to see the inside of his study, but fuck that. Now that the drama has been defused, my interest in the proceedings has waned somewhat. I came with the intention of brokering a deal, but apparently, all it took was the prospect of a puppy losing his balls for the most lethal of men to begin to see sense. On the other hand, the prospect of losing the family jewels is enough for any man to break out in a cold sweat.

I raise my glass of whiskey. "Should we drink to the start of a beautiful relationship?"

Sinclair snorts.

Michael glowers. "It's eleven-fucking-a.m.," he says through gritted teeth.

"It's 5 o'clock somewhere. Besides, the two of you need to chill before you burst a coronary." I curve my lips.

"At your advanced age, I'd say you're the more likely candidate for cardiac arrest," Sinclair scoffs.

"I only have fifteen years on you, ol' chap, and ten on you, I believe," I retort as I nod in Michael's direction.

He firms his lips. "How the fuck do you know so much about us?"

"The same way you know so much about me. Let's not waste each other's time. None of us would be alone in a room with the other if we didn't know exactly who we were dealing with."

Both stay quiet. The silence continues for a beat. Another. I sniff the whiskey in my tumbler.

"A word of advice? Never take your anger out on the whiskey, ol' chaps." I glance between them. Neither makes a move. "No?" I shrug. "Your loss." I raise my glass. "Cheers, or as my old man would say, Cheers to *Debeers*." I take a swig of the whiskey and the notes of aged oak and spices permeate my senses. "Hmm," I sniff at my drink appreciatively. "Nothing like aged Macallan to cast a golden glow on all that I survey."

"Do you always talk like that—like you're in a bad British sitcom?" Michael murmurs.

"There are no bad Brit situational comedies, ol' chap. Only cleverly executed, extremely witty, banter-filled shows. Perhaps you were referring to the piss-poor American versions of what passes for comedy programs?"

Sinclair whistles. "I'll drink to that."

"You do realize my loyalties lie with both Uncle Sam and my motherland?" Michael says slowly.

"Given you speak with an American accent, I'd assume no less." I smirk.

"Unfortunately, the Brit sense of humor is the only thing I respect about your culture," he retorts.

"You mean you're not an aficionado of traditional British pub grub, or an eager participant of our quiz nights, or for that matter, the sportsmanship qualities of a game of five-day cricket matches."

Sinclair winces. "Five-day matches? My grandfather, if I recollect, would faithfully attend them at Lords. Me personally? I'm all for the Twenty20 format of the game."

"Cheap entertainment." I wave my hand in the air. "Five-day matches are the true test of an athlete's mettle."

"Or patience," Sinclair coughs.

"Hold on, you mean to say there are cricket matches that go on for five days?" Michael looks at me like I said I cut my pasta with a knife.

"A true gentleman's game." I smirk.

"You're talking to someone for whom football is as sacred as the Santa Maria herself. I am, after all, Italian—"

"But with American sensibilities," I remind him.

"I attended university in the US." Michael raises a shoulder. "But I'm not here to talk about myself or the Brits' strange taste in sports, am I?" He glances between us.

Sinclair swirls the whiskey in his tumbler. "While I'm with you on the footy, I take umbrage at your questioning our tastes—"

"Or lack thereof," Michael mutters.

"Heard you, ol' chap," Sinclair drawls.

"Wasn't trying to hide my words, *ol' chap*." Michael's lips curl.

"Children, children." I lean forward. "As Michael alluded to, we're here not to insult each other's cultures. Personally, I have no issue with it, but could you do that on your own time? The quicker we can find a middle ground here, the quicker I can leave."

"Getting late for you, old man?" Sinclair makes a show of glancing at his watch. "Time for your *Horlicks* and silk slippers in front of the fire?"

"Horlicks?" I stare.

"Horlicks?" Michael lowers his eyebrows over his nose.

"It's a malted drink favored by children and senior citizens," Sinclair explains.

I scoff. "Your insults are a clear sign that you're envious of my position in life."

"And what might that be?" Sinclair drawls.

"Experienced enough to know when I need to forge an alliance with the enemy."

Silence descends. The men narrow their gazes on each other.

"It's not enough." Sinclair tightens his fingers around his glass. "You think you can come in here and swear your loyalty to me and my friends and wipe out everything that happened?"

Michael's jaw flexes. A nerve pops at his temple. "Let me make one thing clear." He leans forward on the balls of his feet. "What my father did to you and your friends" —he holds Michael's gaze— "was wrong. Nothing I and my brothers can say or do will ever make it up to you."

When Sinclair and his friends were school boys, they were kidnapped by Michael's father and his associate. Yes, I know everything about both of these men, right down to their sexual preferences. I never do business, legal or otherwise, with anyone unless I have them thoroughly researched. So, did I know that Michael's father kidnapped the Seven? Let's just say, it's my business to see patterns where others normally don't. I'd suspected it, but even I couldn't say with confidence that Sovrano Sr. was the responsible party. Not until now, when Michael admits it.

Sinclair's features harden. The muscles on his neck stand out in relief. His jaw moves. He's so tightly wound; I'd be surprised if he hasn't already cracked a molar.

"You have the gall to walk into my house and confess to your father's sins?"

"I am not my father. It's why I'm here." Michael widens his stance. "That, and the fact that Karma wants to spend time with her sister. Much as I'd like to deny it, the reality is that we are linked by family. For the sakes of our wives, we don't have a choice but to find a peaceful resolution."

Sinclair's expression grows even more resentful. "If I didn't know better, I'd think you planned it this way."

Michael drags his fingers through his hair. "When I kidnapped Karma—"

"—the fuck?" Sinclair moves so quickly, his glass turns over. He grabs Michael by his collar and hauls him to his feet. "You kidnapped her?"

Michael glances down at where Sinclair's fingers are fisted in the front of his shirt. He raises his gaze to Sinclair's face. The men exchange looks of anger and hatred, tinged with frustration. I lean forward to intervene, when Sinclair releases Michael. The Don straightens his collar with a flourish.

"Karma more than held her own. The moment I saw her, I knew life was going to change. I just didn't realize how much. I took her to Sicily, married her, and fell in love with her, but not before she stabbed me with my own knife."

"She stabbed you?" I chuckle.

Michael grins wryly. "Perhaps it's why I fell for her. That woman would never allow herself to be in a position of weakness. She's my other half, my soul mate." Michael surveys Sinclair's features. "A sentiment you're familiar with, too, I believe."

Sinclair rolls his shoulders. "My wife is my world. She's my North Star. The reason for my existence. Without her, I'm nothing."

"And without her sister, I'm nothing," Michael murmurs.

"Doesn't change the fact that your father kidnapped us. He held us for nearly a month. He tortured me and my friends, in ways we can never share with anyone. He changed the course of our lives. He traumatized us as children. We bear the scars of it, and could have well turned out to be the kind of people who would have been a menace to ourselves and others. We were lucky we had each other to turn to. More importantly, we found our better halves—the women who reached in and unlocked the empathy we'd hidden for so long, we'd forgotten it existed. It's thanks to these women that our lives were turned upside down... for the better. If we hadn't met them... If I hadn't met Summer, I'd have killed you as soon as I saw you."

"And I'd have shot you as soon as you socked me earlier." Michael lowers his chin to his chest.

"Then we both have much to live for." Sinclair cracks his neck.

"Much to look forward to." Michael looks at Sinclair in a considering fashion.

"There's one way you can make up for some of the things that happened," Sinclair says slowly.

"We work together rather than against each other." Michael drums his fingers on the counter. "And we'll be strengthened by blood ties."

I glance between them. "Whatever it is, the two of you owe me a part of it."

The two scowl at each other, then at me. Sinclair's glare deepens. "You're a motherfucking cunt."

I reach for a cigar from the box under the bar, and using the cutting tool, snap off the end. "Takes one to recognize one."

Sinclair frowns at the cigar. Sure, it's not my house, or my den, or my cigar box, but considering I'm here to broker peace between these two, they owe me.

"We don't owe you anything." Michael shoves his hand into his pocket.

"If it weren't for me, you wouldn't be here in the first place," I point out.

"Speaking of" —Sinclair grips the edge of the bar counter— "how did you find your way past my security?"

I stare at him.

His scowl deepens. "Which one of my motherfucking employees is on your payroll?" Sinclair growls.

"The same one you sent to spy on him." I jerk my chin in Michael's direction.

"Wait—" Michael swivels toward him. "You have a spy in my team?"

"Have had one for the past three months—" Sinclair turns on me. "How the fuck did you track him down, anyway?"

I reach for the lighter—also Sinclair's—and rotate the edge of my cigar through it.

"Oh, *now* he goes silent," Sinclair says in a disgusted voice.

"If we're on the same side moving forward" —I switch off the light — "which I assume we are, there should be no secrets between us."

"This sounds like a nightmare." Michael rubs the back of his neck.

"Why do I feel like I'm not going to like whatever it is you're going to say next?" Sinclair glowers.

I glance between them. "I'll tell you who the spy is, on the condition that both of you guarantee his safety."

3

A day later

Lena

"This is your home?" I stare up at the three-story building that looms above me. It's a Victorian-era building with turrets and spires and even a small tower at one corner. It's set against sprawling grounds with a tree line that runs around the border of the estate. There are more trees that surround the driveway we drove up. I also noticed wildflowers on one side of the driveway, and a duck pond on the other, including a fountain. An honest-to-God fountain with a mermaid set in the center. To think, we're in Hyde Park, in the center of London. I didn't think people were allowed to own property in the park, but clearly, I was mistaken. In fact, the noises of the city don't even reach the premises. A bird trills somewhere nearby. That, combined with the pitter-patter of the fountain is the only sound in the space.

"It's my father's home," Isaac snaps.

I shoot him a sideways glance to find his features twisted. He has a

glower on his face, his bottom lip thrust out in a pout. There was a
time I used to find his little temper tantrums cute, but the novelty wore
off very quickly after his fifth or sixth outburst, all directed at me.
Apparently, triggered by something very inconsequential I did.

"I didn't realize you were so well off," I admit.

"My father's well off, not me," he shoots back.

O-k-a-y, then.

"Maybe I shouldn't be here," I glance at what must surely be a
heritage building in front of us.

"You're my girlfriend. Of course, you should be with me. Besides,
where would you go, considering you didn't get the job after
completing your internship?"

I swivel to face him. "Are you blaming me for it?" I demand.

He raises a shoulder. "You're too sensitive, babe. All I meant was, if
you'd gotten that job, we wouldn't have to move in here."

"You could have pulled your weight, too, you know? While you
waited for inspiration to strike, you could have gone to work and
banked the pay." I tighten my lips.

"Oh, so you think it's my fault we couldn't pay the rent on our
place?" he snaps.

"It wouldn't have hurt for you to turn up more often at your job.
No wonder you got laid off."

"It was a construction job. It didn't count." He rolls his shoulders.

"Didn't count? For what? Every job counts. Every bit of money you
brought in would have helped. But you never did take paying the bills
seriously. You just let me pay the bills and were happy to coast along.
And now, I know why." I jerk my chin in the direction of the house.

"What do you mean?" He frowns.

"Clearly, you were brought up in the lap of luxury. I'm guessing
you were spoiled, and that's why you don't know the value of money."

His features twist. "That's not fair, Lena. You know how much I
have sacrificed to stay on the artist's path. I have to be true to myself. I
need to experience true despair, true angst to be able to paint."

"So why not take yourself off to a third-world country and live like
a backpacker? Living in a studio in Hackney with your girlfriend
paying your rent is not exactly slumming it."

He stares at me for a second, then chuckles. "This is why I keep you around. You always manage to put me in my place."

I stare at him, catching a glimpse of his sense of humor, which I had once found so attractive. That, and the fact that he doesn't give a damn about rules of any kind. He has a fearlessness about him that appeals to me. He wasn't worried about paying bills, or having a career, or any of the myriad of things I worried about all the time. I also resented him for it because it meant I had to shoulder the responsibilities for both of us.

I'm partially to blame, though. I might have encouraged him to spend more time on his art. I love the fact he's creative; I often wish *I* could be more creative. Which is probably why I ended up working for an advertising agency after my expensive university education. The fact that I had even managed to become a part of the internship program with them had been an achievement. Too bad I didn't make the cut to be offered a job. So, it's back to the drawing board—or rather, the computer—to send my resumes off to potential employers.

Isaac takes my hand in his and tugs.

"Hey." I lose my balance and fall against him. He wraps his arm around my waist and hauls me to my toes. Which still means I only reach somewhere in the vicinity of his chest. At six-foot, three-inches, he's much taller than my five-foot, four-inch height. I'd never thought of myself as petite until I ran into Isaac.

He lowers his head and brushes his lips over mine. "I'm sorry I've been such an asshole. I know I've been self-indulgent in staying focused on my art. You know us artists; we're essentially selfish people." He smiles that charming-as-hell smile of his, and my heart melts a little. I'm such a pushover. I dig my fingers into the hair at the nape of his neck and tug.

"Ow." His grin widens. "What was that for?"

"Don't think you can bedazzle me into forgiving you for your assholeness."

He laughs. "So, I bedazzle you?"

I scowl, "I mean it, Isaac. I refuse to become one of those women who's continually making excuses for her boyfriend."

"Aww, babe, but I love it when you take care of me." He tickles my side and I can't stop the giggle that bubbles up my throat. "There she is." He lowers his head and brushes his lips over mine again. Soft, pleasant, so familiar. I flutter my eyes shut and sink into the ease of the kiss. Undemanding, so normal, just how I like it. Of course, I still have to find a job, I can't stay here for too long. That's assuming his father allows us to stay at all. Lord knows, there's space here for all of us, and if he doesn't, well... I'm not sure what I'm going to do, to be honest. I—

The sound of the door opening reaches me. I try to pull away, but of course, Isaac doesn't let go. He tightens his grasp on me, holds me in place, and deepens the kiss. I dig my fingers into his shoulders and push, and he finally releases me.

"So, you decided to show up?" a man's deep voice states from the doorway.

I pull away, wipe the back of my hand over my mouth, then turn toward the new arrival. I have to tilt my head back, and farther back, to meet his gaze. Dark eyes, coal black; there's not a shred of emotion in them. Thick hair cut at the sides and slightly long on top, all combed back from that cruel face. With streaks of gray at the temples that only add to the sense of authority he carries about him. Is this Isaac's father? If so, there isn't much resemblance with his son, except for the height, and maybe around his eyes. This man is way more confident, more self-possessed, more dominant. His shoulders are broad, broader than Isaac's, and thickly corded. He crosses his arms across his chest and his biceps stretch the material of his suit. The jacket is as black as his eyes and definitely stitched by a master tailor on Savile Row. A blue silk tie is knotted around his collar. Who wears a tie at home? Apparently, this man does. It suits him, though. It completes his Lord of the Manor look, along with the snowy white shirt that is a stark contrast to his tanned features. He looks me up and down and a sneer twists his lips. Then he turns his attention on Isaac. It feels like someone dumped a bucket of cold water on me. *What the hell? Did he just judge me and discard me like I'm of no consequence? How dare he?* I open my mouth, but Isaac grabs my wrist and pulls me close. The man's gaze drops to where Isaac's fingers curl around my wrist. His frown deepens. Once more, he glances at his son. Then pushes away from the door. Without another word, he pivots and walks away, leaving it to us to follow.

What the—? I stare after him, trying to shut my mouth.

"Don't mind him. He always has a giant stick up his arse," Isaac whispers.

It's more like he has the entire Big Ben stuck up his backside.

I step over the threshold, and Isaac follows with my suitcase. "What do you have in there, bricks?" He pants.

"Books," I reply, taking in my surroundings. Hold on. "Is that an original?" I point to the painting by the doorway.

"It's a Monet."

My jaw drops, "Your father has a Monet worth millions?"

"Billions," he corrects me.

"Billions." I wince. "In the hallway."

"So?" He raises a shoulder.

"So?" I shoot him a sideways glance. How did I not know my boyfriend is loaded? Is that why he refused to hold down a nine-to-five of any kind to pay the bills? Is he that spoiled? Do I even know this man that was my friend before he became my boyfriend?

"I don't know why you have to carry books around. Why not throw them away and—"

I march toward him and grab the handle of my suitcase. "Give that to me."

"Lena, I only meant, why do you have physical books? Why don't you get a Kindle?"

"Because it's not the same thing."

"Eh?" He blinks. "They would carry the same books in electronic form."

"You wouldn't understand." I annotate my favorite spicy scenes in the paperbacks. Technically, you could do that also in a Kindle, but they're not visible until you open them. Not like a physical page where you can see both the printed part and the handwritten note on the side. When I tried to explain this to Isaac, his eyes glazed over.

"The amount you've spent on these books... We could've paid another month's rent with the same money," he mutters.

I scowl, maybe he's right but I refuse to feel guilty. These books are my best friends. When I get upset with the world, when I'm pissed about anything, I can retreat between the pages and everything seems so much better.

I begin to roll my suitcase forward, but Isaac stops me.

"I shouldn't have made that comment about the rent. I'm sorry." He cups my cheek. "I really am."

I blow out a breath. That's the thing with Isaac. He can be a bitch, but then he also knows how to make up for it.

"Here, let me help you." He takes the suitcase from me, and this time, I don't stop him.

"I know how much you love to read. In fact, my father has a library full of books stacked floor to ceiling. I'm sure you'll love it."

"Assuming he lets me enter the room." I glance around the space again. "Are you sure he wants us here?"

Isaac scrunches up his features, looking younger than his twenty-four years. "Only one way to find out."

JJ

"So, you want to move in here?" I narrow my gaze on my son. I'd led them into my study and taken the chair behind my large antique desk. And I hadn't invited them to sit, either. Not that it had prevented Isaac from dropping into the chair opposite me.

His dirty blond hair flops over his forehead and he brushes it away. The gesture is so familiar. I've seen him do this when he gets excited, when he's anxious, when he is nervous... And right now, he's all three. Maybe unsure, more than anything else. He should be. He left home at twenty-one, vowing never to return. Three years later, he's back and with a girlfriend in tow. The girl has the decency to remain standing, at least.

I rake my gaze over her features. Skin the color of honey, auburn hair pulled back from her temples, and big brown eyes that flash with irritation. Her waist is narrow enough I imagine I can span its length with my palms, and her hips... They flare out and are currently encased in jeans that she seems to have painted on. On her feet are faded Chucks with butterflies drawn on them. Butterflies? She's young enough to believe in butterflies, and probably rainbows and first loves, as well. I suddenly feel old and jaded.

"Does your family know you're here with him?" I snap.

She stiffens. "My family doesn't have a say in how I live my life."

"Figures." I flick my gaze in my son's direction. "You're with him, after all."

My son arches an eyebrow, but before he can say anything, she bursts out, "He's your son. How can you speak this way about him?"

"He's my son. Which is why, if I were your father, I'd order you to stay away from him."

"You're not my father," he spits out.

Thank fuck for that. I raise a shoulder. She's right. It's her life, and if she wants to waste it by being with him, who am I to say otherwise? I turn to Isaac. "You can stay for as long as you want, on one condition."

"If you mean you want me to come into your office and work with you—"

"That's exactly what I mean."

"Fuck this." Isaac jumps up with such speed, his chair crashes to the ground.

The girl shoots him a worried glance. "Isaac, please—" She walks over to touch his arm, but he shakes it off.

"You can keep your charity. I don't want any of your money or any inheritance." He scowls.

His American accent is even more pronounced—a dead giveaway that he's pissed off. That's what I intended, isn't it? To prod him until he loses his temper? Why is it that when I'm with my son, I can't seem to stop myself from falling to his level? Why is it that I have such a difficult time remembering that I'm supposed to be the adult in this relationship? It's not only the fact that hearing his accent reminds me of how my wife insisted on sending them to the American school in London. Insisted that my kids speak in an American accent. I worked myself to the bone to pay the fees for their school, to give them a life-style I could have only dreamed of growing up in myself... And yet, somehow, they both resent me for it. And now, my son is back under my roof.

I draw in a breath. "And yet, you're here," I murmur.

"And now, I'm leaving." He spins around and begins to walk away, but she runs over to him.

"Isaac, stop." She grips his arm, and this time, he allows her to stop him. "We can't afford to piss him off," she says in a low voice, but I can still hear the conversation. "We need this, Isaac."

"I don't need him for anything," my son growls.

I wince.

She stiffens. "So, what are you going to do? Spend the night on the street, or in a homeless shelter?"

"There has to be another way." He drags his fingers through his hair.

"You know there isn't. You're struggling to sell your paintings, and I don't have a job. We need him, Isaac."

"Fuck," my son growls. "Fuck, fuck, fuck."

"Glad to see your vocabulary is as varied as I remember it to be," I drawl.

"Can you stop already?" She pivots to face me. "We're trying to figure this out, okay? You don't have to plant your big foot in the middle and make it worse."

I blink. When was the last time anyone spoke to me in that tone of voice?

"Can you give us a few minutes?" she says through gritted teeth.

I tilt my head, waiting.

"Please?" She finally forces out the word.

"You have five." I lean back in my chair.

She stares at me.

If she thinks I'm going to leave this vastly entertaining spectacle and have the decency to give them some privacy, she is sadly mistaken.

"Four minutes thirty-eight seconds now," I announce.

"Asshole," she says under her breath.

"What was that?"

She covers her mouth with her hand. "I said thank you."

"Four minutes and ten seconds." I tap my watch, "Tick-tock, girl."

She looks like she is about to protest, then grabs Isaac by his wrist and hauls him to the other end of the room. A whispered conversation ensues. I watch with interest as she speaks animatedly, and Isaac listens. He shakes his head, then turns to leave, but she blocks his way. She throws up her hands. He scowls. She stabs a finger in his chest. He hunches his shoulders. Interesting.

My son has always been willful and adamant. When he was a child, I didn't spend much time with him, too busy building my empire. I wanted to give him everything I never had. Turns out, the one thing I should have given him was my time. When he was little, I spent too much time working, spent too much time away from him. The result? I never managed to bond properly with him. I threw enough money at my kids to make sure they'd never want for anything. By the time I realized I didn't really know him, he was already a teenager, and the distance between us kept increasing. I had failed as a father, but perhaps it's not too late to try to build some kind of relationship with him? Maybe this is the opportunity to do so. But I can't allow him to just waltz in here and think he can simply get access to his fortune. He needs to work for it. It's the only way he'll realize the value of what's being handed to him.

Isaac finally nods. She straightens, then turns and marches over to me, with him in tow.

"I'll do it," she declares.

"Do what?"

"You wanted Isaac to come to work with you?"

I nod.

"He can't, but I will."

I blink. "Let me get this straight, *you* are going to come to work for me?"

"He's an artist. You can't expect him to sit behind a desk from nine to five. It would kill his creative spirit."

"Would it now?" I place my fingertips together.

"It would. I, on the other hand, have experience working in an office. My last job was an internship with SGA."

"The advertising agency?"

She nods. "I completed the program, but they didn't have any open positions for me. I'm looking for a job, anyway, so this works out."

"And what would you do for me?"

"I assume you must have a marketing and promotions department. Perhaps, I could get a role in that?"

"The role I was going to offer Isaac was that of my executive assistant."

"You mean, your secretary?" she asks.

"More like my chief of staff. You'd be sitting in for me in meetings, you'd vet all my emails, accompany me to my various engagements. In short, you'd get to shadow me. You'd learn on the job, and yes, part of the role includes doing what an assistant would do when it comes to managing my workload."

"Oh." She blinks rapidly. "That's quite a big role."

"I've never had anyone in that role before. It's been reserved for Isaac, to help him understand the complexities of the business enterprises I look after."

"You mean, learn about the shady dealings that your company is involved in?" Isaac snorts.

I glare at him. "I mean, become conversant with what it takes to run my varied operations."

"Is that what you're calling it these days? Don't think I don't know about the illegal arm of your conglomerate."

"Are you accusing me of something, Isaac?" I say slowly. "If so, I'd rather you come out and say it outright."

He opens his mouth, then seems to think better of it. He firms his lips, then juts out his chin.

I blow out a breath. "This isn't getting us anywhere." I rise to my feet. "It's probably best the two of you—"

"Wait, I'll do it. I'll take the job. I'll be the best chief of staff you'll ever have. Also, I want the role. Even if I went job hunting, I'd never get a position like this. I'll learn on the job. It's the best damn experience I'll ever get. And you'll have someone to fill the position."

"Hmm," I drum my fingers on the table. "And what about you, Isaac. What do you intend to do while we're at work?"

"I—" He opens his mouth, but she cuts him short.

"He'll do you a series of paintings exclusively to be placed within your offices."

"What would I do with his paintings?" I snort.

"I'm sure you've heard of art investment? One day, his paintings will be worth a lot, and you'll be getting in at the ground floor, so to speak."

I turn toward my son. "Is that right? Is that something you want to do?"

He hesitates.

"If you don't—"

"He does." She nudges him. "Tell him, Isaac."

He draws in a breath. "It's true. I'll do the installations for the offices of Kane Enterprises."

"Is that right?" I narrow my gaze on him.

Isaac's features redden. "I told you already I would, didn't I?"

"We know what we are, but know not what we may be," I murmur.

"Shakespeare?" The girl blinks.

I arch an eyebrow. "Very good. Perhaps you'll do better than I think in the EA role."

"Was that a test?" She frowns.

"Maybe, maybe not." I can't stop the smirk that curls my lips. Why do I feel the need to get a rise out of my son? It's not that I don't empathize with him; I do. Hell, if anyone knows what it is to be misunderstood by his parents, it's me. And here I am, repeating the same cycle with my son. Why is it that I can't do a better job of being a good parent? I tip up my chin at the girl. "So, in return for allowing you both to stay under my roof, you'll come to work for me as my executive assistant." I turn to my son. "And you'll furnish all of my offices around the world with paintings?"

"Yes," the girl nods.

My son hesitates, then jerks his chin, "Yes, that's right."

I glance between them. "I accept your proposal, on one condition."

4

Lena

Now what? Can't he make anything easy for us? Does everything have to be not only on his terms but also the result of him driving a hard enough bargain that the other person is left in no doubt as to who holds all the cards?

I scowl at him. His grin widens. His features light up, and for a moment, he looks younger than his years. Is this how he was before he took on the responsibilities that brought him to where he is now? Then, a canny look enters his eyes, and I realize it's all a front. He turns on the charm when he needs to disarm his opposition. No doubt, he uses the tactic in his business meetings. No doubt, that's all this is to him. Another negotiation. It doesn't matter that it's his son's life he's toying with. All he's concerned with is winning.

"Well?" I jut out my chin. "What is it?"

"Just a little thing, I have a gathering for my friends to celebrate their wedding tomorrow night. The two of you will be there."

"You mean your business associates, don't you? Since when do you have friends?" Isaac sneers.

His father purses his lips. "These people started out as business associates but they have become friends. Apparently, even I can't go through life without forging the odd friendly relationship along the way." His voice is self-deprecating.

For a second, I glimpse a man who's lonely. Someone who's perfected the skill of building walls between himself and the world. Someone who doesn't want to let people get close to him... Not even his own family. Maybe it's not all that surprising how mixed-up Isaac is. If this is how his father treated him growing up, Isaac didn't have a chance.

In the ensuing silence, Isaac glowers. His father adopts a look of boredom. Does he really not care if his son has a roof above his head? The tension between them builds until my nerves threaten to snap. Anger pours off of Isaac's body, while his father lounges in his seat.

Isaac opens his mouth, but before he can say anything, I cut in, "We'll do it."

Isaac whips his head in my direction, his features angry. I hold his gaze, a pleading look in my eyes. "Please, let's not make this more difficult. You know we need this," I whisper.

He seems like he is going to protest, then nods. "Fine."

"This is your room?" I glance around the suite which is ten times the size of the crappy apartment we'd been living in, and I'm not exaggerating.

His father called for one of his staff to help us with the luggage, then he turned back to his computer in his study. Basically, we were dismissed. Isaac and I exchanged a glance, then I followed him out. He greeted the man who met us outside the study with a warmth I hadn't noticed when he met his father. Isaac hugged him, then introduced him as Craig. Isaac explained that Craig and his wife Miriam took care of the housekeeping. She also did the cooking while Craig looked after the upkeep of the house and the grounds. He also welcomed me—

something Isaac's father hadn't done. Not that it mattered. We have a roof over our heads, and I have a new job.

Wait! I didn't ask his father how much he would pay. Of course, I assume it must have a good paycheck. Executive assistant roles normally do. A good EA can ease the role of a senior manager in a very effective manner. Provided the chemistry with the manager is right. Something I'm going to find out tomorrow, no doubt. Although, given the way things had been with his father today... maybe not.

"This is where I grew up, yes." Isaac gives his surroundings a cursory glance, then walks over and flings himself on the bed. His bag and mine have been placed just inside the room by the door. Craig offered to unpack for us, but I waved him off saying I'd do it myself.

Now, I wheel my suitcase over to the side by the wall, then place it flat on the floor.

"Use the closet," Isaac pipes up.

"Eh?" I glance in his direction.

He stabs his thumb in the direction of a door set not far from the bed. "It's a closet."

"Oh, okay." I straighten, then wheel my bag to the closet. When I push it open, my breath catches. I step inside a space that's about half the size of our studio. I hoist the bag onto one of the low-slung counters, then open it and hang up my clothes. When I'm done, my one good skirt and blouse, my spare pair of jeans, a few tops and sweat shirts, and my one formal dress have taken up a tiny portion of the space, along with my one pair of Louboutin's, which I spent nearly three months' salary on. But darn it, I wasn't going to buy a fake now, was I? Besides, I feel powerful when I wear them.

I turn around and walk out of the closet to find Isaac on his phone, texting away.

I walk over to him and he glances up, then places the phone aside. "So, what do you think?"

"I think you need to start thinking about what you're going to paint for your dad's offices."

"Ugh, don't remind me." He plumps the pillows behind him and leans back. "I mean, what do you think of the pad?"

"Pad, huh? Are you trying to tell me all this wealth is second nature to you, so you're not affected by being surrounded by luxury after months of living cramped in a studio with your easels for company?

He laughs. "Your sense of humor is your best asset, you know?"

"Gee, thanks." I sit down on the bed next to him. "Seriously, though, you need to start painting again so you can keep your end of the bargain to your dad."

"You know he doesn't care either way, right? He'll probably never see what I paint."

"Are you sure? He can't be all that callous," I murmur.

"Wanna bet?" He sits up. "You think I'm being overdramatic in how I act toward him. You probably think I'm ungrateful, even. After all, a man who gave me all this" —he circles the air with his finger— "can't be all bad, right?"

"You have to admit, this seems like being brought up in the lap of luxury," I agree.

"Ah, so now you think I am a spoiled little rich brat who doesn't value what he has?"

"I never said that." I reach for his hand, but he pulls away.

"My earliest memory of my father was me performing at a school play and waiting for him to turn up, which he never did. Then, there was the time I earned top honors in my class. I came rushing home, eager to show it to my father. I walked into his home office in the middle of a conference call, and he simply gestured for someone on his team to lead me out. I didn't see him for days after that. Not to mention, the number of cricket games I played which he never attended. The only time he seemed to take an interest was when I told him I wanted to be a painter."

"I take it, he wasn't happy about it?"

"That would be an understatement. He was vehemently opposed to it. No son of his was going to follow a creative profession. He told me he would cut off my inheritance unless I went to business school and spent a minimum of two years working with him."

"And you—"

"Defied him, of course. I don't want his money or anything to do with him. Craig and Miriam were more parents to me than my own ever were."

"Your mother?"

"She divorced JJ when I turned eighteen, but even before that she wanted nothing to do with me or my sister. She was too busy with her social life and JJ was away traveling more often than not. It's Craig and Miriam who brought us up."

"You have a sister?"

He nods. "She's older than me. In many ways, she was my father's favorite. Not that he had more time for her, but she seemed content with whatever affection he deigned to bestow on her. That is, until she finished business school and decided not to join his business."

My gaze widens. "She didn't join his company?"

"Decided she'd rather carve out her career on her own. She wanted experience working in a place where she wasn't related to the boss."

"Sounds reasonable," I say slowly.

"Tell that to my father. He was seriously pissed about it. The two of them got into a huge row. It's the only time in my life I've seen my father actively get upset with either one of us. Clearly, he cared more about her leaving than my becoming an artist. She left in a huff, and as far as I know, she's never seen him since."

"When did this happen?"

"About three years ago, when she turned twenty-one. And yes, he did cut her out of his will, too."

Isaac pulls me into his arms. I cuddle in. Being with him has always been nice, comfortable. Like being with a brother.

Eh? Why did I go thinking that?

I mean, the sex with him isn't bad. He's a considerate lover. Maybe too considerate. I think I'd prefer someone more dominant. Someone who'd surprise me, and throw me on my back and fuck me until I can't think straight. With Isaac, it's always been… Not bad. Which is the same as it being good, right? What we have is good. It is.

I wrap my arms around him and pull him closer. "I feel sorry for your father. All alone in this big pile of stone. He has all of the luxuries in the world, but no one to share them with."

"You don't need to feel sorry for him. He's always been a hit with the ladies. After our mother left there was a never-ending stream of women he dated." He uses air quotes after that last word.

I lean back in his arms. "So, he brought these women home?"

"No, he made sure to keep his private life separate, but the newspapers always carried pictures of him with whoever his latest squeeze was."

A hot sensation tightens my chest, and I push it away. "At least he was thoughtful that way. He made sure not to expose the two of you to any more emotional turmoil," I offer.

"No, just having him for a father was enough," he scoffs.

"Maybe, now that you're living back home you could try to make amends with him?"

He stares at me, then bursts out laughing. "You're so cute. You don't get it, do you? My father doesn't need anyone. He's fine the way he is. All he needs is his business, and now, apparently, these friends he's gathered along the way. He'll probably make sure to write his will and gift all his wealth to bring down the national debt or something like that."

"You're kidding, right?"

"Nope." He pushes me onto my back and covers my body with his. "Absolutely not." He bends and brushes his lips across the base of my throat. "He's never going to forgive me or my sister Tally for not wanting to join his business." He fits himself firmly between my legs, and the column in his pants nudges my center.

"You need to unpack," I murmur.

"It can wait." He presses kisses up the side of my throat. I stare up at the ceiling. He brushes his lips over mine, and I turn my head.

"Stop, Isaac. I'm really tired."

"I know exactly how to relax you." He reaches for the neckline of my top and I grab his hand.

"Don't, please."

"What's wrong?" He glances between my eyes. "You're never in the mood lately."

"Probably because I've been too busy trying to pay our bills and keep us afloat."

"I never asked for you to take over that responsibility."

"We did share a flat together, so it was in my interest to keep our rent paid so we didn't get evicted."

"Clearly, you didn't succeed, because here we are," he retorts.

I stare at him, then shove at his shoulder. "Get off of me."

"Aww, come on, doll, you know I'm joking."

"No, I don't, and I hate it when you call me doll."

"You do?" He frowns.

"Yes, and I've told you so many times. And still, you insist on using that stupid term of endearment."

His face falls. "I didn't mean to upset you."

"Well, you did." I'm being uncharitable. It's not his fault that I haven't felt like sleeping with him in a while. Stress at work, combined with the worry of keeping a roof over our heads... I'm just so wrung out. And being here is a temporary solution, at best.

He could have helped, of course, but I knew what I was getting into with him. Isaac's anti-establishment, anti-system, and hates rules. No wonder, because he's spent most of his life rebelling against his father. I don't need to be a shrink to figure that out. And it's part of what attracted me to him, especially because I had been so focused on making something of myself. So, his easygoing nature had come as a relief. That is, until I was faced with the mountain of bills, and he remained carefree and irresponsible. Of course, I could have asked my parents for help, and they would have helped, but they're not well-off. I have two siblings who are still in university, and my parents are paying part of their tuition. I refused their help with my school bills, and took out a loan instead. Another bill. So, the only way out is to rely on Isaac's father for a little while, just until I get back on my feet.

"I'm sorry, Lena. I've been a terrible boyfriend, haven't I? But I promise, I'll make it up to you."

"I know you will." I lean up and kiss his cheek. "Now, I'm going to shower, then get something to eat. Do you want something?"

5

JJ

A sound reaches me. I glance up from the spreadsheet I was studying. Did it come from outside the study? I pull out the drawer on my right, grab my gun, and slide it in the waistband of my pants. The fire my housekeeper built up earlier has all but died down. The glow from the embers fills the space with a warm orange light. What time is it, anyway? I rise to my feet and creep to the doorway. The corridor is silent. I pause, my muscles tensing. The hair on the back of my neck rises. There's someone out there. I pull out my gun and cock it, then keeping close to the wall, I prowl down the corridor—past the living room and the conservatory, the dining room, and toward the kitchen. The sound of someone moving around reaches me. I curl my finger around the trigger of the gun and move forward, reach the kitchen, and slip inside. I point my gun in the direction of the sound and freeze.

She's bent over, taking something out of the fridge. Her perfect pear-shaped bottom stretches the shorts she's wearing so I can see the plump cheeks of her arse. As I watch, she wriggles it to one side, then the other, then the other way again. The sound of her humming reaches me. A tune I can't identify. She continues to bop that fleshy backside, swinging to a rhythm I can't hear. Then she straightens, and bursts into song, *"Whenever, wherever, hmmmmmm, mmm, I'll be there, you'll be here... and mmmmmmmm—"* She arches her back, thrusts out her butt, and shimmies it.

The blood drains to my groin. My cock thickens. I watch, fascinated, as she launches into a full body sway, doing some kind of action that has her arse wriggling around like it has a life of its own. Sweat beads my forehead. Heat flushes my skin. My thigh muscles harden and my stomach clenches. The crotch of my pants is suddenly too tight for me. I take a step forward, then another, until I'm halfway across the kitchen. I can't tear my gaze off that luscious backside.

"Tada tedium, ahahahah, tada, tadum. I'll be there and you'll be—" She turns around, holding a bucket of ice cream, with a spoon in the other hand.

I jerk my chin up to her face in time to see her gaze widen. Liquid gold eyes. Like the most expensive whiskey. No, like melting chocolate and— She screams, the spoon slips from her hand and crashes to the floor. I blink, follow the direction of her gaze to see I'm still holding the gun. I instantly engage the safety and pocket it. I glance up just as the bowl of food tips over.

I close the distance between us, slip on the patch of ice cream on the floor, and lurch forward, crashing into her. The bowl of food upends its contents on me, then crashes to the floor. The tub of ice cream slips from her hands and bounces off my shoe. That unbalances me more and I lean further into her. The world tilts as we hit the floor. I twist my body at the last moment so I take the full weight of her body. My back hits the floor, and she falls on me. Her elbow wedges into my stomach and I huff. Her breasts flatten into my chest, her pelvis pressed perfectly into my crotch. I bring my palms down to grip her hips, and hold her in place. It's pure reflex, I swear. By the time I realize I have her fitted into my now completely aroused cock, it's too late. The warmth of her pussy sinks through the thin fabric of her shorts and envelops my cock.

Jesus-fucking-Christ. My entire body goes on alert. My biceps turn to steel. All my senses hone in on her. She stares down at me, and flickers of silver flash deep in her golden eyes. Her breath hitches, and a pulse flares to life at the base of her throat. Our gazes clash. Something primitive stirs inside of me. Something I didn't even think existed. A chill runs through my body. My grasp on her hips tightens, and she shudders.

She lowers her head slowly, slowly. Her hot breath sears my cheek, and her nose bumps mine. Her mouth is right over mine. All I have to do is lean up and—something creaks. I glance past her to see the refrigerator door slam shut. The sound ricochets through the space.

I blink. So does she.

The next moment, she pushes against my shoulder. "I'm so sorry. I didn't mean to spill all of my food on you. It's just, you scared me and—"

"It's fine. I forgot there was someone else in the house."

"Wha—?" She gapes.

"I thought I was alone." I flip her over on her back, then rise to my feet.

"You forgot Isaac and I were under your roof?" She huffs.

"It would seem that way." I hold out my hand to her.

She ignores it and scrambles up to her feet. We stand there with assorted foodstuffs on my jacket and on her T-shirt. Her very skimpy T-shirt which is currently sticking to her tits. They're nice breasts, too. Supple and firm, and just right to fill the palms of my hands. As for her nipples? They are diamond hard and currently poking through the fabric of her top. She's not wearing a bra.

Fuck. She's not. Wearing. A bra. If I thought I was hard earlier, the sudden clenching of my guts, and the thickness that tents my crotch and threatens to poke through my pants, tells me I was wrong. I resist the urge to adjust myself.

"What were you doing in my kitchen?" I ask in a hard voice that is totally unnecessary and meant more to divert attention away from the blood that seems to have collected between my legs.

"Why do you have a gun?" she retorts.

"I need it to protect myself."

"How many enemies do you have?"

"I am in a position of power, where sometimes even a friend can turn out to be a foe," I murmur.

"That was almost poetic," she murmurs, then blinks. "I'm sorry I spoiled your clothes."

I'm not sorry I got to see your tits. "For the purposes of decorum, I suggest you wander around dressed a little more appropriately."

Her gaze widens. Her features flush further. "I'm dressed appropriately enough." She scowls.

"Not going to debate this with you. My house, my rules. I'd prefer you be fully clothed next time the urge to have a midnight feast strikes you."

She stiffens. "Do you always sound like you're reading from a Victorian text?"

"Do you always sound like you have a problem with authority?" I snap.

She raises her shoulders, then lowers them. "I'm sorry. It's been a lot to take in. And seeing you with a gun completely took me by surprise." She yawns, then claps a hand to her mouth. "So sorry."

"Stop apologizing, it's bloody annoying. Also, let me not keep you from your bed," I say through gritted teeth.

"Oh, but the mess." She glances around her. "I need to clean this up." She begins to lower to her haunches. The wet T-shirt pulls tighter across her tits. Her shorts hitch up those thick, gorgeous thighs. My cock twinges instantly. Fuck, I need to get her out of here and take care of this urge.

"Just go to bed." I grab her arm and haul her to her feet. A sizzle of electricity seems to shoot out from the point of contact. A wave of emotion slams into my chest.

She gasps, her eyes so wide they seem to fill her face.

What the—? What was that? I drop her arm and take a step back. "Leave." I jerk my chin toward the entrance.

She heads for the doorway, then stops. "Just so you're aware—" she glances at me over her shoulder "—the name's Lena."

She waits a second as if waiting for me to introduce myself. When I glare at her, she huffs, then pivots on her feet and flounces away.

Don't look at it, don't. I track her lush curved behind as it twitches and swings as she sashays out the door. I draw in a deep breath, then another. *What the hell just happened?*

I pull out my phone and shoot Craig a message, knowing he'll take care of it right away. Then, I walk around the spilled mess on the floor and out the door. Thankfully, the girl is no longer in sight. Hopefully, that means she's back in her room and in bed.

I head up the steps, past the second floor where Isaac and his girl-friend are staying, and to the third floor toward the double doors that lead to my room. The doors swing shut behind me and I walk directly toward the bathroom. Stepping inside, I peel off my jacket, my shirt, toe off my shoes and my socks, then along with my pants and boxers, I dump my clothes into the laundry basket. I walk directly to the shower, flick it on, and step under the warm spray. I slap my palms against the wall of the shower and glance down at my angry cock jutting up between my legs. My fingers tingle to squeeze myself from base to head, but I resist. *She's your son's girlfriend. Younger than your daughter.* That's a new low, even for me.

I've been attracted to women and bedded them at will. Most throw themselves at me wherever I go. The position of power I hold, and the fact that I'm still attractive—only stating a fact—is a combination most can't resist. Still, I pride myself on sleeping with women closer to my age. I'm not one of those men nearing fifty who acquire eye-candy in the quest to rejuvenate their mojo. I'm still virile. I have no trouble keeping pace with women half my age, which makes them twenty-four years old. She has to be younger, considering my son is only twenty-three.

Fuck, this… is crazy. I can't possibly be entertaining these thoughts. It's probably because I haven't been with a woman in the last month. A combination of work, and then being called on by Massimo Sovrano to help him track down his kidnapped wife, has kept me busy. Still, I delivered, didn't I? I helped him find his wife, and in return, I earned their loyalty. Now, they're my partners, ready to invest in my business and partner in my latest venture, an exclusive gentlemen's club designed as a meeting ground for the most influential, most powerful, and those who are exceptional. Membership is based not only on how much money you have, but on what value you have contributed to the world.

Ambitious, maybe? Idealistic, definitely. Clearly, I'm getting old if, for the first time, I'm putting my ideals before money. But it seems after building an empire, then legalizing the more illicit companies into tax-paying entities, and making enough money to benefit not only my heirs but their heirs, assuming either of them ever have children, I need a different kind of rush. Mental stimulation. An impulse to give to those who most deserve it. Oh, I still want to make money, don't get me wrong, but I want the payoff to be more than monetary. Exactly what that is, I'm still trying to define, but the club is the first step forward in that direction.

I thought I'd found a way to fulfill the ache that's lodged in my gut in the past year, but meeting her, and that reaction to her, seems to indicate otherwise. I need more… excitement, I need to feel more motivated. Maybe I need a bigger challenge. Perhaps I'll pursue the takeover in LA I've been putting off for so long? Yes, that's it. But first… I need to take care of something more urgent. I drop down on the bench in the shower, spread my legs, and grab my cock.

6

Lena

I'd come back to the room I shared with Isaac to find him busy with his phone. I tried to tell him about what happened with JJ but when he seemed to be more intent on his screen than me, I gave up. More resigned than upset, I walked into the bathroom.

Now I yank off my soiled sleeping shirt and my sleep shorts, and dump them in the laundry basket.

Maybe I should have pulled on a sweatshirt before I traipsed down to the kitchen, but I hadn't expected to run into anyone. In my defense, this is what I wear to bed every night, and it covers more than what a bikini would. So why did he go all extra grumpy on me? Might have been something to do with my spilling the pudding on his jacket. I shouldn't have gone for that and the ice-cream. But I had been starving, and the food had looked so enticing. Also, I'd been sure he wouldn't mind my helping myself to it.

I mean, the man has money oozing out of his pores... His very manly pores, I might add. He felt all hard and massive and so solid under my palms. His chest was broad enough that I felt surrounded by his bulk. His stomach was flat, and between his legs... Yeah, the size of what he was packing in his pants is now imprinted on my flesh. The man's an XXL in every which way. His son is pretty well-endowed, but I'll wager his father is... Well, in more ways than one. And he was aroused, all right.

He noticed the state of my undress and registered my nearness, and those dark eyes of his lightened to an indigo—an intense shade of blue I swear I've never seen before. His eyes aren't as dark as I originally thought, apparently.

I lowered my face to his, scented the whiskey and the notes of sherry oak on his breath, and it had gone straight to my head. And to other parts of me, too. He felt all man. All woodsy and strong and unshakeable... and I wanted to crack that composure of his. I wanted to perforate that confidence, peel off the mask he wears to the world, and expose the man he is inside. Primal, crude, basic... As rough-hewn as an oak tree in the wild. As majestic as a lion in the Sahara. As...

What the? Hold on. Why am I going all gaga over this man? He's my boyfriend's father. My boss. Not to mention, he's old enough to be my parent. But it didn't feel like that. It didn't feel wrong to be in his arms. It felt forbidden, taboo, and so very sensual. It felt different than with anyone else I've been with. And his touch... It had snaked a thrill of excitement down my spine. He is one fine specimen of manliness. And completely off limits.

If nothing else, I need the job he offered me, and nothing is worth endangering my position before I've even started with the company. I need the money, so I can get out from under his roof and begin to salvage the remnants of my life. Best to put what happened behind me. Chalk it all up to an inappropriate accident and move on.

As to him having a gun? Well, he is a high-powered businessman. It makes sense for him to be armed, I suppose...

I step under the shower, then towel off and pull on the bathrobe I find behind the bathroom door. I step out of the bathroom, and find Isaac is fast asleep and snoring lightly. About to go to bed I pause. I never did ask JJ what time I need to be ready tomorrow. Also, does he want me to get to the office on my own steam? Or is he going to give

me a lift, and where is the office anyway? I glance at the bed and find
Isaac fast asleep under the covers. It won't help to ask him.

My phone vibrates and I pick it up, see the missed calls from my
mom, and the notifications for the messages that have popped up in
the group chat I have with my family. Jeez, you'd think I was missing
or something. I've only missed messages from the group for the last
twelve hours. I probably need to update them on where I am. I reach
for the keypad, then hesitate. Maybe later. First, I need to figure out
what I'm going to do about tomorrow. I place the phone on the nightstand and begin to pace.

Of course, I could simply get into the bed and try to sleep. Which is
going to be impossible because I'm too stressed thinking about what
I'm going to do about tomorrow. What if I oversleep and miss Isaac's
father before he goes to the office? That'll never do for the start of a
new job.

No, I'm going to have to suck it up and track him down and ask
him myself. I spin around, walk to the door, then out into the hallway. I
head downstairs and find all the lights are off. So I walk back up the
steps. To the right is my and Isaac's room. So I guess JJ's room must be
to the left. I hesitate. If I go to sleep without talking to him I'll not
know what time to be up tomorrow. Not that I want to meet that
patronizing prick, especially after what went down earlier but I don't
have a choice, do I? I turn left and head up the corridor. I reach the
door to a room, and peek inside. It's empty. The two other rooms that
are smaller than Isaac's, but still spacious, are not his, either. Which
means, his father's room must be on the top floor. Okay then. I walk
up the steps then down the corridor and to the double doors. These are
the only doors on this floor, which means they have to be his. The
doors do have the feel of a master suite about them, too.

I knock on the door and it swings open. Huh? It's not locked? I step
into the dimly lit space and gasp. Holy shit. I thought Isaac's suite was
big. But this? This is at least twice, or maybe three times, Isaac's space.
It's a complete apartment. There's no one around, but I can hear the
sound of the shower from the slightly open door in the far corner.
Guess he must be taking a shower?

I glance around the room, unable to stop myself from taking a closer look. On the left is a large living room space with a sectional and a massive TV on the wall in front. Right ahead is a large desk with a laptop on it. On the right, the entire wall is covered with books from floor to ceiling. Beyond the desk is a large window through which I can see the lights of the city. I knew the house was on elevated land, but I didn't realize it gave a clear view of the metropolis.

I take a step forward and my feet sink into the heavy, steel-gray carpet. The soft material seems to envelop my toes. It invites me to sink down and pat it with my hand; that's how lush it feels. No doubt, it's made of some hideously expensive material which I can't even fathom. My eyes are drawn to the massive bed pushed up against the wall on my right. It's a super king-size, at least. I'll bet it's some custom-size larger than anything the rest of us mere mortals can get. The pillows are large and fluffy. The covers are a midnight blue and turned back in a very inviting fashion.

Also pushed up against the wall on the far side is a large rectangular tank. There're rocks and vegetation in it and a basking lamp. I walk toward it and peer inside, then blink. There, on the sandy floor, is a tortoise. I kid you not. It's a tiny tortoise, about five to seven inches long and could fit into the palm of my hand. It's frozen there, I imagine, terrified by my presence. The hard shell on its back has whorls of a repeating design on it. I stay there, unable to move, and it slowly begins to crawl forward. A breath I'd not realized I was holding rushes out of me. I don't know what I expected. It's not like I see tortoises every day. Actually, I don't think I've seen one before this. Which begs the question, what is a tortoise doing in JJ's room? Is it his pet? Does the grouch alphahole have a turtle as a pet? Surreal.

I turn and, once again, glance at the bathroom door. My shoulders slump. I can hardly go in there and bother him. Guess I don't have much choice but to walk down in the morning and take my chances. Maybe I can ask Craig for the office address, or Isaac might have it. I have to assume they start at 9 a.m. Yeah, that's the best I can do. I turn to leave when the shower cuts off.

In the silence that follows I hear a sound. The sound of it can't be him touching himself, can it? I really should leave. I take a step forward when a groan reaches me. The hair on the back of my neck rises. My nipples tighten. I should leave; I really should. Another groan, and this time, his voice is deeper as if he's in pain. My scalp tingles. I am going to hell for this.

I tip-toe toward the open doorway of the bathroom.

The sound of flesh hitting flesh grows louder. My mouth goes dry. All the moisture seems to have drained to between my thighs. My panties are smoking. I rub my sweaty palms on my bathrobe, then slide into the gap between the door and the frame. The heat assails me, surrounds me, swirls over me. The fragrance of spicy soap envelops me. Bergamot and mint and the bite of something darker. Something more potent. Like sherry oak and cinnamon, with a dash of dark chocolate. The scent of his skin.

My mouth waters. A pulse flares to life in my core. I take another step forward, peer through the steam, and spot him. He's in the shower cubicle. The walls are fogged up, but there are enough clear patches left for me to make out that his shoulders are moving. His chest heaves. His biceps strain. His arm moves faster—and fuck me—the steam covers the most vital portion, his center. The wet sound of flesh hitting flesh seems to deepen. The thick notes fill the space. *Slap-slap-slap.* The tendons of his gorgeous throat flex. His jaw tightens, and color smears his cheeks. His hair is slicked back from his face, and maybe that's water clinging to his face, but maybe it's sweat? My fingers itch to touch him, and I curl them into fists at my sides. I narrow my gaze as his entire body jerks. His movements get even more frantic. Little dots of fire dance across the surface of my skin. Ohmigod, this is the most erotic thing I've ever seen. I squeeze my thighs together, bite down on the inside of my cheek to stop myself from moaning aloud.

"Fuck," he growls. "Fuck, Lena, fuck." He throws back his head and shouts as he climaxes.

Wait, what? Did he— Did I hear that right? Did he just say my name? A shudder grips me. My toes curl. I watch as he continues to jerk himself off, his movements growing slower, until finally he hits the wall with a thud, his eyes closed. His features compose into serene lines. There's a small smile on his face. He's more relaxed than I've seen him. Admittedly, I've only just met him, but the tenseness of his body and the way he held himself, all sharp angles and strained tendons, indicated this is a man who never lets down his walls. Except for when he's jerking off, apparently.

How would it be to see him come apart as he rams into me? As he buries his fat cock inside my pussy and drills into me over and over again. As he squeezes my breasts and drags his thumb down the seam of my slit and into the most forbidden part of me. "Oh god!" I gasp, then clap my palm over my mouth. But it's too late. He snaps his eyes open and his gaze locks with mine.

7

JJ

That was yesterday. I'm not sure if I should be pissed off at her for sneaking a peek at me as I jerked off, or if I should be pissed off at myself for finding the entire incident so hot. But then, I am one depraved motherfucker. On the other hand, I've never brought my sexual proclivities to my house. So what if I live alone? This is the house my kids grew up in, and as long as they were around, I ensured no woman ever came home with me. I've kept my tendencies to outside my place of residence. Believe it or not, I've never before jerked off in my own home. I didn't need to. There are enough women to bed outside the house to keep my sex drive satisfied. This month of being celibate, by chance, is definitely playing havoc with my libido, especially considering I'm still turned on this morning as I drink my tea and stare at the garden from the kitchen window.

"Good morning," a chirpy voice greets me.

I turn to find Lena walking into the kitchen. She's wearing heels which help snap back her shoulders and her butt, her suit jacket is conservative and buttoned in the front... But her skirt? It comes to just above her knees, which is perfectly acceptable. But the fabric is cut so it clings to her thighs, and there's a slit up one side that opens to reveal the smooth, brown skin of her thigh before pulling back together and covering it up again. Fucking hell, I bet she wore it just to taunt me.

She keeps her back turned to me as she reaches the counter. She glances around, then leans down to pull out a drawer below the counter. The skirt stretches tight across the perfectly lush curves of her butt. And just like that, I'm erect again. *Jesus Christ, can't I control myself around this woman at all?*

"What are you looking for?" I snap.

She stiffens, then draws to her full height before turning to face me. "Who pissed in your coffee?" She scowls.

I'd like to piss on you, actually. A-n-d, moving on swiftly. "There's tea. You're in England, remember?" I raise my cup, toast her, then take another sip.

"You drink tea in the morning?" Her features are creased in an expression of horror.

"What about it?"

"And from a cup and saucer?" She glances at said objects in fascination.

"So?" I drain the cup and place it on the saucer, then pull up the cuff of my sleeve to glance at my watch. "It's getting late. Let's chat on the way."

"But coffee—"

"Make sure you get down here earlier if you want to get your fix." I grab my briefcase from the island and turn toward the door.

"It's barely seven," she protests.

"It's three minutes past seven, actually, and I'm already late." I stalk toward the door and hear the clip-clop of her heels against the wooden floor as she rushes to keep up with me. I don't slow my steps. Not because I'm a sadist—well, not this time anyway—but because I'm not going to make this easy on her. If it were anyone else in that role, they wouldn't get concessions, so I don't see why I need to bend the rules for her. Just because she's my son's girlfriend—*fuck, she's my son's girlfriend.*

A crater seems to open up in my chest. She's not mine. She belongs to someone else, and not just anyone else, but my own son. The same son I've been estranged from for years, and with whom I've thought I'd never have a chance to mend our relationship. I need to keep my eyes and my hands off of her.

What happened last night was a one-off. An incident I need to move on from. Only, I can't pretend it didn't happen at all. Not when jerking off to her brought me to orgasm in a way being with other women never has.

I stalk toward the entrance of the house and walk out. I take the steps two at a time, aware that she's on my heels. I reach the bottom just as Leo, my chauffeur, drives up with my car. I open the door, and turn in time to see her trip on the last step. I move so fast my feet don't seem to touch the ground and catch her. Her soft curves seem to melt into me. Her scent—strawberry and passionfruit— fills my lungs. My throat closes. My cock lengthens. Every inch of my body seems to light up like it's the Fourth-of-July and Christmas rolled into one. Fucking fuck.

I place her aside, holding onto her shoulder until I'm sure she's steady on her feet. She shoves her hair from her face and her fingers tremble. The feel of her shoulder is permanently etched into my finger-tips. The air between us seems to sizzle with unspoken emotions. She draws in a shaky breath and so do I. The silence stretches for a beat, another. It's she who recovers first, while I stay frozen like a teenager caught in the proximity of his first crush.

"Thanks," she murmurs, not meeting my eyes, then brushes past me. Like a fool I take in another deep inhale of her scent, before she slides inside the car with a flash of her luscious thighs. She pulls her legs in and I close the door, then walk around and seat myself next to her.

I raise the partition between the driver's seat and the passenger seat. She glances at me then away as Leo eases the car forward.

We drive in silence for a few seconds, then she clears her throat. "Do you always leave for your office this early?"

"I'm late today, in deference to you joining me. Starting tomorrow, we leave at 6 a.m."

"What the—?" She swivels to face me. "Why do you bother coming back home? Even you—"

She takes in the smirk on my face and her features redden. "Haha, very funny." She scoffs.

"You're easy to get a rise out of," I admit.

"So, you do leave for work at this time every day?"

"Not for the last few days. I was busy helping Massimo rescue his wife, who'd been taken by the man she'd been promised to before Massimo came along and married her."

"Eh?" Her gaze widens. "Did all that happen, for real?"

"Afraid so. When you're in a position of power, you're bound to rub people the wrong way. People who then take revenge by hurting those close to you. That's why it pays to make common cause with those who's enemies are the same as yours."

"So, you're in an organized crime group?"

"Would it make a difference to you if I said I was?"

She appears to think it over then shakes her head. "Frankly, no. You are the CEO of your business and a rich man. You couldn't have gotten to that level without bending the law at some point."

I tilt my head. "Astute observation. Apparently, you're not just another pretty face."

She flushes. "That's a very chauvinistic remark. I look good, so it automatically means I can't think for myself, right?"

"I didn't say that."

"You implied it."

I raise my hands. "All I meant was that was an insightful remark for someone as young as you."

"Don't be fooled by my youth. I was born wiser than my years."

My lips twitch. "That's why you turned and ran after you came across me last night?"

She flushes, then dips her head so her thick auburn hair falls over her face. "That was different," she coughs.

"How is it different? If you had experience, you'd have managed the situation a little more like a grown-up."

"I didn't mean to barge into your room like that. I only wanted to ask what time you planned to leave for the office today."

"And now, you're trying to change the topic."

She reddens even more, if that's possible. Her brown eyes flash at me. "I am not. I'm simply trying to explain why I walked into your room to find you—"

"Jerking off?"

Her breath stutters, then she tips up her chin and meets my gaze. "I was going to go with wanking, but sure, we can call it jerking off."

"Did you enjoy it?"

"Excuse me?"

"It's an easy enough question. Did you like what you saw?"

"You do realize I'm your son's girlfriend?" She swallows.

"And both of you need a roof over your heads, not to mention, the job I offered you."

"So that means you can say anything to me and I have to take it?"

I stare at her, and she firms her lips.

"You do realize, you're crossing all kinds of lines here?" she says in a low voice.

"I've crossed lines all my life, what's one more?"

8

Lena

So that wasn't awkward at all. I'd hoped he'd just not allude to what happened; that he'd pretend it never took place and then, we'd drive to work and he'd tell me about my new role and what he expects from me... Instead, after that excruciating exchange, which left me uncomfortable and with misgivings—and I hate to say, a little turned on, too —he seemed to lose interest in me and focused on his phone for the rest of the trip.

The fact that he'd brought up our little encounter surprised me so much I'd forgotten to ask him about the turtle. Well, it's something I'm going to bring up... at the appropriate time. Nothing like being armed with knowledge, right?

After a mostly silent trip—where I had tried hard not to take a lungful of JJ-scented air, how creepy would that have been? — we arrive at the offices of his company, and he hands me off to his HR manager. For the next three hours, Jillian walks me through a quick introduction to the company, has me sign the employment contract—

which all seems above-board, except when I come to the part about the salary. The figure I see makes my heart stutter. It's five times what I expected to make in this position. I check with Jillian and she confirms that, indeed, that is the salary for the position. It's the amount he would have paid Isaac, supposedly. The rest of the session passes without incident. All too soon, she's walking me to the top floor of the building, and down a corridor so hushed the pads of my heeled feet on the carpet seem to echo around the space. We walk past rows of offices with glass doors through which I see people at work on computers, then a massive conference room packed with stony-faced, suited executives, until finally we arrive at double doors with handles of which is carved *Kane*. Very subtle. I snort to myself and Jillian glances at me curiously.

"Sorry." I roll my shoulders. "I'm nervous, is all."

She nods. "You have good reason to be. This is a brand-new role where you will be working in close proximity with him. I can't say I envy you."

Is that supposed to be reassuring?

We pause in front of the desk next to the double doors, and a blonde haired, blue-eyed woman glances up from her computer. Her makeup is perfect; winged eyeliner graces her doe eyes. She ignores me and frowns at Jillian. "He's busy."

"He also instructed me to bring her to his office as soon as I completed her orientation."

She looks me up and down then scowls. "Who's she?"

What's up her ass? Does everyone who works with this man have an attitude or what?

"I'm Lena. Lena Richards, Mr. Kane's new executive assistant."

She ignores my proffered hand. "I'm Karen Day, his *personal* assistant," she replies in an icy voice that implies, somehow, being his personal assistant is much more important than being his executive assistant. *Whatever, sister. I have no wish to be his secretary. That position is all yours.*

Jillian blows out a breath. "You know he doesn't like to be kept waiting, Karen," she warns.

Karen tosses her head, then presses the Bluetooth receiver in her ear, "Yes, Mr. Kane. Jillian is here with your new executive assistant."

Her face falls as she listens, and she touches the earbud, then nods toward his door. "Go ahead."

"Good luck," Jillian whispers.

"Wait, you're not coming in with me?" Why do I sound so panicked? I'm a professional, about to start my first day on a new job. I should be happy. This job is everything I've always wanted. It's my chance to leave my mark on the world. All I have to do is see this through, make enough money to be able to pay the rent and deposit on a new place, and Isaac and I will be out of this asshole's hair.

"You'll be fine." Jillian squeezes my arm. "And if you need anything, just call me. My office is down the corridor."

"Thanks." I draw in a breath, then turn and pull open the door.

I step through, and the door closes behind me with a soft click. The hair on the nape of my neck stands on end. Why do I feel like I've walked into the den of a predator? If I thought the corridor outside was hushed, boy, this room is completely silent, except for the hum of the air-conditioning and a very faint voice that sounds like a tiny man trapped inside of a tin can. Rays of sunlight pour through floor-to-ceiling windows that constitute the far wall. In front of the window is a massive desk with at least three computer screens. And between them is my boyfriend's father with his back to me. He's speaking on the phone.

"No, that doesn't work for me. Tardiness will not be tolerated. Make sure the shipment reaches me on time, or the deal is off." He disconnects, then swivels around to face me. He's wearing eyeglasses —square, black-framed, Clark Kent-style specs that turn him from gorgeous to sinful, all the way to number eleven on my imaginary scale. Jesus, is there anything this man can't do to make himself even sexier?

He sits down behind his desk and pulls up sheets of paper. He begins reading through them as I stand there wondering what to do next. Didn't he notice me? I'm sure he did. Maybe this is his way of telling me I don't matter? Well, big fucking deal. He's paying me. It's up to him how he decides to use my time, right? I march up to his table and rap my knuckles on it. "Excuse me, Mr. Kane—"

"JJ," he snaps.

"Eh?" I blink.

"My name is JJ," he says with exaggerated patience.

Fine, if that's what he wants me to call him, I can oblige. "JJ," I begin again, "what do you want from—"

His phone rings again, and he picks it up and listens to the person on the other side. "No, that doesn't work for me. It's a million. That's my final offer; take it or leave it." Once more, he disconnects and drops his phone on the table, then leans back and places his fingers together. "I suppose you want me to tell you what the scope of your role is going to be?"

"That would help, yes." I feel my eyebrows scrunching up into a scowl and smoothen out my forehead. "You offered me the role, so it would be best if we establish what you expect from me."

"Hmm..." A glint appears in his eyes, but when he speaks his voice is professional. "I expect you to fill in for me in meetings I can't attend, to be the first point of contact for my team, to intercept emails before they get to me, to be my chief of staff, and to make decisions as needed. In short, you serve as the primary point of contact for internal and external constituencies, serve as a liaison to the board of directors and senior management teams, and oversee special projects. You'll do everything except the administrative duties, which will be fulfilled by Karen, who from now on, will be reporting to you."

"She will?"

"You are the gatekeeper of my time and you'll ensure it's stream-lined so I get the most out of it." He jerks his chin toward a desk I only now notice in the far corner of the room. "That's your work station. Your email is set up and you've been copied on different task lists already."

I blink, then whip my face in his direction. "Wait, we're working in the same room?"

"It's how I always intended my executive assistant to work."

"But why? Isn't it better if I worked from a different room?"

"It's more convenient this way. We'll save time by being able to discuss things without my having to hunt you down."

I hunch my shoulders. Dammit, he does have a point. I hate it when he sounds so logical. I have no reason to challenge him.

"Okay," I breathe out, then turn to head to my desk.

"If you could, ask Karen to get me a coffee while you get started."

An hour later, I stretch my arms. I managed to log into my computer without any issues. The password the IT department had given me actually worked. Imagine that? I ordered his coffee and Karen walked in within minutes, swishing her ass in a way that was designed to grab the attention of every man and woman within a mile. To his credit, JJ paid no attention to it. He was buried in whatever it was he was working on in between answering phone calls. I managed to keep my eyes off of him and focused on the emails that were coming thick and fast into my inbox. The scope of the businesses he handles is mind-boggling. From Trinity Media, one of his most profitable ventures, to interests in a series of amusement parks, to the ownership of one of the biggest advertising agency networks, which he took over recently, and investments in various well-known social networking platforms, not to mention an upcoming joint venture with 7A Investments, the man is running a conglomerate.

My opinion of him has certainly changed by the time I shoot him a glance to find him staring back at me.

I frown. "Was there something you wanted to talk about?"

9

JJ

"You could start by being a little more polite toward me. I do pay your salary."

"Like I could forget," she mutters under her breath.

"What was that?" I scowl.

She clears her throat. "I meant, is there anything I can help you with?" She smiles sweetly.

"Anyone ever tell you you're a terrible liar?"

She grimaces. "Something you need my help with? Else..." She turns back to her computer.

"Lunch." I rise to my feet, then walk around the desk. "I have a lunch meeting with some of the partners of 7A Investments and I need you there."

"Okay." She trails me as I head for the exit. I hold the door open for her, and she breezes past. The scent of strawberries and passionfruit singed with something spicy fills my senses. I'm instantly erect. Goddamn. Somehow, I've managed to keep my attention off of her and focused on my work thus far. I almost changed my mind about having her seated in my room, but convinced myself that I could hold out against her appeal. Now, I wonder if I made a mistake.

Of course, I had intended for whoever was my EA to work out of the same room as me, and I wasn't lying when I said it was for the sake of convenience. I'd hoped it would be my son and that I could use the time to repair my relationship with him. Now I know what a bad idea that was. It would have been even worse to have Isaac seated where she's been and glowering at me. We couldn't have gone ten minutes without disagreeing on things, forget an hour.

And with her? I'm not sure I can ignore how her presence lights up the space or just how aware I am of her every move—of how she squirms around in her seat trying to get comfortable, how she sighs when she's focused on reading something, how she ties her hair up with a hair restraint when she wants it out of the way, then stabs a pencil through the mass of hair when she's trying to figure out a problem. Yeah, you see what's happening here? I ended up studying her more than reading my documents over the past hour. I tried and failed to keep my attention off of her, so sue me. Following her out, I raise my hand when my other assistant tries to tell me something.

"Not now," I mutter in her general direction, then follow the vixen who's walking forward with that twitch to her hips that's guaranteed to drive me crazy. Maybe it wasn't such a good idea to have her take on this role? Maybe I should have simply allowed her and Isaac to move into the house and asked them to keep their distance from me. But that's not me. I don't just give people what they want without getting something in return. I'm too hardwired to not strike a deal when I see an opportunity.

No, this is the best way forward. This way, I have Isaac doing what he loves, while still under the umbrella of my company, and I have his girlfriend—and I need to keep reminding myself of that—filling in for him while getting much-needed experience out of it. No, I simply need to keep my perspective and my distance from her. And I can do that much, can't I? After all, I've negotiated mergers, and I struck a deal with the *Bratva* and the *Cosa Nostra* to launch my most successful company in Trinity Enterprises. I even managed to lock down a meeting with the notoriously reticent owners of 7A Financial Services. It's going to my biggest coup to date when I get them on board for my newest enterprise. And I need my executive assistant in on the details. It's the only way to ensure that I stay on top of her—I mean on top of day-to-day decisions.

With the proliferation of my business interests, even I have to admit that I can't be in two meetings at the same time—imagine that—and I need to delegate. Hence, the creation of the position of my Executive Assistant. The position really is more of my Chief-of-Staff, as I mentioned to her, but I'll hold back the title until she proves herself, starting with the meeting we're headed for now.

I join her as the lift to my private elevator arrives. She steps in, I follow and punch the button for the lobby level. The silence stretches as the numbers count down on the indicator. That's when her stomach rumbles.

She gasps, them murmurs, "Sorry."

"You're hungry, I take it?"

"I didn't have breakfast because someone was in too much of a hurry."

I shoot her a sideways glance and find her watching the indicators with a look of complete focus.

"Make sure you are ready by 6.30 a.m. tomorrow," I retort.

She winces. "Don't you ever sleep?"

"Sleep is for losers." I scoff.

She shakes her head. "You do realize Gordon Gekko went out of fashion in the nineties, and *The Wolf of Wall Street* is considered in bad taste by those of our generation."

I shoot her a sideways glance when my phone buzzes. I pull it out of my pocket, then listen to the head of my US office tell me why it's a bad idea to expand into financial services. I interrupt him halfway through the conversation, "Winnie, the difference between you and me is that I have the long game in my sights, while you're not able to draw the most obvious conclusion from what is right in front of your nose."

I disconnect before he can respond. The indicator dings and I indicate for her to precede me.

"Do you talk like that to all your employees?"

"Like what?" We exit through my private entrance to one side of the lobby as Leo brings my car around.

"Like you don't give a damn about retaining them."

"They are grown men. I pay them well enough and give them enough responsibility that they'd never get such plum positions anywhere else. On the other hand, if they leave, I have ten other people waiting in line to replace them; so, if they want to leave, they are most welcome to do so."

She firms her lips. I pull the door open, indicating for her to get in, then walk around to slide in next to her.

"I did have one more question," she murmurs.

"What's that?"

"Why do you use a dumbphone?"

"A what?" I frown.

"A non-smartphone." She gestures to the phone I'd just pocketed.

"Because I have an executive assistant who is supposed to screen my emails. And this way, I can focus on the more important decisions, rather than getting dragged into the nitty gritty of everyday operations."

As if on cue, the new smartphone I'd had waiting for her at her desk and which she'd picked up earlier buzzes. She pulls it out and gasps, "What the—"

"Problem?" I drawl.

"What? No." She scowls at the phone. The color fades from her features. She gapes at her screen, then gets busy with her fingers flying over it. I'm sure the emails are hitting her inbox. Chances are good there are at least fifty new emails clamoring for her attention in the ten minutes it took for us to get to the car from my office.

Hopefully she's answering the ones she can, and forwarding the rest to me. I'll find out when I get to my office, no doubt.

"We're here," I murmur.

"What—" She glances up and her eyes widen. "Already?"

I push the door open on my side, step out and walk around to find she's already on her feet. She glances up at the building we've come to.

"We're at *The Shard*?"

She blinks. Is she impressed? She should be, not only is it the tallest building in London, it also has the most expensive and well-known restaurant in the city. It's also one of the few venues exclusive enough to afford me privacy, which is why I'd chosen it for this upcoming meeting. It wasn't to impress her, not at all.

The security guard at the entrance snaps to attention.

"JJ, good to see you again, Sir."

I clap him on the back. "Good man, how are you, Gerard? How are the children?"

"I'm good, and they're not children anymore. Sabrina's off to university, and Samuel is in his final year of school."

"No way." I stare. "Seems like only yesterday when they were born," I say slowly.

"Tell me about it. Time sure doesn't wait for anyone." Gerard smiles.

"Not even for those who have money. That's why it's best to go for what you want in life. You never know, it might all be taken away tomorrow."

"Wise words, Sir." He holds open the door and Lena precedes me.

"Send my regards to the family." I wave my goodbye then guide Lena past the bank of elevators to the private one at the far side. I press the button and the elevator doors open. I gesture for her to step in and punch the button for the top floor. Yeah, time sure does go by, and we often don't even realize it. I was twenty-four when I had my daughter Tally and twenty-six when I had Isaac. I threw myself into building this business, wanting to give them everything I'd never had. In the process, I ignored my wife and children, and by the time I realized it, my kids were teenagers and I'd already lost them. Then next thing I knew, my wife and I were divorced, and my kids were leaving home. While my daughter was more open to having a relationship with me, Isaac refused to have anything to do with me. Yeah, time sure does fly, especially when you're busy chasing a mirage instead of focusing on what you have under your own roof.

We ride in silence for a few seconds, then she glances at me. "That was a nice thing you did."

"Eh?" I blink then meet her gaze. "What's that?"

"What you did back there—acknowledging the security guard, asking him about his family; that was very generous of you."

"Because I spoke to him?"

She nods. "Not too many people in your position would do that. Plus, you seemed to know a lot about his family."

"He's an old friend," I raise a shoulder.

"Don't know of many billionaires who'd call a security guard their friend," she comments.

"How many billionaires do you know, anyway?" I shoot back.

She glowers at me.

"That's what I thought." I turn to face forward again. "There are fifteen more seconds to go until we reach our floor. You should put them to good use and get through the emails, which I'm sure are hitting your inbox as we speak."

Her frown deepens. She opens her mouth to speak, when her phone buzzes. She glances at me, then a small smile curves her lips. *The fuck? Who's messaging her? Is it my son? He has a right to, though, after all. She's* his *girlfriend. His* girlfriend. *And* my *employee. That's* all *she is.*

The elevator slows down and comes to a stop. The doors swish open. I indicate for her to go through, and once more, I follow her to the reception desk in the corner.

"JJ," the hostess greets me. "It's been a while since we last saw you." She walks over to me, and reaches up on tiptoes to press a kiss to my cheek.

Behind me I hear her inhale sharply. *Good, she's jealous. I hope she's jealous. Why the hell do I care if she's jealous?* This is not like me. So focused on a woman. And one who belongs to my son, no less.

I wind my arm around the hostess's waist with more gusto than necessary and kiss her on both cheeks. "Daisy, my dear, you're looking as gorgeous as ever."

Daisy blushes, then pats my cheek. "You're a charmer, JJ." She steps back then tilts her head in Lena's direction. "Miss, welcome to H2O lounge. Is this your first time here?"

She nods.

"May I take your coat?" Daisy asks.

Lena begins to take off her overcoat and I step forward. "Allow me."

Lena stiffens, but she allows me to ease the coat off of her shoulders. My fingers brush against her palm, and she shivers.

"You cold?" I frown.

"A little." She glances away.

It's April but the weather has turned chilly the way London often does in early spring. "Could you turn up the heating in here?" I hand Lena's coat to Daisy, then shrug mine off and hand that to her, as well.

"Of course, JJ." She turns and hands our coats to another uniformed girl who has come up to stand behind us. Then, she leads the way to the low table in the far corner with chaises on either side of it. A couple is already seated on one of the sofas.

Daisy smiles at me with more warmth than the situation demands. "I'll leave you to your guests." She turns and leaves.

The man on the sofa rises to his feet. He glances between us, his gaze assessing, then he holds out his hand. "JJ."

"Sinclair," I shake his hand. "Good to see you again."

10

Lena

"So, how long have you worked for him?" The pretty pink-haired woman leans in toward me. Her name's Summer and she's Sinclair's wife. Sinclair, as I've learned, is one of the owners of 7A Investments, one of the leading financial service companies in Europe, as I gathered from one of the emails sent to me earlier. Good thing I scanned through it before leaving the office. JJ could have warned me this meeting was about a potential merger. Not that he'd have thought to do that, of course.

"Would you believe it if I told you today is my first day at his office?" I raise my glass of water to my lips.

"No." Summer glances from me to JJ, then back to me. Her eyes gleam. "He's hot, eh?" she says in a low voice.

The water goes down the wrong pipe, and I burst out coughing. I spill some of the water on myself.

"Ohmigosh, I'm so sorry." Summer uses her napkins to dab at the front of my blouse.

I continue to cough, and some more water spills from the glass I have in my hand. "Shit." I place it down on the table, then press my knuckles to my mouth in a bid to stop coughing. A large hand slaps my back, and again. The water finally slides down my gullet and I stop coughing. Tears wet my cheeks, and I accept the napkin from Summer and pat my them dry.

"You okay?" JJ rumbles.

"Yes, of course. Sorry. Carry on." I ball up the napkin and fix a smile on my face.

"I'm so sorry," Summer whispers to me. "It's being pregnant..." She motions to the barely perceptible bump around her middle. "Afraid all I have is sex on my mind."

I choke back a laugh. She's direct—I'll give her that—but her manner is so self-deprecating, I can't bring myself to take offense.

"Don't worry," I whisper back.

"You sure you're okay?" JJ's voice is laced with concern, and perhaps, frustration. I risk a glance at him, and his forehead is furrowed. His glance is tinged with impatience. Of course, we're here to talk about a very important deal, and here I am, totally messing this up.

"I'm good," I say in a firm voice and straighten my back. "Sorry about that."

"Oh, please don't apologize. That was my fault entirely." Summer turns to JJ. "Please forgive me. I distracted your associate."

JJ's lips kick up. "No harm done," he says in a gentle voice, then turns to Sinclair. "As I was saying, I'd very much like to invite 7A Investments to be one of the first to back Club Infinity."

"You're starting a nightclub?" I burst out before I can stop myself.

"A gentleman's club, actually," Sinclair murmurs.

"A gentleman's club which is also open to the ladies, surely?" Summer pipes up.

JJ glances toward her. "You're right, it's a club that's open to everyone who qualifies. The only criteria behind memberships is that they're limited to those nominated by an existing member, and to be eligible to be a member, you need to have made a difference in your particular field."

"Hmm," Summer presses a finger to her cheek, "so it can be a contribution in any form? Not just cash?"

"Definitely not just cash. The club will not distinguish between people based on their monetary worth. It's not just their net worth but the value they've added in terms of their art or their service to people, or what they've given back to the community."

"And who would have the final approval?" I ask.

"Me, of course" —JJ's lips twist and he turns his attention back to Sinclair— "and if 7A agrees to back the club, you'll get one person nominated to the board who will have the right to veto the membership."

"Who else is backing the club?" Sinclair's eyes gleam. Good God, the man's hot. With his dark hair, chiseled cheekbones, those broad shoulders which stretch his tailor-made jacket, and his thick thighs spread wide apart, he takes up most of the space on the settee. In comparison, his wife is petite, and with her mischievous eyes and boho style clothing, she couldn't be more of a contrast to him. He wraps his arm around her and pulls her close. She all but melts into his side. He looks down at her, and his features soften.

A ball of emotion clogs my throat. Gosh, the two of them look so much in love. Will I find someone who looks at me the way Sinclair looks at Summer? I do have a boyfriend, though, don't I? Does Isaac look at me like that? Like he can't get enough of me. Like he'd do anything for me. Like he can't stop himself from touching me, and can't take his eyes off me. Like the world begins and ends with me. A ball of emotion clogs my throat. My heart thrums like the wings of a butterfly. I glance toward JJ to find him staring at me.

I scowl at him. He narrows his gaze. There's a considering look on his face. "It's not for public disclosure yet." He turns to face the Sterlings. "But for you, I'm making an exception. Investors include the Sovranos and the Soloniks."

Sinclair straightens. "You mean the *Cosa Nostra* and the *Bratva*?"

There's no change in expression on JJ's face, but the very fact that his features grow impassive warn me that he's on alert. "Is that a problem?"

Sinclair's shoulders tense, then his features relax. "On the contrary, the Don of the *Cosa Nostra* and I are bound by marriage now, so this will help consolidate the relationship."

"You mean this will help you keep an eye on their goings on, don't you?" JJ smirks.

"I mean—" Sinclair bares his teeth in the semblance of a smile, "—since the *Cosa Nostra* have been legalizing their businesses, I'm sure the Don and I will be happy to have more dealings in common."

At this point, a waiter wheels over a bucket of ice and a bottle of champagne, along with champagne flutes that he places on the table. He opens the bottle with a pop and pours it into our glasses.

When he leaves, Sinclair raises his glass of champagne. "To new associates."

JJ clinks his glass with Sinclair's. "And to old friends."

———

Two hours later, we're on our way back home in JJ's car. After the toast, JJ and Sinclair discussed some other business while Summer told me more about the Seven and their wives and girlfriends, and how over the moon she is that she and Karma are pregnant together. The meeting wrapped up shortly after. Summer kissed me goodbye and exchanged numbers with me. All in all, I enjoyed myself. It was 5.30 p.m. and JJ indicated he was ready to head home. I expected him to return to the office, but I'm more than happy to turn homeward instead.

"Sinclair's wife is lovely," I murmur.

JJ doesn't reply. He glances out the window, his forehead furrowed. His suit jacket is unbuttoned to reveal his crisp white shirt. There's a slight shadow over his chin and cheeks, which is the only indication that it's the end of the day and not the beginning. The rest of him is as put together as if he were on his way to the office instead of on his way home.

"What do you make of Sinclair?" He turns to me.

"Eh?" I blink. "You're asking me?"

He scowls, "Do you see anyone else here?"

A-n-d, there he is. The alphahole I've come to expect. Clearly, he was on his best behavior because of the company we were in.

"Well?" His scowl deepens. "I asked you a question, girl."

"I do have a name."

"What's that got to do with anything?"

I firm my lips. *I will not get angry. Will not get angry.* Jerk-ass is my boss. And he's given me a roof over my head. He was probably born with a bad attitude. There's nothing he can do about it. I should pretend he's a child. Yeah, a grumpy, petulant kid who has yet to learn his manners. Yes, that's what he is.

I stare straight ahead. "I think he's as much of an ornery, uncompromising business man as you. As confident as you about his ability to influence people so they fall in with his plans. He must believe in your vision for he agreed to invest in your initiative. Also, I think he trusts you."

"Why do you say that?" he asks.

The curiosity in his tone makes me shoot him a sideways glance. "Because he brought his wife along for the meeting. He strikes me as the type who'd never agree to his wife meeting a person unless he had complete faith in you."

"Or he was using it to put me at ease, while he plots a way to ambush me," JJ says almost to himself.

This time I turn to face him. "You really don't trust anybody, do you?"

"Not a soul." His tone is matter-of-fact.

My phone—my personal phone— buzzes again. I pull it out and peek at the chat notifications in my family group.

Josh: Lena where are you?

Josh: Lena

Mira: She's probably shacked up with a boyfriend. Do you have a new boyfriend Lena?

Josh: Lena?

Seema: Lenny baby what's the goss?

Mom: Leave her alone, you guys. She must be busy with a new assignment. That is all it is, right, Lena?

Josh: Lennaaa?

Mira: Think we should try calling her?

Josh: Let's

Seema: Oooh better still maybe we should take that trip to London and surprise her

Wha-a-a-t? My gaze widens. No, no, no, I can't have my siblings landing here. I begin to type—

Me: STFU you guys. I'm alive just busy

Josh: Lenaaa hey is it true that Guinness tastes better in London than anywhere else in the world?

Mira: You're talking about Ireland specifically Dublin you dumbass

I laugh aloud.

"Something funny?" JJ's voice cuts through my thoughts.

"What? No, it's nothing." I pocket my phone, then glance out the window. I was only messaging my family. That's allowed, right? So what if I'm technically still at work and with my boss?

"Was that Isaac?"

I blink, then blow out a breath. "No, not Isaac."

He pauses as if considering my reply, then, "Are you seeing someone else? Is that what this is about? Because if you are being unfaithful to my son, I promise you, that's not a good idea you—"

"How dare you accuse me of cheating? Also, it's no business of yours. It's between me and your son."

"And I am invested in my son, so it's my business. Is that what this is about?" He leans in closer. His dark eyes are stormy, like the darkness at the bottom of a well when you peek over the side. Something ugly stirs in them, like the eels which dart through the surface of still water. "You taking advantage of my son? Moving in with him, getting him to give you a roof over your head, then going off and being with someone else? You fucking someone else, Lena? Is that what you're doing?"

"And if I were?" Anger crowds my chest. My throat is choked up with a strange feeling I can't define. Heat flushes my skin and I feel the rage vibrating off of me. "What's it to you? You may have given me a place to stay and a job, but you don't own me. My personal life is my own."

"No, it's not. Not as long as you're my son's girlfriend."

"What the—" I gape. Did he really just say that? He couldn't have said that.

Something ugly twists in my stomach. I lean in close enough so my face is only a few inches from his. "I'll fuck anyone I want," I say through gritted teeth.

His features harden. "What did you say?"

He lowers his gaze to my mouth, and liquid heat squeezes my belly. *What? No.* You can't have that reaction to this... this... douchebag. Asshole thinks he owns me? Well, I'm going to set him straight.

"I said, I'll. Fuck. Anyone. I. Wa—"

He clamps his fingers around my neck, and yanks me to him.

11

JJ

Don't do it, don't do it. She's Isaac's girlfriend. Your son's girlfriend, you sick fuck. I squeeze my fingers around the nape of her neck and hold her so close that our eyelashes brush against each other's. Her breathing grows ragged, and her golden-brown eyes lighten until they are amber. The pulse at the hollow of her neck beats like a trapped bird.

"Do it, and you'll not only lose your position in my company, but I'll also make sure Isaac doesn't get a chance to have his paintings displayed in my offices."

Splotches of color smear her cheeks. "You wouldn't," she chokes.

"Try me," I say through gritted teeth.

She sets her jaw, then juts out her chin. "You're a heartless bastard."

"You have no idea how true that is." I release her, and the car draws to a stop in front of my home. I shove the door open, walk around the car, and without waiting for her, walk up the steps. When I reach the

top, I turn to find she's pushed the car door open and is standing at the
foot of the staircase.

"I'll see you and Isaac in the conservatory in an hour."

"Fuck you," she throws back at me.

I laugh. "I could have you fired for swearing at me, but I guess I'll
keep you around for amusement."

The door opens and Craig steps back. I brush past him and stalk
over to the stairs, taking them two at a time until I reach my suite. I
walk in and head straight for my bathroom, stripping off my clothes as
I go along. How dare she say that she can fuck anyone else? She
belongs to my son; she can't go around doing something that would
break his heart. I won't let her hurt him. That's all this is. I was
protecting Isaac from any more heartache. God knows, I've given him
enough to last a lifetime. I'm not going to let her compound it by
sleeping around.

That's the only reason I'm angry. It has nothing do with the red-hot
rage that filled me at the thought of her sleeping with someone else.
I'm angry on his behalf. That's why my guts are churning, and that's
the only reason my chest feels heavy like I had swallowed a stone. Yep.
And I did the right thing by warning her off. I was making sure to safe-
guard my son's future, is all.

I prowl into the shower and stand under the heavy jets, letting the
streams of water beat on my shoulders. I press my palms into the wall
of the shower and glance down to where my cock springs up from
between my legs. Jesus, this constant state of arousal around her is
becoming a nuisance. One whiff of her strawberry-passionfruit scent,
and all the blood drained to my groin. It's part of the reason I lashed
out at her. That, and because she dared to defy me. Instead of agreeing
she'd stay loyal to my son, she challenged me. She's so damn aggravating, so full of life, so vital, so stubborn. What she needs is a good
spanking to get her in line. My fingers tingle. I will not jerk off to her
again, *will not*.

The thought of my palm prints on that curvy, dusky ass of hers
sends a shudder of desire down my spine. My cock thickens until it
fucking hurts. Goddamn her. I grab my dick and massage myself with
strong, hard swipes. From the root of my shaft to the swollen head,

and again... Honeyed skin, rosebud lips, dilated pupils that stare up at me as she drops to her knees and opens her mouth to take me in. As she swallows me down, and I swell to fill her throat. I wrap her hair around my palm and tug her head back, then forward, as I fuck her mouth. My movements grow faster. She digs her fingers into my thighs and holds on as she stares up at me with those big, brown eyes of hers. Tears squeeze out from the corners of her eyes and trail down her cheeks, leaving black tracks of her mascara. Her eyelashes are spiked, her color high. Her tits heave. Then she releases her hold on me, only to weight my balls and squeeze. My cock extends, the tension at the base of my spine splinters, and with a groan, I empty myself down her throat. The climax goes on and on, and I come so hard I see sparks at the edges of my vision. I squeeze my shaft from base to tip and shake off the last remaining drops of my cum. The water continues to beat down on me. I stagger forward and press my forehead into the wall. Jerking off in my bathroom like I'm a teenager... This is crazy. I need to find a way to take the edge off of my sexual frustration. Call any of the women who'll be only happy to spread her legs and give me a warm hole to fuck. Just until I get my equilibrium back, is all. I switch off the shower, dry myself, and get dressed. Then, I make the call.

———

By the time I walk down to meet my guests, I feel more like myself. I head toward the conservatory and the buzz of voices reaches me. I wanted to host this party for Massimo Sovrano and his new wife Olivia, not only because I had played a role in bringing them together, but also because it had put the Sovranos in my debt. One I intended to claim. When the doorbell rings, I veer toward it, glad for the interruption. I wave Craig off en route, then open the door.

Massimo and Olivia stand locked in a kiss. A plaster covers one side of his face. Asshole cut his cheek with his own knife, so it'd match the scar on Olivia's cheek—the one she'd gotten when one of the *Cosa Nostra*'s enemies had fired at her while she was on stage. She'd survived it, come out stronger, and been reunited with Massimo. They faced the challenges together and found each other. Now, he wraps his arm around her and hauls her close, then bends her over his arm and kisses her more deeply. The kiss seems to go on and on. The two of them are so lost in each other, they don't notice me. My chest grows heavy, and my guts churn. A hot sensation, very much like envy, infiltrates my veins. This is bullshit. I am not jealous of them. I'm not. I had my chance at having a wife and kids, and look how I screwed that up. I watch Massimo tilt his head further and Olivia moans. For fuck's sake if they want to make out couldn't they have stayed home? I clear my throat. "We do have bedrooms here, if you'd like me to show you one?" I mutter.

Olivia yelps, tries to pull away, but Massimo continues kissing her for another second or more. By the time he releases her, she's flushed, panting, and her eyes have a glazed look. She blinks up at her husband, who smirks.

She scowls back, then laughs, her features lighting up. Massimo's throat moves as he swallows. He seems like he's been struck by lightning or by love. A look I am never going to wear… A look I don't want to wear. That heavy sensation in my chest sinks to my stomach. I square my shoulders. "You guys ready to come in?"

12

Lena

"Had a good time at the office?" Isaac mutters from where he's flung himself on the bed.

I shoot him a glance, then blow out a breath. "You're not even dressed yet?" I complain.

"I am not going to this... this thing."

"You mean to this event which your father made us promise we'd go to?"

"Fuck that." He picks up his phone and begins to play with it.

I glance at my reflection. I'm wearing the one formal dress I have along with the same *Louboutin's* I wore to the office. Given the choice, I'd sleep in them; that's how comfortable they are. I've twisted up my hair into a sleek hairdo, refreshed my makeup, and overall, I look good, if I do say so myself. "Isaac." I turn and walk over to my boyfriend. "Please don't be difficult."

He continues to play with his phone. Honestly, sometimes it feels like I'm raising a child on my own, rather than cohabiting with a grown man.

"Isaac," I say in a warning voice.

He doesn't reply.

"Isaac, if you don't talk to me right now, I'm going to grab that phone from you."

He scoffs.

"Don't say I didn't warn you." I snatch his phone from him and he yells.

"Lena, what the fuck?"

I hold it behind me and back away from him. "I told you I would do it. Now that I have your full attention—"

He lunges toward me. I scream, then turn and race toward the door. I hear his footsteps stomp behind me a second before he wraps his arm around my waist.

"Isaac, stop it," I pant, holding the phone away from me. He reaches for it, so I move it to my other hand.

"Lena, give me the phone right now."

"No way." I try to wriggle out of his hold, but he tightens his grasp on me.

"Give me the phone," he says in a tight voice. "Right now."

"Why don't you get it from me, huh?"

He releases me so suddenly, I stumble. My hold on the phone loosens, it slips from my fingers and crashes to the floor facedown.

"Oh shit." I stand rooted to the floor.

He jumps past me, picks up the phone, then growls, "You fucking cracked the screen."

"I am so sorry," I say in a low voice. "Really, Isaac, I didn't intend for that to happen."

He turns to me. "I told you coming here was a bad idea. I'd rather have been homeless in the park than stay under the same roof as him. But you had to insist, didn't you? And now look what happened."

"Hold on, you're being unreasonable. We can repair the screen of your phone, okay, or God knows, your father can buy you a new one."

"I don't want anything from him. When will you get that through your head?"

"Isaac, please." I bite the inside of my cheek. "I am really sorry I dropped your phone. It was an accident. You know that, right? As for staying with your father, it's only temporary. Just until I've earned enough money so we can move to our own place. Also, this way you get to paint, and you have a ready audience for your creations—"

"You mean in his stuffy offices."

"It's going to be seen by people. Isn't that what you want? It's a win-win for everyone."

He blows out a breath. "You mean a win-win for you. You get to work for him and get experience that will help further your career."

He pockets the phone then begins to walk to the door.

"Wait, where are you going?"

"To this gathering. You wanted me there, right?"

"Only because it's a condition of your father's. And you can't go down dressed like that."

He glances down at the jeans which mold to his thighs, and the frayed jacket he wears that stretches across his shoulders. He doesn't look bad. In fact, he looks sexy in a bad-boy way—a look I don't mind. It's just... He appears way too underdressed, which, considering JJ didn't specify a dress code, is probably something he can get away with. It's just, I don't want to anger JJ any further. And given how formally he was dressed, chances are the rest of his guests will be similarly dressed.

"Can't I?" Isaac's eyes gleam. He spins around and heads out the door.

"Isaac, stop." I race after him, but his long strides eat up the distance. He walks to the stairs, taking them two at a time. By the time I reach the bottom of the stairs, he's already at the doorway to the conservatory.

"Oh, hell." I break into a run, but by the time I reach the conservatory, he's already halfway across the floor. I glance around and take in the men dressed in tailor-made suits and the women in elegant dresses. In one corner, a man kneels next to a little girl. There's a cat next to her and she's petting it. Except for them, every other person's gaze is on me. I blow out a breath and resist the urge to glance away from the sea of designer suits and elegant dresses. So what if my own is an off-the-rack charity shop dress. I look good in it. I do. The hair on the back of my neck rises. A shiver snakes its way under my skin.

I jerk my chin up to find JJ glaring at me from across the room. Eh? As if it's my fault his son decided to gatecrash his party dressed like he's going on a hike. I refuse to feel guilty about that. I am not his son's keeper. I am his... Girlfriend? I *am* his girlfriend. Doesn't mean I should have to continuously try to keep him in line. Especially when JJ himself seems to go out of his way to antagonize Isaac. I purse my lips, and JJ's glare deepens. I tip up my chin, turn my gaze toward Isaac and groan. He's at the bar, pouring himself a drink. I cross the floor to reach him, conscious that every gaze in the room is on me.

"Isaac, what are you doing?" I hiss.

"Having a drink. What does it look like?" He tosses back the whiskey, then grabs the bottle of Macallan and pours himself another healthy portion. He raises it to his lips and I grab his arm.

"Please, Isaac, don't get drunk."

"It's only my second drink."

"You know you don't have a great tolerance for alcohol."

"Afraid I'll make a scene and my father will throw us out?"

"You know it's not just that. I care about you, Isaac. I don't want you to make a scene in front of these people."

"Like I care." He glances around the space then back at me. "Remove. Your. Hand. Lena," he says in a hard voice.

I stare at him, then release my hold on his arm. He tosses back the drink, then reaches for the bottle of Macallan again. This time I snatch it from him.

"What the—!" Isaac swoops down, manages to get his fingers on it.

I twist my body, turn away and wrestle the bottle from him.

"Fuck!" His features contort. He raises his arm.

13

JJ

Isaac raises his arm, and the breath slams into my rib cage. The rest of the room fades away. All I can see is Isaac and his girlfriend. All I can think is he's going to hit her. My guts churn, adrenaline laces my blood, and my feet seem to move of their own accord.

"Get away from her." I hear my words but am not aware of having spoken them aloud. Then, suddenly, I'm standing between my son and his girlfriend. I grab Isaac's arm and shove him away.

"What the?" Isaac gasps in surprise. He jerks his chin up and his gaze meets mine. He must see the anger in mine, for he pales. He glances from me to his girlfriend, then back at me. "Did you think I was going to hit her?" He sounds shocked. "Really, JJ?"

My heart twists. He started calling me JJ when he was five years old. I'd come home after another business trip which had kept me away for a month. I'd walked into his room that night, hoping to put him to bed. But he'd glanced up at me and begun to cry. He hadn't wanted me in his room. He hadn't recognized me. I'd told him I was his father, but that had only made him cry harder. He'd only settled down after I'd left. He'd never called me father after that. I had decided to be a better parent after that day, but I hadn't been able to keep my promise. Not to him, not to myself. Now, here I am, holding his arm because I thought he was going to hit his girlfriend.

"Of course, you'd believe the worst of me, wouldn't you? Easier to label me the culprit than giving me the benefit of the doubt. Well, you and your so-called friends can go fuck yourselves." He brushes past the both of us and stomps toward the door.

"Isaac," I take a step forward, but he's already marched out of the room. The door slams behind him. Every single person in the room is watching us, but the fuck do I care?

"Now look what you did." She turns on me. "Why did you have to interfere? I had it under control."

"Oh, yeah?" I look her up and down. "From where I was, it seemed like he was going to hit you, and I'm not going to stand by and watch that happen in my home."

"Isaac is a lot of things but he has never physically abused me. Ever." She huffs.

"What about emotional and mental abuse?" I retort. I wish I could say that my son wasn't capable of it, but the fact is, I don't know him at all. Isaac is more of a stranger to me than the Sovranos, with whom I've spent a hell of a lot more time in the past few months.

She hesitates.

"That's what I thought."

"This is your son we're talking about," she protests.

"All the more reason he should behave." I draw myself up to my full height. "As long as the two of you are under my roof, my rules apply. And that includes him being civil to you."

She juts out her chin. "You have no idea about the relationship between the two of us. I know I'm living under your roof, so I don't want to appear ungrateful—"

"You already do, but that's not going to stop you from saying whatever it is you're going to," I mutter.

"—but you coming in between us is not helping at all. It's only making things worse. So can I request that you stay out of our dealings and let us work things out?"

What the hell? Did she just sass me? She did *sass me. Why is she upset with me? I was only trying to help her, after all.* I open my mouth to tell her off, but before I can speak, she turns and stomps toward the doorway. *What the fuck?* No one turns their back on me. Not when I'm speaking. And definitely not someone who is my employee. Not to mention, she is half my age—*less* than half my age. I wince, then stiffen my spine. "Girl," I call out after her.

She pauses, then scowls at me over her shoulder. "I do have a name, old man."

Old man? Who the fuck is she calling old man? I'm not old… Not in years and not in virility. I have more stamina than a twenty-three-year-old, and staying power, not to mention experience.

"Don't walk away while I'm talking to you," I say through gritted teeth.

She laughs, then raises both her middle fingers. "Try and stop me." Turning, she stalks out.

"What the fuck?" I take a step forward but a hand on my shoulder stops me. I turn to find Adrian, Michael's youngest brother at my elbow.

"Steady there, you don't want to say or do something you might regret later," he murmurs.

"So, what's new?" There's already so much I regret. One thing more is not going to make a difference. I shake off his hand and move toward the doorway, but he walks around to stand in front of me.

"Don't do this; have a drink and cool off, *stronzo*."

I glare at him. "Out of my way, Sovrano."

"He has a point," Michael joins him. He hands me a glass of Macallan. "You made it a condition that we attend this celebration for Massimo and Olivia's wedding. You'll be failing as a host if you leave now."

I glance past him toward the door, then back at him. "You heard them. They defied me, and in my own home. I need to ensure it doesn't happen again."

"And if you go after them and tell them off, they'll end up hating you even more," Adrian remarks.

"And I don't need to listen to this bullshit from someone young enough to be my son," I growl.

Adrian merely laughs. "It's because I'm young enough to be your son that I can tell you it'd be a mistake to follow them now. Give them time to cool off; then take it up with them.

I narrow my gaze on him.

"Adrian's young, but unlike the rest of us, he's levelheaded." Michael raises the glass toward me. "Take it, old man. Enjoy the evening with us. You going after them is only going to make things worse. Give them, and yourself, the evening off."

He has a point. They both do. Also, I'm not sure what I'd say once I caught up with the two of them. I was never around long enough to reprimand Isaac when he was younger. Starting now is only going to piss him off further. I need to figure out another way of communicating with him, and I'm not sure confronting him about his behavior tonight like he's an errant child is the way forward.

Her, on the other hand… I intend to teach her a lesson so she never sasses me again. I glance toward the doorway one last time, then reach for the champagne. "Fuck it. Let's drink."

14

Lena

I glance down from the window to where the party continues on the deck outside the conservatory. It's chilly in early March, but the slight breeze through the open window is refreshing, and heaters have been placed around the perimeter of the area. The men and women I saw earlier mill around. The little girl is playing with the cat on one end of the deck. The cat jumps off, then races across the grass.

"Andy," the girl calls. She goes to step off the deck but a woman, presumably her mother, hauls her up.

"It's time for bed, sweetie."

"But Andy—" She wriggles in her mother's grasp.

"It's your bed time, Avery," her mother protests. She turns to walk away, but the little girl bursts into tears. "A… Andy," she blubbers. "Andy. Meow. Kitty."

A tall, broad-shouldered man walks over to Avery. "What's wrong?"

Without waiting for her to reply, I grab my phone, then turn and dash out of the room. Isaac left earlier. We fought, as expected, and he stormed out of the house in a huff. After which, I didn't want to return to the party so I came up here to observe the proceedings from afar. It's not like I spent any time stalking JJ as he stood talking with two other men. No, I didn't notice how his suit outlines his broad shoulders, or how his jacket stretches tightly over the planes of his back when he slides his hands into his pocket, or how the seat of his pants clings to that tight ass of his. And holy shit, I've already seen how magnificent that part of him in between his thighs is, too. It's etched into my brain, if I'm being honest, and the images troubled me throughout last night.

I shove them to the side as I dart down the steps and past the conservatory, then through the kitchen, past Miriam and the catering staff, to the door at the back. I slip out, then walk outside of the golden glow cast by the lights on the perimeter of the decking.

"Hey, Andy, here boy," I say in a low voice as I walk past the bushes. "Where are you, Andy?" I open the torch app on my phone, then shine it into the undergrowth. There's a skittering in the bushes. The light catches Andy's eyes and reflects back at me. He mewls, then walks over to me, his tail high in the air. "There you are." I switch off the flashlight and squat down to his level. Andy rubs up against my leg. I scratch him behind his ears and he purrs loudly.

"Gosh, you're happy, aren't you?" I scoop him up, then straighten. I turn and bump straight into a hard brick wall. Correction, a warm brick wall, with planes so well-defined I can feel them through the fabric of the jacket and the shirt stretched across it. Big hands descend on my hips. The heat sinks into my skin, straight to my core. The complex notes of sherry, oak and chocolate, laced with the aromatic fragrance of cinnamon assault my senses.

Of course, I know who it is before he growls, "The fuck are you doing here?"

Andy yowls in protest. I pull back, and he releases me enough that I glance down to find the cat has dug his claws into the front of JJ's jacket. He's also glaring up at JJ with a displeased look on his face.

"I don't think he likes you."

"What are you doing here?" JJ snaps.

I blow out a breath. "We can have a normal conversation without one of us losing our temper, you know."

"Can we?"

Something in his voice makes me glance up. Dark eyes, so black they seem like infinite pools of possibility in this light. Or black holes. Aren't both the same? Once you fall into a black hole, you'll never find yourself again. Once I glance into his eyes, I can't look away. Golden flares spark deep inside. A nerve throbs at his temple. There's so much intensity in his gaze, so much authority, so much pain. I blink. The man's suffering and he'll never talk about it to anyone. I raise my hand, maybe to touch his cheek, maybe to clasp his shoulder, but he steps back. He lowers his arms to his sides, and I shiver.

"You're cold," he growls in an accusatory tone.

"It's early spring in London, and I'm outside without a wrap or a jacket. Of course, I'm cold."

"You need to get inside," he says in that same snarly voice.

I resist the urge to roll my eyes. "No shit," I say under my breath.

"What did you say?"

I cough. "I meant, you're right..." *Daddy.*

His shoulders go solid. The planes of his chest seem to freeze. His dark eyes seem to darken even more, until they become black holes.

"What did you call me?"

My gaze widens. Good God I didn't say that aloud. I *know* I didn't. But he must have heard what I implied. And he doesn't seem upset about it. Disturbed, maybe. Turned on, definitely. But he seems more surprised by it than anything else.

"Lena." He lowers his voice to a hush and little slivers of delight pierce my skin. This is so wrong. So very wrong.

"Tread carefully, little girl, you are in dangerous territory," he says in that same thick voice.

My core clenches and I glance away. "I'm sorry," I mutter. And I am.

I don't understand why I feel the need to constantly provoke him. Must have something to do with that tightly held control of his. It tempts me to chip away at it and expose the emotions that bubble underneath. I brush past him, and to my relief, he doesn't stop me. Andy gets restive and I bring him up against my chest. "I'll get you in there, little buddy. Are you missing your little play partner, hmm?"

I step onto the deck and past the men engaged in discussion. I walk inside the house, and the warmth instantly envelops me. I hurry over to the couch where the little girl bawls in her mother's arms. "Here you are."

Andy jumps out of my arms and onto the couch. He brushes up against the girl who instantly stops crying. "A… Andy," she sniffles.

"Oh, I'm glad you found him." Her mother sighs in relief. "I thought, for sure, I'd have to send her father in search of the cat."

"I saw him wander off into the undergrowth from upstairs, so I went after him." I smile down at the girl who's rubbing her palm over the cat's forehead.

"I appreciate that." She holds out her hand. "I'm Elsa, by the way."

"Lena." I grip her slender fingers.

"And I'm Sebastian," the man towering over the two of them says.

"Pleased to meet both of you." I release Elsa's hand and take a step back. "I guess I'll leave you to it."

"What nonsense." Elsa rises to her feet. "You should stay and enjoy the rest of the party."

"Ah, no. I mean, thank you, but no. I mean, it's a work day tomorrow, and my boss insists on an early start."

"Your boss also insists that you stay for a while longer," JJ drawls from somewhere above and behind me.

I stiffen. "Thank you, but no thank you," I say politely. "This is your party."

"And I invited the two of you." He steps closer. "Isaac already broke his word and left the party." He lowers his voice so no one else except me can hear it, "I trust you won't do the same."

I swallow. "And if I do, I'm sure you'll say that our deal is off."

"You said it, not me."

I shoot him a sideways glance. "Don't worry, it won't come to that. I'm here now, aren't I? Also, for the record, you don't have to resort to threats every time. If this is how you brought up your son, then it's no wonder he hates you."

He draws in a sharp breath. Anger vibrates off of him. His already tense muscles seem to coil further. Shit, I guess I hurt him. Shit, shit, shit. "I'm sorry, I didn't mean—"

"You did, and I deserve it."

"Eh?" I glance up at him.

"I've forgotten what it's like to have someone else at home. Forgotten that when you have friends and family, you can ask them for things you wouldn't normally ask of another, so I ask you now, girl, will you stay and have a drink with me?"

15

JJ

The fuck? I apologized to her. I. Apologized. To her. I've never asked anything of anyone before. I've always preferred to carve my way forward on my own merit, without anyone else's help… and I had requested she stay and have a drink with me.

I see the surprise reflected in her eyes. She searches my features, hesitates. I'm sure she's going to refuse, when she finally says, "One. I'll stay for one drink."

My lips kick up. *That's what you think.*

"On one condition," she murmurs.

My smile fades. No one negotiates with me… Well, except for maybe Michael or Nikolai, the head of the Bratva. Add to that, Sinclair Sterling, the CEO of 7A Investments. He's going to be a tough partner, that one. But I'm sure I'm going to relish the challenge he poses. Other than that, no one has dared to lay down stipulations with me… until her.

When I don't reply, she chuckles. "Don't worry, it's nothing major. All I ask is that you call me by my name."

"If you stay for three drinks."

"Two."

"Done." On cue, Craig materializes at my elbow with a tray of drinks. I snatch up a glass of champagne and offer it to her, then one to Elsa. Seb takes a glass of whiskey, as do I.

"What are we drinking to?" Lena tips up her chin.

"To… new alliances," I say without taking my gaze off of her face.

"To my new job," she counters.

I laugh. "Stubborn, aren't you?"

"No more than you."

Seb clinks his glass with mine. "Thank you for hosting this gathering. We're going to finish this drink and leave."

Elsa takes a sip of her champagne. "I needed that."

"Mama." Her daughter reaches for the champagne, but Elsa holds it out of her reach.

"Uh-oh, that's not for you, Avery. Not yet, at least," she laughs.

"Mama." Avery pouts.

"Do you want something to drink?" Elsa asks.

When Avery nods, Seb ruffles her hair. "I'll get you some juice, but you're not having anything more after that or you won't be able to sleep." Seb turns to leave. Lena sinks down on the cushion next to Avery. She pets the cat, which arches into her touch.

"How long have the two of you been married?" Lena asks.

"Not long," Elsa laughs. "It was love at first sight between Seb and Avery, though."

"Eb." Avery nods enthusiastically. "Eb."

"Yes, baby, Seb's getting you your drink." Elsa pats the little girl's cheek.

Lena frowns. "Love at first sight? You mean—"

"Yeah. He's not her blood father, but he's done more for her than her real father every did. He's her father in every way, really." She bends and kisses her daughter's cheek. "We were lost and then Seb came along. I wouldn't say he rescued us. That's doing Seb, and us, a disservice. It's more like" —she glances between me and Lena— "like all three of us got a new lease on life. We found each other, you know? We fit, and that was it. There was never any question that we fit together, though I admit I resisted it. All the way to the bitter end. But Seb was persistent. He saw our future so clearly. He was so confident we were a family, right from the beginning. I don't know why I fought it so much now." Her smile widens and she glances back at me. "Know what I mean?"

I frown, then turn my gaze to Lena, who's staring up at me. Her golden-brown eyes seem like they are on fire. The space between us seems full of unsaid things. Forbidden things. Things I dare not name. Things that will haunt me even though I will not acknowledge them. Lena's lips part. I squeeze my fingers around my glass.

Elsa clears her throat. "I think I'll go find out what's keeping Seb." She scoops up the girl and the cat and walks past us.

I stand there, not sure what to do. If I sit down next to her, I'll be too close to her. And for propriety's sake, that's not right.

Lena watches me from under hooded eyes. I try to leave, I do. I even turn my body away, but my feet are anchored to the ground. I blow out a breath, then lower myself to the sofa, but on the opposite side from her. I keep the length of the cushions between us. There, that's safe. I hope.

"JJ, I really am sorry for what I said earlier. I was out of line," she murmurs.

"And I'm sorry I was so unpleasant. It was a shock to open the door and find Isaac on my doorstep. I'd reconciled myself to never having him home again..."

"When was he last here?"

"He left for university, and that was it." I glance down into the depths of my glass. "It's my fault, of course. I should have been a better parent to him and my daughter. I failed."

"There's still time to make up for things."

"There's too much water under the bridge. Too many things said. And unsaid. It doesn't help that even while we were married, their mother didn't want anything to do with them. Isaac blames me for that. He thinks I treated her wrong because of which she ignored her own kids."

"Did you treat her wrong?"

I wince. "I wasn't a good husband. Oh, I provided everything she and my children materially needed. But I was never around. I married her simply because I knew I needed children to further my legacy."

She draws in a sharp breath. "That's—"

"Cold-hearted? Bloody-minded?"

"I was going to say understandable."

I turn my head to glance at her. "What do you mean?"

"That many people marry because they want a family."

"Only, I was never there emotionally for them." I take a sip of my whiskey. The flavors of oak and vanilla swirl around my palate.

"Things happen, JJ. You built this home, made sure you put a roof over their heads. I bet you sent them to the best schools, ensured their education was top-notch. If they blame you for how they turned out, then that's their problem."

"That's your boyfriend you're talking about," I remind her.

She glances away. "Which is why I can see his faults all too clearly. Both of you are too stubborn to make the first move."

"Maybe he already has." I tap the side of my glass.

"Eh?" She squints at me. "You mean—"

"He did agree to stay under my roof. There was no reason to do that."

"Oh, I insisted. Trust me, Isaac didn't want to. But I couldn't see any other way out of our financial difficulties."

I wince.

"I don't mean it that way. I mean, you were the last resort, but I figured it was the logical route to stay here until we're back on our feet. And it's only until we're back on our feet, you know. We won't mooch off you forever."

My stomach churns. Goddamn, am I getting an ulcer? Also, is she talking about moving out, because I'm not letting that happen. Not until I figure out what this thing between us is all about. I scowl at her. "It's not like I gave you a free ride. Remember I get something in return, too."

"To be fair, you are paying for me to be your executive assistant. And you are giving Isaac the opportunity to have his paintings exhibited in your offices, which is prime real estate. Just having them there will make them sought-after."

I raise a shoulder. "The least I could do."

"You're a good father, JJ."

I laugh. "You have no idea what you're saying."

"Oh, I do, and more than you realize. I see how you sometimes look at him with regret. It's written in your eyes how much you love him and want to put things right."

"You're imagining things."

She shoots me a glance. "You know I'm not, but I'll let you get away with it… This time."

"You're letting me get away with it? I'll have you know, if you saw any emotions on my face, it's because I wanted you to."

She tries to hide her smile and fails. "If you say so." She sips from her champagne and her gaze widens. "Oh my god, this is delicious. What is it?" She takes another sip, then moans. The sound travels straight to my cock, which instantly perks up. She takes another sip, rolls it around in her mouth, then swallows. "I think I just came," she groans.

The blood drains to my groin. Images of her panting, head flung back, tits thrust out, sweat trickling down her throat as she shatters around my cock, assail me. *Jesus fucking Christ.* Does she have any fucking idea what she's doing to me?

She glances up at me. "I… I didn't mean—"

"I know exactly what you meant." I clear my throat, then toss the rest of my whiskey back. "I think you were right. You shouldn't stay any longer."

"Excuse me?"

I jerk my chin toward the doorway. "Time you left."

"B… but I thought you said you wanted me to stay a little longer." She blinks.

"I lied. Chop-chop. It's bed time for you, little girl."

Her face pales. Her chin trembles, then she firms her lips. "Asshole." She tosses the rest of her champagne at me.

"The fuck?" The liquid drips from my chin, splashes onto my jacket, and some of it stains my pants. "What was that for?"

"For being an obnoxious, offensive, objectionable jerk."

At least she knows me well.

She places her empty glass on the side table and jumps up to her feet. Silence falls across the room. I'm aware of my guests watching with interest as she strides away.

"Oh, and girl... Don't be late tomorrow."

Without turning, she raises the middle finger of her right hand above her shoulder.

16

Lena

I turn over on my side. How dare he call me little girl? And tell me to go to bed like I was a kid? He's my boyfriend's parent, not mine. An absentee boyfriend, considering I've barely seen him since we moved in here. Isaac still hasn't returned from wherever he went off to earlier.

So, I stomped upstairs to our bedroom, had a shower, and threw myself onto the bed. That was three hours ago. I've been unable to sleep, though. Every time I close my eyes, dark eyes fill my vision. Dark eyes that look like my boyfriend's gaze, but they're not. Dark eyes under thick eyebrows, with wavy hair swept back from that intelligent forehead. Dark eyes that seem to either consume me or look past me like I don't exist. Does he hate me? He certainly gave that impression when he told me to leave. It's like he didn't want me around for a second longer.

Guess that comment about 'coming' from having swallowed the champagne was over-the-top, but I meant it. I'm sure he chose the champagne, and I was applauding it. Perhaps I acted up because I wanted to see how he'd react to it. Now I know, it made him uncomfortable. He was definitely turned on by my words, though. Maybe he was imagining how I look when I come? God, I hope so. He deserves to go through the agony I suffer every time I look at him. And fine, I admit, it's not the kind of comment one would make in polite company. But JJ isn't exactly polite company, either, is he?

Giving up all pretense of sleeping, I snatch up my phone and open my family group chat.

No new messages. Apparently, even my family has forgotten me. It happens sometimes. We exchange a flurry of messages, then everyone gets caught up in their own lives. Guess it's time to stir the pot.

Me: I have noose
Me: I mean news *wink emoji*

I stare at the screen for a few seconds, but no one responds. It must be evening in LA. Maybe my siblings are out having fun, and my mother could be out with her friends? I pout, then close the chat window. I toss the phone onto the bedstand, then throw off the covers and rise to my feet. I walk over to the window on the side opposite from the one I looked out of earlier. I push aside the curtains and look down. "Oh!" I can see the pool from here, and next to it, a pool house. If I remember correctly, Isaac mentioned that it houses a sauna, too. I must use it, at some point. I'm living here—might as well make full use of the facilities, right?

The lights are on in the pool, and a lone figure cuts his way across the length. Strong shoulders, chiseled arms which cleave the water. JJ kicks back, the muscles of his thighs ripple, and he propels himself forward. He reaches the end of the pool, turns, then swims to the other side. And again. And again. I count thirty laps before he swims over to the edge of the pool closest to my window. He grabs the edge, treads water, probably catching his breath. Waits a beat, then another. Then he hauls himself up and over the side.

He straightens and the water pours off of his shoulders. He walks over to the towel on the lounge chair, snatches it up and begins to dry himself. Sweet Jesus. That ass. He has the tightest, hardest ass I've ever seen. And his thighs? They are heavily muscled. They flex and bend as he dries his upper body. His shoulder blades are defined and stand out in relief. With that narrow waist and trim hips, the man is in prime shape. He towels off his hair and I swear all the moisture he's mopping up seems to appear between my legs.

I squeeze my thighs together, and because I can't stop myself, I shove my fingers inside my sleep shorts· and being to rub my clit. Sensations ripple out from the point of contact. My toes curl. He crosses over to the house and disappears from sight. I lean my forehead against the window and shove two fingers inside myself. Jesus, I'm soaked. I've never felt this way. So on edge, so… electrified. The pores on my skin pop. This is wrong. So wrong. I shouldn't be masturbating to thoughts of my boyfriend's father. Shouldn't be shoving my fingers inside my pussy as I pretend it's his digits in me, his lips on me, his gaze staring deep into mine as he digs his fingers into my hips to hold me in place. As he presses his thumb into my engorged clit and circles it, as he pulls my leg up and over his hip, spreading me open for his ministrations. As he curls his fingers inside me and hits that spot deep inside.

"JJ, ohmigod, JJ..." The sound of my breathless voice drives me over the edge. My nipples peak and my thighs contract. The pressure in my core explodes, moisture drips from my slit and I come, clenching down on my fingers. I stay there gasping as sweat slides down my throat and between my breasts. My legs tremble. I pull my fingers out, bring them to my lips, and suck on my arousal. The sweetness of my arousal fills my palate. It only seems to arouse me further, and I just came. I orgasmed, and without a vibrator, which has never happened before. The man hadn't even touched me. Just thinking of him and pretending that he was finger-fucking me was enough to make me come. My heartbeat stays elevated and I draw in a breath, and another. Goddamn, I need a cold shower.

I turn, and my gaze clashes with his burning one. "You? What are you doing here?"

JJ pushes away from where he's leaning against the doorframe.

"It's Jack."

"Jack?"

"Jack." He prowls over to me. I slide back, hit the window, and sensations seem to explode down my spine. "If you're going to cry out my name, you may as well get it right."

"I don't know what you're talking about." I shake my hair back over my shoulder.

"Liar," he says in a casual tone. "I heard you, girl."

"It's Lena. The least you can do is get my name right," I spit out.

One side of his lips quirks. It's not a smile. Oh, no, JJ never smiles. It's more an action resembling a grimace. Or the sly smile of a panther, all sleek and hard as he stalks me. He closes the distance between us until the tips of his toes brush mine. I shiver. Oh, did I mention that he's wearing a pair of gray sweatpants and a black T-shirt? Black ink peers out from under the neckline. This is the most casual I've seen him, and let me tell you, casual JJ is even more sexy than JJ dressed in his formal suit. The heat from his body reaches out to me. And his scent, sherry oak and cinnamon notes underlaid with the scent of the pool water and the lingering fragrance of his cigar smoke.

Fuck me, right now. How's a girl supposed to resist a man who looks like he's her every wet dream come true? I've never had a thing for older men, honestly. But JJ redefines the meaning of 'old.' He's not old as in ancient, but old as in seasoned, experienced, more ruthless, more focused, more dominant. He's just more. More everything. My ovaries quiver.

He bares his teeth, then leans in and runs his nose up my cheek. A moan bleeds from me. *That's not me. That was. Not me.* How embarrassing. He inhales deeply and my pussy clenches. I swear, I can feel the cream ooze out from between my thighs. I am ready for him. He hasn't even touched me, and I'm ready for him. *Fuck, fuck, fuck.* I am crushing on my boyfriend's father. Someone who is almost the same age as my own father. The father, who cheated on my mother and left our family to start a new one. Is it genetic? Is that why I'm so close to cheating on my boyfriend? And with his father, no less.

"Stop," I say through gritted teeth. "We can't do this."

JJ stiffens. He doesn't move away, though. He stays there, with his nose buried in my hair.

"JJ," my voice cracks. I clear my throat. "Please."

"Say my name first." His big shoulders bunch. His muscles are so coiled that they seem to be made of rock. His chest rises and falls. His breath lifts the hair at my temple. "Say. My. Name."

"You first," I whisper. *What are you doing? Why are you having this conversation with him? Why can't you simply walk past him and tell him to leave?* I raise my arms to push him away, but instead, place my hands on his chest. Every part of him seems to go on alert. The heat from his body seems to intensify. And oh, god... He's so hard, so sculpted, so perfectly formed. I spread my fingers and push down to feel the resistance of those cut pecs.

"Lena," he says in a tortured voice.

My stomach jumps. My heartbeat races in tandem with the beat that has been activated between my legs.

"Lena," he growls. And a thousand little fires light up my skin. My nerve endings seem to detonate.

"Jack." I sway toward him, but he steps back so suddenly that I stumble. He touches my shoulder to right me, then pulls back as if it burns him. I am burning up. The air between us is rife with so much unsaid. "Jack." I tilt my head back to search his features. "It suits you."

His dark eyes burn into mine. He seems to be eating me up with his gaze.

"Jack," I whisper.

"Next time you masturbate, at least own up to who you were thinking about when you came."

"It was Isaac I was thinking about," I insist.

"Like I said, you're still a little girl. You don't have the courage to own up to the attraction between us."

"There's nothing between us. You just happened to walk in at an inopportune moment."

His features twist. He looks me up and down and shakes his head. "Is that the story you're going with?"

"It's not a story," I hiss.

"And I'm not stupid. You haven't been able to take your eyes off of me since we met."

"Speak for yourself." I curl my fingers into fists. "You saw me and wanted me. You don't care that I'm your son's girlfriend. It's why you agreed to having me as your executive assistant. And why you insist on having my desk in your room in the office. You want to make it almost impossible for the two of us to spend any time apart. We're together almost the entire day. It's no wonder we're attracted to each other."

"So, you think I'm to blame for the chemistry between us?" he growls.

"Aren't you?"

He holds up his hands. "Grow up." He spins around and walks toward the door.

What the—? I leap forward. "Don't you dare walk away from me, JJ."

"I'll do what I want, when I want. And one more thing..." He glares at me over his shoulder. "Find your own way to the office tomorrow."

17

JJ

I stare out the window of my bedroom at the lights of the city in the distance.

I'd walked into their room to make sure she was okay. I shouldn't have entered it, but I was on my way back from the pool, and I should've walked past their floor but my steps had slowed.

I only wanted to make sure Isaac was back. At least, that's what I told myself. And maybe I should've knocked first. I stood outside the partially open door with my hand raised to knock, and I heard a sound. Heard what seemed like a moan, and my imagination had filled in the gaps. Was he in there... fucking her? Was she on her own... masturbating? I wanted—no, I needed—to find out for myself. If it meant I went straight into stalker territory with that, so be it. I entered the room and found her pressed up against the window with her hand down her panties, the movements unmistakable. She *was* masturbating. She'd been watching me and masturbating.

Fuck! All the blood drained to my groin at once. As I watched, her actions grew frantic. Her entire body shook. She wiggled her hips, squeezed her thighs together—thighs clad in those minuscule sleep shorts. Did she wear those to mess with my head? Then she moaned my name. Goddamn, she moaned *my* name, then her entire body stiffened, and she came. She took another minute to find her equilibrium, then she brought her fingers to her lips and sucked on them, and fuck me, but I had almost come right then. The sweetness of how she would taste filled my mouth, a band tightened around my chest, and it took all of my self-control not to pull her fingers out of her mouth and put them in mine. I could barely breathe, and that's when she turned.

Her gaze clashed with mine, and I saw the guilty look in her eyes. Oh, she denied that she'd been jerking off to images of me, but I'd heard her say my name and seen the evidence in how she flinched when she saw me. And when she called me by my first name, I almost threw her over my shoulder and stalked out of there, and… It was wrong. It's all wrong. She was right when she said I'd maneuvered things so we'd spent the entire working day in close proximity to each other. Maybe I hadn't overtly planned it. After all, the position of my EA was supposed to go to my son… Only she took his place. And she's the one who offered to take the role. I didn't force her to work for me, but yes, subconsciously I knew exactly what it meant.

I knew we'd be spending a lot of time with each other. I felt the attraction flare between us the moment our eyes connected, and did nothing to mitigate it. She's right. I didn't care that she's my son's girlfriend. Didn't care that this would hurt him. Didn't care that she was less than half my age. Not that that would have stopped me, in all honesty. It's the fact that she belongs to my son that makes this scenario a bitch. I have to walk away from her. Have to find a way to limit our interactions. If I have any hope of forging a relationship with my son, I have to nip this—whatever it is between us—in the bud.

I push away from the window and walk into my bathroom to take another cold shower.

The next day I head to work on my own, leaving at the crack of dawn. I have her desk moved to a cubicle on a different floor with the rest of my marketing team. I convey all of my messages to her via email, and through my personal assistant. And when I return home, I keep to my study and my bedroom, making sure not to pause on their floor. I manage to avoid her, which also means I don't see my son. I know he leaves home every day to shoot photographs as inspiration for his paintings, and since he refuses to use the studio on the top floor of my house, I've made sure he has access to a studio on the other side of town. If that means he's away from the house most of the day and late into the night... Well, that's not my problem, is it?

I have also taken to working late in the office. Most days, I send my assistant out to get me lunch and make sure I'm out of the office for lunch appointments so I don't have to see *her*. And when I wrap up work late at night, I head home, swim my fifty laps, and then fall into bed exhausted. I manage to make it through three entire days without allowing myself to see her. On the fourth day, my business meeting finishes earlier than expected, so I reach home sooner than planned.

Thunder rumbles outside. It's going to rain soon, so instead of using the pool, I head for the gym. I put in my time at the rowing machine, then begin to work out with my weights. Chest press, arm extensions, ab roller, then the bench press. By the time I'm done, my muscles burn, and my entire body is covered with sweat. Wiping my forehead with a towel, I walk up the stairs and toward my room. The entire house is quiet. Isaac isn't home yet. I know this because I have eyes on him. Only because I needed to ensure my son is fulfilling his commitment. That's the only reason I have men following him. Anyway, I know he's still at work in his studio.

I also know *she's* eaten and gone to bed because Miriam messaged me to confirm before she left for the evening. It's only the two of us here. Alone. My footsteps slow as I pass their floor. *Keep going, don't stop.* I force myself to put one foot in front of the other. 'Force' being the imperative word. Goddamn, my feet feel like they are weighed down by anchors. I pause with my foot on the step above. Lightning flashes through the window on the landing. It seems to illuminate the path to their room. *Oh, fuck it, who am I kidding? I am just going to peek in and make sure she's okay.* And while Craig and Miriam give me regular updates on her, I haven't spoken to her or checked in on her at all. I'd be failing in my duties as host if I didn't at least ask her how she's doing, right? I won't stay for more than a minute. That's it. Peek in, make sure everything's fine, then leave. That's it. In and out. Yep, it will all be okay. I pad toward their door, then push it open.

The curtains are pulled back, and another flash of lightning illuminates the room. I spot her sprawled out under the covers. Her thick auburn hair flows out over the pillows. Her arm is flung out, reaching toward the empty side of the bed. *His side of the bed.* Where Isaac would be laying, before he reached out to her and hauled her close then kissed her, touched her, sucked on the curve where her neck meets her shoulders. He'd squeeze her plump tits, before he shoved her thighs apart and positioned himself against her opening and—pain slices up my arm. I glance down to find I've curled my fingers into the palm of my hand and squeezed with enough force to break the skin. I rub my palm against my gym shorts, then step inside the room. I toe off my sneakers and socks, drop my towel to the floor, then pad over to stand over her. On the bedstand next to her is a pile of books, many of them annotated. Why hadn't she told me that she likes to read?

Thunder rumbles again, and she stirs. I jerk my attention back to her face. Her eyelids flutter and she sighs, then throws off her covers. I hold my breath until she stills. Glance down to find her fingers are inside her sleep shorts. *Jesus, fuck!* The movements of her fingers make it clear she's fucking herself. Again. She squeezes her thighs together, wriggles her hips, trying to get more friction against her clit. I'm instantly hard. I squeeze my fingers into fists as I watch her shoving her digits inside herself. She turns to face me, and I freeze. Her eyelids stay closed, her lips part, and she brings her free arm up to dig it into the pillow beside her. Her movements grow more frantic. I grit my teeth and force myself not to move. Force myself to watch as she continues to ride her fingers. A moan bleeds from her lips and something inside me snaps.

I round the bed, slide in next to her. I wrap my fingers around her wrist and tug gently. She sighs, then her arm goes slack. I pull her fingers out from between her legs, and raise them to my mouth. I wrap my lips around her digits and lick off her cum. Sweetness, the taste of strawberries and honey, rolls over my palate. A groan wells up and I swallow it back. My cock thickens even more, and the crotch of my shorts tightens. I place her arm across her stomach, then slide my fingers under the waistband of her shorts and between her pussy lips. She's so damn wet. I circle her clit; she inhales. I glance at her face to find her eyelids shut. I slip my fingers across her slit and she parts her thighs. I ease my finger inside her wet opening, and her pussy clenches down on my digit. So tight, so fucking hot. I ease my finger in and out of her. In and out. She wriggles her hips. I add another finger and a third, then begin to thrust them in and out of her. Each time I push them in, her moisture coats my fingers; each time I pull them out, she chases my digits with her cunt. She juts out her bottom and presses her cheeks into the hard column in my pants. I keep my gaze on her face, noting the flush that steals across her cheeks.

"Isaac," she mumbles.

I freeze. Anger twists my guts. My heart begins to thud in my chest. I'm in Isaac's bed, with my fingers inside his girlfriend's pussy, about to make her come, and God help me... I'm not sorry. I've never in my life been so attracted to a woman. Not Isaac's mother, not any of the other women I've slept with. I've never wanted a woman so much, I'm willing to risk one of the most important things in my life—the relationship with my son—over it. A relationship I haven't done enough to salvage, a relationship that is most certainly doomed after my actions now, a relationship I do value. *I do...* and yet, I can't stop myself from continuing to finger fuck her. From increasing the pace of my movements as I shove my fingers in and out of her. As I twist my fingers inside her and hit that spot deep inside of her. As she moans, then throws her arm up and around my neck and turns her head so her lips meet mine.

And what do I do? I kiss her. I slide my lips over hers once, twice. When she opens her mouth, I slide my tongue inside and dance it over hers. I suck on her essence, swallow down that honey and strawberry taste of hers and commit it to memory, so I'll always have it in me, a part of me from now on. I continue to plunge my fingers in and out of her, push down the pad of my thumb into the nub of her clit, then scissor my fingers inside of her. Her back arches, and a shudder runs down her body. Outside, there's another flash of lightning, then rain-drops patter against the windowpane.

A groan wells up her throat, I swallow it down, and she comes. Her moisture gushes around my fingers, down my wrist. I continue to work my digits in and out of her, slowing the movements as I fuck her through the aftershocks that ripple down her spine. She sighs and slumps against me. I pull out my fingers, kiss her one last time, then ease away from her. She turns her face away from me and into her pillow. Her breathing deepens.

I slide off the bed and straighten, then suck on my fingers. Her taste sinks into my blood and my already hard cock seems to lengthen even further. Sweat beads my shoulders, my chest, and it's not from my earlier gym session. I head for the doorway, pausing to pick up the towel and my socks and shoes, then slide out and shut the door behind me. I walk up to my room, take a cold shower, and slide into bed. Not that it helps defuse my raging hard-on.

Clearly, I'm going straight to hell. I toss and turn, unable to sleep. I made her come. I don't regret it, though. I eased her discomfort and allowed her to sleep peacefully. That's the most important thing, or so I tell myself. So what if it means I'm going to hell for my actions? I am never going to tell her what I did. It's going to be my secret.

I bring my fingers to my nose and sniff; despite my shower, the faint scent of strawberries teases my nostrils. My cock instantly springs to full mast. Jesus Christ, I'm never going to sleep now. My fingers tingle to reach between my legs and relieve myself, but I restrain myself. I deserve to stay in pain for what I did to her without her knowledge. If only things were different. If only she weren't Isaac's girlfriend. But she is. And now, I know how she tastes, how she feels as her pussy flutters around my fingers as she comes. How hot and tight and wet she is. How I can't wait to finally be inside of her. *Fuck, fuck, fuck.* I need to stop this line of thinking.

I throw off my covers, rise to my feet, and pull on my clothes. Then

I walk down past the floor with their room and down to my study. I pass the kitchen, and finding the lights on, walk in to find Isaac standing at the counter, a sandwich in front of him.

He glances up, sees me, and his eyebrows draw down. "What are you doing here?"

18

JJ

I prowl past him and head to the refrigerator to pull out a carton of milk, because that's the kind of man I am. I just had my fingers inside my son's girlfriend and now I pour some milk out into a glass, pick it up with that same hand, and place it next to his sandwich.

Isaac looks at the glass, then huffs, "I'm not twelve."

"You'll always be twelve to me."

His scowl deepens. "Don't pretend to be concerned about me. We both know you don't have one fatherly instinct in your entire body."

"You're right."

He blinks. "I am?"

I nod. "I was too young when I became a father. Oh, I know I was twenty-four when we had your sister. And that's not young in terms of years. But I wasn't emotionally ready for the responsibility of having a child. So I coped with it the best way I could."

"By making sure we'd never see you," he says bitterly.

"By throwing myself into my work, and building up my business so the two of you lacked for nothing."

"You mean building your organized crime syndicate, don't you?"

I wince. It's true, of course. I had worked on the wrong side of the law for a long time, until I found the balls to legitimize the business. The Sovranos' decision to go legit might have something to do with it, too. Seeing the brothers find their soulmates and decide to change the nature of their business in order to protect their families had a bigger impact on me than I'd realized. It's why I made the decision to transition myself.

"I am the CEO of one of the fastest growing media companies in the world—one I built from the ground up and through my own sweat and blood. One I'd like very much for you or your sister to run one day."

"You can forget about me. I have no interest in it," he bites out.

"I know that now."

"Eh?" He blinks up at me. "You're okay with that?"

"I wasn't. Not for a long time. But I realize now that you need to do what makes you happy."

He gapes at me. "You're kidding me, right? All those years of refusing to accept what I wanted to be, and now suddenly, you're fine with it? What changed?"

I reach for the glass of milk I'd placed next to him and take a sip, then make a face.

"Yeah, it's gross, isn't it?" He smirks. And goddamn, in that moment, he looks so much like me, I could be looking at a mirror and seeing my younger self. Cocky, but yet to find my confidence. Wanting to charge into the world and slay my demons, but not exactly sure what I truly wanted, either. Yeah, I was one mixed-up, confused man in my twenties, and then the kids had come along. In a way, they had centered me, though. I knew my duty as a father was to provide for them. It's what made me responsible, but also what got me started on founding the Kane company. I'd never intended for it to be involved in illegal activities, but I hadn't shied away from cutting corners, either. And before I knew it, I'd become someone who competed with the

Mafia instead of competing in business. But all that had changed a few
months ago.

I began offloading my dodgy business dealings and started to focus
on my legal enterprises, which had already been doing well. I wasn't
lying when I told Isaac that my media business had been built from the
ground up. I'd ensured it wasn't tainted by my shadier dealings. And
my newest venture, Trinity Enterprises, is a collaboration with the
Sovranos and the Soloniks, one I intended to keep above-board and
use to diversify into new markets. I have a lot of plans and now…

I have a woman, too. Only, she doesn't belong to me… yet. She
might never belong to me. *For fuck's sake, I didn't even want one, but here
I am.* I might be too old for her. She might not want to be with me,
but… I have to try. I've never given up on anything without trying.
Never wanted something and not gone after it. I'm certainly not going
to start now. Except, it means hurting my son in the process. Can I live
with myself after that? Can I live with myself if I don't try to pursue
my woman? Is there a way to do it without causing my son grief? Is
there any way to do it? I don't know, but I'm going to find out. And
that means bridging the distance between my son and myself first.

I spin around, walk over to the shelf in the far corner and pull out a
bottle of 24-year-old Macallan. I pour a healthy measure into two rock
glasses, then slide one over to him.

He glances at it, then at me. "Whiskey?" He scowls.

"My best whiskey," I correct him.

"And you're going to share it with me?"

"You do realize, one day soon, a lot of what I have will belong to
you, too," I murmur.

"I don't want it." He glowers back at me.

I open my mouth, then shut it. "Maybe that was the wrong thing to
say. It's just whiskey, son." I raise my glass. "If you don't want it,
there's more for me." I raise a shoulder.

He continues to stare at me, then finally relaxes his shoulders. "I
suppose I could have a glass."

"Go on then." I clink my glass with his, then take a sip. The complex
notes of sherry oak and cinnamon laced with citrus and wood smoke
tease my tastebuds. I roll the whiskey around my mouth and swallow.

"Go on." I gesture to his untouched glass. "Taste it."

He narrows his gaze on me, then raises his glass to his mouth. He takes a cautious sip, then blinks. His gaze widens. He holds the liquid in his mouth, then swallows. "Wow," he breathes. "This is—"

"Fucking good." I take another sip, let the layers of the whiskey coat my tongue.

He does the same.

We sip our whiskeys in silence for a few seconds. Then I point to the sandwich, "Don't you want that?"

He places his whiskey down on the counter, snatches up the sandwich and demolishes it in three large bites. It's my turn to blink. The appetite of youth. Was I ever that hungry for food? Did I ever eat it with such relish? Is this what it means to grow older? To take things for granted, and lose your zest for things in life. Is that why I'm so attracted to her? A mistaken attempt at holding onto what's left of my life? Not that I'm that old, but I'm not getting any younger, either. Am I about to become a caricature of an older man who can't stop lusting after a woman much younger than him? My head spins. Isaac raises his glass and tosses back his drink, then splutters.

I wince. "That's not how you're supposed to drink Macallan."

With tears running down his cheeks, he scoffs, "Says who?"

"Says me, but you know what?" I glance at the glass, then at him. "Maybe it's time I broke some of my own rules."

I raise my own glass and toss it back. The alcohol burns its way down my gullet. It hits my stomach and sets off a fireball of heat. My skin flushes, sweat beads my brow. "Fuck," I growl.

"Indeed," he laughs.

I grab the bottle of whiskey and top up both our glasses, then nod to his glass. "Follow me."

19

Lena

I come awake with a start. The scent of sherry oak and cinnamon laced with sweaty man, the rasp of a whiskered jaw against my cheek, the thick rough fingers inside me fucking me until I'd come. I glance down to find my fingers are inside my panties. Again. Shit. I pull my hand out, hold it up to my nose, and the scent of sex teases my nostrils. I was masturbating again. OMG, I was fucking myself with my own fingers. I was sure Isaac had come to bed and fucked me. It had felt so real… So much better than real, actually.

The last few times Isaac and I made love, he'd seemed to be in a hurry. As usual, once I pretended to come, he finished quickly, then pulled out, and was gone without any post-coital cuddles. He used to hold me close after sex, in the early days of our relationship. He doesn't bother with that anymore. There have been times when he's thrusted inside, not bothering to find out if I was even wet. It was a relief when he finished, then pulled out and left. I must have been imagining that it was him, but it had felt so real.

I shake my head. I must be losing my mind. I haven't seen Isaac over the last few days, and come to think of it, I haven't seen JJ, either. He moved me out of his office to a cubicle, and that had been a relief.

He also started to communicate through his personal assistant, which is good because that means I don't have to speak with him. On the other hand, Karen—yeah, her name really is Karen—speaks to me like she's doing me a favor. In a word, she is insufferable.

I've been spending long hours at work and using the tube to commute. At least I don't have to spend time in close proximity to *him* in his car. Not that I'm a fan of the tube, but the commute gives me time to steel myself before I get to work, just in case I end up seeing him. Similarly, on the return journey home, I have the chance to strengthen my resolve not to be affected by being under his roof. And it hasn't actually been necessary because I haven't run into him at all. All in all, things have been so much more peaceful. Maybe even... lonely. I grab my phone, pull up my group chat and check the messages.

Seema: News? What news?
   Josh: Lenaaaaaa
   Mira: Bitch, what's the goss? Did you finally hook up with someone hot?
   Seema: She has a boyfriend.
   Mira: Who, Isaac? Is he even a real boyfriend? He's barely around for her.
   Seema: Stop talking shit about him, he's a good boy.

Yeah, that's what he is—a boy. His father, on the other hand, is all man... And so not right for me. Neither of them are, actually. Isaac is too impetuous; his father's too controlled. Isaac's too involved with his creative pursuit; his father's too involved with his business. Both are workaholics, too. Once Isaac gets involved with a project, he tends to forget to eat and drink, let alone remember that he has a girlfriend. JJ? He seems equally absorbed with his company. Karen had taken great pleasure in telling me that his breakfast, lunch, and dinner meetings were all taken up so he didn't have time for me—yes, I had tried to set up a time to meet him. And it's not because I've missed him or anything. I just need to run an idea past him—something I thought of that would benefit his business. Only, the time slot I was given is for two weeks from now. Two weeks! Imagine that. It's bullshit, come to think of it.

My phone vibrates.

Josh: Lena?
    Josh: Lena. Lena. Lena.
    Josh: Lenaaaaaaa are you there?

I blow out a breath.

Me: I'm here
    Mira: Heyyy! What's the goss? You can't leave us hanging like that
    Seema: Is it to do with Isaac?
    Me: Yes. No.
    Clarie: Knew it. Are you breaking up with him? Not that he's a bad sort or anything. I just wonder if he really appreciates you for who you are

Jeez my siblings really are more observant than I give them credit for.

Me: Nothing like that. We got evicted from our home.
    Mira: Whaaat!
    Seema: Are you joking?
    Josh: No way Dinky

Mom: Oh my goodness, honey! Are you okay? Do you need money or anything?

Me: No, I'm good. We moved in with Isaac's father actually. Turns out Isaac has more money than I thought

Mira: Ooh, how old is his dad? Is he a dirty old man?

Umm, yes?

Me: No, of course not. He's been very generous allowing us to stay under his roof for as long as we want. He's also given me a job in his company

Seema: Holdonasec so his dad has his own company?

Me: Kane Enterprises.

…

…

Mira: You mean THE Kane Enterprises

Me: The media company, yes

Mira: STFU his father is the head of an international media organization?

Me: Yes?

Seema: So does this mean Isaac's loaded?

Me: His father is...

Mira: You know what I said earlier about the dirty old man? I take it all back. If he's loaded then—

Mom: Mira, stop that, don't go putting ideas into your sister's head

If she only knew.

Me: Chillax guys, I barely see him. He goes to the office and I work on a separate floor as his executive assistant

Mira: HE MADE YOU HIS EXECUTIVE ASSISTANT?!

. . .

Shit, shouldn't have mentioned that, but it's too late now.

Me: It's fancier than it sounds, and it's not glamorous at all. He makes me work all day. Man never takes a break, and I don't even have enough time for lunch.

Mom: It can't be healthy if you don't have time to eat.

Me: Oh it's fine. I manage to eat a sandwich at my desk.

Mom: It sounds like hard work. You sure this is what you want?

Me: Mom, you know that's why I studied for an MBA. I've always wanted a career in a big corporate company.

Josh: And I've always wanted to steer clear of those behemoths. But if it works for you...

Me: It does. I'm learning so much.

Seema: So, his father is letting you live with him rent-free, and in return he's being a slave driver?

Me: He's also given Isaac a chance to get his paintings displayed at his offices. And I discovered he has ten offices around the world! So it's a big break for him.

Seema: What's the catch?

Trust my older sister to read between the lines.

Me: No catch.

Seema: There's always a catch Dinky

Me: Not this time. It's all going swimmingly well.

Mom: Goodness, you sound so British. You've been away far too long, honey.

Me: I'm just getting started on my career, Ma.

Mom: You always were the ambitious one.

Josh: Hey have you forgotten who has his sights set on becoming a pilot?

Mira: Umm, Josh, you never did make it through flight school...

Josh: Their loss is the army's gain. I can't wait to leave on my first tour.

Mom: You know I'm proud of your choice Josh, but I wish you didn't have to leave so soon.

Josh: Aww Mom don't go all emo on me now

Mom: Emo, me? Ha! I'm the first to support my children on whatever their career choices are. I'm all for you leaving the nest so I can get my life back.

Josh: You say that but you're gonna miss me when I'm gone

Seema: Mom never tells us how much she misses us, but I did catch her putting away your clothes when you were in training Josh.

Josh: Knew it! Mom you promised not to fiddle around with my stuff

Mom: I was only putting your washed clothes in their place.

Josh: Mom you promised not to come into my room

Mira: Don't worry, Mom knows that you watch pron.

Me: Ewww, can we not have this conversation? Or at least not in front of Mom.

Mom: I'd rather you not hide anything from me. And it's not that I don't know about your smutty books, either

Me: Wait what?

Mom: You do realize you share your Kindle with me?

Me: What? No I don't!

I scramble up from the bed to snatch my laptop from my bag.

Mom: Relax. Of course you don't share your Kindle with me. Just kidding.

Me: MOM!

Mom: Sorry, couldn't resist. But you think I don't know that all four of my kids are now sexually active and—

Mira: Okay bye

Seema: *face palm emoji* I'm gone, too.

Josh: *hand waving emoji*
Me: Bye, Mom.

I log out of the chat, then drop my phone on the side table. My family can be crazy, but I do miss them and their sense of humor. When we're together, we're always kidding each other and our group chats are often hilarious. It never fails to perk me up. I glance at the other side of the bed. The pillow is slightly indented. I lower my nose to it and sniff. The faint trace of detergent reaches me. Even though I'd been dreaming of JJ, I'd been so sure Isaac was in bed with me, but that doesn't smell like him. Where is Isaac anyway?

I swing my legs off of the bed, pull on a pair of yoga pants, T-shirt and socks, then creep down the steps. When I hit the landing of the ground floor, I hear voices. I head toward them, past the kitchen where the lights are ablaze, past the dimly lit conservatory and the living room, and into the study. I pause at the entrance, then rub my eyes. *What the—? Am I still dreaming?* Maybe I'm stuck inside one of those dreams where you think you woke up and started doing regular things, only to wake up a bit later and realize you'd been sleeping.

I find JJ and Isaac seated at a side table. The same one where I'd noticed the open game of chess. They're seated across from each other, an ashtray on the side. Both have a cigar stuck between their lips. As I watch, JJ pulls out the cigar and lifts his head. The tendons of his gorgeous neck tighten, then he blows out a perfect smoke ring. He clamps the cigar between his lips again as he considers the chess pieces in front of him.

Isaac moves a piece. He must capture one of JJ's because he fist pumps. "Yes! Got you!"

"Only because I let you," JJ growls. His eyebrows draw down and he focuses on the board.

Isaac shoves the hair back from his face. The gesture is so familiar, a ball of emotion clogs my throat. How many times have I watched him do that when he's focused on playing a video game or cleaning his brushes? Or sometimes, when he looks through the viewfinder of his camera and asks me to push the hair off of his forehead so it doesn't interfere with his shot.

Isaac lowers the cigar from between his lips, then takes a long drink from his tumbler of whiskey. He wipes the back of his hand across his lips. "Goddamn, JJ, this whiskey gets better with every mouthful."

"It's the best there is," JJ says simply. He moves a piece on the board, taking out one of Isaac's pieces this time.

"Fuck," Isaac swears.

"I've got a lot of life in me, boy." JJ smirks.

He called Isaac boy. He calls me girl. Does he think of me as someone that young? I mean, I am that young in age, but really, I've always felt much older in spirit than my friends. Or in comparison to Isaac, for that matter. Age-wise, I am closer to Isaac, but on a soul level, I might as well be in an older age bracket. But JJ can't see that. All he notices is me in the role of Isaac's girlfriend. I'll never be more than that to him. So why am I still thinking of him?

I walk over to the nearest shelf and run my fingers across the spines of the books. *Moby Dick, Don Quixote, Crime and Punishment* by Dostoevsky—to be expected. Also, Dickens, Tolkien, Aldous Huxley, Leo Tolstoy, Harper Lee, Jules Verne, Bram Stoker—which I didn't expect. And volumes of Shakespeare. He did quote the Bard earlier, but I didn't think he'd have studied his works in such detail. I pause. A space has been cleared in the shelf below it. Maybe he's looking to buy more books?

"That space is for you."

I glance over my shoulder to find JJ's gaze on me.

"Excuse me?" I mutter.

"Your books—" He tilts his chin in my direction. "You like reading books, don't you?"

"Given the choice, she'd prefer to curl up with a book than talk to people," Isaac interjects.

"Nothing wrong with that." JJ's lips curve slightly. "Books are far more trustworthy. Also, they don't talk back to you."

I snort. "Leave it to you to take the pleasure of reading and turn it into something misanthropic. Also, thanks, but no thanks. I prefer to have my books close where I can see them and touch them many times a day."

His nostrils flare and his gaze narrows. I know I've pissed him off by turning him down. Also, that came out more suggestive than I'd intended. Or maybe I had wanted him to feel how frustrated I am? Damn, why am I acting in such a contradictory fashion? He's my boyfriend's father. So he's attractive, but he's also an asshole. Someone I need to keep at arm's length. But it's so much fun getting a rise out of him, too.

I walk over to Isaac and touch his shoulder. "Hey, babe, where've you been all this time?"

"Hey." Isaac's lips twitch. He pulls me into his lap.

The hair on the back of my neck prickles. I can feel JJ's eyes bore through me. I ignore him and focus my attention on my boyfriend. "Didn't realize there was a party happening here. Why didn't you invite me?"

I pluck the cigar from Isaac's lips and plop it between mine. I puff on the cigar then blow out a cloud of smoke straight in JJ's face.

His gaze narrows.

I allow my lips to curve, and tip my chin up toward Isaac. "I woke up and missed you. Why don't you come on up to bed?"

20

Isaac

I squeeze my girlfriend closer. Goddamn, but I've missed her. There was a time when we were so close to each other—both of us away from our families. Along with Ben. The three of us were inseparable. We shared a flat and went to university together. Ben was studying to be a doctor, I was pursuing a degree in fine arts, and Lena was focused on getting her MBA. The three of us were so different, and yet we fit somehow. There was never a dull moment when we were together. We didn't have much money, but we made up for it by having parties at our tiny apartment. It was pretty much an open house most days. Or at least, as much as Ben could push us to open it up to the other students. I didn't mind. I was happy to go along with his plans. Left to myself, I'd have spent most of my time painting or taking photographs for inspiration, instead of hanging out with people. With the exception of Ben and Lena, that is. Lena had been different in those days. Much more sociable. Oh, she was as focused on starting a career and talked about the security it would give her, even then. But she took time out to enjoy life. Thanks to Ben's influence. I weave my fingers through hers. "Missed you, Dinky."

She frowns. "I never should have introduced you to my family."

"You've met her family?" my father growls from across the table.

What's crawled up his ass now? For a few seconds there, I thought we were getting along. Almost. I should have known it was too good to be true. I never should have allowed him to lure me into playing chess with him. But, it's one of the few happy memories I have from my childhood—playing chess with my father. It was the one time he seemed to forget about his job and his company, when he focused his entire attention on the chessboard. The one time he was completely present… while playing chess with me.

It's why I agreed to the game. Why I agreed to smoke a cigar with him. Not that it was a hardship, of course. The bastard has good taste when it comes to his whiskey… and cigars… and clothes… and choice of home, I suppose. I fucking loved this house. He may have been gone a lot, but he made sure my sister Tally and I lacked for nothing. Sure, we could have done with his being around more often, but we had enough friends at school and could invite them around any time.

Our mother wasn't very present in our lives, either. She might have been physically in the house but she was too busy with her social life, not to mention her discreet affairs on the side. The only time she brought home a lover, Tally walked in on them. She told our father about it, and JJ was enraged. He told our mother in no uncertain terms that if she brought another one of her boy-toys around, he'd ensure she lost her monthly allowance. That shut things down pretty quickly, I can tell you. Our mom knew exactly how to play the game.

The deal, as we found out later—Mother made sure she told us before she departed—was that she stay home and keep up the pretense of marriage with JJ until we came of legal age, at which time, she could leave with a massive fortune. If she left before that, she forfeited all the money. So she stayed, and she wasn't a bad mother—when she remembered to be one, that is. Part of the deal was that she not flaunt her lovers in our face. Just like he kept his private life discreet. Sometimes I wonder what brought the two of them together. I assume they were in love once. Whatever it was seemed to have faded away very quickly, though, for I have almost no memories of the two of them being together.

After watching the two of them, I swore that when I did marry, it would be to someone I loved more than anything else in life. Someone I couldn't live a minute without. Someone I wanted as much as I needed to breathe air.

While our parents weren't always around, my sister and I always backed each other up. We were each other's best friends, until she finally went off to university. I missed her a lot, and to some extent, the friendship I had with Ben and Lena helped bridge that gap. Those university years were probably the happiest of my life. Maybe that's why I was clinging onto those memories and didn't want to let go.

Maybe that's why I feel this need to be with Lena. Maybe that's why I'm going to try to be a better boyfriend. I weave my fingers through her slimmer ones.

"Yes, I've met her family." I bring her fingertips up to my mouth and kiss them. "Do you know they call her Dinky because she used to be tiny?"

"I grew up." She scowls

"You're still tiny. A perfectly formed body." I smirk.

"I'm more than my body." She shoots me a sideways glance.

"You're also the most hardworking person I know."

She winces. "Now you're making me sound so boring."

"You're anything but. You and your family are a lot of fun, Dinky."

She smiles. "I think so, too. They can be a little extra, though. Comes from the East Indian heritage on my mother's side, but they are a lot of fun."

"Your mother is from the subcontinent?" JJ asks.

"She moved to the US when she was five. My grandparents came to LA with very little. They started a restaurant and brought up my mother and her sister without wanting for anything. My mother met my father when she was very young. He didn't want anything to do with the running of my grandparents' restaurant."

"You're not close to your father, I take it?"

"He left and married someone else. He has his own family now. It's

my mother who brought us up, while running my grandparents'
restaurant."

And I don't need a psychologist to tell me my Daddy issues arise
from having been abandoned by father.

"How many siblings do you have?" JJ asks

"Three. Seema, my oldest sister, is studying to be a doctor. Then
Mira, who's training to be a chef, then me and finally, Josh who's
eleven months younger than me. He leaves for his first tour this
summer."

"Ah, a soldier." JJ stares at the chess pieces, but I'm sure he's
tracking Lena's reaction. The asshole has the senses of a snake, or a
spider. He knows everything happening in his vicinity. He's so damn
switched on, nothing ever gets past him.

"Is your mum worried about him leaving?" JJ taps his fingers on the
table.

Lena knits her eyebrows. "She is, of course, but she's also proud of
him. She always told us to follow our instincts. As long as we're happy
with our chosen professions, she wouldn't dream of interfering. She's
always been very supportive of our choices."

"And does she approve of Isaac?"

I scoff. "JJ, really?"

She hesitates. I turn to find Lena scrutinizing my features. She leans
in close enough so her lips are just a hair's breadth from mine. "She
thinks I could do worse."

"Oh yeah?" I tug her forward. She yelps and loses her balance and
crashes into my chest. I rise to my feet with her in my arms. "Gotta go,
old man, I need to show my girlfriend just how good a choice I am for
her."

"Isaac, what are you doing?" Lena hisses.

I glance down to find her cheeks are red. How cute. The fact that
she still blushes is such a fucking turn-on.

I turn and head for the doorway.

"Isaac," JJ calls out.

I pause and swing around to glance at him.

"Good night."

He sits there in his armchair, cigar clamped between his lips. His jaw is rigid. A nerve throbs at his temple, like he's pissed off about something. His features, though, wear the same emotionless mask I've seen so many times growing up.

"Night." I turn and walk out.

I've only reached the stairs when the sound of something crashing to the floor reaches me.

I pause.

"Should we go and check if something's wrong?" Lena asks.

I glance down at her. "Do *you* want to go and check if something's wrong?"

"Nope."

"Me neither." I lower my head and brush my lips over hers. "I'd rather spend the time showing my girlfriend how much I've missed her."

21

JJ

"Did you hurt yourself?"

Michael Sovrano jerks his chin in the direction of my hand.

"No, I didn't," I snap.

"It sure looks like you cut yourself, ol' chap," Sinclair Sterling drawls from his position near the window of the conference room that adjoins my office at Kane Tower.

Oh, now they back each other up. For men who were once sworn enemies, I'd say I did a good job of bringing them together. When I revealed that the man I had spying on both Sinclair and Michael was none other than Antonio, they were gob-smacked. He was one of Michael's men, whose life Sinclair and his friends had spared on the condition that he spy on Michael for them. And he was spying on both of them for me, for Antonio owed his loyalties to me. Sinclair and Michael were understandably pissed. Michael was the first to admit I beat them at their own game. Sinclair followed suit. They both then promised they wouldn't harm him. Not that I was giving them a chance. I contacted Antonio and ensured him that he and his girlfriend Nina had safe passage to a country of their choice where they could live out their lives in anonymity. So, yep, I won this round.

Now, I glower at the both of them. "Told you, it's nothing."

"Oh, it's something," Nikolai Solonik, the head of the Bratva, murmurs from where he's lounging on the settee opposite me.

"If we're done with this inquisition, can we get onto the business at hand?"

Michael chuckles. "Someone's in a foul mood."

"Who's in a foul mood?" a new voice asks.

I glance up as Hunter Whittington strolls in. His dark hair is perfectly coiffed, the shadow of his designer beard gracing his jaw. He's wearing a three-piece pinstriped suit. Even though he's in his mid-thirties, he dresses like someone who's older. Someone with conservative tastes. Someone who has control tightly reined in. Someone who's just announced his candidacy for the position of Prime Minister of the UK.

Michael and Nikolai fall silent. The expression on Sinclair's features doesn't change.

"I believe you know each other?" I murmur.

Sinclair nods. He rises to his feet and thrusts out his hand. "Councilor."

"Sterling." Hunter's lips quirk. "I should have believed JJ when he said I wouldn't regret making it to the meeting he set up today. Your new takeover is all over the business community."

"As is your announcement for candidacy." The two men grip each other's hand for a second longer, then step back. Hunter turns to Michael.

"Sovrano. Your reputation precedes you. I hear you've been looking to invest in England?"

Michael tips up his chin. He doesn't offer to shake Hunter's hand. The councilor doesn't seem put out by it.

"You do realize this meeting doesn't mean you can bypass any checks and balances before you invest?"

Michael smirks. "Wouldn't dream of it."

He turns to Nikolai. "The same goes for you, Solonik."

Nikolai tips up his chin. The two men engage in a staring match—something to be expected when you have multiple men with big egos in the same room.

"Gentleman, this is a safe space. It goes without saying that whatever is said between these walls stays here."

There's silence, then Hunter nods. So do Sinclair, Michael, and finally, Nikolai.

"What did I miss?" I turn to find Declan Beauchamp entering the room, Adrian Sovrano on his heels. Declan walks up to Michael and slaps him on his shoulder. "Didn't expect to see you here, but can't say I am surprised."

"Glad you could make it from LA," I add.

"I didn't think I could, but something came up." His eyebrows crease. "Turned out, I had to be in London for a premiere. I could juggle around my other engagements to make the meeting."

Adrian walks up to Michael who holds out his hand. "Don." Adrian kisses the ring on Michael's little finger."

If the others are surprised by the gesture, they don't show it.

"I assume you've brought us together for a reason, Kane?" Nikolai turns to me.

"Indeed. If you could all take your seats?"

Declan takes the chair next to Sinclair, and Adrian the one next to him. Hunter walks further to take the chair at the foot of the table.

"Sorry I'm late." Liam Kincaid strides into the room. He grips my hand, then turns to the men. "Gentlemen." He rounds the table and drops into the seat next to Michael.

I glance around at the cast of characters—each one handpicked by me for what they can bring to the table. Each one a leader in his own right. Each one has a unique skill set which the others may not be aware of yet, but which will be revealed in time.

"There are two people missing."

Hunter glances around the table. "From where I am, everyone who matters is here."

"Except me," a female voice calls out, then a woman walks into the room. Dressed in a skirt that reaches to just above her knees, and a fitted jacket with her hair flowing around her shoulders, Zara sashays into the room. She walks over to where Hunter is seated and stares down her five-foot four-inch height at him. "You're in my seat," she says haughtily.

"Am I now?" he murmurs.

"Yes, you are." She crosses her arms across her chest. "If you were a gentleman, you'd have offered me the seat."

"But you're not a lady now, are you?" he drawls.

She stiffens. "You're every bit the wanker I thought you to be, Mr. Whittington."

Of course, Hunter is known by face, but have the two met each other before? The two of them lock gazes; the seconds stretch by. Hunter smirks. She stiffens. Something passes between them.

"On the other hand, my mother taught me better."

He rises to his feet, gestures to the seat he's just vacated, only to move to the seat next to her.

Zara takes her seat. "Thanks for having me, JJ."

"Zara Chopra, she is a leading media personality," I introduce her. She's not as well-known as the rest around the table, yet. But that's going to change. It's why I invited her to join the club. Best to get them in before they embark on the upward slope of their career trajectory.

Zara inclines her head in the direction of the table.

Hunter looks at her with interest, but when Zara turns to him, he changes his expression to one of indifference. *Hmm.*

"Who's missing?" Declan asks.

"Edward Chase."

"Edward?" Sinclair frowns. "You mean the once Father Edward Chase, who has since left the Church?"

I nod.

"*My* friend Edward Chase?" he asks again.

"Precisely. I left him a few messages, but he hasn't responded. He hasn't been in touch with you, has he?"

Sinclair shakes his head slowly. "Not since he went to Thailand. Something about setting up a beach bar, I think. That was a month ago, I haven't heard from him since."

"I'm sure he'll surface at some point," I offer.

"You going to reveal why you wanted us all in one place?" Liam asks.

"What if I said it was for the pleasure of your company?"

There are snickers around the table.

"You gentlemen and lady are right, of course. I've brought you all together because each one of you is unique in your contributions to the world. You come from all walks of life. Arts, business, and politics to name a few."

Liam tilts his head.

"Some of you live on the fringe of society, too."

Nikolai smirks.

"It goes without saying that most of you are personally wealthy, too, but it goes beyond that. Each of you is among the most influential, most powerful, and most exceptional in your fields. You, here, are a veritable roster of who's who. The media is interested in many of you and follows your every move."

Hunter's gaze sharpens. Zara twists her lips.

"For all of you, your home is your sanctuary, the one place you can unwind without scrutiny from peers, or from tabloids."

Declan lowers his chin to his chest.

"Now, you have another place. Here, you can unwind without being worried about the media. A space to entertain and be entertained.

"A combination of comfort, glamour, and intimacy, where what's said and done in the club will stay in the club. In short, this will be the place to meet and network among the tastemakers, the influencers, those whose every choice has a ripple effect on the decisions of millions."

Liam drums his fingers on the table. "Are you talking about a club, because if so, I'm already a member of—"

"Not any club. Call it a league, a coalition, a fellowship."

"So, a society?" Adrian asks.

"A group of people united by common interests," I retort.

"Which is?" Declan narrows his gaze.

"Each of you has a certain proclivity..." A ripple of tension runs around the room. "Including me. And this is the place where you can indulge in it without fear of being judged or exposed."

"And you have this information, how?" Sinclair asks in a soft voice.

"I have my sources. Just as you had me investigated before you agreed to meet me the first time, just as" —I sweep my gaze across the people around the conference table— "each of you had me investigated before doing business with me previously."

"Except me." Declan touches his fingertips together. "We haven't done business, and I haven't had you investigated. Sure, I know of you by reputation, but really, I came along because I was curious."

"And your trust is your strength—"

"Or your downfall," Liam drawls.

Declan chuckles. "You need to have some faith in the inherent goodness of people, ol' chap."

"I don't survive merely on the strength of my looks, pretty boy," Liam scoffs.

"And I don't think everyone is out to get me, though admittedly, there are more people out there who hate my guts than there used to be. The perils of fame." He raises a shoulder.

"You—" Liam frowns, but I cut him off.

"People, I know your time is precious so I won't take up any more of it, except to say, the lot of you have been handpicked to head the board of this league."

"A league?" Nikolai drawls. "Is that what we're going with?"

"For the time being, unless any of you have a better suggestion?"

There's silence around the table.

"Fine. A league it is. New members need to be recommended by existing members. And we meet monthly to review the membership requests that come in. Any board member can veto the entry of a new person. All of us need to agree that the person will be the right fit for this league."

"Is there a name for this league?" Liam asks

"The League?" I offer.

"Right," he says in a skeptical voice.

"Do we have, like, a clubhouse and stuff?" Declan asks.

"For now, we meet here in my offices. But the new premises will be at Piccadilly, right next to the headquarters of the BAFTA."

Zara leans forward in hear seat. "Next to the BAFTA, huh? Fancy."

"What's BAFTA?" Declan quirks his eyebrows.

"British Academy of Film and Television Arts. The equivalent of the Oscars. They're housed at 195 Piccadilly. We'll be occupying the premises next to them."

"Are you sure it's wise to have such a public presence?" Hunter murmurs.

"Are you ashamed of your kinks?" I shoot back.

Zara laughs, then turns it into cough.

"I do have a public image to uphold." He frowns.

"If you were so worried about your image, you wouldn't be here in the first place," she reminds him.

"Who are you? My PR manager?"

"God forbid. And whoever does manage your PR has my full sympathies. He or she must have to spin many plates at the same time to keep your image out of the gutter."

Hunter opens his mouth, but before he can speak, I interject, "If there are no more questions—"

"What exactly is the benefit of being on the board again?" Liam tilts his head. "Other than a direct hotline to those around the table, that is?"

"You mean, a direct communication channel to the kind of power that can sway governments, influence share prices, give you access to secrets that you'd have found difficult to get hold of otherwise, and the chance to do good on a scale that can make a visible difference," I remind him.

"I'm not sold on the idea yet, but" —he raises a shoulder— "I'll give it a trial run. If the club adds value to my business, and indeed, to my life... I'll not only stay on, but I'll recommend the kind of members who'll make a real difference by their very presence alone."

"Is that a challenge?"

His eyes gleam. "If you wish."

I hold out my hand. "If I win, you recommend seven new members to join the league."

"If you lose?" He peels back his lips.

"I won't."

"But what if you do?"

I laugh, "We'll cross that bridge when we come to it."

That's when there's a knock on my office door.

22

Lena

I haven't seen the alphahole in three days. Three full days when it hasn't mattered how early I woke up, by the time I went down to the kitchen, he'd left. I'd tried to see him at work but Karen had informed me, with unwarranted glee, that he was busy. JJ was being a bitch, and I hated it. In fact, it made me so angry that after being turned down yet again by Karen, I grabbed my tablet with the urgent information I needed to share with him, then marched past her and rapped on the door to his office.

"Hey, stop!" She jumps up from her seat, but I shove the door open, step in, and come to a stop.

The men and one woman seated around the table swivel their heads in my direction. Oh, shoot, he really was in a meeting, huh?

"Umm, sorry?" I begin to sidle back toward the door when Karen pops her head around me.

"I'm sorry, Mr. Kane. I tried to stop her, but she kept going, I—"

"It's fine, Karen," he says without taking his gaze off of me.

"If you want me to tell her to leave—"

"You can go now."

"Okay. Awesome." I turn to leave when his voice rumbles behind me.

"Not you, Lena."

Oh shit. Next to me, Karen shoots me a nasty look. I glower right back at her. She retreats out the door, and shuts it behind her. I draw in a breath, square my shoulders, then spin around.

"I wanted to ask you about the Delancey pitch, but it really wasn't urgent." I shuffle my feet. "It can wait."

"Why don't you come on in and take a seat?" He gestures to me.

"Eh?" I glance around the room, taking in the curious faces of those around the table. "Really, it's nothing important."

"Important enough to barge in, at any rate." His lips twist. Douchebag smirks as if he knows exactly how frustrated I am that I couldn't get an appointment to see him. And how urgent it was to get his signoffs so I didn't miss the deadline on this particular proposition. And that's the only reason I'm pissed off with him. That's all, I swear.

"Besides, my guests were leaving," JJ drawls.

"That's true." The man seated next to JJ rises to his feet. He nods at JJ, then turns away from the table and heads for the door. It's Declan Beauchamp, whose face is on the cover of almost every tabloid and online magazine, thanks to his recent streaming hit. I try my best not to stare at him, but as he passes by, he winks, and I flush. The others rise to their feet, too. One of them seems vaguely familiar. Maybe I saw something written about him in business magazines? He's wearing a tailor-made suit and is handsome in a standoffish kind of way. I also recognize a potential prime ministerial candidate, another man with dark looks and a swarthy countenance, as well as the man next to him who I'm almost sure belongs to the mob—not that I know what a mob boss looks like, but there's something about him that screams predator. I step back and give them a wide berth as they head toward the exit.

The only other woman among them is tall, statuesque with a striking mane of dark hair that flows past her shoulders. She sniffs at Hunter as she brushes past him and heads out the door. The fine hair on the nape of my neck rises. I know he's watching even before I turn and my gaze clashes with those black holes that are *his* eyes. Only this time, there's something burning in their depths. The nerve at his temple pops. Is he angry with me because I broke up his meeting? Not that I asked him to. I did offer to leave, didn't I? So why is he looking at me like he's about to shout 'off with her head'? I scowl at him.

He sets his jaw, then crooks his finger at me. "Come 'ere," he growls.

My stomach seems to hollow out. A frisson of awareness runs up my spine. I try to move, but my feet are stuck to the floor.

"Lena," he says in a hard voice, then points to the space in front of him.

I blink rapidly, forcing myself to move. I close the distance between us, and stop when I'm in front of him. "I swear I didn't mean to intrude on your meeting."

"Sure, you did. You were feeling left out, weren't you?"

"What? No," I choke out. "I was worried about the deadline on the Delancey project, that's all."

"Hmm." He looks me up and down. "Fine, I believe you."

"You do?"

"Of course, not."

I scowl. *Jerk.*

"You're my executive assistant. That's why you wanted to meet me. And you were right not to wait, not if it meant compromising on the success of such an important project. But that doesn't mean you didn't want to get my attention because you feel I've been neglecting you."

"You're right about the first, wrong on the second."

His grin widens. "If you say so."

"I do." I set my jaw.

He jerks his chin to the chair next to him. "Take a seat and let's discuss it, shall we?"

I take him through the pitch that the team and I have put together. He listens to me with complete focus and gives me feedback that's on point. Feedback that tears the work I've done so far to shreds. I stare in disbelief as he goes through each page on the presentation, pointing out my flaws, telling me what I could have done better, explaining why my assumptions were wrong... Why the creative was off direction... Why the copy used for the campaign we were presenting was drab and how it had bored him to tears. By the time he's done, my stomach is in knots and my guts churn. Anger squeezes my rib cage so hard, I can barely breathe.

"It's not that bad," I say around the lump of disappointment in my throat. My first project that I've worked on with the team, and he's torn it to shreds.

"Oh yeah?" He leans back in his seat. "This is the worst pitch I've come across in all the time I've headed up Kane Enterprises. I don't know what kind of work you're used to doing, but any presentation that leaves my office is world-class in quality. Our advertising clients expect the best, and this is far from the standards they are accustomed to from us."

I squeeze my fingers together in my lap. "It's really not that bad. It isn't."

"Are you trying to convince me or yourself?"

"I am not trying to convince anyone. Also, there isn't enough time to make all of the changes you've indicated."

"When's the deadline to submit this?"

"Tomorrow morning."

"Well then, you'd better get started. You have" —he looks at the watch on his wrist— "precisely eighteen hours to get it right."

"At this rate, none of us will be able to leave the office tonight."

"Not my problem. It's not my fault you couldn't track me down earlier for feedback."

"You were busy. Every time I called, you were in a meeting. Karen wouldn't let me see you."

"Try harder next time." He pushes back from the conference room table and rises to his feet. "If that's all—"

"No, it's not all. You're being unreasonable. There's no way we can make the changes in the given amount of time."

"Are you saying you're not up to the challenge?"

I glower at his handsome face. The gray hairs at his temples only add to his appeal. How I hate his smirking, gorgeous visage. How I want to wipe the smile off of his face and show him I'm not a light-weight. That I can take the criticism he's thrown my way, and turn this project around. I want to make him eat his words—*and my pussy— No, not my pussy!* How can I even think of his sex appeal and sex with him at a time when my career is in jeopardy?

"I am saying" —I rise to my feet and grab my tablet— "that it would help greatly if you would call the head of Delancey Products and ask for an extra day so we can get this right."

"No, absolutely not. Kane Enterprises has never been late with a presentation. We take pride in delivering the most effective advertising campaign within the given time."

"I wasn't in on the early meetings when the deadlines were set. If I had been, I'd have asked for a longer lead time."

"And I want to triple my turnover in the next year, but not all of us get what we want."

He pivots and walks over to his desk on the other side of the room. "Now, if you'll excuse me, I have things to attend to."

He leaves me standing where I am, sits down at his desk and busies himself with his computer.

I stay there for a beat, another. He begins tapping on his keyboard like he's already forgotten I'm there. What a wanker.

I grip the frame of my tablet so hard my fingers ache. I'll show him. I'll deliver the best presentation that's ever gone out from this office. I spin around and head for the door.

"Oh, and Lena?"

I pause.

"Next time, I'll make you pay if you barge into my office."

23

Lena

That alphahole. That gloating, self-satisfied, smug-assed… charismatic hunk of masculinity. *Gah! Stop that, don't go there. Focus on how much you hate the guy.* And I do. I press the heels of my palms into my burning eyes. I'm so tired. After walking out of JJ's office, I called an emergency meeting for the creatives and gave them JJ's feedback. To say they weren't happy about the changes he wanted was putting it mildly. The head creative threw a fit. He'd refused to work on the copy and threatened to walk out, until I'd promised him I'd get him a commission if we won the account. Not that I have the authority to do that, but if we don't win this account, my days at Kane Enterprises are numbered. So, I stretched the truth and incentivized him. He finally got down to work, and after brainstorming with the rest of the creative team, he sent me the revised copy. By which time it was already 6 p.m. I ordered pizza for the team, on the office account—which JJ could well afford—then buckled down with the design team to mock up the ad images. I had these in place by 8 p.m. Then I returned to my desk, and surrounded by the now empty cubicles of my co-workers, I started reworking the presentation.

It's nearly 10 p.m. now, and I'm not even halfway through the slides. *Fuck, fuck, fuck.* My nose itches, my throat aches, and my eyes burn. I lean my head back against the seat and take a breath. *I can do this. I want this. I do.* My stomach grumbles. When's the last time I ate? Breakfast was a banana as I rushed out of the house, and then... I haven't eaten anything since. No wonder I'm feeling faint. I need to get through this presentation, though. I can't fail at my first assignment at Kane Enterprises. I square my shoulders, then look up and cry out, "What the—"

"Sorry, I didn't mean to scare you," JJ murmurs from his position next to my cubicle. "Just got you this." He places a paper bag next to my computer.

I glance at it, then at him. "What's this?"

"You skipped lunch."

"So?" I fold my arms cross my chest. "What's it to you, anyway?"

"You need your strength to work on the presentation. Can't have you keeling over now, can I?"

"Of course not." I turn back to the computer and begin to type onto the keyboard.

"Eat first," he growls.

"I'll eat when I'm taking my next break."

"Eat. Now," he snaps.

I stiffen. "I told you. I'll eat when I'm ready."

He moves forward. The next second he's grabbed the back of my seat and turned it around so I'm facing him.

"What?" I scowl.

"Don't disobey me."

"Who do you think you are that I should obey you?"

"I'm your boss and you live under my roof. Also..." He hesitates. "I'm your boyfriend's father. It's in my interest to make sure you are taken care of."

I stare at him, then burst out laughing. "Really? Really, you're going there now?"

"There's nothing to laugh about. Eat your dinner first, then continue working."

"Okay, Daddy," I murmur. There it is. I said it aloud. There's no going back now. But damn if I care anymore.

His nostrils flare. His dark gaze grows intense. He lowers to his knees and glares into my features. "What did you say?"

"You heard me." I toss my hair over my shoulder. "You're the one making moves on your son's girlfriend, I hope your conscience can cope with that."

"You're the one who can't look at me without blushing, who shuffles her feet and can't stop twitching her butt whenever she's in my vicinity."

"Hey, don't blame your stalker tendencies on me."

He stiffens, then draws himself up to his full height. "Are you implying I'm watching you?"

"Aren't you?"

"I haven't seen you in three days."

"The very fact that you went out of your way to avoid me is another sign that you feel an affinity for me."

"I'm not sure I'd call it an affinity; more like an itch I need to scratch."

I gape at him. "Seriously? Did you just say that to my face?"

"Best to be up-front about what this is. Explosive chemistry. Nevertheless, it's only a physical attraction. If we fuck it out of our systems, we can both move on."

"A-n-d, I can't believe you'd stoop low enough to proposition your son's girlfriend."

"At least I am being up-front about what I want. I'm not the one lying to myself and those around me."

"I'm not going to stay here and listen to you insult me. I—"

I begin to rise to my feet, but he firms his lips. "Sit down, Lena."

I sit. *What the hell? How can he control me this easily? I am not a pliable woman. I'm not. But with this man? I want to resist him, but everything in my body insists I obey his commands.*

"What do you want?" I glance up at him. I really shouldn't be talking to him. In fact, right about now I should be rising to my feet, brushing past him and out the door. I shouldn't engage with him, except as necessary for my job. Which, to be fair, is what I've been doing so far. But when I didn't see him for a few days, I admit, I missed him. Isn't that screwed up?

I peer into his face, and everything I'm feeling is reflected there. Damn, this is not helping things at all. I'd hoped I could resist him, but the more days I spend under his roof, the more I sense his presence in the same space—even when I'm not in the same room as him. What a mess.

"What do you want, JJ?" I whisper.

He growls, "I told you, it's Jack."

"I can't call you that."

He bends his knees and looks into my eyes. "Why not? Why can't you call me by my name?"

"Because everyone calls you JJ."

"You're not everyone."

"You can't say things like that," I protest.

"Why the fuck not?"

I narrow my gaze. "Because it gives the wrong impression."

"And what impression is that?"

"That there's something more between us."

"Which there is."

"And I'm your son's girlfriend," I shoot back.

"How long do you think we can tiptoe around whatever this is between us?"

"For as long as I possibly can. I can't do this, JJ. I can't betray Isaac. And with his own father." The pressure behind my eyes builds, and I look away so he doesn't see how close I am to tears.

Of course, jerkface notices.

"Lena, look at me," he growls.

"No." I sniffle.

"Lena," he warns in that hard voice—that Dad voice of his I'm beginning to think of it as— not that I'll ever tell him that.

"Look at me, right now," he snaps.

I do. I turn to him and he peers between my eyes. His jaw flexes. The muscles above his cheekbones flex. A sure sign he's gritting his teeth. If he does this too many more times he's going to crack a molar.

A teardrop squeezes out from the corner of my eye and he looks stricken.

"Lena, please." He reaches over, and before I can pull out of his reach—not that I want to, which is why I'm a second too late—he's already brushing the space below my eyes.

"Don't cry, please." His voice sounds anguished.

"I'm not crying." I shove his hand away and swipe at my face, then paste a fake smile on my lips. "See? No more tears."

"That's a terrible smile." His own lips quirk a little.

"Yours isn't much better," I point out.

He wipes the half-smile off his face and narrows his gaze. "Let me help you, Lena. All you have to do is tell me you want to leave him, and I'll support you in this. I'll talk to him on our behalf—"

"Don't you dare." I shake my head. "Don't say anything to him, JJ, please don't." I lock my fingers together. "Promise me you won't breathe a word of this to him."

"Breathe a word of what?" a new voice says. Both JJ and I turn to find Isaac standing in front of the cubicle.

JJ straightens.

I stiffen. The blood rushes to my cheeks. I jump up, brush past JJ and head to Isaac. "What are you doing here?"

"I came to see you."

"To see me?" I blink.

"I was in the building dropping off the first set of my paintings for Jillian to take a look at."

"You were here to meet my HR manager?" JJ asks.

"You did ask me to use her as my point of contact," Isaac points out, before turning to me. "I thought I'd come by and see how you were doing." He glances between me and his father. "Guess I'm not the only one who had that idea."

My cheeks warm further. I didn't do anything wrong. I didn't. *I was only entertaining sinful thoughts about your father, that's all.* I shove my hair back from my face. "I won't be done for hours more."

"And I was just leaving." JJ nods toward Isaac, then walks past the both of us. My heart flutters in my chest. And all because he brushed past us. Apparently, not even the fact that his son, my boyfriend, is standing near me is going to tamp down this magnetic pull his father exudes over me.

Isaac searches my features. "Are you okay? You look flushed."

To be fair I'm probably flushed because I'm tired and hungry so I don't need to lie to him but what comes out is, "Ah, it's only because the air-conditioning here hasn't been working properly." Jeez, talk about having a guilty conscience.

"Oh yeah?" He looks around the space. "Feels fine to me."

"Have you eaten dinner?" I blurt out.

"Eh?"

"Dinner?" I mimic shoveling food into my mouth.

"Not yet."

"Wanna share mine?"

"You have your dinner here?"

"Ah, your father—" I bite the inside of my cheek. If I tell him his father got me food, that would sound weird, right? "I ordered food which just got delivered," I lie.

"You ordered food?" He narrows his gaze on me.

"I knew I was going to be working late, and I didn't eaten lunch, so —" I raise a shoulder.

He seems like he's going to protest, then nods. "Sure. Why not?"

I pull him in the direction of my table. "Let me get you another chair." I grab the one pushed up against a corner of my cubicle, and place it next to mine. "Sit."

He seems dubious but slides into the seat.

"Wonder what's in here?" I pull out the cartons stamped with the logo of a restaurant that specializes in Indian-Chinese food.

What the—? How does he know I'm addicted to Indian-Chinese food? A particular kind of fusion cuisine popular in the subcontinent and available from a select few outlets in London. And he ordered from the one that's my favorite. My fingers tremble. He's messing with my head. Bet he's having fun with whatever game he's playing with me. And that's all I am to him—a game. He has no compunctions about desiring me, no matter the forbidden nature of our relationship. He's playing with my life, my career, my connection with Isaac—all of it—and he doesn't give a damn.

"You don't know what food you ordered?" Isaac's voice cuts through my thoughts. I glance at him from the corner of my eyes.

Shoot, I knew I shouldn't have said that aloud and trust Isaac who's normally only half present when he's with me to notice what I said.

"Of course, I do." I tilt up my chin. " I just forgot because I'm so tired. And hungry. You know how absentminded I can get."

His muscles stiffen. He narrows his gaze on me. "Lena, you are the most put-together person I know. You're very focused, very ambitious, very driven—the exact opposite of me. It's why I was so attracted to you."

"And I you." I turn and take his hands in mine. "I like the fact that you're easygoing and don't take things too seriously. I like that you give me my space, and let me be."

"Maybe I'm giving you too much space, eh? Maybe I need to be more demanding of you."

He reaches over and tugs the container of food from my hand, then places it on the table. He turns and takes my hands in his, then tugs me forward. I fall against his chest. He wraps his arms around my waist and pulls me even closer. "Kiss me," he says in a hard voice.

I plant my palms on his chest and try to push away, but his grasp tightens.

"Does it turn you on when I'm rough with you? Do you prefer it when I don't give you a choice? Would you rather I demand your attention, Lena? Is that it?"

"Isaac, stop, what are you doing?"

"What I should have done a long time ago. You think I'm a pushover, Lena? You think I like the fact that I don't make enough money to keep a roof above our heads?"

"I never said that, Isaac."

"But you implied it when you all but forced me to ask my father for help."

"I did it because there was no other way out."

"You could have asked your family to help out."

"They're in LA, and not exactly rolling in money," I protest.

"And my father is," he retorts in a flat voice.

"I had no idea how well off he was until we reached his home, and you know that."

"And now you've lost all respect for me because we're living under his roof." His jaw tics.

"Isaac, please. I'm not judging you at all. This is just temporary, until we get back on our feet."

"So why are you avoiding me?"

"I thought you were the one avoiding me." I protest.

His eyebrows draw down. "I've been home the last two days and I haven't seen you."

"Only because I've been busy. I've been working on this pitch and I need to get it right, and at the last minute, your father changed everything so I now have to rework it and—" To my horror, tears squeeze out again from the corners of my eyes. "Oh shoot." I turn my head and try to pull away from him, but he doesn't let me. "Please, Isaac, let me go."

"No." He removes his arm from around me and pinches my chin. "It's okay to show you're vulnerable. It's fine to share what you're going through. You don't always have to be strong for me, you know."

"Don't I?" I rub the back of my palm across my nose. "You're so busy chasing your muse, you haven't exactly pulled your weight when it comes to paying the bills."

"That's all you think of—paying the bills, cleaning the home, meeting the rent for the month."

"Well, someone has to," I snap.

"There you go, all passive-aggressive again. You clearly don't have a single good word to say about me."

"I'm here, aren't I?"

He pauses. "Do you not want to be with me? Is that it? Would you prefer to be with someone else, Lena?"

"What?" I gape at him. "What are you talking about?"

"You're the one who's implying that you're doing me a favor by being here with me." His jaw hardens. "I know I haven't been the best boyfriend, but if you have an issue with being with me, I'd rather you come out and say it than slyly hint about it."

"I'm doing no such thing." I wriggle in his grasp, and this time, he releases me. I pull away and rise to my feet. "Did you come to pick a fight, Isaac? Is that why you're here?"

"I came to meet you because I missed you."

I stiffen.

"I do, Lena. I miss what we had. We said we'd always be there for the other, remember?"

I glance away, unable to reply. A ball the size of Earth seems to have lodged itself in my throat. I swallow but it does nothing to ease the pressure.

"Lena, you mean so much to me." He takes my hand in his.

I glance at the tiny tattoo on the back of my right wrist, the twin of which is on his left wrist. The tattoo of the outline of a swan. We'd been so happy that day watching the swans swim in The Regent's Park. We'd rollerbladed in the park, eaten ice cream, read on the park bench, then napped on the grass. And we'd laughed so much. I'd been sure I'd found my soul mate. He must have felt the same way, for on our way back as we passed a tattoo shop in Camden Town, he'd pulled me in and surprised me with the tattoo on his wrist. To end a perfect day with the perfect girl, he'd said. In a burst of spontaneity, I'd asked for a twin of the tattoo. I'd been sure I'd end up with him for the rest of my life that day. Now, I'm not so sure.

"Do I?" I take a step back from him. "You have a funny way of showing it."

His gaze narrows. "What do you mean? Did I not accept the job with my father for you? Did I not come by here to check on you and see how you were doing?"

"You didn't have to do that, and you didn't have to oblige me by taking the job with your father for me. Do it because it's going to help your career, Isaac. Don't do it for me."

Isaac flexes his shoulders. He opens his mouth as if to say something, then shakes his head. "You know what? Forget it. I knew I shouldn't have come here today. This is so pointless." He brushes past me and begins to walk away.

"Isaac." I race after him. "Isaac, stop, please."

He heads to the elevator and punches the button.

"Isaac, say something."

"What's there to say, Lena? We can't seem to have a simple conversation without arguing. All I wanted was to see you and say hi to my girlfriend. Instead, as usual, it's turned into a shouting match."

"It wasn't a shouting match. We have differences. It happens. It's normal for a couple to go through ups and downs."

"We've been so down for so long, I can't even remember what up is anymore."

"Isaac, don't leave like this, please."

The elevator dings, the doors open, and he steps inside.

"Isaac, please." I slap my hand on the door to stop it from closing. "Don't go."

"I think it's time I did." His features wear an expression of resignation. "I wish things between us hadn't deteriorated to this stage."

"We can salvage things, Isaac. We can."

"As always, you're the optimist, Lena. It's too bad this time... I'm not sure if I feel the same way."

"Isaac—"

He shakes his head. "I'll see you at home."

The tension in my shoulders leaches out. He's going home. I'll see him at home. He's not leaving me... Yet. I step back and the doors swoosh shut. I spin around and walk back to my cubicle. My knees feel wobbly and cold sweat pools under my armpits. The stress drains out of my muscles and I yawn. I didn't realize just how wound up I'd been from Isaac's visit until now. I yawn again, then slam into a hard wall. A warm, ripped, hard wall. My nose connects with the front of his chest and I draw in large gulps of sherry oak, cinnamon and dark chocolate. My mouth waters. Large warm palms clamp down on my hips, jerking me out of my strange reverie. I glance up to meet his dark gaze.

"What are you doing here?"

"I stuck around to make sure you were okay."

"Of course, I'm okay." I step back, and JJ releases me at once. I walk around him, continuing to my cubicle.

"Have you eaten?"

I drop down into my seat and focus on my screen. The words blur in front of my eyes, but I continue to stare at it.

"Lena, you need to eat to keep up your strength."

"Please stop with your fake concern."

"It's not fake. I'm worried about you. About both of you."

I still. "You heard us arguing?"

He doesn't reply. He doesn't need to. Of course, he did.

"It's impolite to eavesdrop on other people."

"You're *my* people."

"Like your son, you have a strange way of showing concern. And I don't need it. I just want to be left alone so I can carry on with this pitch, okay?"

"Eat first."

I throw up my hands. "Oh my god, you're so annoying." I reach for the container of food, but he snatches it up, then the bag with the rest of the food.

"What are you doing?"

"Follow me." He stalks back toward the elevator.

"Hey, stop." I spring up and run after him. First the son, then the father—these Kane men are really annoying.

He walks to the elevator, presses the button and the doors open. He steps in, then holds it open for me. "Come on."

"Where?"

"A place where you can enjoy your food in peace."

"I'm not sure it's advisable for us to be alone."

"We're alone on the floor, in case you hadn't noticed."

"I mean alone in an enclosed space." I jerk my chin in the direction of the elevator.

His lips curl. "I confess, I've wanted to push you up against the wall of your cubicle then lift your skirt and spank your lush butt before I fuck you from behind, but this is not one of those times."

"Oh." My jaw falls open. *Did he just—? He did, didn't he? How could he?* "You—"

"Get in the elevator, Lena. I promise not to touch you." He lowers his chin to his chest. "Not unless you want me to," he mumbles under his breath.

"Eh? What was that?"

He fixes me with that glare. "Get. In."

24

Lena

I polish off the food, then lean back with a sigh. "That was good."

"Here, finish this." He pushes his untouched plate over.

"Oh, I can't."

"You're still hungry."

"If I eat any more, I'll fall asleep in my chair."

"You can take a nap on the couch." He jabs his thumb over his shoulder toward the settee in a corner of his office.

We're in the adjoining terrace, with floor-to-ceiling windows that open onto the lights of the city. A table and chairs placed around it invite people to sit down and enjoy the view. Which I never have, until now. And only because he's here with me.

"Why are you being nice to me?" I frown.

"Because you're my—"

"Employee, and you need the pitch done on time. Got it. Speaking of, I really do need to get back to it." I begin to rise, but he presses down on my shoulder.

"Sit down and finish your food first."

I don't even bother arguing with him. I know better. All he has to do is glare at me and order me in that dominant voice of his, and every single shred of feminism in my body goes out the window. So annoying. Also, I don't want to miss out on my favorite food. If it had been anything but Indian-Chinese I might have objected, but seriously, I love this cuisine. I dig into my veg fried noodles with my chopsticks and tuck in.

"You really love this cuisine, eh?"

"Of course." I try to say with my mouth full. It comes out as "Uff —cooos."

I chew, swallow, then shove another mouthful in and another. When I'm done, I place my chopsticks down with a sigh. "This particular confluence of Indian flavored Chinese food is something I discovered in London. They don't have this in LA. It has the flavors of my mother's cooking but with a Chinese base which is so unique. It reminds me of home, but it's also so exotic."

"Like you."

"Eh?" I jerk my chin in his direction. "Did you say something?"

"Just that it's refreshing to come across a woman who relishes her food and eats without compunction."

"You mean eats too much, right? Of course, that was after you insisted I eat." I make a face. "But that's why I can never get rid of these curves."

"I love your curves."

I flush. "I wasn't fishing for compliments. And you shouldn't speak like that."

"Just telling you the truth. You're the most perfectly-formed woman I know… when you're not speaking, that is."

"What the—" I gape at him. "That was so sexist. So inappropriate. But why should I be surprised? It's exactly the kind of thing you would say. And just when I was thinking that, perhaps, you're not that bad a person. I really don't get you." I pat my mouth with a napkin, then drop it on the plate. "You get me my favorite food—I don't know how you found out it's my favorite cuisine. It's something I rather not know actually—and then you compliment me and insult me in the same sentence. It's messing with my head. You—" I stab my finger in his direction "—are messing with my head. It's time for me to get back to work."

I rise to my feet, and this time he doesn't stop me. I brush past him when warm fingers circle my wrist. "I'm sorry."

"Excuse me." I whip my head around. "Did you just say what I think you did?"

He rubs the back of his neck. "I didn't mean for it to come out that way."

"Sure, you did."

His lips twitch. "Yes, I did. I'm old-school. I believe a woman's place is in the home."

"Don't you mean barefoot and pregnant and cooking for her man in the kitchen?"

"That, too."

I scowl. "And having a hot meal ready for the hard-working husband who comes home in the evening."

"Err, yes?"

Anger flushes my chest. My stomach flip-flops. I don't find the thought of cooking for him a turn-on. I don't. I pull at my wrist but his grasp tightens. "Why are you upset?"

"I'm not upset." I toss my head. "Why should I care that you have such an archaic, outdated, pre-historic view of the world?"

"Would you rather I lie to you?" he asks softly.

"I'd rather you not talk to me at all," I say through gritted teeth.

"I tried that. Didn't work, remember? It only had you getting your knickers in a twist."

"My knickers are fine, thank you very much."

He opens his mouth, and I raise my finger. "And not one more inappropriate comment from you about my knickers, *Mr. Kane.*"

He seems taken aback, then mimes zipping his lips. And when I tug on my hand, he releases it. Why is he being so compliant? It's a ruse, it has to be. Jerkass is playing another game with me, no doubt.

"I really do need to get back to work to finish that pitch," I mutter.

"Your boss is a slave-driver, huh?" he murmurs.

I blink. Is that JJ being nice? And did he just make a crack at himself? That is so weird. And I'm too tired to deal with him right now.

"Can I get back to my work now please?"

"Why don't I help you?"

———

Two hours later, I lock my fingers together and stretch my arms above my head. "I'm beat." I yawn so long, my eyes water.

Daddy J—I'm definitely exhausted which is the only reason I called him that—glances up from behind his desk where he's putting the finishing touches on the presentation on his computer. After dinner, we moved to his desk, where we worked in almost complete silence. We were very productive. What would have taken me a minimum of five hours to complete on my own had been done in less than half the time. The man's brain is razor sharp. He was always ten steps ahead of me. In fact, it felt like he was holding back and waiting for me to catch up as we'd worked on the pitch. Now, he narrows his gaze on me. "Why don't you take a nap while I wrap this up?"

"I can help," I protest.

"You've done a lot already."

"All I did was work out the outline of the revised deck. It's you who's been filling in the words."

"They were my ideas to begin—" he points out.

"Yes, but I fleshed them out further."

"And now I'm folding them into the presentation. This won't take long and you look beat."

"I am." I yawn again.

"Go on." He nods toward the settee in the corner of his office.

"You sure?" I say doubtfully.

"Relax, I'm not going to make a move on you while you're asleep, if that's what you're worried about." He smirks.

I scoff, "That's not what I'm worried about. It's just... I don't want you to think I'm slacking off or anything. After all, I was supposed to complete the pitch."

"And we did it together."

"You won't hold it against me or anything, will you?" I shuffle my feet.

"Are you doubting my word?"

"No, it's just... It doesn't feel right for me to sleep while you're still working." I yawn, this time so loudly my jaw cracks.

"Go on," he chuckles, "it's nap time for you, young lady."

"Hmm." He does think of me as someone much younger than him. At other times, it feels like he treats me as his equal. And this chemistry between us? It's so unexpected. Somehow, his age and his maturity, not to mention his confidence and complete assurance in everything he does, is so appealing. And it's not just his looks, which of course, are not a deterrent. There's something else about him, something lost, something wounded inside of him that seems to call to me every time I see him. It's the same thing I'd sensed in Isaac. Only, there's a lot more anger in Isaac. In JJ, though, it's settled into something darker, edgier inside of him. Something that identifies him as a predator. A person who doesn't trust anyone easily due to his experience.

"Lena?"

His voice cuts through my thoughts.

"Yeah, okay. I'll take a short nap. Wake me up when you're done, okay?"

25

JJ

"Lena? Lena." I stand over the sleeping girl.

She's sprawled out on her side on the settee, her thick auburn hair around her shoulders. Her palm tucked under her face. Dark eyelashes fan her cheeks. There are smudges under her eyes.

So far, she's managed to rise to every challenge I've thrown her way. I hadn't meant to help her out with this presentation, but when I heard her and Isaac arguing I felt... Angry. With him. With myself.

It's not right that she's being pulled between us. It's not right that I'm still entertaining thoughts of her. I tried to distance myself, but look how well that turned out. She feels the pull between us and is as helpless against it as I am. Yet, she doesn't want to acknowledge it. And I get it. I really do. Isaac has youth on his side. He has his future ahead of him. Me? I'm set in my ways. I'm in the stage of my life where I should be thinking of my son's wedding. Instead, I'm eyeing his girlfriend. But it's not my fault.

I wasn't looking for this kind of attraction. I wasn't searching for something to add depth to my life. I wasn't looking to find someone who'd occupy my thoughts. Someone I yearn to catch sight of every day. Someone I want to hold in my arms and kiss, then throw down and fuck until she can't remember the name of any other man but me. She brings out a possessiveness in me, the likes of which I've never felt before. Not with any woman. Definitely not with the mother of my children. Not even when she was pregnant with them, and that's just wrong. How can I have such visceral feelings for a stranger? How can I feel so possessive about her, to the extent that I'm ready to fight my own son for her affections. This is insane.

I drop down on my haunches and whisper, "Lena?"

She doesn't stir. It's been two hours since she crashed. Two hours since I continued to work on the presentation while shooting glances at her, and throughout that time, she hasn't moved. Her lips are parted; her chest rises and falls in her sleep. I rake my gaze down her shoulders, the curves of her tiny waist, the flare of her voluptuous hips which ensnared me from the moment I set eyes on them. I push a strand of hair that's fallen over her cheek behind her ear. She continues sleeping. I reach out to touch her, then hesitate.

Yes, I touched her when she was in bed, under my roof. And no, I'm not going to apologize for that. My fingers tingle. My skin feels too tight for my body. I lean in closer, until my nose is at the hollow of her throat. I draw in a deep breath, and the scent of strawberries and passionfruit goes straight to my groin. My cock stirs and my heartbeat accelerates. *Jesus fucking Christ, how could smelling her turn me on so much?* ·

I lean back on my heels, then lower my head to the apex of her thighs and draw in another breath. The sweet scent of her pussy, combined with that deeper scent of her arousal, sinks into my blood. My dick instantly stands to attention. *Fucking fuck.* I shouldn't have done that. Shouldn't. She's asleep in my office. I told her I wouldn't move in on her while she was asleep. *I lied.*

She's never going to be mine. She's never going to leave Isaac. The only way I'll get to be a part of her life is through deceit. There, I've admitted it. It doesn't excuse what I'm about to do, but fuck that. I flip up her skirt. Her thighs are that rich warm brown that make my mouth water, and her panties are pink. Of course she wears pink panties with little white hearts on it. My dick lengthens. Jesus-fucking-Christ I'm going to hell for this. I brush my fingertips over the shadowy cleft between her butt that's visible through the fabric. She doesn't stir. *Nice one Kane. This is what you've been reduced to. Feeling up your son's girlfriend while she's fast asleep on your couch in your office.* And I'm a dirty old man. Might as well conform to the stereotype fully.

I ease my hand under the waistband of her panties, cup her pussy, and she moans. I freeze, stare at her features. That's when she turns on her back. She turns her head in my direction, her eyes still closed. Then she parts her legs. I stay where I am with my fingers up her skirt and in her knickers.

My chest hurts. My stomach is tied up in knots. A bead of sweat runs down my spine and… this is bullshit. I'm the CEO of a multi-billion-dollar company. I'm the head of one of the most notorious underground syndicates in the world. And I'm standing here, moping over the fact that I can't have this girl? This is insane.

I'm about to pull my hand back when she squeezes her legs together. She rubs her thighs, trapping my palm between them. She pushes up so her pussy is nestled firmly in my palm. Oh, fuck. I watch her face, but she's still asleep. She parts her legs again, then subsides. Her breathing deepens again. I bend on one knee, continue to survey her features. I circle her clit, strum her pussy lips, and she moves restlessly. Bloody hell, I'm going to have to be quick about this. I ease a finger inside her pussy. And so help me God, but she's wet. So wet. So hot. I slide another finger in, then a third. I weave them in and out of her, in and out, never taking my eyes off of her features.

She wriggles her hips, moans again, but doesn't open her eyes. I plunge my fingers into her pussy and twist. And her entire body shudders. Her breathing grows labored. Her chest rises and falls; the peaks of her nipples stand out against the fabric of her blouse. I want to tear off her blouse, rip off her bra so her full tits spill out. I want to fuck her tits and come in her mouth. But since I can't, I'll settle for making her come on my fingers instead.

I increase the intensity of my actions, then rub the heel of my palm into her clit. Her mouth falls open, a low cry emerging from her lips.

She bows her back and her entire body shudders as she comes, with her pussy fluttering around my fingers. I continue to finger fuck her gently through the aftershocks running up her body. Then, I pull my fingers out and ease my arm out from under her skirt. I bring my fingers to my mouth and suck. Her sweetness coats my tongue and goes straight to my head. She tastes like goddamn strawberries. I straighten her skirt, but before I can draw up her zipper, she turns on her side facing me. I pause, but she doesn't move. I reach over to raise her zipper, but she brings up a knee. Fuck. I manage to pull up the zipper. She shifts again. I pause again. Best not to push my luck. I rise to my feet, turn to leave, then hesitate. I shrug off my jacket, then bundle it up and lift her head to place it under her neck. She sighs, then snuggles into the jacket. Her breathing deepens.

I glance around, then walking over to the closet in the corner of the room, I open it and pull out one of the blankets I keep there for the nights I've needed to spend in this office, too. I turn back, reach her, and cover her with it. I'm only doing it so she doesn't get a cold because she's the one who has to present this pitch tomorrow. Yeah, that's all it is. I rub my chest, then spin around and walk over to my desk.

"JJ! Hey!" I snap my eyes open to find Lena staring down at me. The dawn light filtering in through the window highlights her features.

Her hair is mussed, her cheeks are flushed, but she looks rested. Her shoulders are relaxed. Good. She glances from me to the computer, then back at me. "Did you finish it?"

"What time is it?"

"6 a.m."

I crack my neck, roll my shoulders, then rise to my feet. "I've emailed the deck to you. Go over it once, and be ready to present the pitch by 9 a.m."

"I need to go home and change."

"So do that."

I brush past her, heading for the door.

"JJ, wait."

I turn to find her walking over to the settee. She holds the balled-up jacket out to me. "You forgot this."

I close the distance between us, take the jacket, and shrug into it.

"Thanks for letting me sleep here."

I shrug.

"And thanks for loaning me the jacket, and the blanket."

"It was an afterthought," I assure her.

"I slept really well, actually." She eyes the couch with a puzzled look. "In fact, I could have sworn I dreamed that—"

"What?"

"That..." She purses her lips, then shakes her head. "Nothing, forget it. I've been dreaming a lot lately."

"Good dreams, I hope?" I can't stop my lips from twisting.

Her cheeks pinken. Then she tips up her chin. "It was all right."

"Just all right?" I frown.

"What's it to you?"

"Me?" I raise my hands. "Nothing at all. I'm glad you're rested. It'll help you win this pitch."

"Right." She draws in a breath. "Are you going to give me a lift home so I can change my clothes?"

"Oh, I'm not going home today. I keep an apartment just above my office."

"You do?" She blinks.

"You can find your way home on your own, I assume."

She scowls. "Can I use your car and driver?"

"Nope."

I turn to leave.

"Jerk," she mutters under her breath.

I pause, glare at her over my shoulder. "What was that?"

She frowns at me. "Why are you acting like a grouchy-ass bear again? I thought we'd reached some kind of understanding last night?"

I have... with your body. Too bad it isn't with the rest of you.

"Nothing's changed, girl. I'm still your boss, and you're my son's girlfriend. And I need to get going, or I'll be late for my breakfast meeting."

"So, it's back to calling me girl, is it, and—" Her eyebrows knit. "You have a breakfast meeting before the 9 a.m. pitch?"

I glare at her.

She pales, then glances away. "Of course, you do." She squares her shoulders, then walks toward me. "I'd best get my handbag and get home so I can return in time for 9 a.m."

"You'd best." I hold the door open as she passes. Then walk with her to the lift. The doors slide open, and she enters, then turns to face me.

"You may have gotten me dinner and covered me with a blanket while I slept, but you're still a selfish prick."

"And you're still an immature girl who doesn't know what she wants."

"Now that we've gotten that out of the way." She stabs the button on the lift and the doors begin to close. I plant my foot in between them, forcing them to stop.

"I'm still your boss. Treat me with respect."

"And I'm still your son's girlfriend, as you like to remind me so often. Treat me with the necessary decorum."

"Fine," I snap.

"Fine," she huffs.

I step back and the doors close. Fuck this shit. Fuck my fixation with her. Fuck the fact that she still has feelings for my son. That she can tell me off, and I don't have the guts to fire her because I want her in my orbit. The thought of not having a reason to meet with her, not being able to see her every day, is beyond my imagination. Bloody hell, I need to get a grip on myself. I need to break this hold she has on me. I need… a distraction. Something… *Someone* to take my mind off of her. She wants decorum? She'll get it. In spades. I pull out my phone and call a familiar number.

26

Lena

"So you see, Kane Enterprises is the best place to represent your brand in the market. It's not an exaggeration when I say we have the best creative brains in the world working on your campaign. You will not regret choosing us as your agency."

I pause, then glance around the table. The one woman and three men who represent the client meet my gaze. Silence descends. Is that good? Is it bad? I glance toward JJ, who's been sitting in silence on one end of the table. He prowled in at exactly 9:01 a.m., shook hands with the most senior member of the team, then introduced me and handed the floor to me. I hesitated initially, then picked up speed as I found my flow. I walked the team through the presentation and answered all of their questions. I've done my best... I did a great job... I think?

I try to read JJ's expression, but he doesn't give anything away. I try to signal with my eyes that he needs to do something, to break the building tension in the room. But does he? Of course not.

The woman who leads the client's team taps her fingers on the table. "Lena, isn't it?"

I nod.

"You make an eloquent case for Kane Enterprises."

I tip my chin down. "Thank you."

"But I'd prefer to have a word with JJ about the possibility of using Kane Enterprises as our advertising agency."

"Oh, but—" I begin to protest, but she's already dismissed me.

She tosses her blow-dried, chin-length hair over her shoulder as she turns to JJ. "In private."

JJ seems taken aback, then nods.

"If everyone else doesn't mind stepping out," he murmurs.

The woman snaps her fingers, and the men who've accompanied her jump up to their feet and head for the door.

I grip my fingers together and look between them. The woman is in her early forties, dressed in a skirt that shows off her shapely legs and a blouse tucked in at her waist to show off her figure. Her blonde hair is cut in a blunt bob that swings around her shoulders. Her make-up is perfect. Perfect eyeliner. Perfect lipstick. Perfectly manicured nails. I fold my hands behind my back. I can't remember the last time I got a salon manicure, preferring to take care of my nails by myself. She's well put together, confident, glamorous, and closer in age to JJ than me. She eyes him with a hungry look. No doubt, as soon as I'm out of the room, she'll make a move on him. And he—? JJ leans back, a slow smile tugging at his lips. He all but preens under her attention. It's like the two of them have forgotten about me. I clear my throat.

The woman turns to me. "This is a private conversation," she reminds me.

"Oh, don't mind me. I'm just going to take notes."

She frowns. "This isn't that kind of a meeting."

"Oh, aren't you going to be talking about the campaign? In which case, I really do think I need to be here. I'm Mr. Kane's Executive Assistant and the Account Manager on this, after all."

"And we don't need you here for whatever is to be discussed. Go on, shoo." She snaps her fingers.

What the—? If she thinks I'm one of the emasculated men on her team who's going to snap to attention just because she says so, she's got another thing coming.

I draw myself up to my full height, "Shoo? Did you say shoo? I don't think—"

"Lena." His deep baritone rumbles across the space. "You need to go."

"What?" I turn on JJ. "This is my account. I helped put this presentation together, and if I need to debrief the team later, I need to be in on all aspects of the meeting. You know that, JJ."

He hesitates.

The other woman's frown deepens. "I need to speak one-on-one with you, JJ." She straightens her spine. "Or do the client's wishes not count anymore?"

JJ tilts his head, then nods. "Out, Lena."

"But—"

"Now." He lowers his voice to a hush, and that dominance in his voice—oh, God… My nerve endings seem to fire all at once. My thighs clench, and I'm sure my panties are soaked. I could stand around all day listening to him scold me, and have spontaneous orgasms just from listening to him.

"Go." He jerks his chin toward the door.

I spin around and march toward the exit. Goddamn him and that bitch. I step outside the conference room, and to the side. Then, because I can't stop myself, I pull my phone from the pocket of my skirt and pretend to study it as I watch the two of them from the corner of my eye. The woman rises to her feet and walks over to stand next to JJ. She leans a hip against the conference table and speaks to him. JJ nods occasionally as she continues talking. Then she puts out a hand and touches his shoulder. I stiffen. Bloody hell, is that normal? Touching a business associate like that? And JJ doesn't pull away. He smirks up at her.

The woman laughs. Anger squeezes my chest. They definitely know each other outside of work.

"They make a good couple, don't they?" A man steps up to join me. He's one of her team. One of the men she dismissed earlier.

"Sylvie's always had a thing for JJ," he adds.

Like I care. Why is he telling me this anyway? When I don't reply he shuffles his feet. "It's one of the main reasons she prefers to attend the meetings with Kane Enterprises in person, you know? So she can meet with him. She also thinks she has a better chance at influencing him."

"Indeed."

Sylvie leans in closer. She runs her fingers down JJ's collar. Every muscle in my body tenses. *Whoa, hold on. Why am I getting all twisted out of shape?* It's JJ's business if he wants to sleep with his client. It shouldn't matter to me. Except I put in a lot of work on this deal. He may have completed the presentation last night, but I put in days' worth of effort behind it, as did the rest of my team. I owe it to them to step in and find out just what's going to happen next.

I put my phone away and straighten. The man next to me tenses. "You're not going in there, are you?"

"I don't see an alternative. This pitch is important to me and my team. I need to be able to add input to it."

I knock on the door to the conference room, then twist open the handle, and step in.

"—I'd love to grant the account to Kane Enterprises." Sylvie straightens JJ's tie. "It doesn't come down only to the ideas presented, which weren't bad, by the way, but—"

"Not bad? Those were bloody good ideas," I exclaim.

Both of them turn to face me. JJ has an expression of boredom on his features. Sylvie looks pissed. Good. She still hasn't let go of JJ's tie. *Bitch.*

"And it wasn't just me working on it. It was the entire team. And JJ, too."

She turns to face him. "You worked on the presentation yourself?"

He arches an eyebrow.

"Really?" She blinks rapidly. "Since when does JJ Kane, head of the Kane Company, work on presentations hands-on?"

"Since now?" He brushes off her hand and rises to his feet. *Finally—fuck!* "I understand why you'd want the personal touch, Sylvie, but we do also need to keep the team in the loop." He jerks his chin in my direction.

"But we haven't concluded our discussion," the woman whines. I don't know her well, but I'll bet she's a hard-ass career woman. And given how she treated her team, I'll bet she eats men's balls for breakfast. And she's actually pouting? Is this the effect JJ has on the female population? Do all of them forget every single feminist lesson they've learned and get their panties wet around him? Do all of them find him that attractive? Do all of them stare at him with greed in their eyes like they want to lick him up all over? *Is that how I'm staring at him right now?*

"I believe the presentation is complete and now you do need to make a decision... over" —he looks at his expensive-as-fuck watch— "considering it's already eleven a.m., an early lunch."

"Lunch?" she breathes.

"Lunch?" I yelp.

"Lunch." He smiles at her. Asshole gives her his trademark smirk, and her bosom wrapped in that tight shirt heaves.

"Lunch, right." I draw in a breath. "Let me grab my purse, and I'll be right back." *Give me patience. Give me patience. Won't kill me to go to lunch with them.* It's work, a job, the job that'll make me independent enough to get away from him and be able to rent my own place. *And you'll miss him when you do that.* Eh? Of course not! Why should I miss his alphaholish ways, his domineering tendencies, his larger-than-life persona, his gorgeous profile, his beautiful throat, his reassuring presence, his—

"Oh, you're not coming to lunch with us," JJ states flatly.

I whip my head in his direction. "Excuse me? What did you say?"

"This lunch is for me and Sylvie to catch up and seal the deal. You know how it is."

"No, I don't know how it is." I pull myself up to my full height. "I worked on this account. You know how much effort I put in—"

"And you did well."

"—I should be there for the final negotiations."

"These are delicate discussions, things that Sylvie and I need to discuss as the heads of our companies."

"Things that an employee such as yourself doesn't need to worry your pretty little head about." The woman sniffs. "Run along now, and make sure our cars and drivers are ready for us, will you?"

I curl my fingers into fists at my sides. "How dare you?" I narrow my gaze on JJ. "How dare you treat me like this, you son of a bitch?"

Sylvie gasps. JJ's features harden. Yeah, so maybe that was a little out of line. Big fucking deal. He deserved it, right? And I bet no one's every spoken to Mr. Stick-Up-His-Ass-Billionaire—who's giving me serious whiplash with how he's behaving—like this. One minute, he's helping me with the presentation, the next, he's acting like a douchebag of the first order. *What the hell is wrong with him? What the hell is wrong with me that I'm still standing here when both of them insulted me in the worst possible way?*

"I recommend you return to your office, Lena," JJ says, using that condescending voice I hate. The voice that makes me feel like I'm twelve. The Dad voice he likes to use to make a point about the age gap between us... When it suits him. *Dick.*

"I recommend the two of you call up your own chauffeurs. I'm no one's personal assistant."

I spin around and am about to leave when— "Oh, and Lena?" His voice rumbles behind me. "Use the time to get started on your next brief, will you?"

27

'She loved me for the dangers I had passed, And I loved her that she did pity them'
(Othello – Act 1, Scene 3)

Lena

I did *not* start on the next brief. In fact, I stayed for hours at my desk, staring at my screen and conjuring up all of these scenarios in which that bitch Sylvie was all over that douche-bagel, JJ.

By the time four p.m. rolled around, he'd fucked her too many times to count—in my head—while her shark-like smile taunted me. I was too sick to my stomach to eat any lunch, either.

What a pathetic, little idiot I am. I was mooning over my boyfriend's father, who's my boss. Just because he was nice to me last night and helped me with my presentation—after telling me to change it all at the last minute—I thought... I don't know what I thought. That he felt something for me? That he and I would... What? Have a chance together? How did I allow things to get so out of hand? And I'm still Isaac's girlfriend.

My stomach had bottomed out as my guts churned. If I'd sat there any longer, I'd have broken something, or been physically sick, or both. So, I opted to grab my bag, avoid the questions from my team on how the pitch had gone—which I'd managed to evade all morning—and marched out of the building. I raced home... To the dickwad's home, that is, and found I was alone. For once, I was happy that Isaac wasn't around. It meant I could indulge the anger I felt toward his father.

It meant, after a quick shower and changing into my pajamas, I could walk down to the cellar—which I'd heard about from the house staff—choose a couple of bottles of wine, and carry them back to the living room. It's not even six p.m., but what-fucking-ever. After the day I've had, I'm entitled to get drunk. Speaking of, they went out to lunch at 11 a.m. and he' s still not home? That motherfucking, dick-sucking, sleazeball!

I pour wine into a glass and try to watch a movie, but my mind is racing. I can't focus. How many times have the two of them fucked by now? And isn't JJ getting along in his years? How often can he get it up anyway? I hunch my shoulders.

He's gorgeous, though... and so hot. Like this wine, I'll bet he's only gotten better over the years. Bet he's fan-fucking-tastic in bed. Bet we'd be incendiary together, given the chemistry between us. *No, don't go there. Stop it already.*

I turn off the TV to play some music, but that doesn't help, either. I settle for shutting down all sources of entertainment, and instead, proceed to get steadily drunk. At least the wine is top-notch. A vintage year, if I'm not mistaken. It must have cost a bomb, but fuck that. Bet the alphahole can afford that, and more. And why isn't he home yet?

I pour another glass of wine, then sink into the armchair in front of the window. I glance out at the driveway and the tree line beyond it. I'm not waiting for him. I am not. I finish the glass of wine, top it up again, then yawn. Some of the tension drains from my muscles. It's been a long day and I didn't sleep that well last night, either. I finish off this glass of wine and set it aside. My limbs feel so heavy. I yawn so loudly that my jaw cracks. Maybe I can grab a quick shut eye while I wait for JJ… and Isaac… Yeah, I'm not waiting only for my boyfriend's father, my boss, to return. I'm waiting for Isaac, too. *What a lie.* It's not a lie. It's not. I'm waiting for both of them to return. Meanwhile, I'm just going to shut my eyes for a few minutes.

The next thing I know, I'm being lifted and carried. Strong arms cradle me against a solid chest. I try to open my eyes, but my eyelids are so heavy.

"Isaac?" I murmur. There's no reply. I turn my face into the sculpted planes. I draw in a deep breath, and the scent of sherry oak and cinnamon fills my senses.

"JJ?" I breathe. The muscles against my cheek seem to ripple. He still doesn't say anything, though. This is so wrong. He shouldn't be carrying me like this. I wriggle, and his arms tighten around me. I manage to crack open my eyelids and peer up to catch a glimpse of that sculpted jaw. I reach up and run my fingers over his five-o'clock shadow. He flinches but doesn't pull away.

"You're gorgeous," I mumble.

A chuckle rumbles up his throat. "And you're drunk."

"Am not," I hiccup. *Damn it.* I bite the inside of my cheek and lower my arm, only to place my palm over his heart. *Thud-thud-thud.* His heartbeat doesn't change as he mounts the steps of the staircase until he reaches the landing, then walks down the hallway and enters the room I share with Isaac. He approaches the bed and lowers me onto it. He begins to straighten, and I grab his tie. "Don't go."

"You're inebriated," he growls.

"Not enough." I hold his gaze as I search his features. The heat in the room seems to increase in intensity. A thousand little sparks of fire blow on my skin. "JJ—" I swallow.

His gaze narrows. He searches between my eyes, his expression predatory. A nerve pops in his jaw and I know he's controlling himself as much as I am. Or, at least, as much as I was. I'm not exactly controlling myself now, am I?

He grips his tie and tugs it from my grasp, then stands.

The cool air rushes between us, and I shiver. Suddenly, I feel wide awake, like I've been roused from a dream. "Where were you all this time?"

He arches an eyebrow. "You know where I was."

"You spent half the night with that… that… trollop?"

"It's barely midnight, and we spent some time discussing the pitch, yes."

"Took you most of the day to convince her to sign the account to us? You must be losing your touch."

His jaw tightens. He turns to leave, and I jump up on the bed.

"Stop, JJ."

He continues walking to the door.

"Stop, or you'll regret it."

He pauses, then scowls over his shoulder. "Are you threatening me?" he asks in a low voice.

Goosebumps pop on my skin. Oh, my. JJ is, of course, one-hundred percent alpha male predator, but when he stares at me with such unnerving focus, when he looks at me like he can't wait for me to challenge him further, it's heady and exciting and so… so stupid. This is a game I'll never win. He's my boss, my boyfriend's father, and he just carried me to bed.

"Why did you do that?" I scowl.

"Why did I do what?" His eyebrows knit.

"Carry me to bed." I tip up my chin. "Why didn't you just leave me where I was?"

"Clearly, you were waiting up for me—"

"I was not."

He tilts his head. "And if I had left you to sleep there, you'd have woken up with a crick in your neck."

"So?"

"So, I figured you'd be more comfortable in bed."

"You could have woken me up," I point out.

"You were fast asleep."

"What do you care about that?"

He blows out a breath. "Is there a point to this conversation?"

"Yes, yes, there is. I'm tired of fighting this, whatever it is, between us."

"Oh?"

I nod. "And I hated thinking of you out there at dinner with that… that woman."

His eyes gleam. "You were?"

I walk over to the edge of the bed. "I wanted to find out where you went to dinner, and tear your eyes out."

His lips quirk. He doesn't seem bothered by my outburst. If anything, his chest seems to swell, and he turns around to face me fully. "So why didn't you?"

"I had no idea where you'd gone. And it's not like your assistant would have told me."

"So, you settled for waiting up for me?"

"I wasn't—" I purse my lips. "Fine, okay, so I was waiting up for you. Did you only discuss work or—"

"Or?"

"Or was there other stuff that the two of you spent time on?"

"Why don't you come out and ask the question that's bothering you, hmm?" He slides his hand into the pocket of his pants, all smug. *What a jerk. What a beautiful, hunk of a jerkass he is, too. And I can't resist him. I can't.*

I cross my arms across my chest. "Did you fuck her?"

"No."

The tension I hadn't been aware I was holding in my shoulders drains out. I draw in a breath, square my shoulders, then brace myself. "Do you want to fuck me?"

28

JJ

Do not answer that question. Don't. It's a trap, any which way you look at it. Say yes, and you're damned. Say no, and you're even more damned. So, what's it going to be, eh?

"Yes." I widen my stance. "I want to fuck you."

"Oh." She draws in a sharp breath.

"But I'm not going to."

Her chest rises and falls. "Don't tell me you're getting an attack of conscience all of a sudden."

"I'm not a good man. I've done many things that are in the morally gray space, I admit. And it's not the fact that you're my son's girlfriend that's stopping me, nor our age gap."

"What then?"

I hesitate. "If I fucked you, once would not be enough."

Her cheeks color. "What are you trying to say?"

"I don't believe in relationships."

"It's not like I'm looking to marry you, either." She scoffs.

"I don't sleep with a woman more than once, and with you, somehow I know that I'd break that rule."

"So, you don't mind that you and I would be cheating on your son and my boyfriend, but there's some silly rule you've made up that's stopping you?"

I raise a shoulder.

"This is stupid. Have you even heard yourself?"

"Have *you* heard yourself?"

"Have *you*?" She props her hands on her hips.

"We can't go on like this." I rub the back of my neck.

"You're telling me." She laughs bitterly. "This crazy chemistry between us, then having to see you in the office. And then, you belittling me in front of the client I'll have to work with moving forward."

I blow out a breath. "I'm sorry about that. I should have invited you to dinner with us."

"You think?"

"But I know Sylvie. She wanted alone time with me, and her company is our biggest account." Lena opens her mouth and I hold up my palm to stop her. "Doesn't mean what I did was right. I should have handled the situation better. I apologize."

She blinks rapidly. "Can you repeat what you said?"

"I said, I apologize," I say through gritted teeth.

"The great JJ Kane, actually apologizing?"

"I see no shame in doing so when I am wrong. And I was in the wrong. While I'm coming clean, you may as well know, it was me who called and asked Sylvie to attend the meeting."

"Eh?" She frowns. "You… you made sure she attended the meeting? I don't understand."

"I wanted to ensure they renewed the account. Also, I may have been curious about your reaction when she came onto me." I rub the back of my neck.

"You knew she'd come onto you?"

"I expected it, yes."

Her jaw slackens. "And you wanted to see how I'd react to her being all over you."

"You were jealous of her attention toward me."

"I was not." She huffs.

I laugh. "You can deny it all you want, but I saw how pissed off you were when she put her hand on my sleeve."

"It was the wrong kind of behavior for an office," she says primly.

"That all it was?" I arch an eyebrow.

"That's all it was." She juts out her chin.

I stare at her, then shake my head. "Still not buying it. And just so we're clear, none of this means I'm going to sleep with you." I take in her still flushed features, those golden-brown eyes alight with the possibility of a fight, her thick dark hair a halo around her shoulders. She's a vixen, a siren, a vision I'm going to carry around with me. A woman I'd love to bed, to own... To possess... And then, I'll never be able to let go of her. I meant what I said earlier. As I sat there and watched her deliver that presentation, I felt a flush of pride, an emotion very close to protectiveness. A thrill ran through me at the thought that I'd helped her with the presentation. Imagine that? Clearly, she's broken through the walls I've built between myself and the world.

After how my first wife left me, I convinced myself I wasn't made for relationships. She makes me want to believe there's a better side of me that I've yet to find. She makes me want to be someone she can depend on. She makes me want to be the kind of man who'll be there for her. She makes me want to be better... Period. Fuck. I'm losing myself. I don't want the complications that would come with being with her, even if it means for only one night. I wouldn't be able to walk away, and that would change everything. I don't want that kind of impediment in my life right now. It's best I leave. While I still can. "Goodnight, Lena."

I turn and walk toward the door just as Isaac strolls in.

He pauses; so do I. Behind me, I sense Lena stiffen.

"You?" Isaac scowls. "What are you doing here again?"

"I—"

"Oh, we were discussing the pitch I presented this morning," Lena interrupts as she hops down to the floor. She moves toward him, then rises up on tiptoes to brush her lips over his. "So happy you're back, Isaac."

My guts churn. My chest tightens. I ignore the hollowness in my stomach and head for the door. As I walk past the two of them, Isaac frowns. "Do you make it a habit to come here often?"

"Yes, Isaac. I come in here every night to check on you and make sure the boogie-man hasn't taken you away," I scoff. *Jesus, man, do you have to resort to sarcasm to deflect the conversation and with your own son?*

His frown deepens. "Can't the two of you keep your work dealings to the office? Do you have to come to our room past midnight?"

"You're right. It's nothing that couldn't have waited until tomorrow. It won't happen again." I step out of the room and shut the door behind me. Then, like a coward, I wait. There's silence, then the low murmur of voices. The creak of the bed, then silence again. I press my ear to the door. The sound of her gasp reaches me. *Motherfucker.* My fingers tighten on the handle of the door. The bed creaks again, then she moans. *Don't go in, don't give yourself away. Have some pride, you loser.*

I don't step into the room. I don't leave, either. I stay there like a motherfucking twat, unable to move. Unable to stop listening to the sounds that emerge from behind the closed door. Unable to stop my guts from churning. Unable to stop my fingers from curling into fists. Unable to stop my dick from lengthening and stretching the crotch of my pants. Is it wrong that I'm turned on to hear my son fucking his girlfriend… *his* girlfriend, the girl I want to fuck? The sounds of panting reach me, then I hear the unmistakable sound of flesh meeting flesh. My shoulders tense. Every muscle in my body tautens.

Go away, there's still time. Leave. Right now. But do I? Of course not. I stand there through the sound of her mewling, his grunting, then her crying out, and my son's groans as he comes. Silence descends. The blood thuds at my temples. My chest rises and falls. A bead of sweat slides down my throat. Still, I don't move.

Then, I hear the bed creak again, and the sound of footsteps approaches the door. That's when I turn and quietly jog down the steps. Grabbing my keys, I walk to the garage, past the rows of cars, to the dust-sheet-covered shape at the very end. I pull off the cover, and for the first time in a decade, I straddle my bike. Good thing I've kept it in top-notch condition, for when I kick start it, it revs up immediately.

The garage door rolls up, and I pull out. I ride for what seems like hours around the deserted city until, at dawn, I find myself at Primrose Hill.

I park the bike, walk up to the summit and glance down at the city. I grew up in the streets of the East End of London and came of age when my parents were killed in a car accident. They were schoolteachers, honest upright folks who'd saved up for years for a family vacation to the coast. I survived the crash unhurt. I was fifteen, on my own, no brothers or sisters. My mother was an orphan, my father's parents hadn't wanted to take on the responsibility of a teenage boy. As a result, I went into foster care.

My next few years were without incident, but for the fact I insisted on picking fights. With my foster parents, with my schoolmates. My foster family didn't give up on me, though. They were patient, giving me my space, insisting I go into therapy to deal with the aftermath of what had happened to me. Even at that age, I didn't need a therapist to tell me I was acting out to assuage my conscience. *Why had I survived when my parents hadn't?* A question that would haunt me for the rest of my life.

I'd have refused to continue with therapy, but for the fact I'd developed a crush on my counselor. An infatuation that pushed me to complete high school, and to graduate. I turned up at her home, only to find she was already married with two kids and a doting husband. I never forgave her for that… For what I thought was a betrayal.

But did I walk away from her? Hell no. I went back when she was alone at home, and seduced her. Even at eighteen, I was charismatic enough, and she didn't refuse me. I fucked her in her marital bed, then walked away. I never saw her again.

In the years that followed, I began running with a local gang. My parents had been honest to a fault, and what had it gotten them? An early death? That life wasn't for me. I wanted more for myself, and I didn't want to wait until I was older.

My parents were gone before they could live life, and I meant to make use of every second I was alive. I wanted to get rich quickly. It's why I decided to embrace the gray area of the law. I established the Kane company with Kane Enterprises as it's legal front. I decided to do whatever it took to establish myself as the head of the most powerful underground, organized crime syndicate in the country. It included sleeping with any woman who interested me, no matter if they were attached. Not that I had to try hard to seduce them, either. The wives flocked to me, knowing I'd satisfy them physically—something their husbands couldn't do. Only I spoiled them for anyone else, resulting in their marriages breaking up.

I destroyed relationships, wrecked connections between spouses. It was my pattern to go after what was unattainable and prove to myself that I could get it. I specialized in breaking things. In showing people just how fickle their loyalty to their loved ones was.

The only relationships I've respected so far are those of the Sovranos, and now, the Seven. Probably because I have a lot of regard for the men themselves. That's the hard line I drew for myself—never go after women who belong to my work colleagues or friends. Of course, many of my so-called colleagues also belong to organized crime syndicates. They're the kind who are more prone to draw a gun on anyone who messes with their women, and I don't have a death wish. And, to be honest, the thought has never crossed my mind anyway. I've never been attracted to any of them. Not until *her*.

I drew the line at not going after women belonging to colleagues or friends, but forgot to include family. But how could I have ever foreseen this happening? It's like a plot out of a movie. And it looks like, once again, I've been cast in the role of villain.

I'm about to cross the line I set for myself. I'm going after her. After what I heard tonight at their bedroom door... After losing all of my dignity by spying on them... I realize, now, I never should have held myself back. I've never felt such a powerful attraction to anyone, and it's thrown me off my game. She's just another woman. In this case, she also happens to be my son's girlfriend, which may be the only reason I find her attractive.

So, maybe I'll sleep with her more than once—enough to fuck her out of my system. I'll still be able to walk away. I always have. If that upsets Isaac, that's life. He's young and he'll get over it. So will she. Besides, I'll compensate her enough so she'll never have to work a day in her life. She'll be able to afford a comfortable lifestyle. She'll be able to move out of my house, find a place of her own, and have enough time to find a job that she truly enjoys. No more working late nights on a pitch that she's not appreciated for. Yep, that's it. It's all going to be all right, and I don't have to deny myself, either.

The early morning rays of the sun slant over the city. Saint Paul's Cathedral glistens in the distance. Not far from it is the phallic-shaped Gherkin, and near that, the angular springing-into-the-sky icicle that is the Shard, which marks the financial district of the city. Technically, the businesses I own are a part of that cohort, but I've never felt more removed from my day-to-day role as the CEO of Kane Enterprises as I do at this very moment.

That's how much this girl has twisted me from the inside out. It's why I've been acting out of character. Perhaps some sliver of decency in me has held me back from taking the final step, the one that will ensure the final rift between my son and myself. And I do want a relationship with him. I will still have a relationship with Isaac.

Once I've fucked her out of my system. Besides, they're not suited for one other. I've barely seen them together since they moved in. It's as if he's avoiding her. Plus, he's only now finding himself. Once he's a better-known painter, he won't have a problem finding women, either. I'm doing them both a favor by following my instinct and going after what I want. Which is her. One day, they'll thank me.

I spin around, walk down the hill, and ride my bike home. I shave, take a quick shower then walk into the kitchen. I greet Miriam who's already at work preparing breakfast. I grab a cup of tea and turn to leave when Lena walks in.

29

Lena

"Good morning," JJ's dark voice rumbles across the space.

I stiffen. "Morning." I keep my gaze lowered as I shuffle over to the electric kettle that's plugged in on the side of the counter.

"There's coffee for you," Miriam volunteers.

"Eh?" I squint at her. "Coffee?"

She nods in the direction of the brand-new coffee machine that's appeared on the other side of the counter. It's not your average drip-coffee maker, either. It's one of those fancy, shiny machines that looks like it's straight out of a sci-fi movie. I stare at it. "Uh, how do I operate it?"

"Let me." His voice vibrates up my spine. I stiffen. My eyelids snap open. All remnants of sleep drain from my eyes like sand through an hourglass. I spin around and almost face-plant into the wide chest that seems to loom above me and to either side of my line of sight.

"Excuse me," I say stiffly.

"Ah, but I'm just about to get you your morning cup of joe." He leans around me and the scent of his aftershave, something complex and dark and spicy, just like him, assails my senses. My head spins. Must be because I forgot to eat dinner last night, not to mention the drinking. Also the angry words Isaac and I exchanged after we'd fucked hadn't helped. The act in itself had been satisfactory, if a little emotionless. Luckily, Isaac's been blessed with a big enough cock and he knows how to use it. *Imagine how much more honed his father's technique would be, eh?*

"Did you say something?" JJ straightens.

Heat flushes my cheeks. "Coffee, just need my cup of brew," I choke out, then slide out from between him and the counter and stumble toward where the cups are kept.

"Are you okay, Lena?" Miriam asks in a kind voice. "You seem exhausted."

"Yes, Lena, did you sleep well?" The smirk in JJ's voice has me shooting him a sideways glance. His lips twist. There's a knowing gleam in his eyes. Does he know I've been thinking about a particular asset that both he and his son possess? *Am I really thinking about both JJ and his son in the same breath, the same line, the same sentence? Next to each other? Jesus H. Christ.* I need therapy. And coffee. "Coffee?" I croak.

I hear the gurgle of the coffee machine, the hiss of steam, and turn to find JJ holding a cup under the machine. I leap toward it, and even before the dark brew has stopped trickling out from the spout of the fancy-ass contraption, I've grabbed the cup and raised it to my mouth. I take a sip, then gasp. "Ow, it's too hot." I fan my mouth, then race toward the sink where I start rinsing my mouth with cold water, swishing it around, spitting it out, then swallowing the cool liquid to soothe my throat. I turn to find both of the other occupants staring at me.

"What?" I scowl.

Miriam shakes her head and turns back to the counter where she's making omelets.

JJ merely smirks. "You could have waited until the coffee cooled."

"Where's the fun in that?" I walk over to the table on the other side of the island and drop into a chair. "I haven't seen you in the kitchen this early before, Miriam."

"JJ wanted me to come by and make sure I had breakfast ready for the both of you."

"Both of us?" I scowl at JJ.

"You're riding with me today," he announces.

"I am?"

He nods.

"Oh."

His grin broadens, the flash of his perfectly white teeth between those lips that look so hard, but are actually quite soft, seems more than a little predatory. A frisson of uncertainty crawls up my spine. Why is he looking so happy with himself? What's going on in that head of his?

"Hmm." I raise my cup and take a sip of the brew which is now the correct temperature. The scent of rich dark soil, the feel of green moss weaving through my fingers, and the sound of thunder as water pours onto rocks far below sweeps through me.

"Wow," I breathe. "This coffee is amazing."

"It should be, it's made from the poop of Thai elephants."

I choke on the mouthful I've barely swallowed. "You're shitting me."

"It's the shit of the elephants, actually," he drawls.

"You're kidding." I scoff. When he doesn't reply, I blink. "Right?" I ask.

"Right." He smirks.

"Oh, thank God." I glance at the coffee then place it back.

"It's actually extracted from Indonesian cat poop."

"Excuse me?" I whip my head back in his direction. "Now you really are joking."

"'Afraid not. It's the second most expensive coffee in the world."

"O-kay." I place my hands in my lap and stare at the remainder of the dark liquid in my cup. "I... I'm not sure I want to drink the rest of it."

"You just said you loved it."

"That was before you gave me the lowdown on what it's made from."

"Relax, it's rich Colombian coffee from a private plantation." His eyes gleam.

"Why don't I believe you?" I scoff.

The machine runs again, I glance over my shoulder to find he's filling another cup with the dark liquid.

"Thought you didn't drink coffee?"

"I don't."

Huh. Does he mean that he bought the coffee machine for me?

Miriam plates out the food, then slides it onto the table. "If that'll be all?"

JJ nods. "Thanks, M."

She smiles at me, then leaves by the back door. JJ fills the cup and prowls over to stand next to me. He blows into the cup and the steam rises. The bittersweet scent of coffee intensifies. Mixed with the spicy scent of his aftershave, it's a potent combination that sinks into my blood and arrows straight for my core. I cross my legs and his gaze sharpens. "You seem restless this morning."

"I'm fine," I snap back.

"Where's Isaac?"

"He, ah, left earlier to get some early morning shots," I lie. He left last night after our argument, when I accused him of not being completely there when we made love. I couldn't really call it making love. More like, fucking? No, not even that. He penetrated. I faked an orgasm. The usual.

"Trouble in paradise?" JJ drawls.

"None of your business," I shoot back.

"You're wrong. Everything about you is my business."

"I don't know what you—"

"Open your mouth," he growls.

"Excuse me?"

"Open. Your. Mouth. Lena."

I do.

The next second, he takes a sip from the cup, then leans over and dribbles it into my mouth. My gaze widens. My stomach clenches. An insidious heat flares to life between my legs. I hold those dark, fathomless eyes of his as the liquid pools on my tongue. His gaze deepens further.

"Swallow." He lowers his voice to a hush, and my pulse rate rockets through the roof.

I close my mouth, do as he commands. The thick taste of him combined with the aromatic notes of the coffee is an aphrodisiac that leaves flashbulbs of desire popping in its wake. He lowers his gaze to my mouth, and I realize my lips are parted, waiting… Waiting for him to take another sip, swill the coffee in his mouth and dribble the now lukewarm liquid onto my waiting tongue. I close my mouth, swallow, then part my lips a third time. He inhales sharply and his chest planes swell until I'm sure he's going to burst out of the seams of his jacket. He places the cup on the table, then lowers his mouth until his lips are poised over mine. His hot breath sears my cheek. Goosebumps pop on my skin.

"I heard you last night. Heard you as you moaned for him. Heard you as you opened your thighs for him."

I gasp. "Wha—"

He pinches my chin so I can't speak. I try to pull away, and he grips my shoulders, holding me in place.

"It made me want to walk in there, turn you on your front, pull you up to your hands and knees, and fuck you until you screamed *my* name. If it had been me, you wouldn't have been able to walk this morning. You wouldn't be able to speak, except to ask for my cock. You wouldn't be able to sit down—I'd have reamed your arse and made you come on my dick so many times, you'd still be floating down from the endorphins saturating your bloodstream… Until you've forgotten everything except the shape of my face, the feel of my shaft inside you, the essence of me coursing through your veins as your heart opens to the only man who'll ever be able to satisfy you again."

My entire body seems to detonate into a million little flames. Sweat beads my brow. I draw in a breath and my lungs burn. My toes curl. "JJ, what are you—"

"I *am* going to have you, girl."

30

JJ

Going to have you. Going. To. Have. You. Goingtohave—

"Check!"

"Eh?" I glance down to find my queen exposed. "What the fuck?"

"Your mind's many miles away. Maybe it's with a certain young, dark-haired girl?" Liam drawls.

There's only the two of us at this table on the main floor of the 7A club in Mayfair.

Turns out, Sinclair Sterling had seen enough potential in my venture to buy 49% of the club. He wanted 51%, but I refused. He settled for 49% with the stipulation that the club be named after the investment company he and his six partners ran. Who was I to argue with that? He'd paid enough to have the venture turn profitable from day one. He also wanted each of the Seven to have veto powers on who to approve to the club, but that was fine by me. The club was going to pay in dividends many times over if the interest levels among those who had been invited to join was anything to go by. So far one of the biggest rock legends, a leading paleontologist, and a Pulitzer Prize winning war journalist had already agreed to be part of the fraternity. If they came to the club's premises even once in the next three hundred and sixty-five days, it would benefit every single one of the core board of members. So, this startup had matured straight out of the gate. Which couldn't be said about my current chess game.

"Shut your trap," I say blandly. I move my knight into position, then smirk. "Checkmate, motherfucker."

It's Liam's turn to scowl. He glares at the chessboard. The seconds tick by then he tips his king over. He holds out his hand and I shake it.

"Well recovered," he says mildly.

So, I haven't lost my balls completely. "It was close," I concede, then reach for my cigar and offer him one. "How're the wedding plans coming along?"

His features darken. He leans forward and I light his cigar. He straightens, puffs out a cloud of smoke, then pulls the cigar from his lips. "It's not the wedding that's a problem, but the wedding planner."

"What do you mean?"

"A wedding planner engaged by my bride-to-be who has to be the most annoying, most exasperating, most aggravating woman ever. She turns every wedding rehearsal into a cartoon show. She sets my teeth on edge, has my blood pressure going through the roof. I fear, at this rate, by the time we make it to the wedding, *if* we make it to the wedding, only one of us will remain standing, and it's not going to be her."

I whistle. "That's a little bloodthirsty, don't you think?"

He shoots me a sardonic look. "You haven't met this woman. She's tiny, this tiny" —he raises his hand so it's on level with his forehead when he's sitting down— "but she has a presence that's larger-than-life, a voice that's designed to cut the knees out from under a grown man, and that which distract everyone in sight—men and women. Not to mention, a temperament which has me wanting to push her into the nearest closet—"

"—and follow her in."

"Eh?" He blinks, uncomprehending.

"Sounds like there's serious chemistry between the two of you."

"Oh, there's something between us all right, but it's not chemistry. It's one-hundred percent pure anger. We can't stand the sight of each other."

"Hmm." I take a puff from my own cigar. "You sure about that?"

"Of course, I am. Don't confuse your inability to keep your paws off the woman in closest proximity to you with my problem of wanting to throttle this annoying little hellfire—"

"Shouldn't that be your bride-to-be?"

"What?"

"The woman in closest proximity to you most often, shouldn't she be your bride-to-be?"

His lips firm. "She is."

"What was her name again?"

"You mean Isla?"

"I mean your bride."

"Ah, her name is..." He blinks. "Is..." His throat moves as he swallows. "It'll come to me any second."

"Who are we talking about?" Michael Sovrano prowls over to drop into the third seat at our table.

"I see I made it in time to see Liam at a loss, again?" Sinclair smirks, then eases himself into the only remaining chair at our table.

"The wedding preparations getting to you?" Sinclair glances at the fallen king, then at Liam.

"I'm not the one with the attention span of a lizard, unlike..." He jerks his chin in my direction.

"A chameleon," I offer. "One who blends in with his surroundings and pounces when his prey is least expecting it."

"You planning a coup of some kind?" Michael asks in an interested voice.

"Something like that, yes," I agree.

"Hmm." Liam places his cigar on the ridge of the ashtray. "Sounds more like a takeover to me," he offers.

"Could be." I raise a shoulder. "But we were talking about Liam's upcoming nuptials."

"Who's the unlucky bride?" Sinclair asks.

"That's what I was trying to find out. Seems he doesn't have the foggiest idea who he's going to marry."

"A woman of good blood and high status with all the pre-requisites needed to become a good hostess and the mother of my children," Liam declares.

The three of us stare at him.

"What?" He frowns.

"You been watching a lot of *Bridgerton*?" Sinclair finally asks.

"My sister likes to watch it, yes. How do you know about the series anyway?" He frowns.

"Summer and her sister Karma have been bingeing it, and I'm afraid I may have been coaxed into sitting in on some of the episodes," he explains.

"The one time I'm glad I wasn't there to accompany my wife." Michael's features wear an expression of horror.

"So, Summer and Karma are sisters? Which makes you" —I glance between Sinclair and Michael— "family."

"Brothers-in-law, as it turns out," Sinclair confirms, scowling at Michael, who returns the gaze with an expression of mild dislike.

This should be interesting. The two men are equally matched in power. Sinclair with his extensive interests in the business community in Europe, and Michael with his grip on organized crime, though he's legalized the vast majority of his businesses. Still, can one actually walk away from one's roots when they've been part of not only your life but also that of your forefathers? For decades, Michael's family has been synonymous with the *Cosa Nostra*. Could he really move them into more legalized businesses? And isn't it useful that the man who can play a key role in that is also his brother-in-law?

My phone buzzes. I glance at the tracking app to find the golden spot that represents Lena pop up very close to my location. "Eh? What is she doing here?"

"Who are you talking about?"

The door to the room swings open, and she steps in with a bag slung over her shoulder and a tablet in her hand. "There you are." She heads straight over to me. "I'm afraid this pitch can't wait. You need to take a final look so I can send it off."

"You could have called or emailed."

"I did."

"Eh?" I close the app and find she's right. Two missed calls, two missed texts, a bunch of emails. All from her.

"Is it already time to send off the Delancey campaign?"

"It's Friday the thirteenth," she reminds me.

"Of course, it is. And if you had gotten through to me, I'd have told you that I didn't need to look at it."

"But you must; this needs to be sent before the end of the day, and—"

"You've seen it. What do you think?"

"That the team has outdone themselves. The creatives are fresh, the copy is witty, and the concept, you have to hear it—"

"If you're happy with it, I'm fine with it."

"What?" She gapes.

"You, clearly, think it's a stellar pitch. I believe in you, so send it off."

"You… you're sure?" Her voice is low, "Are you really sure?"

I smirk. "Of course, if you'd rather not—"

"What? No!" She draws herself up to her full height. "It's good. I'll, uh, just shoot off the email to them then. Sorry I bothered you." She finally glances around the table, noticing the other men. "Good day, gentlemen." She walks around them and toward the door.

"Wait for it... wait for it," Michael murmurs under his breath.

"Do you think he'll last until she reaches the door?" Sinclair asks in a lazy voice.

"And I thought I was the one getting married. This man may beat me to it." Liam smirks.

"Shut the fuck up," I snap, then spring up to my feet. "Lena, hold on, you can ride home with me."

———

"You didn't have to ferry me back to your place."

"It's your home, too," I point out.

"Temporarily," she shoots back.

"Of course. I was done anyway at 7A. No sense in you taking public transport back when I'm headed the same way by car."

"Have you ever driven or been driven in anything else except this —?" She gestures with her hand to the confines of the back seat of my Rolls.

I'd like to drive my cock into you. "What's wrong with my car?" I drawl.

"Nothing." She looks away. "If you don't mind the agony of being unfashionable."

"What did you say?"

"Eh?" She coughs into her hand. "Me? I didn't say anything."

"You're being a brat again," I warn.

"Just stating a fact, is all. This ride of yours..."

"You mean my Rolls?"

"Is not exactly the height of being 'with it.'" She makes air quotes with her fingers.

"It's a Rolls," I counter.

"Exactly. If it were a Porsche—"

"Too small," I retort.

"Or a Lamborghini—"

"Too predictable," I scoff.

"An Aston Martin?"

"And invite comparisons with Bond?"

"How about a…" She pushes her finger into her cheek.

"A Jaguar?" We both say at the same time, then look at each other in surprise.

"That's so you." Her cheeks curve.

"Is it?"

She nods. "Stylish, sporty, with presence, yet lots of speed, and a certain sleek machismo about it."

"You think I'm macho?"

She rolls her eyes. "You know you are, and if you dare repeat what I said to anyone else, I'll deny it."

"Even if I told your boyfriend?"

Her features shutter.

Goddamn, did I have to bring up my son? And how long am I going to put off this conversation?

"You realize the fact you're his girlfriend is not going to stop me from pursuing you?"

"I... I gathered," she swallows.

"Maybe it's because you're his girlfriend that I find you even more attractive," I murmur.

"What?" She whips her head around in my direction. "That's just—"

"Hot?"

"Twisted," she corrects me.

"You mean forbidden... taboo... socially unacceptable, don't you?"

"What, are you a walking thesaurus?"

"I'm walking orgasms for you, baby."

She inhales sharply. Her pupils dilate. "Now you're being corny."

"I'm being truthful."

"It's not truthful when you set out to seduce your son's girlfriend," she bursts out.

"No law against it."

"But it's not right. Can't you see that? We can't keep doing this behind his back."

"So... tell him, Lena."

I glance out the window. "I... I can't."

"Why not? You can't turn your back on our connection. I won't let you do that. And it's going to come out in the open at some point, and then it's only going to hurt more. It might be best if you told him upfront. Or"—I tilt my head—"maybe I should? Is that what you've been waiting for? Do you want me to reveal what's been happening between us?"

"Nothing has happened, and don't you dare say anything to him."

"If nothing's happened, why do you care if I speak with him?"

"JJ, no." She locks her fingers together. "Please don't do anything like that."

"Then you tell him."

She glances away, then back at me. "Give me time, okay?"

"I'm tired of waiting, Lena, tired of hiding the fact that I want to fuck you."

She winces. "No one can accuse you of being romantic."

"If you wanted romance and poetry and sweet nothings, you'd have stuck with your boyfriend. You want more, Lena. You want to know what it feels like to lose yourself in the kind of passion that comes along only once in a lifetime."

Her breath hitches.

"You want to find out how it feels to be possessed by a man. To drown yourself in a sea of emotions where your body leads and you follow, to stop thinking and allow yourself to be led, to fold into a tapestry of sensations that will consume your mind and body and soul."

She squeezes her thighs together.

"You want to feel the touch of my fingers on your skin, my lips on yours, my tongue laving your curves, my palm gripping your hip, my thighs forcing yours apart and—"

"Stop!" She reaches over and claps her palm on my mouth. "You can't talk like this."

I place my hand over hers then kiss the inside of her fingers.

She shivers. "Stop, JJ." Her voice is weak. "Please don't say anything more."

I lick the dip where her fingers meet the flesh of her palm. She closes her eyes.

"JJ," she breathes.

I close my fingers around her wrist and tug. She falls against me. I clamp my hands on her hips, then lift her up so she straddles me.

I lean in toward her, but she turns her head to the side.

"Look at me, Lena."

She shakes her head.

"Look. At. Me."

She looks at me.

"Good. Now, tell me you don't want me."

Her brow furrows. A look of misery twists her features. I should feel pity for putting her in this situation. I should spare her the anguish of being torn apart by her feelings. Only, I don't care. I want her. I am going to have her. End of story. I'll just have to make it up to my son…

Later. For now, though, I'm going to ensure she finally tells me what I want to hear.

I kick forward my pelvis and grind my dick into her center.

She shudders.

I grip her tiny waist and push down so every centimeter of my throbbing column is pressed against her core.

Her face flushes. She opens and shuts her mouth but no words emerge. Her golden eyes darken until they seem like pools of amber. *Once I'm caught in them, I'll never be able to escape.* Don't be ridiculous. She's a woman. And like most, she has an expiration date. Maybe it'll take me a little longer to tire of her. But eventually, I will. I always do. There's no place for another in my life. I wasn't even able to share myself with my children when they were growing up. So, why would I open myself up to this stranger? I'll have my fill of her in every sense, and then I'll bid her goodbye, after compensating her, of course. She'll be happy to see the last of me no doubt. As would I.

"JJ, I—" She swallows. "I—"

I lower my voice to a hush, "Say it, Lena. Tell me what I want to hear."

"I don't want you."

31

Lena

"Excuse me?" His eyebrows draw down. Those dark eyes flare with anger and something else. Hurt? For a second, he seems vulnerable, then his lips twist.

"I understand it's difficult for you to admit what you're really feeling, but—"

"I don't want you. I ache for you."

His gaze burns into me, then he wipes all expression from his face.

"When I see you, I want to throw myself at you and wrap myself around you. And when I'm not with you, I am so aware of the JJ-shaped void in my life. I see you at your desk, and I want to throw myself on it and spread myself for you. I see you in the conference room and imagine you pushing me up against the window and taking me from behind. I see your son, and I see you. I see you and understand where Isaac gets so many of his traits."

He opens his mouth, but I shake my head. "Let me finish, please." I draw in a breath and fortify myself. "It's the very traits that attracted me to your son that also attract me to you. Only, they've matured in you, of course. Both of you are strong individuals, adamant about getting your way, headstrong and obstinate, to the extent that sometimes I want to knock your heads together and shake some sense into you. It's no wonder that you don't get along. You're too similar."

"Including the fact that we're attracted to the same woman."

I blow out a breath. "I didn't say that."

"You implied it." He notches his knuckles under my chin so I don't have a choice but to meet his gaze. "It could have been anyone else, and I'd have still pursued you. It just so happens, in this case, it's my son. I don't take no for an answer."

"No kidding. Sometimes I'm sure the fact I'm someone else's girl-friend is one of the reasons you want me. You want to acquire the prohibited, the out of reach, the thing that you can't have."

He blinks, and I know I'm right.

"That's it, isn't it? It's because I'm a challenge to you that I caught your eye."

He doesn't deny it. Anger travels up my spine. A heavy weight crowds my chest. I turn and begin to pull away, but he doesn't let me.

"I admit, it's one of the things that I find alluring. When the odds are against me, I fight better. When I'm told I can't have something, I fight harder. When everything pointed to the fact that I shouldn't think of fucking you, it made me even more determined."

I squeeze the bridge of my nose. "So, this is all a game to you? You'd screw up my life and the chance to have a good relationship with your son because you can't resist the challenge?"

He doesn't say anything. But he doesn't need to. The evidence is clear, and it all points to the fact that he can't resist the prospect of taking me away from his son.

"Does my choosing you over your son mean so much to you?"

His head snaps back like I've slapped him.

"The fuck you talking about?"

"Do you think you're in competition with your son? Is that what this is about?"

"You have no idea what you're saying."

"Don't I?" I tip up my chin. "You're facing the inevitability of life, realizing you have less than half your life left in front of you. You're confronting your own mortality when you see your son, and you want to deny it. It's why you want to fuck me so badly. It's not anything to do with your son, as you say. It's about you facing yourself. Your regret over your past. Your helplessness over your future. You can't bear the thought of growing old, and shagging a woman less than half your age is your way of trying to stop the wheel of time from turning. You think you're reinventing yourself, but I have news for you. You're pathetic, JJ. A cliché." My breath comes out in pants. My heart oscillates in my rib cage like the pendulum of a clock that's counting down… Toward what, though? I stare into his perfectly black eyes and notice slivers of silver in them. It's as if he's mirroring the agitation I feel in myself. I just insulted him in the worst way I could think of and he's not reacting at all. Is that good or bad?

Then his fingers tighten on my hips with enough force that I know he's left marks there. Good. I want him to mark me. I want him to tear through my objections and fuck me. I want him to see past the bluster, the spiel I've launched at him, and kiss me.

"Kiss me," I croak. "Do it."

He peels back his lips. His teeth glisten. He's a predator, a ravager, a marauder who's going to plunder me of every last shred of self-respect and reveal what I truly am. A willing sacrifice at the altar of his lust.

I move; so does he.

Our mouths clash. Our lips fuse together. Our tongues tangle. I kiss him fiercely and he kisses me with the kind of hunger that sweeps through me, sinks into my bones, tears through my cells, leaving a zip of fire in its wake that unravels with such speed that my entire body seems to detonate into flames.

He yanks me to him so my breasts are crushed against the wall of his chest. I dig my fingers into his thick, dark hair and tug. He growls deep in his throat, and the vibrations run down my body. My nipples peak, and a heavy pulse fountains to life between my legs. Liquid heat sizzles up my thighs and I grind down on the thick, fat column that stabs up and into my core. A groan wells up, and he deepens the kiss. He holds my hips in place and slants his head so his tongue fills my mouth. He sucks from me, seeming to draw out all of my hesitation, the last vestiges of shame, of doubt and indecision, and lighting them up with the fire of his intent. The flames of our pent-up desire sweep through me, turning everything into ash, which is swept away in the tsunami of emotions that invade every pore of my body. My breath comes in pants, my muscles quiver, and every cell in my body seems to have tuned into him. His scent, his taste, the feeling of his hands on me, the sensation of his big, hard body that cushions me. The massive steel rod in his pants that fills the space between my legs, hinting at how good it would feel without the barrier of the clothes between us.

"Hurry," I gasp.

At least, I think I do. He's still eating my mouth like he's been deprived of any sustenance for decades. He must understand, though, for he grips the front of my blouse and yanks. The buttons pop, the front panels part. White-hot lust cleaves through me. My head spins. I try to breathe and my lungs burn. He tears his mouth from mine and glares at me.

"I hate you for how you make me feel," I burst out.

He peels back his lips. "I'm going to fuck you now."

32

JJ

Her gaze widens. The black of her pupils has bled out until only a circle of gleaming brown remains around their circumferences.

"I'm going to fuck *you*." She wriggles her hips over the throbbing tent at my crotch. I thrust my hand up her skirt, grip her panties, and tear them off.

She gasps. "You're an animal. A filthy, salacious beast who—"

I fit my mouth over hers with such force our teeth clash. She bites down on my lower lip and I taste blood. It only adds fuel to the desire raging through me. The need to punish her for driving me to this state. The insatiable craving to bury myself in her and find out what I've been missing. I shove my hand down between us and lower my zipper. My cock springs free. She glances down and her eyes widen.

"What the fuck?" She tips up her chin. "If you think I'm going let you fit that… that monster dick inside me, you're—"

"I am going to stuff my cock inside you, and you're going to take every inch, like a good little girl."

She draws in a sharp inhale. "Why do I find that so hot?"

My heart slams into my chest so hard, I'm sure it's going to break through my rib cage. "Because under those prim suits and that career-focused mind, you're a filthy slut who finds the thought of fucking her boyfriend's father a huge turn-on."

Color smears her cheeks, then she slaps me. Pain rings through my head, then I laugh. "Fucking hell, you're a little hellion, aren't you?" I straighten my features. "You've done it now. I'm not going to stop until I've fucked every last bit of defiance out of you."

Her breathing grows erratic. Her color deepens. She glances to the side, then at me. She turns her body, and I grab her hips, raise her, then slam her down on my cock.

"Oh, my god," she cries out. Her entire body shudders. She grips my shoulders, and I hold her in place over my swollen shaft.

Hot, wet, and tight—so goddam tight… Being bare inside her is like coming home. I freeze.

She grips my shoulder. "It's okay. I'm on birth control."

"I know," I growl.

She blinks. "You knew I was on birth control?"

I clear my throat. "I guessed."

She blinks. "Also, I'm clean and Isaac and I… We—" She glances away, then back at me. "He's always used a condom."

My chest hurts. My stomach feels like I've swallowed a vat of concrete. Of course, she and Isaac fucked. He was her boyfriend, for fuck's sake. He's still, technically, her boyfriend. But I'm the one fucking her right now. I'm the one holding her down on my cock. I'm the one who's going to make her come like she never has before. I thrust up and into her with enough force that her entire body jolts. She gasps, and her gaze widens.

"Ohgod, ohgod, ohgod," she chants. "You're too big JJ."

"You can take it."

"It hurts."

"Good."

She blinks, then slaps my shoulder. "What the fuck?"

I begin to laugh and she firms her lips. Then she wriggles around, and the sensation of my flesh sliding against the walls of her moist channel sends a rush of sensations crawling up my spine. My laughter disappears and I glare at her. "I'm going to have to punish you for that."

She makes a rude noise.

"I'm going to fuck you now," I warn her.

"That's what you said earlier."

"I'm barely halfway in."

"What?" Her eyes round. She stares down at where my flesh joins hers.

"Omigod." She gulps. "You weren't kidding, were you?"

"Hold on."

She glances up. "Wait, what—?"

I thrust up and into her. "JJ!" she screams. "You're going to slice me in two."

"I fucking hope so." I stay there, allowing her time to adjust to my size. A quiver grips her. She trembles and groans. Her fingernails dig into my skin through the shirt I'm wearing, and still I don't move. I grit my teeth, dig my heels into the floor of the car. "How do I feel?"

"Like you're filling me up, you're stretching me... You're so damn huge, you're consuming me."

"Good."

I lift her off of my lap then I lunge up into her, seating myself to the hilt. A groan bleeds from her lips. She opens her mouth and a low keening sound emerges from her throat. Good thing I raised the barrier that demarcated the back seat from the front earlier, sealing us off from my chauffeur. Still, I'd prefer for him not to hear her, either. I close my mouth over hers to absorb her cries. Then I begin to fuck her in earnest. Long, smooth strokes that plant my cock in her melting pussy. Each time I plunge into her, she groans. Moisture bathes my shaft. A bead of sweat slides down my spine. I continue to push up and into her again and again. Her body trembles and her thighs clench. Her pussy squeezes my cock, and fuck me, I can feel the tension building at the base of my spine. The ball of lust squeezes in on itself, and I know I'm close. I release her mouth, glance at her closed eyes. "Look at me," I growl.

She raises her eyelids and her golden-brown eyes shine.

"You're going to come with me, Lena," I order.

She shakes her head. "It's too much," she croaks. "Too much."

"Can't keep pace with a man more than twice your age, eh?"

She scowls. Her eyebrows knit, then she firms her lips. There she is. The stubborn, headstrong woman with a spine of steel. "Keep pace with you? I'll show you how I keep pace with you." She rises up, then slides down, impaling herself on my cock.

A growl rips up my throat. She grinds her hips down, taking me even further inside of her just as I power up and into her again. I hit a spot deep inside of her. She shudders, then gasps; so do I.

I hold her gaze and increase the intensity of my movements. I power up and into her, and again.

"Oh god, Jack," she whines.

"I like the fact that you have God and my name in the same breath. Though I'd prefer you call out to me first."

"You're insane," she moans.

"I am, when it comes to you." I propel up and into her over and over again, hitting that same spot inside her.

She holds my gaze and scrunches up her features, and I know she's so close. I squeeze her hips, power up into her one last time, then growl, "Come with me."

She throws her head back and cries out, "Jack, oh, god... Jack." She arches her spine and her pussy flutters around my cock as she comes.

I continue to pound into her over and over again, fucking her through the aftershocks that roll up her body. The ball of tension in my lower belly explodes and I shoot my load into her. I place my forehead against hers as she slumps into me. For a few seconds, we stay that way.

Outside, the streets of London whizz by as the Rolls continues its journey home. Everything is the same, and yet... not. I've changed. From one second to the next, my priorities have shifted. Something inside of me insists what just happened was more than just fucking. I push her hair back from her face, then lean back and peer into her features. "You okay?"

She draws in a breath, then begins to rise, but I stop her.

"Lena, are you okay?"

She doesn't meet my gaze.

I pinch her chin, then stare into her eyes. "Speak to me."

She shakes her head.

"Tell me what you're feeling."

She squeezes her eyes, and a single tear slides out.

I bend, lick it up.

She flinches. "Don't do that." She clears her throat.

"Why not?"

"We fucked, JJ. That's all it was. Fucking."

"So why can't you meet my gaze?"

"Because I can't." She pushes off of me, and this time, I don't stop her. I straighten my clothes and she pulls the fronts of her blouse together, holding them in place, because, of course, I tore off the buttons. Satisfaction heats my chest. I scrutinize her features but she keeps her gaze averted.

She begins to scoot away from me, but I circle her wrist with my fingers. "Tell me what's wrong."

"Nothing," she spits out.

"Liar." I pinch her chin so she has no choice but to glance at me. I search her features. "I felt it, too," I mutter.

"What?" She frowns. "What are you talking about?"

"That was more than fucking, Lena."

"No, it was not."

"It was, and you know it."

She tosses her hair over her shoulder. "You have no idea what you're talking about."

"On the contrary, this is one time I know what I'm saying. One advantage of being older than you is that I have enough experience to know when something out of the ordinary happens and this" —I gesture between us— "is one of those times."

"You've lost your mind."

"For the first time in my life, I'm thinking clearly."

33

Lena

This was more than fucking, Lena.

This is the first time in my life I'm thinking clearly.

I stand under the shower and let the hot water pour over me. When the Rolls had come to a stop outside JJ's house, he tried to loan me his jacket. I refused. The last thing I want is to be caught with any item of his clothing on me. Instead, I pulled out the safety pins I keep in my bag—something my mother insisted I never be without—fixed myself up, then jumped out and ran up to my room. I couldn't bear to talk to him... Not after what we'd done. I fucked him. I fucked my boyfriend's father and OMG, it was so hot. So much hotter than any sex I've ever had before.

At least he remembers my name. That's something, I suppose. As for the rest of what he said? Bet he's doing it to screw with my head. No matter if it did feel like it was a lot more than fucking for me, too. That orgasm I experienced? I've never felt anything so intense before. It was the kind of bone-rattling, mind-numbing, emotion-wrenching climax that would have swept me off my feet, if I'd been standing, and catapulted me to somewhere high in the stars. It shattered me, blew me to smithereens. Until I couldn't remember my name... or who I was... or who he was... or where we were. I came to my senses to find I was slumped against him. He cradled me in his arms, his forehead pressed to mine, and when he asked me if I was okay, his voice sounded worried. He sounded concerned about me. And that was my undoing.

I much prefer it when he's glaring at me, or looking at me with cool disdain. When he's being mean to me, and I'm fighting him back, I'm able to resist him. I'm able to focus on something other than how attractive he is. How dominant he is. How overpoweringly handsome, how charismatic, how there's something about him I can't resist. How it's not just his physical attributes that attract me to him—I feel safe with him. I hunch my shoulders.

There... that's it. The thing I wasn't able to articulate, even to myself, earlier. My father left when I was only three and we grew up without a father figure. My family overcompensated by sticking tightly together, but we never really got over the loss of him at such an early stage in our lives. I often felt my older siblings tried to overcompensate for it by trying their best not to let me and Josh feel his gap in our lives.

Technically, I shouldn't have missed my father at all. After all, I didn't even know him that well. And yet I did miss him—every day. And meeting JJ only brought home just how much I missed having an authoritative male figure in my life. Someone I could look up to. Someone I knew would have my back, no matter what. Someone who would watch out for me, protect me. The way JJ did when he thought Isaac was going to hit me. He intervened that day at the party. He stepped between us to shield me. It was then that things shifted into place inside of me, and my attraction to JJ bloomed to life. An attraction I've been fighting with since... A connection I gave in to earlier when I fucked him. A shrink would have a field day with the situation I'm now in.

I switch off the shower, dry myself, then step into the bedroom and pull on a pair of yoga pants and top. I've just switched off my hair dryer when the door to the bedroom opens, and Isaac steps in. I avoid his gaze and continue to style my hair.

He places his camera and equipment on the table by the door, then shrugs off his coat and drops it to the floor before he walks over to stand behind me. He puts his arm around my waist and draws me close. "Mmm, you smell good." He kisses the top of my head, then moves over to the bed and flings himself down on it. "I'm exhausted." He stretches his arms over his head. His T-shirt rises to reveal the sliver of skin over his flat stomach.

Isaac does work out, as well, and he has a six-pack to prove it. He's as tall as JJ, but leaner. And his shoulders are not as thick as his father's. But he's as good-looking as JJ, albeit in a different way. So why am I not attracted to him the way I am to JJ? Why can't I feel half the attraction toward him that I feel toward JJ?

He must sense my gaze, for he lowers his arms and smirks. "Come 'ere," he drawls in a low, hard voice. And in that moment, I see the kind of man he's going to mature into. The kind of self-assured, commanding, controlling man that JJ is today. Only, he's not there yet. I want someone to take care of me, not be the person who has to take care of another. JJ can do that. He can take care of me. He knows what I want. He satisfies me the way Isaac never has. He's not half the man JJ is yet, but he will be, someday soon. And he'll find the kind of woman who'll feel toward him the way I do toward JJ. But I'm not that woman, and I never will be. I may have been drawn to Isaac, but it's nothing compared to the sheer primal pull JJ wields over me.

I place my brush on the dressing table with a soft thump, then walk toward him. When he holds out his hand, I take it and allow him to pull me onto the bed next to him. He folds me in his arms and tucks my head under his chin. For a few seconds, we stay that way. He sighs deeply. "This is nice," he says in a drowsy voice.

"Too nice, maybe."

"What's that supposed to mean?" he murmurs.

I open my mouth, then close it. I'm not sure I'm ready to say this, but I must. No putting it off further. I can't fuck his father, then lay in bed with Isaac and pretend everything is fine. Not when it hasn't been for a long time.

"Isaac?"

"Hmm." He sounds like he's half asleep.

"Isaac." I pull back, and he groans then turns over onto his back.

"I'm exhausted, Lena, can't this wait?"

"Why are we still together, Isaac?"

"What do you mean?"

"Why are we together? It's not like we're attracted to each other anymore."

He throws his arm over his eyes. "I'm trying to sleep."

"And I'm trying to have a conversation."

He makes a sound of frustration. "What is this, an inquisition into our sex life? We just had sex, Lena."

"Yesterday. We had sex yesterday, and it was over before I even came."

He lowers his arm and glances at me. "What do you mean? You came, Lena."

I narrow my gaze. He blinks.

"I mean, you did come, didn't you?"

"I've never come when we've had sex," I inform him.

"You haven't?" He scowls. "That can't be right." He glances past me and I sense him searching through his memories. "No, definitely not. That first time—"

"You were comforting me, when Ben" —I glance away— "when Ben was in the accident."

"We came back from his funeral, and we were both so upset. I found you sobbing in your bed and held you."

"And one thing led to another, and we had sex. We found comfort in each other."

"Nothing wrong with that," he points out.

"We should have never gotten together, Isaac."

"Hold on." His scowl deepens. "I wasn't in love with Ben."

"But he had a crush on you. I knew it—" I explain.

"And it's why you never responded to my overtures. But after he died—"

I wince.

"After his accident" —he softens his voice— "you were lonely. And I felt terrible for you."

"You felt sorry for me. What we had was a pity fuck... Which became a habitual fuck."

This time he winces. "I wouldn't call it that."

"It's time someone put a name to what we have."

"And I suppose you're going to do that?" He lowers his chin to his chest, a long-suffering look on his face.

"I have to, Isaac. It's high time. Every time I've tried to talk to you in the past, you've changed the topic or been too bored to discuss it, but this time I'm going to say my piece."

He heaves a long-suffering sigh, but doesn't stop me.

"We drifted into this relationship. Initially, I let it happen because I was alone, and while I wasn't completely comfortable with it, I also knew you hadn't had the same feelings for Ben that he'd had for you. But I have to admit, I felt guilty because I knew that if he'd been alive, he'd have been pissed at us."

"And he'd have come around to it, too."

"Ben?" I laugh. "You know he'd have held a grudge for a long time. He'd have never forgiven us if we'd gotten together, Isaac."

"I'd have convinced him. We'd have convinced him, Lena."

"Maybe I wouldn't have wanted to convince him."

"What are you talking about?" He drags his fingers through his hair. Some of the strands flop onto his forehead, and he seems even younger than he normally appears. Or maybe, it's just me. Maybe I'm already so spoiled by JJ's mature countenance that everyone else looks immature in comparison.

"You know what I'm trying to say, Isaac."

"No, I do not."

It's my turn to flop onto my back. "If Ben had been alive, we'd have never gotten together. I wouldn't have felt so responsible for you, and we'd never have ended up living under your father's roof."

"But he *isn't* alive. And we *did* get together, and now we're here."

"Living under your father's roof," I point out.

"Why do you keep bringing that up? You were the one who wanted us to go to him for help."

"Only because I didn't want to end up homeless."

"That would never have happened."

"No, it wouldn't, because I'd have inevitably found a way to pay our rent."

"I knew it." He slaps his hand on the mattress. "You've come back to the same point in a roundabout way. You want to guilt trip me, yet again, for not taking my responsibilities seriously. For not paying my half of the rent. For not pulling my weight when it came to the bills."

"That's right." I jackknife up and spring out of bed. "And you don't have to make it sound like it was wrong of me to expect that."

"I'm not saying that. It's just that I needed time to get my shit together," he protests.

"And, in the meanwhile, you let me shoulder our problems."

"As you constantly remind me. You're beginning to sound like a broken record," he snaps.

"And you're sounding like the spoiled brat that you are."

He pales. "That's not fair, Lena, and you know it."

I deflate a little. "You're right, it's not. I hate it when we fight like this."

"So, let's not fight."

"It's unavoidable when whatever little feelings we had for each other are no longer existent."

He stares at me. "What're you trying to tell me?"

"I want to break up with you."

"Excuse me?" His gaze widens. "Why... why would you say such a thing?"

"Because—" I squeeze my eyes shut. "I slept with your father."

34

Isaac

"You what?" I blink, then burst out laughing. "I know you're pissed at me, but c'mon. This isn't the kind of thing you should joke about."

"I'm not joking."

I wipe the smile off of my face. "I don't understand, Lena."

"What's not to understand?" She jumps up and off the bed, then begins to pace. "I slept with JJ. I fucked him. I had sex with him."

Anger squeezes my rib cage. My heart jumps into my throat, blocking off my airflow. I try to say something, but nothing comes out of my mouth. My brain cells seem to be unable to create a single thought.

She turns and surveys my features. "Why aren't you saying anything?"

I shake my head to clear it. "You slept with JJ?"

She nods.

"You fucked my father?"

She pales, but doesn't glance away. "That's what I said."

I sit up, then drag my fingers through my hair. "When... when did it happen?"

"Just now, on our way back from the office."

"You fucked him... In the car?"

"In his Rolls." She locks her fingers together. "It's only happened once, Isaac."

"Are you in love with him?"

She stares at me. "What? No, of course not."

"So why did you sleep with him?"

"We were attracted to each other. And the, uh, connection between us has been growing over the last few days. We've been spending so much time in each other's company—in the office, in meetings... It... just spiraled out of control. But I swear, I'm not going to sleep with him again, Isaac. I'm going to do my best to avoid him. I—"

"Bullshit." I spring up and face her across the expanse of the bed. "Look me in the face and tell me you don't want to fuck him again."

She opens her mouth, then shuts it.

"That's what I thought. You're not the kind of person to make impulsive decisions, Lena. It took me years of getting to know you before you agreed to sleep with me, and you've fallen into his bed within days of meeting him? You must feel something for him. That's the only reason you'd allow him to fuck you, unless—"

"Unless?" She scowls.

"Unless it's his money. The security he can provide you. You're always worried about having a roof over your head, about paying your bills. It's why you've been so focused on your career. You hate having debts, Lena. You lay awake at night, unable to sleep, wondering how you're going to pay it off. No doubt, his wealth played a factor in your letting him seduce you."

For a few moments, she seems speechless, then she bursts out, "You're accusing me of being taken in by his affluence? By his position and his riches and" —she waves her hand in the air— "by all this?"

"You wouldn't be the first. And it's okay, I get it. It must be a lot coming from a background like yours..."

"And what background is that?" she asks in a low voice. "What are you trying to imply?"

"That you're just another gold digger. I thought you were different, Lena. I thought you saw through the masks people wear, to what's true underneath it all. I thought you weren't the kind of woman who'd be taken in by status and money, but I guess I was wrong."

"It's not like that, Isaac. Truly. It's just this… this chemistry between us."

"Chemistry?" I laugh. "If that were the case, you wouldn't have cheated on me."

"That's not true. What we have, it… it's not enough, Isaac."

"Are you saying you never had any feelings for me?"

"No, that's not what I'm saying. I care a lot about you, Isaac. You're probably my best friend. In real life, outside of my books. "I love you, and I never wanted to hurt you."

"But you have. And it looks to me like you have the hots for my father's wealth. How he can wipe away all your debts in one go. How he can, no doubt, take care of your family, too. Have you planned it all out, Lena? Have you decided to get pregnant while you're at it, too? So you can lure him into marrying you and setting yourself up for life, you—"

"Stop it." She marches around the bed and raises her hand, but I catch her wrist.

"Going to slap me now?"

She tugs at her hand. "Let me go."

"Why should I? You're my father's whore now. Maybe I should fuck you one last time and send you back to him with my scent on your skin. Would he like that you think?"

"Stop." She tries to pull away, but I tug on her arm, then twist it behind her back. I tug and she falls against me. Her breasts smash into my chest, her hips cradle mine, and my cock instantly snaps to attention. She must sense it, for her eyes widen and her cheeks redden further. Her breath comes in small gasps. "Don't you dare, Isaac."

"Oh, yeah? Give me one reason why I shouldn't fuck you? You cheated on me, so you owe me, Lena."

"I don't owe you anything, Isaac. I was the one who supported you when you were too lost in your head to figure out how to pay your bills or keep a roof over your head."

"That's why you fucked my father? As payment for all the times you took care of me?"

She furrows her forehead, a look of abject helplessness on her features. "I know you're upset and you want to hurt me, but you have to know that's not why I—"

"Shagged my father?"

"You know that's not why I did it, Isaac. I didn't mind taking care of you. It was my role as your girlfriend—"

"You're no longer my girlfriend."

A drop of moisture squeezes out from the corner of her eye. "I'm so sorry, Isaac."

"Well, you can apologize by fucking me one last time." I begin to shove her toward the bed, and she resists.

"Stop. Stop it, Isaac." Her voice rises in pitch.

The band around my chest tightens further. *Why are you doing this? Why are you scaring her? Let her go already. She doesn't want you, she's made that abundantly clear. And she wants him instead.* Once more, my bitch of a father has managed to get the better of me, just like he did when I was growing up. He won almost every fight I had with him then, and he's managing to do it now, too.

I shove her back. The backs of her knees hit the frame of the bed, and I push her onto it. She falls onto the bed. I throw myself on her, covering her body with mine.

"Isaac, what are you doing?" she pants. Her features are flushed and her pupils are dilated. You might be fooled into thinking she's aroused, except for the fact that she slams her fist into my shoulder. "Let me the hell go," she snaps.

"No." I first grab one arm, then the other, and twist it over her head. "You slept with my father; now it's my turn."

"This is not some competition, you asshole."

I stare at her, then chuckle. "Of course it is, sweetheart. Haven't you realized that by now?"

"Wait, what?" She blinks rapidly. She surveys my features and understanding dawns on hers. "Is that why... No, it can't be..."

"If you mean, did I bring you here with the notion of flouting you in front of my father, then you're right."

"What?" she chokes out. "I don't believe you. You had feelings for me, Isaac. We felt… something for each other. We've always been friends. I was worried about you, about us. I'm the one who insisted we approach your father for help."

"And I saw the wisdom in that," I agree, "and we were friends. So, it's not like I set out to show you off to my father. But then I saw the way he looked at you. Saw how he couldn't keep his eyes off you. Hell, he didn't stop himself from interrupting when we fought in front of him. So, I knew you'd caught his attention. For once I wanted to show him that I had something he didn't. That I was better than him. I thought I had youth on my side. He may have money—"

"Which you're going to inherit one day."

"And which I'll donate to charity right away, but that's not the point. The fact is, for the first time in my life, I had one up on him. I had something he coveted. For once, I was better than him. At least, I thought I was. I was sure you'd choose me over him."

"This is crazy." She shakes her head as if to clear it. "If you knew he wanted me, then why did you agree to me taking the job in his company? Why were you fine with me working with him? With me accompanying him to the office... with working in such close quarters with him?"

"Because I wanted to make a point. I wanted to rub his nose in it. I wanted him to realize I had won this round."

"This is not a competition," she says in a harsh voice.

"Apparently not. I never stood a chance. I never thought that you'd fall for him. I should have realized you'd turn out to be like every other woman. Show them a loaded wallet and they can't see anything else. I thought you loved me, Lena. I thought you were on my side."

"I am," she cries. "I am, Isaac."

"Until you weren't." I set my lips. "I'm going to fuck you, Lena. I'm going to show you that I'm every bit as good as my father— No, that I'm better than that bastard. I can do better than him, Lena." I square my shoulders. "I'm going to do better than him. Just you wait." I lower my head to hers.

She turns away. "Stop, Isaac, stop."

"Kiss me, Lena, just give me this chance to prove myself."

"No, get away from me. Please."

"Just one kiss. That's it. A kiss." *When did I start yelling?*

She strains under me. "No, Isaac. You've lost your mind."

"I've lost my mind? I'll show you—" I press my lips to hers. The next moment, I'm hauled away from her. I hit the floor, and the back of my head smashes into the hardwood. The breath rushes out of me. Stars fill my vision. When it clears, I stare up into the angry face of the bastard who calls himself my father.

35

JJ

"You. Keep your hands off of her." I stab my finger in the direction of my son.

Isaac sprawls on the floor next to the bed. He glares back at me with an expression I recognize. It's very similar to the one I saw on a daily basis when he was a teen.

He jumps up to his feet and rushes me, but I'm ready. I bend, and lift him up and over my shoulder.

Lena screams.

Isaac crashes into the nightstand. The jug of water overturns and smashes into the floor. Shards of glass glisten amidst the pool of water.

Isaac groans, then lurches back to his feet. "I'm going to kill you," he growls.

"I'd like to see you try." I crack my neck, then beckon to him.

He bares his teeth, then jumps forward. *What the—?* He lands a fist in my cheek. My head snaps back, and stars fill my vision. Pain shoots down my spine. I stumble, evade his next hit, snap out my fist and land it in his nose. The sound of cartilage being smashed fills the space. To his credit, Isaac doesn't cry out. Blood drips from his nose, down his chin and onto his shirt.

"Stop it," Lena yells.

Isaac shakes his head, drops of blood flying off his face and blotting the floor.

"Still haven't learnt to fight, have you?" I shake out my fingers, then beckon to him again. "Think you have it in you to hit me again?"

"Stop, JJ, you're going to kill him," Lena pleads.

I ignore her, narrowing my gaze on my son. "I should have done this a long time ago."

"You mean hit me? That's all that was left. You ignored me for most of my life, and when you finally decide to notice me, it's to fuck my girlfriend. You don't have a shred of decency in your body, do you?"

"I don't," I concede. "It's winner takes all, boy. You take your eyes off the prize and you lose it. Surely, you know that by now."

"I'm not a prize, you assholes," Lena cries.

"I fucking hate you." Isaac peels back his lips. "I'm going to smash your head in."

I chuckle, "I'd like to see you try."

He takes a step forward. So do I. That's when Lena jumps down from the bed. The sound of shards of glass being crunched underfoot reaches me. I wince. Lena gasps. I follow her gaze to where she's standing on slivers of broken glass.

"Jesus, Lena!" I leap toward her and pluck her off the ground.

"Let me go," she huffs.

"No fucking way." I head away from the glass and into the bathroom, then deposit her on the edge of the bathtub. "Stay there."

She scowls. "You can't order me around."

Before I can reply, Isaac's petulant voice interrupts me from the doorway of the bathroom. "He's right… On this occasion."

Both Lena and I whip our gazes in his direction.

I stare.

Lena glowers at him. "You're agreeing with him?"

"Unfortunately, yes. But it's about your safety, so I don't have a choice." He glances down at her feet. "You're hurt."

"So are you." I jerk my chin toward the bathtub. "Have a seat, I'll get some antiseptic for the both of you."

He opens his mouth, no doubt to protest, but I spin around and walk toward the cabinet on the far side of the spacious bathroom. What a mess. I shouldn't have fucked her, but I don't regret it. It was worth every fight with my son, every possible breakdown in the relationship with the one person I wanted to have some kind of a connection with. *Was it, though? Was it all right to choose his girlfriend over him? Is that what I did, though?* That's how he's going to see it, but really, I followed my instinct. The two of them are wrong for each other, I can see it, but can she… Can he? *And you're right for her?*

I'm better at taking care of her than Isaac, any day. *And you're not looking for a relationship; not with her, not with anyone else. But if you were looking for some kind of bond, some kind of association, a companion for a short period of time, then…* I'd choose her, in a heartbeat. That I'm not going to fuck her and leave, I accepted a while ago. But this… This need to hold onto her for some period of time, to risk a liaison of the kind I've never allowed myself before, would be… Dangerous. Unprecedented. A first, of sorts. A chance to redeem myself, perhaps? I grab the antiseptic, the bandages, and the first aid box, then turn toward them.

The two of them are seated as far away from each other as the length of the bathtub will allow.

I reach Isaac, hand over one of the bottles of antiseptic, some cotton and bandages, then walk over to her. I squat down in front of her and spread out a clean towel to place my supplies on it.

"Let me." I reach for her foot, but she shies away.

"Lena" —I tip up my chin— "I won't hurt you."

"Not more than you have already," she mutters.

I wince. "I need to pull out the glass pieces and disinfect your foot."

She blows out a breath. "I can do it myself."

"Can you?" I narrow my gaze on her.

She firms her lips.

"Jesus, woman, let me help you, okay?"

She folds her arms across her chest.

"He's right," Isaac mutters. "He's a bastard, but again, he's right. He needs to remove the pieces of glass, Lena."

She blows out a breath. "Fine, do it then."

I circle my fingers around her ankle. Goosebumps pop up on her calf. I place her heel gently on my thigh, then glance at the sole of her foot. Several shards of glass are embedded in the tender flesh. I wince. I grab the other to check, then heave a sigh of relief when I find the skin is not broken.

"What is it?" she asks in a worried voice? "Is it okay?"

"It will be. Do you have tweezers?"

"In my cosmetic bag." She nods toward the counter by the sink.

"I'll get it." Holding a balled-up towel to his nose, Isaac hops up and walks toward the cosmetic case. He brings it over to her. Lena pulls out the tweezers and I take them from her.

I glance at her, then at Isaac. "You might need to distract her."

Lena starts, "What do you mean? Is it going to hurt? Is that why—"

"—hold on, Dinky." Isaac clambers into the bathtub and stands behind her. "Is it okay if I touch you?" he murmurs. "I swear, I won't hurt you. I'm sorry for earlier. I just lost it, you know? When you told me you... you slept with him—"

I glare up at Isaac, but his attention is focused on Lena.

"—I just sort of lost my head. All I could think was that you'd broken my trust. You hurt me, Lena."

She blows out a breath. "I know. I'm so sorry, Isaac— Ouch."

I pull out a piece of glass and shake it out on the towel.

She glowers at me, but I ignore her and focus on my task.

"You don't need to apologize. I mean, you do, but I bet he seduced you. I bet it's mainly his fault."

I grit my teeth, swallowing down the anger that bubbles up, and pull out another piece of glass.

"Ow, that hurts," she whines.

I glance up at Isaac, who meets my gaze and nods. "I'm going to hold your shoulders, okay? Just to support you. Is that okay?"

Lena nods. I take in her pale features. Her eyes glisten as she stares at her foot. It's a good thing she can't see the shards of glass. I pull out another piece. She moans, and my heart slams into my rib cage. Jesus

H. Christ. Since when did I become such a wuss? I drop the piece of glass on the towel, and I'm not surprised to find my hand is shaking. Should have had a drink before I embarked on this. Hold on. It's just some pieces of glass stuck in her foot. And she's bleeding. Blood trickles down her foot and onto the floor. My guts churn. I focus on the task at hand. *Focus, focus.* I grip another piece of glass, but before I can tug it out, her entire body freezes.

"Isaac," I snap.

"Lena, look at me," Isaac coaxes her.

"I don't wanna," she says on a sob. "Oh, god. It's going to hurt. It's going to hurt."

"What's the most idiotic thing you've ever done?" he asks.

"Getting together with you," she replies promptly.

I shake my head. Boy needs lessons on how to occupy a woman's attention.

"If you don't look up at me, I'm going to kiss you," he says.

"What the— Don't you dare." She glances up at him, and I pull out another piece of glass.

"Ow, that hurt." She huffs.

"It's going to hurt a lot more if I don't get all the pieces of glass out," I drawl.

"I hate you," she bursts out.

"Good, we agree on something," Isaac murmurs. "Do you remember the time we went with Ben to the zoo?"

"I didn't want to, but Ben loved it. He was a kid at heart."

"And you could never say no to him."

Ben? Who's Ben? I pull out another shard of glass, and this time she flinches, but doesn't protest.

"He loved the open spaces in this city. It was such a change from New York for him, you know? He was always trying to do new things."

"Remember the ballet class he wanted to try out?" Isaac murmurs.

"I went along with him."

"And I signed up because he dared me to." Isaac winces.

I stare at him. "You joined a ballet class?"

"It was one class." He reddens.

"He was quite good at it, too."

"No, I wasn't," he protests.

"Aww, don't be shy now. The teacher called you a natural."

"And that was the last time I ever put on tights." His flush deepens.

A chuckle wells up. "You wore tights?"

"I might even have a picture somewhere." Lena laughs.

"Don't you dare show it to him, Lena."

"I definitely need to see this." I pluck out the last of the shards from her foot.

She peers up at Isaac with a mischievous look. "If you bring me my phone—"

"No, absolutely not." He scowls down at her. "And if you show him that photo, I swear, I'll tell him how you laughed so much that time we went to the comedy club that—"

"No, stop. Okay, I won't show him the picture," Lena interrupts.

"What happened at the comedy club?" I pull out another small piece. I almost missed it.

"She laughed so much that—"

"No, stop." She grips his hand and squeezes it. I glance at it, and a slow burn begins behind my ribcage. Damn, my ulcers are acting up again. Surely, that's the only reason my stomach feels like it's eating itself.

Isaac begins to chortle.

Her brow grows thunderous.

"Shut up, Isaac." She glowers at him. He only laughs louder. He leans his chin on her head and chuckles until tears run down his cheek.

"Isaac!" she snaps in a warning voice.

"Fine, okay, I won't tell him that you laughed so much that you peed your pants!"

"Isaac, really!" She shoves him away. He's laughing so hard that he sinks down in the bathtub. He holds his middle and guffaws. He cackles so hard that a reluctant smile tugs at her lips. I realize my lips, too, are twitching. I forgot how Isaac laughs with his entire being. Like the mirth wells up from somewhere deep inside and is taking over his entire body.

"Almost done." I lower her foot to the floor.

She begins to rise, but I grip her knees. "You can't put pressure on your foot yet. Also, I need to disinfect and bandage it."

"Oh, okay."

I reach for the antiseptic, then scowl at my still snickering son.

"Isaac?"

He wipes the tears from his face. The blood has stopped flowing from his nose. Guess I didn't hit him that hard, after all. He jumps up and resumes his stance behind her.

"Brace yourself," I murmur.

"What—?" She frowns.

I dab the antiseptic onto her hurt foot and she yells, "It hurts, it hurts." She's holding onto Isaac's hand again. My stomach knots itself, but I ignore it. I really should learn to take time out for lunch. Obviously, that's the reason there's a hollow feeling in my belly. I reach for the bandage and wrap up her foot quickly, then place it on the floor.

I glance up to find tears clinging to her eyelashes. Her features are even more pale, and a drop of blood wells up from her lower lip where she's bitten down on it.

"All right?" I ask softly.

She nods.

I rise to my feet. Then before she can straighten, I swing her up in my arms.

"Hey, I can walk."

"Actually, it's better if he carries you." Isaac glances between us, then he releases her hand and steps back. "I'll let you two go."

"Isaac, no, it's not like that." She raises her hand, then lowers it. "It's really not how it looks."

"It's exactly how it looks. You fucked him, Lena. I haven't forgotten that."

"It… it doesn't have to be this way."

"Are you saying you're not going to do it again?"

"I—" She glances up at me. I hold her gaze for a second, then another. I'm not sure what she sees in my eyes, but she clamps her mouth shut. The silence extends.

Then Isaac blows out a breath. "That's what I thought."

36

Lena

"I'm not going to sleep in your room."

"Yes, you are," JJ says so patiently, I want to punch him in the face.

"You're not listening to me. I am *not* going to sleep in your bed."

"You're going to sleep in my room, and in my bed," he snaps.

"Fine, I'm not going to sleep with you in the same bed."

He walks up the stairs, down the corridor, and uses his shoulder to open the double doors that lead to his room. Then, he crosses the floor and deposits me on his bed. I sit up at once, and swing my legs over the side.

"You are not putting weight on your foot. I forbid it."

I set my lips. "Oh, you *forbid* it? *You* forbid it, eh?"

"I do."

"And what makes you think you can stop me from doing anything?"

"I'm your boss... And the man who fucked you so hard you couldn't stop crying out my name as you spasmed around my cock."

His words sweep through me and arrow straight down to the space between my legs. I have to stop myself from squeezing my thighs together. Why do I find his dirty talk such a turn-on? Is it because of the assuredness with which he speaks those four-letter words? Or the confidence with which he glares at me as if daring me to challenge his order?

I scowl at him.

He raises an eyebrow.

"Are you going to lay back in bed, or am I going to make you lay back?"

"You wouldn't dare."

His eyes gleam. "There's nothing I'd like more than pressing you back onto the bed, then undressing you and—"

"Don't you dare," I say hotly.

"There you go again, daring me." He takes a step forward, and I throw up a hand.

"Fine, fine. I'll lay down. But not with you."

"Where else am I supposed to sleep?"

"Anywhere else, just not here."

"This is my bed," he says in a voice that drips with exaggerated patience. Oh, my god, I hate it when he treats me like I'm a child. I do.

"That is exactly my point. This is your bed. You want me in your bed. And that's fine. I'm willing to sleep here, just not with you."

"This is a big bed. You sleep on one side, and I'll sleep all the way over on the other side."

I glower at him. "Oh, no, you're not pulling that on me."

He raises a shoulder. "You can sleep on top of the covers, for all I care. But you are going to sleep in my bed, and so am I, Lena."

He turns around and heads toward the bathroom.

"Where are you going?" I ask, then snap my lips together. Why the hell do I care where he's going? And why did that come out sounding so needy?

"To get you ibuprofen for the pain," he calls out over his shoulder.

"Oh." I let out a sigh.

He returns a few minutes later with a glass of water and two tablets that he hands over to me. I wash them down with the water.

"Thanks." I place the glass of water on the bedstand.

"I'm going to get you something to eat." He turns and leaves.

I glance around the room. I saw it, of course, the last time I snuck in here, but now, I'm taking in the details. The plush dark blue carpet on the floor. The bookcase that takes up one entire wall. The sectional in front of the fireplace on the far side that makes for a cozy seating area. A door set in the wall on the other side, which I assume leads to the closet. And the bed I'm seated on which is large. It's a super king-sized bed. So wide that we could easily sleep without touching each other. Tiredness pulls at my muscles. My limbs feel like they weigh a ton. I lower myself onto the pillow and yawn. I snuggle into the bedsheets and my eyelids flutter closed.

A delicious warmth cocoons me. Mmmm. I rub my cheek against the soft—no, the hard surface, which is also soft. How is that possible? Thud-thud-thud. The reassuring beat of his heart mirrors the beating of my own. I turn my face into the warmth and inhale. Notes of sherry oak and cinnamon fill my senses. A slow pulse flares to life between my legs. I wiggle my toes and my foot feels fine. Huh? Guess I'm not hurt as badly as I thought I was. In fact, my entire body is tingling with a sense of well-being. I tighten my hold around the wide surface that is also warm. And muscled and—

I snap my eyes open. It's dark in the room, but I can make out the acres of ripped planes. Grooves, divots... pecs. I'm staring at his pecs. His very deliciously-sculpted pecs with a smattering of hair on them and that deep groove that demarcates them. And there are scars. Scars big and small pepper his chest. The skin above his nipple is puckered. Is that a gunshot wound? It *is* a gunshot wound, and it's so close to his heart. My own heart spasms at the thought. How did he get that? Was it in a gang war? I heard Isaac mention that JJ once belonged to an underground gang.

Seeing him in meetings in the conference room of his office, I'd never have believed it. But the marks on his torso are a testament to the kind of life he's had. It doesn't take away from the beauty of his physique. If anything, it lends it a dangerous edge. And his abs? He must work out a lot to maintain the shape of those corrugated abs which dip down and disappear under the white of his sheet. The sheet that outlines the length of his powerful legs as he lays sprawled out on his bed. *His* bed. I'm in JJ's bed… in his room… in his arms. To be clear, I am on *him*. All over him, to be doubly clear. I have my arm flung around his massive chest, my leg flung over what must be his thighs and—I stop breathing. That thick, hard, fat rod that's stabbing into my upper thigh is his cock. He's not wearing briefs. How dare he get into bed without wearing briefs? Also, thank God he's not wearing briefs.

Also, not only am I clinging to him like a python, but *his* python is ready to return the favor, and in spades. I draw in a breath and the scent of him intensifies. Moisture beads my center. Pinpricks of heat shiver up my back. Perhaps he senses it, for his shaft seems to grow even thicker and longer. My fingertips tingle. *Should I? Shouldn't I?* I glance up to find his eyes are shut. His breathing is even. His chest rises and falls, and there's no change in the cadence of his breathing. *Guess he's still sleeping, eh?*

I lower my hand to his crotch. Then, making sure he's asleep, I close my fingers around his dick. It instantly throbs and fills my palm. I try to wrap my fingers around the girth, but my fingertips don't meet. I know… You think I'm exaggerating. But honestly, that's not true. My fingertips. Don't. Meet. Jesus, and he stuck that inside of me? No wonder it hurt… Before it felt good. So damn good. My thighs quiver, and my mouth waters. *How would it feel to have him down my throat, hmm?* Keeping my eyes on his face to make sure he's asleep, I slide down the length of his body, making sure not to touch him, until I'm positioned with my face over his crotch.

I inhale deeply, and his musky scent—a mixture of spice and sweat —sinks into my blood. I lick my tongue over the swollen head, and his column seems to swell further. I squeeze my fingers around the base, then close my mouth over the tip. I swipe my tongue around the rim and his length fills my palm. Jesus, how much bigger is he going to get?

He's carrying what amounts to a baseball bat between his legs. No wonder he has big balls. It's because he *literally* has big balls. It's why

he's so full of himself. Why he comes across as so dominant, so confident, so authoritarian. He can afford to be all of that. Not only does he
have the money to back up his stance, but he has the *cojones* to support
his ego. I tilt my head to take him further inside, and he seems to swell.
He's filling my mouth, pressing down on my tongue, pushing up into
the roof of my mouth. My jaw begins to hurt. Saliva drips down my
chin, and I pull back. My breath comes in puffs. The hair on the back of
my neck rises. I glance up to find him staring at me. My heart flips up
into my throat. Adrenaline laces my blood. I begin to pull back, but he
digs his fingers into my hair and holds me in place.

"Why don't you finish what you started?" His hard voice rumbles
across the space, and my nerve endings crackle.

I tighten my grip around the base of his cock, and he inhales. His
chest planes seem to harden, and his shoulders swell. He seems to
grow bigger. A plume of heat seems to rise off of his body and slam
into my chest. I gasp. My core clenches, and I'm ashamed to say my
panties are now completely wet. I squeeze my thighs together, and one
side of his lips kicks up. He seems to know exactly the kind of effect he
has on me.

"Suck me off, little girl," he says in a hard voice, and pinpricks of
heat dot my back. "Now," he commands.

I drop my head, close my mouth around his cock, and swallow. A
groan rips up his chest. I bob my head and take him down my throat,
making his thigh muscles go solid. I gag, then swallow, and he slaps
his palm into the mattress. Something like victory courses through my
veins. This is Mr. Big Balls JJ and I have him where I want him. At my
mercy. With his dick down my throat. Bet I can make him come
quickly, and hard and long. Bet I can make him lose control the way
I've often wanted to see him come undone in the office. I bring my
hand up and cradle his balls. I squeeze them as I continue to suck him
off. In-out-in. With long sweeps I pull out until the tip of his cock is
balanced at the edge of my mouth, then lean in and swallow around
his shaft.

He growls. "Fucking hell, Lena, do that again."

He wraps his fingers around my throat. I lower my head until he
slides across my tongue and down the column of my throat.

"I can feel my dick down your throat." His voice is thick with desire… and lust… and strain. Like he's still holding back. I pull back, then plunge down, again and again. Spit drools down my chin. I scoop it up, then slide my digit up the valley between his ass cheeks. I brush his puckered opening and he stills. I slide it inside and brush his prostrate, then massage his balls. At the same time, I swallow around his cock and his entire body seems to shudder. "You're killing me, girl."

He tugs on my hair, and my scalp tingles. I increase the intensity of my motions, and every muscle in his body seems to coil in on itself.

"I'm going to come," he gasps. I glance up at him, then deliberately lower my chin and take him down even deeper. His dark eyes flash, and a current seems to run from his shoulders to his belly to his thighs. The planes of his chest swell and he shoots his load.

37

JJ

Flares seem to go off behind my eyes. My ears are ringing, or maybe that's my toes. No, I can't feel my toes at all, or my fingers, or my limbs, for that matter. I can't remember the last time I came this hard, and that's saying something. My orgasm seems to go on and on. I come down her throat and she swallows it all and that only turns me on even more. I come until I see black spots behind my eyes. When I finally crack my eyelids open, it's to find her pulling back.

My dick plops from her swollen lips. She wipes the back of her hand across her mouth, and my balls tighten all over again. Her golden gaze meets mine. Her cheeks are flushed, and her hair is stuck to her forehead. A thread of saliva drools down her chin. A fire detonates in my groin. I'm no longer so young that I can go twice back-to-back, but goddamn, if, with her, I don't find my cock swelling to attention. I release my hold on her hair, only to grip her shoulders. In one smooth motion, I pull her up, then flip her onto her back.

Her voice trembles. "What are you doing—?" She stops when she sees I've lowered myself down between her legs.

I slide my arms under her thighs, then pause.

"You went to sleep on an empty stomach," I point out.

"I was tired."

"You're awake now. Are you hungry? I can get you something."

She shrugs. "Not really. I just had a snack." She smirks.

I shake my head and look down at the bandage around her foot, then back to her face. "How does your foot feel now?"

"It's fine."

I frown, and her lips kick up. "No, really. It's fine. I don't feel any pain at all. My pussy, on the other hand—" She bites down on her lower lip. Of course, my gaze lowers to her mouth.

"You trying to be bratty, little girl?"

She shakes her head.

"Don't lie to me. You want me to pull down your yoga pants and bury my face in your cunt?"

She squeezes her eyes shut. "Oh, god, when you talk dirty like that, it really turns me on."

"You don't have to beat yourself up over that, Lena. It's okay to get aroused by filthy talk."

"I know. It's just… I never expected you to be so proficient at it…" She looks away. "Or at other things," she mutters under her breath.

I release her legs, then crawl up her body. I bracket her in with my elbows and peer into her features.

"Look at me, Lena."

She shakes her head.

"Are you ashamed that we fucked in the car?"

She doesn't reply.

"Are you uncomfortable because you like to call me Daddy?"

She peers up at me from under her eyelids. "Are *you* uncomfortable when I call you Daddy?"

I glance between her eyes. What if I said it does something interesting to me? That I find it weirdly hot. What does that say about me? What if I admit it to her, and she finds it creepy?

"I prefer my sex to be rough, but I'm not into the lifestyle, not into setting scenes. I'll always take the lead in bed, but I don't have to resort to whips or chains, or any of the things that younger men seem to find so intriguing. I don't need props, not when I have a hot-blooded, willing woman in my arms, and—"

"Your monster dick in your pants. You only have to unleash that, and you don't need any other weapon to terrorize your sexual partner?"

I choke. "Is that a backhanded compliment? If I'd known the size of my cock would traumatize you—"

"I'm not emotionally scarred from seeing your dick. " Her eyes twinkle. "Well, not completely, that is."

I scowl. "Did I hurt you when I fucked you in the car yesterday? Were you in discomfort when you sucked me off earlier?"

"No, no." She half laughs. "I was too into the moment yesterday in the car. I mean, all that pent-up frustration and buildup. I wanted to fuck you, as well, you know. And earlier today... I woke up with your cock stabbing into my thigh—"

"Not going to apologize for that,"

"—and I wanted to taste you. Though, why you couldn't wear your pajamas to bed, I don't know."

"I don't have pajamas," I inform her. "I'm too set in my ways, and not going to change now. Not even for you."

"Yeah." She scoffs. "I guess you know best—" She firms her lips before she can say that last word, but I know—and she knows that I know—what she was going to say then.

Daddy.

A thick sensation swirls in my belly. My groin hardens, my balls tighten, and I don't need to look down to know my cock is now at full-mast.

"Apparently, you're not *that* set in your ways." Her cheeks heat.

"Apparently not." I lower my head until my eyelashes brush hers. Until I can peer into her eyes and see the flares that dance in their depths. Until her sweet breath sears my cheeks, and her lips part, seducing me to brush my mouth over hers. A whimper spills from her lips. The sound goes straight to my head.

"You can call me anything you want, little girl." I lick her lips.

This time she moans, and my balls feel like they weigh a ton. For chrissake, I just came in her mouth. Clearly, being with her has turned me into a man who can get it up any time. Just for her.

"I am going to eat you out, then I'm going to fuck your tight little cunt, and then I'm going to turn you over and take your ass... If you'll let me."

She swallows and her pupils dilate, a sure sign she's turned on. "JJ," she whines.

"When you pout and moan my name, it fucking drives me crazy."

"JJ," she breathes. The air between us turns thick with erotic intent. "JJ." Her voice breaks. "Jack... please." She thrusts her breasts up so the tips of her pebbled nipples jut out from under the thin camisole top she's wearing.

"What do you want, girl?" I force myself to deliver the words in a voice that comes out in an almost normal tone. 'Almost' being the operative term. Because I'm quickly losing my grip on the control I've held onto for most of my life. The control I drew on to stare down the boys on the street from the rival gang. The control I needed to not cry out when my best friend knifed me and took off with my money. The control I'd sought when I rose through the ranks in the organized crime syndicate I joined. The control I drew around myself in order to commit the crimes needed to get to the top. The very control I leaned on to transition my business from the Kane company to that of Kane Enterprises. The control that threatens to snap when I stare deeply into her honey-gold eyes. I'm losing myself in them... In her. I'm so close to burying myself in her and not letting go for a very long time. And when she calls me by my first name, I'll do anything for her. *Anything*.

"Girl?" I cup her cheek. "Tell me what you need."

"You, Jack, I want every filthy, erotic thing you can do to me."

A fierce sensation coils in my chest. My belly hardens, pinpricks of heat tighten at the base of my spine, and I brush my lips over hers. "Your wish is my command." I kiss her more gently than I intended to. With my mouth, I worship hers. With my fingers, I draw back the hair from her features, then plant my hips in between her legs. I lower my weight into her body, and the softness, the give, the sheer surrender of her body takes me by surprise. Her submission is implicit in the curve of her hips, the way she opens her mouth to mine. How she sighs as I slide my tongue over hers, and allows me to suckle her honeyed sweetness is my undoing. I release her lips, then tug her camisole up and over her head. I toss it aside, bend and suck on one ripe nipple.

"Jack," she moans, and fuck if that doesn't make me hornier. I turn my attention to her other nipple, while I squeeze the first one. I tweak her nipple and her entire body jolts. "Oh, god, that feels so good."

I glance up at her, then massage both breasts before I pinch her nipples. She wriggles and makes those little noises that tell me she's aroused. "You like that, little girl?"

She nods.

"Your breasts are so sensitive." I massage them, run my fingers around the rims of her areolae, and her face flushes. She rises up, trying to get closer, and I chuckle. "What's the hurry? We have the entire night, don't we?"

She scowls. "Stop teasing me, JJ."

"Oh, it's JJ now, is it?" I slide down her body, then shove her yoga pants and her panties down her hips. Rising up to my knees, I pull them down her legs and off her feet gently. I drop them to the side, then raise her bandaged foot and kiss her ankle. Goosebumps rise on her skin. I press little kisses up her slim calf to the inside of her knee. When I turn my face into the soft skin there, she sighs. I continue to feather kisses up her thigh. She squirms and tries to pull away, but I grip her hip and stop her. I bury my nose in her pussy and inhale deeply. She shivers. "JJ, please," she whines. "Please, please, please."

"Please what, little girl?" I blow lightly on her cunt and her entire body jolts.

"Omigod, will you fuck me already?"

38

Lena

Did I just say that? I said that. That needy, demanding voice was mine. It's what this man does to me. He knows exactly how to turn me on, and yet, withholds what I want until I'm on the verge of spontaneously combusting. I reach down to touch my clit, but he brushes away my hand.

"You will not touch yourself, little girl."

"But why not?"

"Because this pussy belongs to me." He glares up at me. I shiver. And here I thought he was going all tender on me. Well, he is, but at his core, he's still the demanding, dominating alphahole I fell in hate with.

Without taking his gaze off of me, he swipes his tongue up my pussy lips.

"Oh, my god!" My eyes roll back in my head. I pant and moan, then bite my lips to stop any more embarrassing noises from escaping.

"Hold on to the headboard," he orders.

I do. I throw my arms up and hold onto the headboard just before he swoops down and begins to eat me out in earnest. No preamble, no warning. He shoves his tongue inside my pussy, then grinds his heel into my clit. Sensations detonate up my spine. I writhe and groan. I throw my head back and bring my thighs together around his head. I know I'm smothering him, but damn if I can help it. He flicks his tongue in and out of me, then flicks the swollen nub of my clit. My nerve endings all seem to fire at once. I arch my back and contort my body, trying to get away from him even as I shove my pelvis up, chasing that wicked tongue of his that's bringing me so much pleasure.

"Jack, please, make me come. Please, Jack."

I sense his growl vibrate through my pussy lips. He rubs on my clit and curls his tongue inside, doing something that sets waves of liquid heat sloshing up my belly. The sensations gather speed and shoot up my spine, and just like that, I shatter. As I float back to Earth, I'm aware of him licking at my slit, cleaning up my cum. Heat flushes my cheeks. I raise heavy eyelids to find him looking up at me. He raises his head, and in a gesture that mirrors mine but, somehow, seems so much dirtier, he wipes the back of his hand across his mouth. He hitches his arms under my knees and shoves them up near my ears. He settles between my legs and the blunt head of his cock nudges my opening.

"I'm going to fuck you now, girl."

Before I can react, he plunges forward and into me. It's as if a missing part of me has slotted into place. Intense sensations shudder out from the point of our joining. He holds my gaze, and it's so hot, so erotic. So very JJ. He doesn't hesitate. Simply pulls out, then thrusts into me with enough force that the entire bed jolts. I slide up the bed and my head would have banged into the headboard; except he's released my knee and slapped his palm between the top of my head and the hard surface of the headboard. He rises slightly on his knees, then grits his teeth. "Let me in, girl," he growls.

"You're in," I gasp out.

"I'm barely halfway there."

I laugh. "That's what you said the last—" I cry out when he sinks in another inch. I groan.

So does he. "Fuck, baby, you feel so good." He squeezes his eyes shut, as if savoring every inch of where his cock throbs inside my most intimate space. A nerve throbs at his temple, a bead of sweat slides down the column of his throat.

Something like tenderness fills me. I reach up and cup his cheek. "Jack," I murmur, "look at me."

He opens his eyes, and his dark gaze fills my line of sight. He turns his head slightly to brush his lips against the inside of my palm, then he leans down to kiss me. He kisses me so deeply, with so much tenderness and heat and authority, that my core clenches. Moisture beads my center, and he sinks in further. I groan into his mouth. Heat flows off of him in waves and sinks into my skin. The force of his personality pushes down on my shoulders and pins me in place. He releases his hold on my other knee, then reaches between us to strum my already sensitive pussy lips.

A tingling shoots out from the point of contact. Sweat clings to my shoulders, and my breath comes in pants. My heart is racing so fast, I'm sure it's going to break through my rib cage. He holds my gaze and begins to fuck me again. Slow, deep strokes. Each time he slides into me, he hits the most intimate part of me deep inside. I dig my heels into his back and lift up my pelvis, trying to take him in even deeper. And he never breaks eye contact, which is more erotic than anything I've ever experienced. He pulls out again, and this time, when he thrusts into me, he pinches my clit. Goosebumps pop on my skin. A thousand embers light up my skin. The orgasm crashes into me with such force, I see stars. My climax seems to go on and on. I feel like I'm floating through space, and when I finally reenter my body, I realize I must have yelled out, for my throat hurts. He continues to fuck me through the aftershocks that ripple through me. I'm burning up—with need, with satisfaction, with an urge to hold onto this moment and never let go. "Jack," I whisper, not sure what I want to say, and unable to stop the tear that slides out of the corner of my eye.

He bends to lick it up, then with one last thrust, he empties himself into me. His features contort with pleasure-pain, and he lowers his head and digs his teeth into the curve of where my neck meets my shoulder. The pain slices through me, straight to my clit. I feel him throb inside of me, and I squeeze him in response. He groans. The pulses mirror the rhythm that thuds at my temples, my wrists, and behind my eyes.

"Jack." I swallow.

He seems to sense the emotions bubbling inside of me, for he raises his head and searches my features. "Don't." He pushes his forehead into mine. "Don't think, not now."

"Then when?" I whisper.

"Not now. Let's give this a little time, eh?"

"But—" He brushes his lips over mine, effectively silencing me. He deepens the kiss, and I feel him stir inside of me again. I scowl at him, and he smirks. With his hair disheveled and the lines around his eyes relaxed, he seems so much younger than his years. He lifts his head, pulls out of me, then rolls over to stand up.

"Stay right there." He stabs a finger in my direction before he turns and leaves the room.

Where is he going? What is he up to? He's back in a few seconds with a waterproof overshoe protector in his hand. "Is that—?" He kneels in front of me, then slips it on over my foot.

Then he bends and scoops me up in his arms. He stalks around the bed and into the bathroom. He deposits me on the side of the tub, then heads to the shower stall. Of course, I can't stop myself from taking in his body. Tight butt, powerful thighs, and a waistline that'd put a man in his twenties to shame. Not to mention the cut abs, the sculpted shoulders, and his arms. Have I mentioned his veiny arms? His forearms flex as he turns on the shower and checks the temperature of the water. He adjusts it until he's satisfied, then lifts me up again and carries me into the stall, which is almost as wide as some of the rooms I first stayed in when I moved to London. This is no ordinary shower. There are eight, no, ten showerheads positioned at intervals above, behind and on the side walls. All of the water streams meet at the exact spot where he places me on the bench built into the side wall.

"Fancy," I murmur, taking in the glittering bathroom accessories. I peeked in on him the other day in the shower, but I was too focused on trying to see the accessory between his legs to notice much else.

"It helps me relax." He raises a shoulder. "I didn't always have such a fancy shower. There was a time when I had to make do with sharing a bathroom with five other men."

"You did?" I blink, trying to reconcile the powerful, remote, authoritarian man in front of me with a younger, skinnier version of him who must have come from humble beginnings. Did he look more like Isaac then? Long limbs, a body beginning to show the promise of the man he'd grow into? And I fucked both of them. Does that make me a slut?

He must see the thoughts reflected on my face, for he frowns. "What did I tell you? No thinking for the moment." He closes the distance between us, then lifts me and spins me around so one knee is supported by the bench, keeping my weight off of my injured foot.

"What are you doing?" I ask breathlessly.

"The only time you don't think is when I'm fucking you, so I'm going to fuck you again."

"Wait, don't you need a break to recover, considering your advanced years?"

A sharp pain splits my butt. I yelp and turn my head over my shoulder to find him palming my ass.

"Getting sassy again, I see."

"Getting horny again, I see." I glance down to where his monster cock springs up from between his legs. I'm still not used to its size. "Is the second J in your name for that?" I ask.

"What?" He blinks.

"The second J in your name—"

"I heard you the first time. And no, I don't indulge in infantile practices where I name my dick."

"I'd have called it JJ junior except, you know, JJ junior is—"

"Let's not bring him into this discussion," he says hastily.

"Why not? I can't hide the truth from myself, can I? I did fuck you, and—"

"Not now," he interrupts me. "We have time to analyze and discuss this situation later."

"You make it sound so cold."

He blows out a breath. "I merely meant, we can talk about what this means for us later. Right now, though…" He feathers his fingers up the valley between my ass cheeks, and a shiver ladders up my spine.

"Has anyone fucked you here, little girl?" he asks in that hard voice that grates over my nerve endings. My thighs clench. Oh, god. When he talks to me in that authoritarian voice, I'll agree to anything.

"Answer me," he growls.

"No. No one has. You'll be the first," I say in a rush.

"Hmm. First, I'm going to teach you a lesson for not doing as I asked."

"I did everything you asked, Daddy. I did."

His muscles seem to stiffen. The heat pouring off of him seems to intensify. He sits down on the bench next to me, then pats his thighs. "Bend over."

"Excuse me?" I stare. He doesn't mean what I think he means... Surely not. I shove back my hair that's clinging to my head, thanks to the shower. "If you think I'm going to—"

"Girl, do as I say." He lowers his voice to a hush.

I do as he says. I bend over his massive thighs, painfully aware of how exposed I am. The water from the shower continues to pound me from all sides, forcing me to squeeze my eyes closed and take sips of air through my mouth. He drags his hand down my spine and I can't stop myself from squirming. He palms my butt, and I freeze. Any moment now, he's going to spank me. I sense him move. The next moment, the shower switches off. Silence descends, except for the water that drips from my hair to the floor. He continues to massage my ass, swiping his fingers in circles. The tension oozes out of my muscles. Degree by degree, I feel my thighs unclench. All of my senses are focused on where he's touching me. Caressing me. Kneading my flesh, reminding me that I belong to him. I am his. I've been his from the moment he stepped between me and Isaac to stop what he thought was Isaac about to hit me. It's the first time I truly noticed him. And I haven't stopped since. His movements continue in ever-widening circles. Despite the fact that I'm naked and wet, warmth pools between my legs. Heat suffuses my skin, and I allow my arms to fall to the floor. Allow my weight to relax fully into his lap. It's like a signal to him because that's when he raises his palm and brings it crashing down on my ass.

39

JJ

Whack-whack-whack. I spank her on alternate butt cheeks without stopping, without giving her time to recover. She yells, tries to move away, but I lean my weight on her back to hold her in place. I continue to spank her until her honeyed skin blushes pink, until her ass is so hot to the touch, it rivals the temperature of the water from the shower. I massage her backside, and she moans. I slide my fingers down the cleavage between her butt cheeks, to her slit, and find her wet.

"You're a filthy little slut, aren't you? You like it when I spank you."

"Fuck you," she spits out.

I laugh. "So much fight in you. It's a bloody turn-on, you know that?"

"Well, you're not turning me on," she retorts.

I chuckle. "Not what your body is telling me, baby."

"Don't call me baby," she says in a petulant tone.

"Do you always deny yourself everything you like?"

"What's this, a lesson in pop psychology?" she scoffs.

"More like a chance for me to learn your body, little one."

I grip her waist, and plucking her off of my lap, I gently place her on her feet. "Does that hurt?" I survey her features.

"Not as much as my butt, you bastard."

I chuckle.

Her frown deepens. "Can I leave?" She shoves her hair back from her face.

"Not yet." I rise to my feet so she has to tilt her head back to look at me. Reaching behind me, I flick on the tap so the water pours over us.

I grip her arse, and she flinches. Fuck if that doesn't turn me on further. The fact that I marked her is the reason she's in discomfort now. It's the reason she's so turned on that her pupils are dilated until they resemble the sun when it's high in the sky. *I'd pluck the moon and the stars for her if she were to ask me.* I shake my head. *Where did that thought come from? I'm not falling for her, am I?* Sure, there's a connection between us. It's why I fucked her, regardless of the fact that she's my son's girlfriend. *Was* my son's girlfriend. Doesn't mean I'm in love with her. Impossible.

It's the sex that's addled my brain. And admittedly, my orgasms with her have been out of this world. Come to think of it, as long as I'm fucking her, everything is okay. I have no time to think, and then I don't have to worry about these soppy sentiments that insist on intruding in my thoughts. Best to keep our interactions to shagging. I mean, that's why I decided to fuck her more than once, didn't I? It's why I brought her here.

"I've never brought any of my women here," I murmur.

"Eh?" She glances up at me, her anger forgotten. "You mean to say—"

"You're the first woman in this room, in my bed... In this shower, for that matter." I scowl down at her.

She relaxes a little. "You don't seem happy about it."

"Can you tell?" I twist my lips. "I'm trying to understand why it is that I can't get enough of you."

"Sexual attraction. It happens. You can't always choose who you have chemistry with," she says in a soft voice.

Tell me about it. "That's why I'm going to take your arse."

She stiffens and I squeeze her shoulders. "Relax. I'm going to make sure you enjoy it."

I walk around to stand behind her, then slide my hand down her knee and push it up so her foot is balanced on the bench.

"You okay?"

She nods.

"Speak to me, tell me you're fine with this."

She glances at me from the corner of her eye. "I'm fine with this."

"Good girl." I push her hair off the nape of her neck, then press a kiss there.

She shivers.

I take her arm and place it against the wall of the shower.

Her shoulders stiffen. That won't do at all.

I reach around and cup her breasts in both of my hands. I balance them, weigh them, then use my fingers to run circles around them. I tweak her nipples, and a shudder runs down her body. "I fucking love your tits." I slide my fingers down her stomach to her pussy. I play with her clit and she gasps. She leans back and into me. I stuff two fingers inside her, and her body jolts. I continue to tweak a nipple, then curl my fingers inside her.

The water pours down on us and steam bellows out. My cock throbs between us, but I ignore it. I continue to finger fuck her, move my other hand down to her pussy to scoop up some of her cream, then bring my hand up to her face. I slide my finger inside her mouth. She sucks on it while her pussy clamps down on my other fingers. "You're so damn tight, girl." I bend and press my cheek to hers. "Gonna stuff my cock in your arse and make you come until you feel me there for the next few days." I slide my fingers out of her, reach to the side and grab the conditioner. I step back and pour it into the valley between her arse cheeks.

"Jack." She swallows. "Will it hurt?"

"I hope so."

She scowls up at me. "That's not reassuring, asshole."

"You walked into that. Again." I smirk.

She glowers at me.

So fucking adorable.

"Relax, baby." I squeeze her reddened butt cheek. Red because she still wears my palm prints. Satisfaction heats my chest. My cock thickens further. "I promise, you'll want more of it when I'm done," I murmur.

"Somehow, I doubt that."

"Don't you trust me yet?" I toss the conditioner to the side then slide my fingers between her arse cheeks. I work one of them into her puckered hole, and she tenses.

"Shh." I kiss her temple then ease my finger farther inside.

"Oh," she gasps.

"How's that?"

"Not too bad," she admits.

I pinch her chin and turn her head toward me, then bend and take her lips. I nibble on her mouth until she sighs and relaxes. I continue to kiss her as I slide my hand down to her clit and apply pressure. She shudders, spreads her legs wider, and I slip a second finger inside her back hole. I continue to kiss her, thrusting two fingers inside her pussy. I curve them and she arches up and against me. I manage to thrust a third finger inside her back channel. She freezes.

"Shh," I whisper against her lips. "Let me in, baby."

A whine spills from her lips. I continue to rock my fingers inside her pussy and her back hole, continue to finger fuck her until she clenches down. The water pours over us, and her cum moistens my digits inside of her. I press kisses up her cheek to her ear, swirl my tongue inside, and she shivers.

"Oh my god, what are you doing to me?" she groans.

"Just getting started, little girl."

I pull my fingers from her puckered hole, then replace them with my cock. When she stiffens, I grind the heel of my hand into her clit while I continue to finger fuck her pussy. Instantly, she relaxes, and I slide my dick inside. She gasps and clamps down on my cock.

"Easy, baby, easy." I rub my cheek against hers, then kiss the edge of her lips. She turns her head, and I lick her mouth. She trembles. I slant my mouth over hers. She parts her lips, and I sweep my tongue inside to tangle with hers. I curl my fingers inside her pussy and a moan wells up. Her entire body seems to grow languid. Her muscles melt, and I slip in through the ring of muscle of her sphincter. She groans, then wraps an arm around my neck. I pause, allowing her time to adjust to my size. I kiss her deeply, and she pushes herself further into my chest. She digs her fingers into my scalp, pushes out her butt, and I slide in farther. She whimpers, and I absorb the sound. The water from above continues to pour down on us. The contrast of the droplets hitting my shoulders, the honeyed taste of her mouth on my tongue, and her tight channel holding my cock in a vise-like grip is too much. My dick swells even further, pushing against her walls, and she moans.

"I need to fuck you, baby." I pull out slowly, then thrust inside her. She shudders. Moisture bathes my fingers as I finger fuck her pussy with greater intensity. I tilt my hips and bottom out inside her. She trembles. I begin to move, ramping up my speed. Long smooth movements where I can feel every millimeter of her melting walls. Each time I lunge into her, the sound of flesh meeting flesh mingles with the sound of the shower droplets crashing onto the floor. The pressure at the base of my spine tightens, and my thigh muscles spasm. Her pussy quivers around my fingers, and I know she's close. So am I.

I pull my mouth from hers and take in her features, her forehead folded into a grimace of pleasure-pain. I pull out one last time, then thrust forward. Her mouth opens and shuts. She throws her head back and cries out as she shatters. I hold her close, absorbing the shudders of her body as I continue to fuck her. The ball of tightness at the base of my spine coils in on itself, growing even more taut, more rigid. One last time, I thrust forward and bottom out inside of her. My balls tighten. Just like that, my orgasm rams through me, and I come with such force, flickers of darkness dot my eyesight. I manage to keep myself upright and hold her close. The aftershocks ripple through her and me. *Through us.* As they fade away, I become aware of the water pouring down on us.

I pull out of her, then turn her around and lower her onto the shower bench. As I begin to wash her, she wraps her arms about my waist and slumps into me. I reach for the shampoo and work it into her thick, beautiful hair. I unwind her arms from about me, lean her back, then pour out the soap and run my palms down her shoulders and to her breasts, down her stomach, between her legs. The water washes it away.

"JJ." She stirs then. "What are you doing?"

"Washing you." I squat down in front of her and kiss her between her thighs.

"JJ." She shudders.

I swipe my tongue up her slit and she moans.

"I want to eat you out until you come on my tongue again."

She grips my hair and tugs, but it's a half-hearted attempt.

I continue to fuck her with my tongue until, with a little cry, she squirts all over my mouth. Then, I wash her some more, until her clit is engorged and she's holding on to me. I rise to my feet, and cup her cheek.

"How are you feeling now, baby?"

"Like I'm flying." Her voice is heavy with lust, her shoulders slumped. She's well and truly relaxed. Good. I squat down, then kiss the inside of her thigh. She shudders, and I straighten. I soap myself quickly, then run my fingers through her hair, washing away the last of the shampoo suds under the water. Then I massage conditioner into her hair, and she sighs. When we're both clean, I turn off the shower. I walk out of the cubicle and return with a towel that I wrap around her. I draw another over her hair and begin to blot it.

"I can do it," she protests.

"Let me," I insist. I pat down her hair, fold the towel around her head in a turban, then draw her to her feet, tuck the other towel under her arms and secure it above her breasts. I quickly dry myself with a towel before I toss it aside. I scoop her up in my arms again, and she laughs.

"I'm fine. I can walk."

Ignoring her, I walk over to the bed, then place her down. I pull off the shower protector on her foot, then unknot the towel from around her.

"Get in," I pull back the covers on the bed, and she slides in. I walk around to the other side of the bed and slip under the covers. I pull her over and curve around her body, spooning her.

She sighs, "This is nice."

It really is. Warmth sinks into my body. My limbs grow heavy. When was the last time I was this relaxed? And it's not only because I came three times in the last few hours. It's her proximity. Having her in my bed with my arms around her. Her head tucked under my chin. My cock nestled in the valley between her butt cheeks.

"JJ, we do need to talk." She yawns so loudly I can hear her jaw crack. "JJ?"

"Not now." I pull her even closer. "Sleep now."

When I awake, I'm alone in bed.

40

Lena

Seema: All okay, Lena? Haven't heard from you in a while.
Josh: Lena?
Mira: Everything okay with you and Isaac?
Mom: Dinky, I'm sure whatever it is you're dealing with it, just know we're here if you need us.
Josh: Lenaaaa?

I blink away the tears in my eyes. My family has always been supportive, so why are their messages of encouragement making me feel so emotional? Also, what am I going to tell them? I'm fine, but am sleeping with Isaac's father? And Isaac and I have broken up? And I have a feeling things are going to get more complicated? I hold my fingers poised over the phone screen, then click out of the group chat. Not ready for this yet. I'll let them know what's happening. Just... not yet.

I place my phone on the kitchen island, then pick up my cup of coffee. I take a sip of the dark liquid and glance out of the window, when a current of electricity runs up my spine. I hear the heavy tread of his feet a second later. He walks over to stand next to me. "Good morning," he rumbles.

My thighs clench. *What is this crazy reaction to his nearness?* This, after he fucked me three times last night. And then washed every inch of my body like he was memorizing it.

"'Morning," I murmur without looking at him.

He bends and presses a kiss to my temple. I flinch. I don't mean to. It's just such a casual gesture. Such an easy gesture. Such an unexpected gesture. My breath catches. I sense his muscles stiffen, but still don't look at him.

"You okay?" he asks in a low voice.

I nod. "I'm good." I take another sip of the coffee.

"How's your foot?"

"It's fine. I pulled off the bandage and the cuts are already closing up."

He glances down to where I'm wearing my ballet pumps. My foot is fine, but I don't want to risk putting more pressure on it by wearing heels.

"You should keep your weight off it."

"I'm fine. Really." I stare straight ahead.

His gaze lights on my features, but he doesn't speak. After a few seconds, he moves away. The tension drains from my muscles somewhat. I hear him move around the kitchen. He fills up the kettle and switches it on, then reaches for the shelf where I know the teabags are kept. The kettle begins to boil, and he pours water into his tea. I hear the clink of the spoon as he adds sugar to his cup, then his footsteps approach. He walks over to stand next to me again. We drink our individual brews in silence. Outside, the birds chirp. The trees are still. It's still early, not even seven a.m.

I woke up to find myself surrounded by him and was so tempted to stay. But the last thing I wanted was to wake up next to him when I'd be seeing him in the office again in a few hours. And that's complicated further by the fact that he's my boss. Instead, I left his warm bed, and crept down the stairs to the room I shared with Isaac. Thankfully, he wasn't there, and the glass had been swept away. I showered and dressed in my office clothes, then grabbed my phone and my handbag before walking to the kitchen.

"You should have slept in," JJ murmurs.

"And take advantage of the fact that I'm shagging my boss?" I press my lips together.

JJ raises his cup of tea to his lips. He doesn't react to my words, and I do regret my outburst, but I was only saying what he was probably thinking anyway, right? It's bad enough he's my boyfriend's father. He had to be my boss, too? Have I not only ruined my personal relationship with Isaac, but also sounded the death knell on my career? Did I get so carried away by my attraction to this guy that I risked everything I've worked so hard to achieve for my entire life?

"I can hear you thinking," he finally drawls.

I turn away, walk over to the island and place my cup of coffee on it. "Look, JJ, last night was fine but—"

"If you're going to pretend it didn't happen—"

"Oh, it did happen." I squeeze the edge of the counter. "And that's the problem."

I hear his footsteps, then he pauses behind me. He places those big warm hands on my shoulders and kneads. "Breathe, girl, breathe."

"I wish you wouldn't call me that."

"You mean, call you 'girl'?"

"It makes me feel like I'm so much younger than you."

"You *are* younger than me," he reminds me. He continues, "Perhaps you're younger in years, but you've demonstrated a level of maturity that I've found very few people, regardless of their years, possess."

I lift my chin, then glance at him over my shoulder. "Was that a compliment?"

The skin around his eyes crinkles. "What do you think?"

"Can't you at least confess that you were being nice to me, without having to always don that big, bad alphahole disguise of yours?"

"Afraid it's not a disguise. And I was being truthful."

I search his features. "I guess." I lower my gaze, then face forward again. "What happens now?" I bite the inside of my cheek. "We fucked.

Many times. Now, do we go into the office like nothing happened? And Isaac? How is he going to take all of this?"

"For one, I'm moving out of our room and into the studio on the top floor," Isaac's announces from the doorway.

I glance up to find him walking over to stand on the opposite side of the island. His gaze lowers to where JJ's hands are on my shoulders. I try to move away, but JJ firms his hold. Isaac's features harden. He grips the edge of the counter in a move that mirrors mine. The skin stretches across his knuckles.

"Isaac—" I begin

"Don't." He raises his palm. "Please don't say anything."

"But—"

He shakes his head. "Do me the favor of not bringing up any excuses. I know I wasn't the perfect boyfriend, but I still don't understand what you see in him."

"It's just... It's difficult to explain." I lower my chin to my chest. "I can only imagine how difficult this must be for you—"

"Honestly, it isn't."

My eyes pop open in surprise.

"I knew when he stepped between us that day at the party that something was up. JJ isn't the kind of man who'd do something that impulsive. It was clear his emotions got the better of him. In fact, I think it's the first time I saw him give in to his compulsions. It surprised me enough that I began to pay attention to the interactions between the two of you. I saw how he stared at you when he thought no one was looking. I also saw how you looked at him."

"Isaac," I whisper. Was I that transparent? Was JJ that obvious about what he felt for me?

"And then, that day I walked into our bedroom to find him leaving..."

"Nothing happened," I murmur.

"Maybe not. But the tension between the two of you was enough to strip paint from the walls. I may have been an absentee boyfriend, but once I started paying attention to the two of you, it's surprising how much I picked up on."

"I wish you'd said something." I bite the inside of my cheek.

"I take full responsibility for what happened," JJ interrupts. "Lena resisted me until—"

"—she couldn't." Isaac's lips twist. "I still don't see the appeal, to be honest. But I'm also not that stupid. I can see how the two of you react to each other. Fact is, we never had that much chemistry, did we?"

"No, we didn't," I whisper.

Behind me, I sense JJ's muscles tense further. He's still holding my shoulders, but his grip feels more comforting, like he's trying to encourage me. Like we're on the same team. Or maybe, it's because the two of us are standing together on the same side of the counter, and Isaac is standing on his own on the other side.

"I want you to complete the project and deliver the paintings to all of my offices," JJ cuts in.

"Oh, I intend to, and it's not because I want to keep my word to you." Isaac scoffs.

"Of course not," JJ drawls.

"It's because I promised *you*." Isaac turns his gaze on me. "I said I'd keep my end of the bargain, and this time, I intend to."

Guilt squeezes my rib cage. My stomach churns. I try to move around the counter so I can get to Isaac, but JJ's hold stops me. Tension radiates from his big body. It's as if he knows I'm torn between him and Isaac, and he's worried about losing me. To be honest, I'm worried about it, too.

What I did to Isaac was wrong, wasn't it? He was a far-from-perfect boyfriend, but he was the only person in my corner when I lost my best friend. *But he took advantage of your grief and made his move on you when you least expected it.* I'd never wanted to be with him, but he was there and it was convenient. And now I'm making excuses for myself. I pull away again, and this time, JJ releases me. I walk around the counter to Isaac.

"Thanks, Isaac, it means a lot to me," I murmur.

Isaac looks between my eyes. "I never deserved you, Lena. I know you're upset with me because I moved in on you so quickly after Ben's passing, but you and I both know, I never would have fallen for him. I may be bisexual—"

JJ stiffens, but doesn't say anything.

"— but he was never more than a friend for me. You, however, refused to look at me while he was alive. And even after, you were so resistant. But I wanted you, Lena."

"Only because you couldn't have me." I swallow.

"You mean, the way my father couldn't have you as long as you were my girlfriend?" He glowers at JJ. "Not that it stopped that asshole from going after you."

"Watch your mouth, boy. I'm still your father," JJ growls.

Isaac scoffs. "That was never true growing up, and it's even less true now."

JJ rounds the counter. He approaches Isaac and I shoot out my arm to stop him. "Don't, JJ, please." I scowl at him from the corner of my eye.

JJ glares at Isaac. The two of them trade the kinds of looks that convey how much they hate the sight of each other. Even more than they did a few days ago. *And I'm the cause of it.* My stomach bottoms out. My head spins. How did I get caught up in all this drama? All I wanted was a roof over my head and a chance to get my life on track. Instead, I've plunged myself straight into the worst situation of my life. *And it's all my fault.* I couldn't control my impulses, and now I've succeeded in driving a deeper wedge between these two men, which hadn't been my intention at all.

"Don't worry, I'm not going to hit you." Isaac narrows his gaze on his father. "I need to care enough to do that, and honestly, I don't. Any relationship between us was over a long time ago, and you've killed any chance of a reconciliation."

JJ's shoulders bunch. Beneath his tan, he pales. He swallows; the tendons of his throat move but he stays silent.

"Isaac, you don't mean that." I turn on him. "He's still your father… your family."

"You were… *Are* my family, Lena." His shoulders deflate a little. "I know I treated you like shit. I wasn't thinking of the effect my actions would have on you. I wasn't thinking of anything but my art. I don't blame you for what you did. I just need some time to get my brain wrapped around everything." He spins around and heads for the door.

Worry knits my insides and bile bubbles up my throat. "Where are you going, Isaac?"

He pauses, then turns to face me. "I'm not going to do anything stupid." His lips twist. "It's best I get on with my paintings, don't you think?"

He leaves, and the ensuing silence is thick with unsaid words. I'm very aware of JJ standing next to me. His entire body seems to have turned to granite. Except for the heat that pours off of him, he may as well be a statue. I wipe my damp palms on my skirt. Apprehension is a stone that weighs down my belly. I draw in a breath, and my lungs burn.

I can neither move my feet nor turn to face JJ. *My fault. This is all my fault.* Why did I have to follow my instinct? It didn't feel like I was doing anything wrong when I was with JJ and yet, technically, I was Isaac's girlfriend when I did. I should have broken things off with him a while ago, but I hadn't had the courage to do it. In my mind, I moved on from him a while ago... Probably the day he said he didn't care if we didn't have a roof over our heads. When he refused to take responsibility for our well-being, I lost respect for him. I stopped seeing him as a partner, and instead, regarded him as more of a responsibility. And maybe that's what stopped me from ending things with him. It didn't feel right to leave when he was trying to figure his stuff out. I thought I was doing him a favor, but I only complicated all of our lives. And now... Things are such a mess. What am I going to do next?

"Breakfast?" JJ asks in a normal voice.

I turn on him. "You had a falling out—likely, a permanent one— with your son, and you want to eat breakfast?"

"You need to eat to survive," he says in that patient 'Dad' voice of his, the one I hate and love because it makes me feel taken care of, but it also emphasizes the age gap between us.

"I don't want to eat."

"You are going to eat." He lowers his voice to a hush and my pulse skitters. He's going to use the force of his authority to make me concede to his wishes again. But I'm not going to let him win. Not this time.

"I'll eat, on one condition."

41

JJ

When Isaac was a toddler, and on the occasions I actually made it back home for his bed time, he'd insist I read to him. It always pissed off his mother. The fact that I wasn't around that much meant that when they did see me, the kids would be all over me, to such an extent that they'd ignore their mother. She wasn't the best mother, but she also wasn't the worst. She never compromised on her social life, but she was there for them. Sure, I compensated her well enough for it, but at least she was physically present for the parenting role, while I was mostly absent. And so, during the times when I was there to read to Isaac at bedtime, he'd fight sleep. When I'd ask him to close his eyes, he'd negotiate with me. *Would I be around in the morning when he woke up? Only then would he close his eyes. Would I read one more book? Would I lay down next to him? Only then would he fall asleep.*

Lena's question reminds me of all those times. Does everything have to be a negotiation with this generation? And how warped is it that I'm comparing her to my son. She's far more mature, more responsible, more worldly wise than my son has ever been. That doesn't change the fact that she's his age. That I moved in on my son's girl-friend and used every charm offensive in my arsenal to seduce her. The inevitable happened, and my son is so pissed off with me, I might never be able to salvage the relationship with him. And yet, I can't bring myself to feel upset about it. Partly, because I'm confident I can win Isaac back. But also, because nothing could have stopped me from going after her.

"JJ?" Her forehead knits. "Did you hear what I said?"

"You won't eat until I give you what you want," I drawl.

She tips up her chin. "Separate bedrooms."

I blink. "What do you mean?"

"I can't stay with you in your room under the same roof as Isaac."

"Why the fuck not?"

She opens and shuts her mouth. "Because I can't be fucking you when he is so clearly hurting," she finally admits.

"So, you'd rather deny what's between us? You'd rather hurt us?"

"If that's what it amounts to, yes. I didn't break up with him before sleeping with you, JJ."

"The two of you didn't even have a relationship."

"We had enough of a relationship to have sex the day before you fucked me in your Rolls."

I wince. "I should have moved in on you before that happened."

"I was still his girlfriend." She firms her lips.

"There was no emotional connection beyond friendship between the two of you. None whatsoever," I growl.

"And there is between us?"

"Isn't there?" I bend my knees and peer into her eyes. "There was something between us from the moment we met. It might have taken me time to acknowledge it, but I have and now, there's no turning back."

She searches my features then swallows. "I... I'm not so sure, JJ."

"What the fuck does that mean?"

"I slept with you; I don't regret that. But I can't keep doing so. Not when he's here and clearly hurting."

My fingers tingle. I want to grip her shoulders, haul her to me, then kiss her so deeply she forgets about everything else in the world but the two of us. I want to throw her over my shoulder, take her to my room, lock her up there and fuck her until she has no recollection of anything but me, can't feel anything but my cock between her legs, can't smell anything but me, taste my lips, hold my gaze as I bury myself inside her and lock her to my side twenty-four-seven.

"If there's to be anything between us, first, we need to resolve what happened with Isaac."

"Are you saying you want Isaac to give his blessing for our relationship?"

She glances away, then back at me. "I hadn't thought about it that way, but now that you mention it, yes." She blows out a breath. "Yes, I want Isaac to say he's happy for us to be together."

I laugh. "That's never going to happen."

"Then we can't be together, JJ."

"Bull-fucking-shit. This is complete poppycock," I protest.

She stares at me.

"What?" I snap.

"Sometimes I forget how British you are."

"Sometimes I forget you don't have the balls to see through what you started."

Her features pale. "That's not fair, JJ."

"And what you're doing to us is?"

"There's no *us*." She crosses her arms across her chest. "Not yet."

"You're wrong, there was an us the moment we set eyes on each other."

"So you keep saying."

I widen my stance. "Are you saying you weren't attracted to me from the moment you saw me."

"I'm saying maybe we should have waited. Maybe it would have been better if I had broken things off with Isaac first."

"Something you weren't going to do for a very long time. All I did was nudge you along in that direction."

She stiffens. "So, you were manipulating me?"

"I was simply making you see how explosive we could be together."

"Sex isn't everything, JJ."

I laugh. "Sex is the bedrock of any relationship. And what we have isn't normal sex." I close the distance between us. "It's a dirty, filthy, forbidden, erotic coupling that gets more intense every time we're together."

Her cheeks heat. Her breathing grows rough. If I glance down, I'll see her nipples bead through her blouse. She's as turned on as I am.

The air between us electrifies. Every nerve ending in my body stands to attention. I've never felt so alive as I have in her presence. It's as if I'm turning back the clock when I'm with her—finding my mojo, rediscovering what it means to want a woman with so much intensity that every part of me seems to be reinventing itself. "Lena," I cup her cheek, "I want you like I've never wanted anything else before. My need for you is more than my urge to succeed. It's more enormous than my thirst for power, more fervent than my ambition to make so much money that no one in this world could ever touch me or my family."

"And yet, you didn't make time for your children."

Pain coils in my chest, and I shove it away. "I was younger, more... foolhardy. I thought there'd be time to get to know them when they were a little older. I was wrong, of course. By the time I realized my mistake, I was too late."

"And you committed the same mistake again when you put your own happiness before your son's."

"He doesn't need you. He's not in love with you, girl," I snap.

"And you are?"

"I—" I open and shut my mouth. *Am I in love with her? Am I?* I hesitate.

Something anguished flashes in her eyes. Her features twist—it's barely noticeable; I almost miss it, and I would have if I weren't watching her so closely—then she composes herself. "Thought not." She takes a step back from me. "Whatever this is between us, JJ, I'm not sure. But I can't be as callous as you. I can't give up all semblance of decency and shack up with you when Isaac is hurting."

"You're wasting time. This relationship with Isaac is a red herring.

You know what we have is the real thing. You know you want this, Lena, so why are you denying it?"

"Because I still care about Isaac. He's my friend. And it seems callous to flaunt our relationship in front of him."

"He'll come around, Lena. He'll understand that this is best for all of us."

"You mean for you. This is best for you," she argues.

"And for you. You know it, Lena."

"All I know is I need time to work through what I'm feeling. I need a clear head to figure things out, which means I need to keep my distance from you."

I curl my fingers into fists. The fact that she needs to keep her distance so she can think things through means she's as affected by my nearness as I am by hers. That means something, right?

"You want us to get Isaac's blessing? Fine. Let's go out to dinner together."

"What?"

"The three of us. You, me, and Isaac—family dinner tonight."

Her features take on a doubtful expression. "I'm not sure if that's a good idea."

"It's just dinner," I say impatiently. "Surely the three of us can sit around a table and have a civilized conversation?"

"Have you managed a civilized conversation with Isaac even once so far?"

I open my mouth and shut it again.

"That's what I mean." She raises her hands. "Dinner isn't going to work. We need something else. Maybe we need to do something where our hands are occupied. Something where we don't have to just focus all of our attention on each other."

"I'd happily focus all of my attention on you," I shoot back.

She scowls. "You know what I mean. We need to do something that involves physical activity."

I smirk. "I know exactly the kind of physical activity I can indulge in."

"Oh, hush." She rolls her eyes. "I mean, something that keeps us busy… Something like… Bowling."

"Bowling?"

"Bowling."

"Bowling," I say slowly. "I'm not sure *that's* a good idea."

"Why? Surely even you're not too old to enjoy it."

I scowl. "Don't sass me, young lady."

"Don't talk to me like I'm sixteen."

"Sometimes you act older than your years. Other times, I swear you act like someone much younger than your years, purely to aggravate me. If you want to be spanked, you only have to ask me and I'll gladly oblige."

Her blush deepens, and her pupils dilate. A telltale sign that she definitely does relish the idea.

"Goddamn…" I shake my head before I bend my knees and peer into her features. "That's what this is about. You like being a brat. You like acting out just to find out if I care. You want me to take charge of you and direct you and command you. You may be career-oriented and independent, but in bed, you're submissive."

She flips her hair over her shoulder. "I have no idea what you're talking about."

"Don't lie, little girl." I move in closer until our feet bump. Until my breath raises the hair on her forehead. Until the nervous tension vibrating off of her body hits me squarely in my chest. My groin hardens. My gaze narrows. A familiar excitement licks my veins. The thrill of a chase. The thrill of closing a deal in the boardroom. Of sitting across from some of the most seasoned gangsters in the land and pitting my wits against them. It's always a mind game. A contest of who's going to blink first. And I never do. I've never lost a challenge before, and I don't intend to now, either—even though all those confrontations pale in comparison to the struggle that shimmers between us.

Run, little girl. If I catch you, you're mine.

"Excuse me." She blinks rapidly.

I peel back my lips. "You want to play? This is your chance. You get to choose the game, and if I win then… *I* win."

"What do you mean?" She scowls.

"You want to go bowling, so be it. But if… *when* I win, you will move into my room, no questions asked."

"And if you lose?"

"I won't."

42

Shall I compare thee to a summer's day?
Thou art more lovely and more temperate:
Rough winds do shake the darling buds of May,
And summer's lease hath all too short a date...

-Sonnet 18, William Shakespeare

Lena

The ball slams into the middle pins and all the pins topple over. "Strike!" I fist pump and do a little dance. I turn to find JJ watching me with a strange look on his face. Isaac is sprawled out on the bench near the control panel where we'd earlier keyed in our names. I booked us into a bowling alley not far from the office. It didn't take much to persuade Isaac to join us. Probably because Isaac's a decent bowler, or so he's told me. As am I. JJ, on the other hand, seems to be floundering. He's dressed in bowling shoes, worn jeans, and a black T-shirt that stretches across his chest. He runs his fingers through his hair and his biceps bulge. It's the first time I've seen him dressed in something other than his suits, and whoa, it takes his appeal to an entirely different level. He was already the sexiest man I've ever set my eyes on, but with his hair mussed up, and that perpetual scowl on his face, now tinged with frustration, he looks younger. Fiercer. Even more determined, if that's possible. My belly clenches. A pulse flares to life between my legs. It doesn't matter what he's wearing; my body clearly digs him.

"Your turn." I stab my thumb over my shoulder, then walk over to grab my beer from the table next to the panel.

JJ rolls his shoulders. He stares down the bowling lane at the new set of pins which have been replaced at the end.

I take a deep pull from my beer bottle, follow him as he walks over to pick up the ball. He turns to the lane, then hesitates. He lets the ball dangle from his fingers as he focuses on the pins. The seconds stretch. A beat. Another.

I sit down on the bench next to Isaac, keeping enough distance between us that we don't touch. "I'm glad you could make it," I murmur, my gaze fixed on JJ.

His shoulders stretch his T-shirt, which molds to the planes on his back. From this viewpoint, the way his torso tapers in at the waist then meets that tight butt of his is pure eye-porn. His jeans cling to his powerful thighs and damn, there's something about how he fills out a pair of jeans. I've always been a sucker for a man who wears his jeans like he was born in them, and considering how much I love JJ in suits, I thought he'd converted me, but JJ in jeans is… A whole new level in debauchery.

"—Lena, you listening to me?"

"Eh?" I whip my head around to find Isaac is scowling at me. His lips turn down in an expression I remember from all the times we fought. His jaw is tight, and a pulse throbs at his temple. He glances to where his father leans forward, his knees bent. His fingers hooked in the ball as he lowers it to his side.

"I'm going to win you back, Lena, I'm not letting you go without a fight."

"Isaac." I turn to him. "Please don't do this. Don't make this situation worse than it already is."

"I'm making the situation worse? You're the one who cheated on me."

"I—" I flinch, then lower my chin to my chest. "You're right. I shouldn't have acted on my impulses—"

"I don't blame you. I'll bet he didn't make it easy for you. Bet he manipulated things so you had no choice but to constantly see him twenty-four-seven in his office, on the way to work, after work. And I wasn't around, Lena. I know I should have spent more time with you and made sure you were settling in. I left you in a strange place on your own and went off."

"You were working on your art, Isaac."

"Art." He blows out a breath. "I've used it as a crutch, as a way to channel all of my frustrations and my sorrows. I've used it as an excuse for too long."

Well, great, now he comes to his senses, when it's too late.

"Isaac, I—"

"You don't need to apologize. You don't need to say anything. I don't blame you. I really don't."

"You should, Isaac. I was as much at fault as JJ. We both wanted each other… We still want each other." I force out the words through the ball of emotion that clogs my throat. I have to say it. I have to be upfront. No more hiding. No more pretending the connection between JJ and me doesn't exist. It's why I called Isaac here today, didn't I? So I could be truthful with him.

Isaac's shoulders tense. He squeezes his fingers around his beer bottle with enough force that the skin across his knuckles stretches white.

"I'm still not giving up on you, on us, Lena."

"Isaac, please, you—"

There's a crash as pins tumble over. Isaac and I turn to find JJ raise his fist in his version of a fist pump. In other words, it's a restrained, leashed gesture that has his biceps bulging. The muscles of his body are coiled. Excitement vibrates off of him. He spins around and his blazing dark eyes meet mine. "Strike."

"It's not possible. Not possible." I survey the scoreboard. JJ leads with 120 points. Isaac is on his heels with 100, and me? I'm at 80—I blame it on being distracted by the sight of JJ's butt. Of course, he's fit and I've seen his ass without clothes and felt how firm and unyielding it is. But seeing it clad in jeans is an entirely new level of eyegasm, honestly.

I lean forward on the bench with my arms balanced on my knees. "You lied to me," I say through gritted teeth.

"I've never lied to you," JJ says in a voice that drips with sincerity.

Oh no, I'm not falling for that.

"You said you weren't good at bowling."

"I never said that."

"You implied it."

"Nope. I didn't."

"There you go, lying again. Can you even hear yourself?" I scowl without taking my gaze off Isaac. Feet apart, stance relaxed, knees bent slightly, he's holding the ball at waist length with his non-bowling hand supporting it from the bottom.

"I said I wasn't sure it was a good idea," JJ drawls.

"You implied you weren't good at bowling."

"That's what you took the implied meaning to be."

"You could have corrected me. You could have told me you were a bowling monster."

"I have news for you," he murmurs.

Just then, Isaac moves forward until he reaches the foul line and releases the ball. It rolls down the lane, curves midway, and hurtles dead center toward the middle of the pin set. All ten pins topple over.

"Yes!" He punches the air, pivots, and does a little victory dance. He walks over to hold his palm out to me. If he thinks I'm going to high five him, he's mistaken.

"You could have told me," I glower at him.

He lowers his arm, a look of confusion on his face. "Told you what?"

"That you and your dad are like *The Big Lebowski?*"

"The Big what?" Isaac asks.

"*The Big Lebowski*. The movie with Jeff Bridges in which he's mistaken for a millionaire by the same name and enlists his bowling buddies for help in tracking down the millionaire's missing wife?" JJ supplies helpfully.

I jerk my head in his direction.

"If you think you can get into my good graces by repeating the IMDB synopsis of *The Big Lebowski,* you're sadly mistaken," I spit out.

"Just trying to help," JJ murmurs.

"Well, don't." I snap at the same time Isaac's frown deepens.

"IMDB? What's that?"

JJ opens his mouth to answer, and I shoot my hand up in the air. "Don't even bother." I jump to my feet, turn, and walk away.

"Where are you going?" JJ calls out.

"Lena, the game's not over." Isaac's voice reaches me.

"It's over as far as I'm concerned."

"Wait, let me call the driver." I hear footsteps approach, knowing it's JJ.

"Don't." I glare at him over my shoulder. "I need some time alone, okay?"

"But—" JJ frowns.

"Hey, let me come with you." Isaac draws abreast.

"No way. I don't want anything to do with either of you right now."

The men exchange glances.

Isaac turns to me. "What did I do?"

"For one thing, you didn't tell me that your father's practically a professional bowler."

"You didn't ask.

"All along, the two of you were laughing at me, no doubt. Was it funny watching my pathetic attempts at bowling when the two of you are clearly such experts at it?"

"It's one of the few activities we did together growing up," Isaac admits. "This and cricket. He" —he jerks his chin in JJ's direction— "was insistent I learn how to play it."

"Not that it did much good," JJ mutters.

"Yeah, well, cricket's a boring game. I much preferred bowling."

"That's because you lot prefer a game which is all brawn. Cricket is much more strategic: so much of it is played in the mind."

"B-o-r-i-n-g," Isaac sings out.

"Whatever. I'll see the two of you back at JJ's place." I half turn, then turn and scowl at both men. "And don't either of you dare follow me."

"I'm so glad you called and came over." Summer West slides a massive glass—or is that a bowl? —of frozen margarita across the counter. We're in her kitchen at the townhouse she shares with her husband Sinclair Sterling. Her hair flows around her shoulders. Slivers of pink stand out among the dark strands. She's wearing a long flowery skirt, a peasant top and ballet pumps. At her feet, Max their dog, pants happily. She raises her glass and clinks it with mine. "Salut."

"Cheers." I take a sip of the frozen liquid. The icy, sweet flavor of strawberries almost masks the tang of the tequila, refreshing as it imparts the warmth I seek. "Yum." I lick my lips, take another sip, then pause. "Should you be—" I jerk my chin toward her barely visibly bump.

"Oh, mine is sans alcohol. Besides, I make these only when I need a brain freeze."

"Clearly you overcompensated for that by dumping your share of tequila into my drink, I take it?"

She giggles. "I might have. Do you mind?"

"Nope, I need it. Also," —I lower my eyebrows over my nose— "a brain freeze?"

She nods. "When I need my brain to stop thinking and want my thoughts to just retreat for a bit. Know what I mean?"

I nod.

"So…" She pulls out a treat from the packet next to her and holds it out to Max. He reaches up, grabs it, then begins to chew it. "Tell me what's bothering you." She turns to face me.

"How do you know something's bothering me?"

She tilts her head, a knowing look on her face. Yeah, okay. Woman's too astute to be taken in by my protests to the contrary.

I take a gulp of the margarita, then cup my fingers around the freezing glass surface. "I, uh… I'm in a bit of a pickle, as you Brits would say."

"Hmm." She plucks the strawberry from the rim and chews on it. "A love pickle, I take it?"

I nod.

"It's JJ, isn't it?"

I lower my chin to my chest.

"The first time I went to meet Sinclair, I was pitching the services of my agency to his company. Turned out I liked him, and not at the opposite side of the table. I'll spare you the details, but suffice to say, I kicked his legs out from under him during our first meeting."

"What?" I choke on the next sip of my drink.

Summer leans over and slaps my back. "Let me back up. That meeting wasn't actually the first time I met him. And the first time didn't exactly go well. Imagine my surprise when I turned up at the presentation to find he was the man I needed to convince to hire my company. And I needed that contract."

"Did you get it?"

"And the man." Her lips kick up. "After, uh, some manipulating on his side, and a whole lot of resistance on my side."

"At least he wasn't your boss," I murmur.

"In a way he was. JJ's the CEO of the company. So what? Is there a clause against dating in your contract?"

"Don't think so, but it doesn't feel right." I wriggle around, trying to get more comfortable.

"Is he abusing his power by sleeping with you? Is that what you're worried about?"

"I would be, except that's not the only complication."

"Oh?" Summer's eyes gleam. "There's more?"

I lower my chin to my chest. *Do I dare say it? I have to say it.* Best to get it off my chest, and to someone who doesn't know me that well. From what I know of Summer, she's chill, so I don't think she's going to get all riled up or judge me. As for my family? They're not the kind to pass judgment, but they've met Isaac. How am I supposed to tell them I'm sleeping with his father? I'm going to have to tell them the status of our relationship at some point. Just not yet.

"There's more." I square my shoulders, then meet her eyes. "I was his son's girlfriend before I slept with him."

43

Lena

Her gaze widens. "So, you and JJ's son—?"

"Isaac." I nod.

"And now, you and JJ?"

I squeeze the bridge of my nose. "I'm a slut; I know."

"Hey, stop." She reaches over and squeezes my shoulder. "Firstly, I'm really glad you reached out to me. I know we've only just met, so I'm honored you trust me enough to confide in me. Secondly, no judgment. You haven't met some of my other friends but we've all been through our own journeys to create the life of our dreams, and it hasn't been easy. We were lucky we were able to support each other, and I'd be privileged if you'd let me do the same for you."

Tears prick the back of my eyes. Guess I miss my family more than I realized. Except, even if they were in the same city as me, I'm not sure this is a situation I'd be able to share with them. Of course, if Ben were alive, I'd tell him, but I did cheat on him, too, in a sense, didn't I? A band squeezes around my chest. Shit, I am a liar and a tramp. I lower my chin to my chest.

"Lena, hey, please don't judge yourself so harshly."

"You don't know what I'm thinking."

"Oh, I think I have a good idea. We women are so tough on ourselves. We never give ourselves a break, do we?"

"Somehow I don't think I deserve it."

"Let me be the judge of that, hmm?" She inches my margarita forward. "Take a sip now, will you?"

"You make it seem almost medicinal." I sniff.

"Oh, it is, I promise." She raises her glass and clinks it with mine. "Bottoms up, then tell me what's on your mind."

I glance doubtfully into the depths of my glass. The frosty pink liquid is deceptively innocent, but I know better. Already, a pleasant numbness permeates my limbs. Also, I don't know how much tequila she put in it, but my vision definitely has a rosy glow around the edges.

"Go on," she urges.

Okay, then. I snatch up the half-full glass of margarita then drain it. So does she. I place the glass back on the counter with a snap before clutching the front of my head. I hear Summer's groan and glance up to find her doing the same. We both burst out laughing. As the pain eases, I realize the numbness has spread to my toes. All of my muscles feel limber. I plant my elbow on the counter and cup my chin. "Hmm, I already feel better."

She tops up my glass from one pitcher and hers from another, then points a finger in my direction. "Come on, fess up, missy."

"There's this attraction between JJ and me. From the moment I saw him, no other man existed for me. It's like I have his features burned into my brain. I carry the imprint of his scent in my veins. I feel his presence as soon as he walks into a room, and when he's not around, I can't stop thinking of him. I can't stop thinking of him anyway." I twist my features. "God, I'm pathetic."

"And you slept with him—"

"Oh, I resisted him and the attraction. Trust me, I tried my best to keep away from him. But it was difficult, considering we worked in the same office, and initially, he'd give me a lift to his office."

"And you're living under the same roof as him."

"It was tough to remain impervious, you know? Everywhere I turned, there he was. His grumpy, glowering face would fill my line of sight. I'd look out of the window and see him swimming. I walked into his room once, and saw him jerking off in his bathroom."

"Wait, what?" It's her turn to choke. "You snuck in on him jerking off?"

"It was a mistake." I huff.

"No doubt." She chuckles.

"No, it really was a mistake. I didn't intend to be in his room. I mean, I went there intending to find out what time he was going to leave for the office the next day, and it's not like his door was locked so—"

"Was it hot?" Her tone is sly.

I blow out a breath. "So hot." I snatch up my glass of margarita and pull on it. "I've never been so turned on in my life. After that, I couldn't see him without imagining him naked, and I was still living with my boyfriend—his son—under his roof."

"I'll bet JJ went out of his way to seduce you. I'm sure it wasn't an error that the door to his bedroom and his bathroom were unlocked, either."

"Hmm, I never thought about that." I hunch my shoulders. "I was so drawn to him that the last time Isaac and I had sex, I imagined it was JJ. Even when I was on my own, I imagined it was JJ."

"What do you mean?"

"There was one time I woke up, sure Isaac was in bed with me, but it was empty. But I was sure he'd been there and made love to me. Only, a part of me convinced myself that it had been JJ."

"Are you sure it wasn't JJ?"

I scowl. "What do you mean?"

"You were under his roof. And your boyfriend wasn't around. You hadn't locked the door. And given he's not exactly a scrupulous person, what's to have stopped him from coming into your bed and making love to you while you were sleeping?"

I blink rapidly. "No, he wouldn't…" *Would he? Would JJ sneak into my room and fuck me while I'm sleeping? Is that why the time I'd come dreaming of JJ it'd felt so good?* I thought I'd been imagining things, which is why I'd woken up so satisfied. And then the time I'd fallen asleep in his office. Both times I'd come so hard, more than I ever had with Isaac. But what if I hadn't been dreaming? What if it had been JJ himself making me come? *It couldn't have been, though… Could it?*

"No, no, no." I shake my head. "It's not possible."

"You're right. He wouldn't do that. He's not as cutthroat as the Seven—that's Sinclair and his friends who run his company with him and whose wives and girlfriends are my very good friends," she informs me.

"I mean, he is rumored to have run an underground organized crime syndicate, so—" I raise a shoulder.

"Rumored? So, you haven't asked him if it's true?"

"We haven't exactly done much talking. Also, I'm still trying to work out what the hell I'm going to do about this situation."

"What situation?"

"This situation" —I wave my hand in the air— "where I want to be with JJ, but I feel sorry for Isaac. I feel responsible for him somehow, you know?"

"You're not his keeper. He's a grown man—"

"Who I cheated on."

"Did you, though?"

"Eh?" I tip up my chin. "I was with Isaac when I slept with his father. In fact, I was sleeping with Isaac, and then I slept with his father."

"And you haven't slept with Isaac since."

I shake my head.

"And you told him—"

"Right away. I couldn't keep it from him. I had to tell him, you know?"

"So, you broke it off with him right after."

"I did kiss JJ before that, and whenever we were in a room together it was as if there was a livewire connecting us."

She fans herself. "That sounds hot."

"You have no idea."

"So, you made out with his father. You were confused. You tried to be a good girlfriend to him—"

"But he was never around. He was too focused on his art, and I get it. It's his art. It's like a third person in our relationship sometimes. And I understand, I really do—"

"Do you?"

I pause. "I wanted to." I stare into the depths of my glass. "I was proud of the fact that he was so talented. I wanted him to be successful. I wanted to support him, but also, I wanted him to understand we had bills to pay. I couldn't completely shoulder it all on my own, you know?"

"It's understandable, Lena," Summer says softly. "You did the best you could."

"I really did. I thought if we stayed in his father's home, it would be a temporary reprieve. Isaac could pull himself together and make a go of his painting, while I tried to find another job and save up to move out of there. I didn't expect to find myself working for JJ."

"Or to fall for him."

"Or to fall for him, and *still* feel responsible for Isaac. He's my friend, Summer. He says he's going to find a way to woo me back. He's moved into his studio on the top floor of the house."

"So, all three of you are still under the same roof?"

I grimace. "It's a mess, right?" I roll my shoulders. "What am I going to do?"

She takes a sip of her margarita. "Maybe you don't need to do anything, for the time being."

"I'm not sure that's an option," I mutter.

"Why is that?"

"I wanted JJ to patch things up with Isaac. They've always had problems. It's nothing new, but this situation has cranked it up to another level. Anyway, we decided to go out bowling."

"Bowling?"

"It was my idea." I blow out a breath. "And JJ, being the master manipulator that he is, insisted if he won then I should move into his room with him."

"With Isaac under the same roof?"

"Exactly. He wants to rub Isaac's nose in it, no doubt. Of course, neither of them told me they were the *Starsky and Hutch* of bowling."

"Isn't *Starsky and Hutch* a buddy cop movie?"

"You know what I mean," I interrupt. "You do, don't you?"

"I think so." She rubs her chin. "I guess you weren't kidding when you said you're in a bind."

"In the mother of all pickles, is what you mean."

She takes a hefty swig of her margarita. "So, what are you doing now?"

44

''...Who could refrain,
That had a heart to love, and in that heart
Courage to make love known?'

-(*Macbeth – Act 2, Scene 3*)

Isaac

I'm not letting her go without a fight. It's the only reason I'm staying under his roof. That, and the fact that this studio is bloody amazing. The first time I entered it, I couldn't believe my eyes. The space is massive. It stretches across the length of the entire floor, with skylights that let in so much light, it feels like I'm floating in a light bubble. There's a bed pushed up against one wall, with a walk-in closet and an attached bathroom. On the other side is a kitchenette with a fully-stocked refrigerator.

As if that weren't enough, there's a separate entrance to the space. So, I can take the steps down and out the side door without running into either of them, if I so chose. In fact, I know she's staying in this house, but I could easily forget about both of them and go for days without seeing either of them. If my brain would let me.

My father might be a bastard, but he got this studio right. He'd created the exact kind of space where I'd love to live and work. To think, I spent all this time running from him... Also, it's exactly why I preferred to keep my life separate from him. He's a canny bastard, and he knew exactly what to say and do to ingratiate himself with me, and I don't want that. I don't want to foster any warm feelings toward him. Don't want to develop a familial sensibility for him. Don't want to feel beholden to him in any way. Staying in the studio seems to come close to that, but goddamn, if this space isn't fine. Best of all, I've been able to create here.

Despite the fact that they're right below me in the house... In spite of the fact that they could be fucking right now... None of that seems to interfere with my creative flow. Which is a massive relief. For the first time in my adult life, I'm able to paint without interruptions. Without worrying about the outside world. Without feeling the obligations I normally felt toward having a girlfriend.

I might have been a shitty boyfriend, but a part of me had tried. Maybe I'd failed, but I'd tried to do good by her. And I was found wanting. It confirms what I've known all along. As an artist, I'm better off being on my own.

My muse is a jealous mistress. She wants me all to herself. I'd been aware of it, but I'd never acknowledged it. And now, I've reached this stage where my own girlfriend preferred my asshole of a father over me.

A part of me doesn't blame her. JJ can be formidable, and despite his age, he's lost none of his appeal. He has a sense of strength about him. A magnetism. Something I gravitated toward, even as a child. He'd made me feel secure, which was why it was a blow when he chose his work over me and my sister.

Bet *she* feels secure with him, too. It's why she's drawn to him. I get it. She didn't have a father of her own, and now she's allowing him to fill that empty space—the daddy-shaped space—inside of her. And that's why I can't give up without a fight. Maybe just to prove a point to her. To show her she doesn't need him, and I'm better than him.

Does it matter? Even if she accepted it, do you see a future with her? Does she see a future with him?

Doesn't matter. Even if I don't see a future with her, I'm not giving up. And I don't care if she imagines a future with him.

I put down my paintbrush and walk to one of the large floor-to-ceiling windows that grace the wall. After Lena walked out of the bowling alley, I began to follow her. JJ stopped me. He asked me to finish the set. I hesitated. He insisted. I gave in and, to be honest, it wasn't too bad. We played that set, and then another. The whole time, we continued chugging beer. And by the time we were done, I had a nice buzz going. I've never gotten drunk with my father, and it seemed significant. Which was the only reason I accepted the ride home with him.

As usual, we ended up exchanging words. He pissed me off when he asked me if I was truly committed to being a painter. Again. It's like the guy doesn't understand me yet. Who am I kidding? He definitely doesn't understand me yet.

Lena had. And I'd leaned on her for support. I'd taken advantage of her good nature. I'd allowed her to shoulder the responsibility of the rent and bills. I'd refused to help her. I had also not been truthful to her completely. I'd fucked the HR manager at JJ's office. The one I was coordinating with about my paintings. And I'd never come clean to her about it. At least she had the courage to tell me when she slept with JJ. It couldn't have been easy but she did it. It's one of the things I love about her. She has more balls than me.

I should complete my paintings, hand them over to JJ's office, and leave. But I can't. If nothing else, I have to show JJ I'm not a loser. That I can still win her over… Sleep with her one last time before I leave.

I glance down at the pool. The blue surface is serene. Next to it, the lights are on in the pool house. It also has a sauna, if I remember correctly. My mother often used it. It doesn't sound like a half-bad an idea. A quick dip in the pool, followed by a stint in the sauna. It'll clear my head, and then I can paint again.

I pull on a pair of swim trunks, grab a towel, then head down. I manage to swim a few laps, before I pull myself out. Grabbing my towel, I walk into the pool house and enter the sauna. "You?" I sneer, then come to a stop.

JJ glances up from where he's sprawled out on one of the benches. Without acknowledging me, he folds his arms across his chest, and closes his eyes. A real piece of work, he is. I stomp over to the bench on the far end and fling myself down. Barely have I sat down when the door opens and she walks in.

45

Lena

Summer had insisted her chauffeur drop me back after that last margarita, and I'd been a bit too lightheaded to refuse. I came home, but despite, or maybe *because* of, the alcohol in my system I was too wired to try to sleep. Isaac's stuff was gone from our room so I knew he'd moved out while I was away. Which was fine. It's what I wanted. Still, I felt a little sad about it. I never thought I'd have a future with him, but he was my friend. The fact that I'm sleeping with his father must have been crushing. I hurt him, no doubt about it.

How am I going to make it up to him? As for JJ? No way am I moving into his room. With Isaac scoring that last strike—he texted me to let me know he'd drawn abreast with JJ in points—it's not like JJ won the game anyway.

How typical of JJ to be so confident that I'd end up doing as he wanted. Well, this time I'm not going to budge. I may have no choice but to stay under his roof, but no way am I moving into his room.

The thoughts buzzed around in my head, and finally, I decided to change into my swimsuit, wrap a robe around myself, and try the sauna. Maybe it'd help relax my muscles and I'd unwind enough to sleep. I marched down and into the pool house and found both of them there.

Now, I look at JJ sprawled in a corner. He's wearing a towel wrapped around his waist. His legs are set wide apart, enough that the towel gapes between them. I spot a flash of his lean brown thigh, the darker hair sprinkled across his legs.

When he sees me, he leans his elbows on his knees. His biceps bulge and his shoulders are still. His chin is lowered and he watches me from under eyelashes. His cheeks are slightly flushed, his hair damp. A lock spills over his forehead, lending a youthful air to his features. A bead of sweat trickles down the demarcation between his pecs. I can't stop myself from following it as it traverses down to his navel, further down to where his towel is knotted at his waist. The muscles of his forearms flex, but the rest of him is a solid, hard, rigid mass of sinews, tendons, peaks and valleys, and divots—which I ran my fingers over the last time I was under him, over him, in front of him, bent over as he took me from behind in the shower. My thighs clench, and the low hum in my core detonates to a high-pitched whine. *Shit.*

A movement catches my attention from the corner of my eye. I tear my eyes from JJ to find Isaac scowling at me. His lower lip juts out, his jaw hard. I raise my gaze to his and find something like helplessness and sadness etched in his features. He, too, has a white towel wrapped around his waist. His body is leaner than his father's, his muscles not as well-developed. His shoulders are as broad, but lack the definition of JJ's. The shape of his jaw, though, is one-hundred percent a mirror of his dad's. And his eyes… Not as dark as JJ's, not as much depth of experience, not as lined around the edges… But the intensity in them is so familiar.

It's as if I'm caught in the crosshairs between them—twin beams of anger and lust and vulnerability. There's this emotion of being unshielded, of being bare to what is to come that emanates from both of them. Heat billows around my feet and swirls about my shoulders.

Sweat beads my upper lip, and pools under my armpits. I walk over to take the bench seat at right angles to both of them.

Turning, I face forward, and flick my gaze from one to the other. Both men are watching me. Neither has spoken a word. Neither has bothered to disguise the interest in their eyes. It doesn't seem to matter to them that all three of us are almost fully naked and in an intimate space. I kick off my flip-flops and my bare feet thud on the wooden floor. The heat slinks up my soles, my calves, my thighs. It could well be the trail left from how both of them rake their gazes up my body. I reach for the bathrobe knotted around my waist, tug on it, and it parts in the front. I sense JJ's body stiffen. Isaac draws in a breath. Keeping my gaze lowered I push the bathrobe over my shoulders, then let it pool around my feet.

I'm still wearing my bikini—it's not like I'm naked—but given how the tension in the room ratchets up, you'd be forgiven for thinking I am. The hairs on my arms stiffen. My fingers tingle and I resist the urge to cover myself. More sweat pours down my back, and all of my pores seem to pop.

I know it's a sauna, but why is it so hot in here? A shiver runs down my spine. Only when my gaze alights on JJ, do I realize I've turned my head to face him. He still hasn't moved from his earlier position, but every muscle in his body is tense. His shoulders are bunched, the tendons of his throat stand out in relief, a nerve pops at his jaw, and his eyes are so dark they seem to be bottomless wells of desire, of lust, of need. Want.

My core clenches, and my toes curl. I take a step in his direction, when a movement catches my attention. I turn to find Isaac sitting upright. His fingers are clenched at his sides. His chest rises and falls. His lips are pressed together, and in his eyes is abject agony.

Something hot twists inside of me. This man held my hand and consoled me when Ben passed. He was there for me when my family was physically in a different space. They were empathetic about Ben's death, but Isaac understood how difficult it was for me to lose him. How I'd always wonder if there was more I could have done to prevent it.

Without him, the two of us were rudderless. We turned to each other, and while I've always wondered if Ben would have been upset if he'd been alive... He left us. He chose to take his own life. He'd been depressed and I hadn't realized it. Neither had Isaac. The two of us bore the brunt of the aftermath. We only had each other then, and we saw each other through the worst.

Now, I'm in love with his father. I stiffen. *Shit, I have feelings for JJ.* Inevitable, perhaps, but did I have to realize that now? When I'm standing in just a bathing suit, in a sauna, with the two of them glaring at me as if they expect me to choose sides.

I turn to JJ. His face is impassive, his jawline even more pronounced with how he's holding himself upright. Everything about him is rigid. Uncompromising. He's a rock. Unyielding. Tough. Immovable. He'd ground me, cocoon me, secure me, take care of me... Maybe stifle me, until I drew the line. He'd be the responsible one. The one who took the cares of the world on himself. The one who'd ensure he'd satisfy my every need... Then walk away. He already broke his rule of never sleeping with a woman more than once. What other rules can I get him to break, I wonder?

Isaac shifts in his seat. I turn toward him and take a step forward. His face lights up, his eyes gleam, and the tension fades from his face. You'd think he'd just been told that his most expensive painting had been bought. "Lena," he breathes.

"Lena." JJ's low voice rumbles behind me. A shiver zips down my spine. *Don't look back. Don't.* I take another step toward Isaac, when— "Lena!" JJ's voice rings out behind me.

Every muscle in my body tenses. Something deep inside of me insists I turn and walk toward him. My feet feel like they're stuck to the ground, I force myself to keep going.

"Lena, stop." The authority in JJ's tone slices through me. My entire body jolts.

"Lena, please." Isaac holds out his hand.

46

JJ

Don't do this. Don't.

Isaac holds out his hand and Lena closes the distance to him. She places her hand in his.

Before I know it, I realize I'm on my feet. My heart is pounding so hard against my rib cage, it's as if I've run a marathon. My pulse thuds at my temples. Steam billows in front of me, and when it clears, it's to find she's sitting sideways in his lap, her arm around his shoulders, his hand on her hip. She raises her head, and he lowers his. Their lips meet.

Adrenaline laces my blood. My chest feels like it's being cleaved in half. I've never lost a business transaction. Never lost a fight with an opposing clan. I've straddled the line between black and white. I've come close to tipping over the edge, to losing the battle of my will…

Once… When I knew I needed to be home more—to salvage the remnants of my family, to tie them together, to ensure my children didn't feel the lack of affection I had growing up. I failed at that.

And I'm failing now. I wanted her to be mine for a little while longer. Until I had my fill of her. And set her up so she wouldn't have to worry about money, or a job, or her future. She'd be free to find another. And then, I'd make things up to my son. Ensure his paintings were seen and enough were sold that he'd be able to launch his career. That's what I had planned for. And now everything is falling apart in front of my eyes.

"Lena," I growl.

She stiffens in the circle of his arms. He doesn't let go of her, though. She leans up and whispers something in his ear. His shoulders go solid. He shakes his head, but she reaches up and cups his cheek, forcing him to meet her gaze. Something seems to pass between them. He nods. When he raises his gaze to mine, he seems unhappy but resigned. She follows his gaze, then holds out her hand.

Eh? What the fuck? For the first time in my adult life, I'm at a loss. I can't believe what I'm seeing. Is she actually holding out her hand to me? What does she mean by that? Does she want me to go over? I glance from her to Isaac, then back at her. She tilts her head, a beseeching look in her eyes. She wants me to go over. I glare at her. The color fades from her cheeks, but she doesn't back down. She looks at me steadily, a determined look in her eyes. She tips up her chin and, in that instant, something inside me melts.

A hardness, an immobile, unforgiving knot deep inside fades. I move, and before I can talk myself out of it, I reach the two of them. I grab her hand and tug. She rises to her feet, her movements graceful. Her bare toes brush mine, and a shiver grips me. She's so close, I can smell her strawberries and passionfruit scent. My cock instantly lengthens. I pull on her, and she falls into me. Her breasts brush my chest, the soft flesh of her core pushed into the space above my groin. She swallows, the sound loud in the space. I dip to brush my lips over each of her eyelids, press a kiss to the tip of her nose, to the edges of her lips. To her chin. She moans then arches into me. "JJ."

"How many times do I have to tell you to call me Jack?" I growl.

She tips up her chin, searching for my lips with hers. I turn my head slightly, so her mouth brushes my cheek. "Say it, girl."

Her chest rises and falls. Her heart thunders in her chest, mirroring mine. I nibble tiny kisses up her jawline. I suck on her earlobe, and a whine bleeds from her lips. "JJ... Jack, please."

I turn my head, close my mouth over hers. I bury my teeth in her lower lip, wanting... Needing to mark her. Maybe it's because I know where this is headed. Maybe I can't believe I'm still here... Maybe I need her to be aware that, regardless of what happens in the next hour, she's mine. *Mine. Mine. Mine.* She gasps, and I sweep my tongue inside her mouth. I suck on her tongue, drink from her, kiss her until her nipples are so hard, they dig into my chest. I continue to drink from her, when she stiffens and thrusts her breasts forward, curving her back.

She unwraps one arm from around my neck. Without removing my lips from hers, I glance up and my gaze clashes with his. Isaac has his hands on her shoulders. One of her arms is twined around his neck. He pushes back the hair from her neck, drops a kiss there, and another to the right and another over the curve of her shoulder. I tilt my head, deepen my kiss, and her entire body shudders.

One side of his mouth twists. He lowers himself to his knees on the floor behind her, and she winds her arm around my neck again. He trails his fingers down her spine to where her hips flare. He slides the bottom of her bikini down her thighs and it pools around her ankles, she kicks it aside. He glances up, meets my gaze. I nod. Without removing my mouth from hers I unhook the top of her bikini and ease it over her shoulders, down her arms, until it falls to the floor.

Isaac's lips quirk. Then he squeezes her arse cheeks apart and, still holding my gaze, he swipes his tongue up the valley. Her hold on me tightens and a cry wells up her throat. I swallow it.

It's fucking hot. Watching my son pleasure my girl as I continue to ravish her mouth. It's wrong. It's dirty. It's filthy. It's against all rules of polite society... A society I never belonged to in the first place. I made my choice a long time ago to do what was right for me. And this...

This is right for me. For us. Maybe this is the way to heal the chasm between me and my son. With the aid of the woman who both of us can't seem to get enough of. If, at the end of this, she decides to choose him... Then I'll accept it. I'll walk away from her, from both of them. I won't interfere in their lives. But right now, I have her in my arms. I have him so focused on her that, for the first time in our lives, he's staying and fighting for what he wants, instead of walking away in a huff. For the first time, we're having a conversation—through her—and I'm going to savor it.

Still on his knees, he continues to lave the cleavage between her butt cheeks. She squirms, and pushes her pelvis into my groin. My cock throbs, hard and heavy between us. The blood rushes to my belly, and my thigh muscles harden. I balance her weight on one arm, and drag my hand up to her breast and squeeze her nipple. She jolts, and a low cry leaves her lips. The sound goes straight to my dick, which lengthens further. Sweat pours down my neck. Moisture beads her shoulders, and Isaac's temples, too, are dotted with drops of perspiration.

It's as if a fine mist of desire covers all three of us, coating us in a bubble that is far removed from the rest of the world. In this sauna room, it's just the three of us, and the erotic, forbidden nature of the act that's going to bind us together. I massage her breast, then slide my hand up to curl my fingers around her throat. I squeeze slightly and her thighs clench. Her pussy lips flutter and I know she wants more. I tear my mouth from hers and glance at the bench behind us, then at Isaac. He seems to understand what I'm saying, for he rises to his feet. He unknots the towel from around his waist and tosses it aside before he seats himself.

I lift her up then lower her over him until she's poised above the head of his cock. He grips her under her armpits and she stiffens. "Jack, I—"

"Shh…" I brush my lips over hers. "You made the right choice."

"I did?"

I nod. "Whatever happens next, I'll accept your decision."

Her forehead crinkles. "But—"

I shake my head. Press a hard kiss to her lips. "Open your legs for him, baby."

She searches my features, then does as I ordered.

"Ready?"

She swallows. "Ready."

I glance at Isaac, who jerks his chin. I lower her until his cock brushes her slit. She bites down on her lower lip, and my cock thrums. I bend my knees, close my mouth over hers, and press down on her hips. She slides down further and her body trembles. I lick into her lips, giving her time to adjust. I bring my fingers between us to strum her clit, and she groans.

I sense Isaac moving and glance up to find he's kissing her shoulders, her neck. I push down on her hips inch by inch, until she's completely impaled on him.

She groans and digs her fingertips into my shoulder. "Jack. Oh, god… Jack," she warbles.

"Let him in, baby."

I push my forehead to hers as I circle her clit, then pinch. She lets out a hoarse cry, then throws her head back. I press little kisses down her chin, her neck, between her breasts. Then straighten. I plant my hand on the wall above them, the fingers of my other hand curled in her hair.

"You going to take care of our girl, Isaac?"

He bares his teeth, then pistons his hips up and into her. Her entire body jolts. "Jack." She grips my hip, tilts up her chin. "Jack."

I hold her gaze as Isaac pumps up and into her, again and again. Each time he thrusts into her, her breasts jiggle. Her lips part and her breath comes out in little gasps. Her pupils are dilated, her color high. Her eyes are dazed and the lust in them heightens my desire.

I bend to latch my mouth around her nipple and suck. She groans and curls her fingers in my hair and tugs. I bite her nipple, and she lets out a tiny scream. I turn my attention to her other breast and give it the same attention. Her flesh swells under my attention. She writhes, then pants. She tugs on my hair with enough force that I raise my head. Instantly, she crashes her mouth on mine. She bites down on my lower lip and my cock thickens.

My balls tighten. It feels like I'm carrying stones between my legs, weighed down by the strength of my need for her. My thigh muscles throb. Pinpricks of fire detonate across my skin. She must feel it, too, for she reaches down and cups my balls.

47

Lena

I must be dreaming. That's the only explanation for why I have Isaac's cock inside my pussy and my hands on JJ's balls. I hadn't consciously made a choice when I had stretched out my arm toward JJ. For that matter, I hadn't meant to walk over to Isaac in the first place. But he'd seemed so sad sitting there on his own, with that look of desperation in his eyes. He'd expected me to go over to JJ. I'd expected myself to go over to JJ. But I also knew JJ was stronger than Isaac. He could weather disappointments, bounce back faster. Isaac was more unsure; he was still finding himself.

I hated the fact that I'd come between them, complicating their relationship further. I wanted to mend the chasm between them. Wanted to find a way to get them back together. All of this had been in my subconscious when I'd walked over to Isaac, then extended my hand to JJ. I didn't think he'd join us. He was always so serious, so set in his ways, so very possessive, I was sure he'd be pissed off with me. I was sure he'd jump to his feet and leave. Only, he walked over to us.

Not only did he join us, but he encouraged me to allow Isaac to fuck me, in front of him. And he added to my pleasure. He touched me and knew exactly how to play my body to enhance my pleasure. No surprise there. Something Isaac never bothered to learn in the time we were together. Oh, he was making up for it now. As if he was aware that this was a turning point for all of us, Isaac was tunneling into me with so much vigor that, between his fucking my pussy and JJ squeezing my tits and fondling my clit, I knew I wasn't going to last long.

Now I glance up into JJ's features. His jaw is set, his gaze narrowed. A nerve throbs at his temple. But his eyes? The look in his eyes is confused, vulnerable. It's uncharted territory for him. For all of us. And JJ's still here. It must be so difficult for him to turn his back on his set ways and do something different, something that wasn't his idea. To hold me, to encourage me, and to be there for me as his son fucks me.

He's willing to do it for me. He's ready to leave the choice of what happens next to me… That's what he meant earlier when he said he'd accept any decision I make. He's doing this for me. And I… I want him to join us, to be with us when we hit that pinnacle. I am not going to leave him behind. It's why I reach for the towel knotted about his hips and tug. The towel falls to the floor and he's there. Or rather his monster cock is there, thick, heavy, standing at attention, precum oozing from the slit on its crown.

The muscles of his groin jump and his thighs flex. "What are you doing, girl?" he growls.

I allow one side of my lips to kick up, then cup his balls in my palm and wrap the fingers of my other hand around his cock. His dick throbs and pushes into my palm. Hot, thick, and so hard. The blood pumps through the organ, the head purple and weeping. The scent of his is sherry oak and musk, with an edge of need shot through it. My core clenches and Isaac's chest planes bunch against my back. I want this. I need this. Without taking my gaze off of JJ, I bend and take him in my mouth. His cock seems to thicken further, pressing down on my tongue and shoving against the roof of my mouth with such force I gag. A groan rips from him. His grasp in my hair tightens. "Girl, you're killing me."

I glance up; a tear drop rolls down my cheek. He scoops it up with his thumb and brings it to his mouth. He sucks on his digit, and somehow, it's more erotic than anything we've done together, including this spontaneous threesome I never imagined I'd be part of.

"You sure, baby?" he asks in a low voice. "You sure you want to do this?"

I allow my lips to curve, then tilt my head and take him down my throat.

"Bloody fucking hell," JJ curses. He pulls on my hair and my scalp tingles. Pinpricks of lust sizzle down my spine. My pussy clamps down on Isaac. His grip on my hips tightens. I'll probably have bruises all over my body tomorrow, but it'll have been worth it if I ensure these two men finally see eye-to-eye. It'll be through the medium of my body and it feels so right. So hot. So primal. My womb quivers. Moisture beads my forehead. I'm so close. Too close. I pull back, then lean in, so JJ's dick slips down my throat again. This time he tugs on my hair so I have no choice but to tip up my chin.

"I want to fuck your mouth, baby."

My gaze widens.

"Nod if you want me to."

I do.

"You won't regret this. I'm going to make it so good for you." He pulls me back then forward, and again. He sets a punishing rhythm that has his cock down my throat and out, and down again. Saliva drips down my chin, and tears flow from my eyes. He doesn't let go; he doesn't let up. His gaze narrows and his eyes burn into me, like he's worshipping me and cursing me in the same breath. I swallow, and his shoulders swell. I hum, and his entire body goes still. His biceps bunch and his forearms flex. He pulls out until the throbbing head of his dick is poised at the rim of my lips.

"I'm going to come." He shoves it down my throat. Then his balls contract and he shoots his load.

Behind me, Isaac seems to increase his pace even more. "I'm

coming, Lena. Jesus Christ, I'm coming." A groan rips from him, his thigh muscles ripple and he comes inside me.

JJ pulls out, then cups my cheek and bends to kiss me tenderly. There's a brush on my shoulder and I realize Isaac is raining kisses on the curve of where my shoulder meets my neck. He slides his hands down to massage my thighs and I slump into him. JJ straightens, then as if he can't help himself, he bends and kisses me on the lips again, before he walks to the door of the sauna. He glances over his shoulder and exchanges a look with Isaac. Something silent passes between them. Isaac scoops me up in his arms and rises to his feet.

"Where—" I clear my throat. "Where are you going?"

"You'll see." He follows JJ out the door and into the adjoining shower room.

Of course, this is JJ's home, so instead of a closet-style shower cubicle, this is a space that's almost as large as the sauna. There's a rain showerhead above us, two on the walls on either side of the handle, and two each on opposite walls of the cubicle. JJ flips a switch and water streams down from all of the showerheads. When he turns to us, my gaze instantly lowers to the monster cock that, once more, juts out from his groin.

You know my question earlier about how often could JJ get it up? Consider that answered.

Isaac sets me down on the floor in front of JJ. The water from the showerheads streams over my skin. Delicious ripples of heat sink into my blood. Isaac's body heat envelops me from behind. JJ's immovable chest covers my line of sight. I feel surrounded by testosterone, cocooned by male intentions, wrapped up in swirls of longing, desire, hunger… burning, itching, needy predilection that's surely going to consume me, chew me up and spit me out.

My head spins. I must stumble, for JJ grips my shoulder. At the same time, Isaac squeezes my hip. Just like that, both of their hands are on me, and the arousal wells up deep inside, swarming my cells, crowding my blood. My entire body is a mass of yearning. My chest feels like it's going to burst. I want it. I want it all. And tomorrow can take care of itself.

"Please," I burst out. "Please fuck me."

48

Isaac

The fuck are we doing? I just fucked her while she sucked off JJ. She swallowed his cum while I came inside her. And then, I followed his lead and brought her into the shower, where the three of us are now naked.

What happened earlier… I hadn't been able to resist. I needed to be inside her one last time before walking away. But this? I have a choice. I am not going to stand around and fuck her and indulge in a ménage à trios with my old man. Jesus, that's downright wrong. I back away and, as if sensing my retreat, she turns to stare at me over her shoulder.

"Stay." She blinks the water from her eyes. "Don't leave yet."

"So we can both fuck you again? Is that what you want, Lena? You want me and JJ to fuck you at the same time?"

She winces, then squares her shoulders. "And if I do? Are you going to guilt trip me about it? I didn't hear you protesting earlier in the sauna."

"That was" —I shake my head— "a one-time thing."

"So is this." She walks toward me, and I throw up my hands.

"Don't, please," I burst out.

She pauses. The water beats down on her from the sides.

"You felt sorry for me, so you fucked me. I get it. It was goodbye sex, but this—"

"This is our way of bonding. Of bridging the gulf between us," JJ rumbles.

"Christ, you really are a twisted son of a bitch, aren't you? You couldn't stop yourself form seducing her, and now you want her to have sex with the both of us?"

"It's what I want," she cuts in. "Don't go putting this on JJ. I'm the one who instigated this, and you know it."

"Well, thanks, but your pussy is not so special that it can overcome years of neglect on his part."

She pales, and my heart contracts. "Shit, I'm sorry. I didn't mean that, Lena. I'm just not sure this is a good idea."

JJ steps forward. "You've always been too worried about the world; that's your weakness."

"And you don't give a damn about anyone or anything. You could, at least, take care of her."

"I intend to," JJ retorts.

"I don't need a man to care for me." She raises her chin. "I don't need someone else to take care of me. I've been looking after myself since I was thirteen, and I can do the same without either of you assholes bestowing your charity on me."

She moves forward, then past me. "This was a mistake. Thanks for making me feel dirty over something that I thought was special to all of us."

I grab her wrist. "It was special." I tug and she turns to face us.

"Not with the way you put it. You're already regretting the fact that the three of us were intimate."

I wince. "It's not that I have a problem with threesomes. It's just that it was him."

"It had to be him," she retorts.

"It had to be the three of us," JJ snaps at the same time.

She glances past me at JJ, then back at me. "Can't you forget about the kind of judgment you think people may pass on us and just let this —whatever this is—heal the both of you?"

I swallow. It's true. Whatever resentment I've harbored toward JJ all this time seems to have lessened. I feel lighter, and it's not only because I just had sex... It's because when he impaled her on me, he tacitly gave his consent to her fucking me. It's because he told Lena whatever happened next is her decision. I've never known him to be so open, so amenable. It's like, for the first time, we're communicating. And it's because of her.

Lena slides her fingers down to twine with mine. She slides back and tugs me. I follow. She takes another step back, then another. "I want you to fuck me." She spins around to face JJ. "I want the both of you to fuck me at the same time."

My heart squeezes in my chest. My groin hardens. A flush of heat sluices through my veins. "Are you sure?"

"Very," Lena murmurs without looking at me.

"You won't regret this?" JJ takes her hand in his and brings it to his lips. "You can walk away, right now. Neither of us will be angry. I won't take it out on you, I promise. You no longer need to be my executive assistant. You can choose any job within the company. I'll ensure the salary covers accommodation for you until you have a chance to get back on your feet. It's included in the package anyway." He glances at me over her head "And the same goes for you, Isaac. It's the least I can do to make up for being the shitty parent I was."

I open my mouth to reply, but Lena shakes her head. "That's very generous of you, but I still want this. I want the two of you to fuck me. At the same time."

JJ's chest rises and falls. He peers into her eyes, and whatever he sees there must satisfy him, for he nods. "Let's show our girl how the Kane men can satisfy her every need." He glances up at me. "You up for the challenge?"

The canny asshole. He's phrasing it so I won't back down. The surest way to get me to comply is by pitching it as a competition. He knows how to wind me up, for we're too alike, he and I. I know his intentions, yet I can't stop myself from taking the bait. "Question is, are you? Let's not forget your vastly advanced age."

JJ laughs. I blink. I've never seen him laugh this openly. His features are softer. He seems years younger, like the father he could have been when I was a child.

In two steps, he closes the distance to her. He plants his hands on her hips and lifts up. She yelps, grips his shoulders, then locks her legs around his waist. In one smooth move, he breaches her.

She gasps. Her body shudders. "Jack, oh god. You're filling me up. You're stretching me. It still hurts, Jack."

He instantly freezes. "Do you want me to stop, baby?"

This time it's Lena who laughs. "You walked into that one, didn't you, old man?"

JJ seems taken aback, then his features light up. "You're learning fast, little girl."

The two of them grin at each other, and something passes between them. It's then I realize how well suited they are for each other. Lena brings out the caring, protective, tender side of JJ—a side I've never seen until now. And he, in turn, makes her feel cherished. He treats her like she's his most precious possession, and she positively blooms under his attention. The chemistry between the two of them is unmistakable. But it's more than that. There's companionship and affection, and the kind of connection I'd hoped to forge with Lena but which I understand would not have been possible. Lena and I were never meant to be together—not as soulmates. As friends, maybe. But not as partners. Not as husband and wife.

I take a step back, but as if he senses my thoughts, JJ snaps his gaze on me. "You going to take our girl's arse? You going to make her orgasm so hard and so many times that she'll forget anything else but this moment?"

My guts protest. Everything inside me insists I show him the finger, then turn on my heel and walk off. But I don't. For her. I can't leave, for this is the way forward. To heal wounds of the past. To move ahead with a clarity of purpose I've never had before. This… is right. It may be unconventional, but it works for us. I didn't get to where I was in my art by following rules, after all. And this is the same.

"I'm ready." I step forward and cup her butt cheeks. Goosebumps pop on her skin. The jets of water pelt down on us. Steam swirls, enveloping us once more in a bubble. I glance around, and JJ holds up the conditioner. He tosses it over her shoulder. I catch it, flip open the lid, and pour the liquid down the valley between her butt cheeks.

49

Lena

Once more, conditioner is poured down the demarcation of my butt cheeks. Only this time, it's the son, not the father, behind it. Is that weird? It should be weird that only the second man who's going to dilate my back channel is related to the first. That's a *weird* thought. As Isaac plays with my back hole, I clench down with my pussy.

JJ groans in response. "You're so tight, so wet, you're milking me, baby."

His cock swells further, stretching me around his girth. The walls of my channel weep in protest. Flecks of pleasure radiate out from the point of contact. "Let me guess, you're not even halfway inside?"

"I wouldn't say that."

"You wouldn't?"

His grin broadens, until his features seem almost wolfish. "I'm only one-third of the way inside."

"Oh, please—" I glance down to where he's embedded in me, and sure enough, jerkface is not joking. His thick column is stuffed inside me, but there's so much of him still not in me. Just then, the blunt tip of Isaac's digit probes my puckered bud. I gulp. This isn't anywhere near the erotic scene I'd envisioned when I'd asked the two of them to fuck me. That's so classic me. Always an overachiever. Always overextending myself, or in this case, trying to fit large, thick objects into my very small holes. "Umm, maybe this wasn't a good idea."

JJ chuckles. "You don't worry about a thing, baby. We'll make it good for you."

I wriggle a little, and his cock slips in a little further. Heat sears my back. Then the blunt tip in my back hole retreats only to be nudged back in.

"Isaac." I try to turn my head, but JJ grips my chin.

"Look at me."

"Jack… I—"

"Shh, I always keep my promises, baby." I raise my gaze and am instantly lost in those dark black holes that are his irises. They aren't completely black, either. It's something I noticed when we fucked the last time. There are tiny silver-gold specks that flare when he's angry or experiencing high levels of emotion, as he is now. He brushes his nose against mine, the action so tender, so real, a melting sensation coils in my chest.

Isaac brushes my hair back and drops a kiss to the nape of my neck. "I promise, I'll take care of you," he murmurs against my skin. He presses little nibbles down the slope of my shoulder. Warmth courses through me. My muscles seem to unwind. The tension drains away, and I slump a little. He slides another finger inside me. The pinch is uncomfortable, but fades away. He begins to move his digits in and out of my back hole. I wriggle a little, and JJ cups my breast. He drags his thumb across the nipple and a whine bleeds from my lips. I lean forward and push my breast into his palm. His lips quirk. He plucks at my nipple, and moisture pools between my legs. He sinks farther inside me, and oh, god, I'm so full. He's so broad, so massive. My pussy quivers, and my shoulders shiver. I lean my head back against Isaac's shoulder and pant.

"You okay?" He presses a kiss to my cheek.

I try to say yes, but all that emerges is a faint garbled sound. My cheeks redden. I sound like I'm being fucked at both ends by two men. Heat sears my features and JJ looks at me with interest.

"Did you think something very dirty just now?" he murmurs.

"And if I did?"

"Then I have to tell you, the reality is going to far outweigh any X-rated thoughts that crossed your mind."

"Hmm." I purse my lips. "Is that a promise?"

He places his mouth over mine. "It's *my* promise."

Isaac withdraws his fingers completely and something much bigger prods at my back opening.

My gaze widens. "Oh, god, Jack, I—"

He closes his lips over mine, then slides his fingers down to my pussy. He rubs the heel of his palm into my swollen clit, and goose-bumps flare across my skin. He continues to kiss me deeply, his cock seeming to throb in tandem to the rocking of my heart. His taste sinks into my palate… his scent surrounds me… his mouth consumes me.

My head spins, and I submit completely. My muscles turn to jelly. Isaac slips in through the tight ring of my sphincter. A moan wells up. Jack swallows it. He pulls out slightly, then pistons his hips forward. My entire body shudders. The vibrations flow over me, down my back, over where I'm connected to Isaac.

He steadies me with one hand on my outer thigh. The other he slaps onto the wall of the shower. He pulls out, then thrusts into me, and the rocking motion swings all three of us forward. JJ curls his fingers around the nape of my neck, holding me upright, then he pulls out and slams into me. The wet sucking sound of flesh meeting flesh is evident over the sound of the shower. Isaac picks up the motion and retreats, then plunges forward again. He bottoms out inside of me, hitting a place deep inside. I gasp, and tendrils of sensation spread out from the point of contact. I feel like I'm caught in the middle of an erotic see-saw. I've never been this crammed. This packed. This stretched with the ebb and flow of fullness that swirls out from my core.

The tension coils harder, faster, higher, brighter. The climax crawls up my legs, my thighs, my spine. My pulse begins to thud faster, the blood pumping harder at my pulse points in my ears. *Th-thump. Th-thump.*

I hear the sound of Isaac pant. Of JJ growl. I'm caught in a maelstrom of erotic impulses, all tendons and skin and electric current that swirl faster and faster. I'm dimly aware of being rocked backward and forward over and over again. It's a smooth, synchronized move which they might as well have rehearsed. That's how much in tandem both of them are.

I can't move, can barely breathe. I am one big mass of lust, of desire, of sensations that are pulling me out of my body. Their movements speed up further, almost frantic now. JJ grunts as he slams into me. Isaac gasps as he propels forward and into me. Faster, faster. My nerve endings all seem to spark at once. My brain cells seem to fire in tandem. The orgasm crashes over me. I open my mouth to scream but JJ is already there.

He absorbs the sounds and continues to kiss me as he fucks me. As his son fucks me. Flickers of darkness flash across my line of sight, and I slump, my arms and legs useless. I'm aware of both of them still fucking me through the aftershocks, then Isaac yells. His dick pushes against my walls, crowding me, sending another burst of sensation up my spine before he groans and comes inside me. Then it's only JJ. He cups my cheek, his touch gentle, as he continues to kiss me, until finally, with a growl, he, too, empties himself in me. I float for a while, unable to move, caught between father and son, with their cocks still pulsing inside me. Isaac is the first to pull out. He pinches my chin, turns my face to him, and brushes his lips across mine.

"Thank you, Lena," he whispers, his voice almost humble.

He positions my body so my head is cushioned against JJ's shoulder. I'm aware of my legs being lowered to the ground. JJ pulls out of me, and already, I feel so empty. I cuddle into his chest, unable to open my eyes as he washes me. Then the shower is switched off. Someone— JJ? Isaac? Both of them rub me down. I'm swaddled in a towel and lifted into someone's arms. The rocking motion of being carried lulls me to sleep.

Voices filter through my subconscious mind. I fight my way up through layers of sleep. I crack my eyelids open, find I'm on my back under the covers. I'm in bed. My bed? I glance around the room. No, not my bed. JJ's bed. There's only one lamp on and it bathes the room in a dim golden glow.

"That's not going to happen again," JJ says from somewhere to my right. I don't dare turn my head, else they'll find out I'm awake.

"I know," Isaac replies. He's sprawled to my left. From my line of sight, I can just make out their legs stretched out on either side of me. Both are wearing identical gray sweatpants. I bet neither has bothered to pull on a shirt. Again, I'm not raising my eyes to take in their naked torsos, as much as I'd love to feast my gaze on that vision. *Haven't you had enough, you slut? You fucked both of them… Or rather, they fucked you. At the same time.* And it was… Incredible.

I come awake with a start to find I'm alone in JJ's bed. I glance around, and the mattress on either side of me is mussed. *Huh? Did they both sleep with me in the same bed?*

I stretch, and my muscles feel limber. I swing my legs over the side of the bed and stand up. My core protests. My back channel twinges. But otherwise, I feel fine. No, I feel great. Like I've had an intensive workout and the blood is pumping through my body with renewed vigor.

I glance around and find my clothes laid out on a chair. Huh? It has to be JJ. It's exactly the kind of thing he'd do. I step toward the jeans and T-shirt laid out. That won't do. It's too casual to wear to work. Speaking of, how late is it? The sun slants through the window, indicating it must be late morning, at least. I walk into the bathroom and grab the first bathrobe I find. I slide into it, and JJ's scent surrounds me. My nipples peak at once. Damn, it doesn't take much for me to be turned on when it comes to him, does it?

I head down the stairs to my room, then take a quick shower before dressing in a pair of slacks and a blouse. I slide my feet into heels, then grab my phone. More messages populate my screen. All of them from my siblings in my family group chat. All of them demanding to know if I'm okay. Shit. I really need to message them—and say what? I slept with my boyfriend and his father? I slept with my boss and his son? At the same time. Whichever way I phrase it, it feels wrong.

I settle for:

I'm good. Busy at work. Will message at length soon. Love you all

Then I drop the phone into my handbag and head down the stairs toward the kitchen. The scent of coffee and cooking reaches me.

As I draw nearer, the sound of voices grows louder. I step into the kitchen to find JJ and Isaac seated at right angles to each other at the island. Their heads are close, their looks intense. They aren't arguing. More like, they're discussing something with such gravity, they don't notice me. Also, Isaac is freshly shaven, while JJ, for once, has a day's growth of whiskers on his chin. He's also dressed in jeans and a T-shirt, as is Isaac.

I walk past them, and JJ is the first to notice me. He drags his gaze down my body and up again. By the time he reaches my face, my blood is pumping fast. Heat flushes my cheeks.

"Morning, did you sleep well?"

An answering throb from deep within my body has me flushing further. "Mmm-hmm. I did. And you?"

"Never better."

"Come sit," he pats the barstool next to him.

I glance at the coffee pot, then back at him. "Wanted to get a coffee."

"Isaac will do that for you."

I blink. "He will?"

"You bet." Isaac flashes me a grin, then hops off his stool. He brushes past and winks at me—he actually winks at me—as he walks toward the kitchen counter.

My head spins. "What was that?" I whisper.

"What was what?" JJ lowers his voice to a hush. "Come, baby, sit next to me."

I've never seen Isaac look this happy or JJ this... mellow. This tender. This... caring. It can't be just the sex we had, though that was phenomenal. Over-the-top. Other-worldly. It was more than sex, actually—more like a bonding experience. Clearly, the men feel the same way, too. I manage to put one foot in front of the other, round the island, and slip onto the barstool that JJ indicated. I place my book on the island.

"Where's Miriam? Doesn't she normally get breakfast? I didn't see her yesterday, either."

"I've given Miriam and Craig the week off." JJ takes a sip of his own coffee.

"You have?"

He nods.

"Why's that?"

"So we have a chance to get to know each other better."

50

JJ

The sex last night was incredible. It was mind-blowing. I had no idea I could come that hard, that long, feel this fulfilled. It was more than sex. It was toe-curling, bone-shattering, mind-jarring, perception-bending shagging.

If anyone had told me I'd share a woman with my son, I'd have shot them first, then laughed. Yet, there's no denying the fact that it happened. And it was mind-boggling. But that's not all. It was a means of connecting with my son. For the first time, I understand just how similar we are. It's why we've been at loggerheads for so much of his life. That, and the fact that I was a shitty father. I've never felt closer to him in my life than I do now. Never realized how much I wanted my family around me until she came into my life.

Oh, I denied the effect it had on me, but after last night, it's clear I'm not letting go of her… Not until I've had my fill of her, which isn't going to happen for a long while. And that means more than just fucking her. It means spending time with her, getting to know her, finding out what her likes and dislikes are. It means having a relationship with her. Enjoying her razor-sharp mind, understanding what makes her tick. What she loves to do. What her dreams are. Her aspirations. Her goals. Who and what she is.

As for Isaac, things are so much clearer. He's a lot like me, yes, but he's also his own person. He has his own individuality, his own personality. His own ambitions. He has the right to live his own life. If I were in his shoes, I'd have been pissed off by how I tried to mold him to fit my expectations. I'd have left home and never returned. But Isaac did...

Thanks to her. Because she was there for him when he needed a friend. She didn't allow him to go homeless or hungry. She took care of him and became the responsible one. She ensured he had the time and space to pursue his craft. I owe it to her for bringing my son back into my life. And as if that weren't enough, she became the medium through which I found my son all over again.

"I'm not sure what you mean, JJ." Lena nods her thanks to Isaac who places a mug of coffee in front of her.

I slide off the stool, fill up a plate with food, then slide it across the counter toward her. "Eat first, then I'll tell you."

She glances at the toast, baked beans, eggs, and hash browns.

"How did you know I like my eggs sunny side up?"

I allow my lips to quirk. "Lucky guess?"

"Hmm." She narrows her gaze on me. "And why are you dressed like that?"

"Like what?"

"Like... so casually. I've never seen you in jeans before today," she says in an accusing tone.

"I'm not going into work today."

"You're not?" She blinks. "What are you going to do instead?"

"As I said, I'm going to get to know you better, Lena."

She glances from me to Isaac, who's digging into his own breakfast. "You have nothing to say about this?"

He pauses with his fork halfway to his mouth. "Me? Why would I have something to say about this?"

"Isaac, the three of us just—" She bites down on her lower lip and my cock twitches. "We, you know—"

"Fucked?" I interject.

Her cheeks pinken. She dips her chin so her hair falls over her face. "Yes, exactly."

"It's not going to happen again," I state.

"Eh?" She whips her head in my direction. "You mean—"

"It was one time. One night. It won't happen again."

She glances at Isaac. "And you're okay with this?"

Isaac places his fork and knife in his plate, then wipes his mouth with his napkin. "I'm not into pity fucks, Lena."

She pales. "It was more than that, and you know it."

"A goodbye fuck then?"

"That's not fair, Isaac." She grips her mug between her palms. "I didn't want you to feel—"

"Left out? Lonely? A third wheel?" He smiles gently. "I'm a grown man, Lena. It's time for me to take on my responsibilities and behave like one. What happened last night... I don't regret it, but I also know there's no future for the two of us."

She turns to me. "This is your doing. You're the one who's upset him—"

"No, I'm not upset. And I take full responsibility for my actions." Isaac reaches over and places his hand on Lena's. "Thanks to you, I have a channel of communication open with my father. I owe you for that, Lena."

I can't take my gaze off of where his fingers are curled around her wrist. Anger thrums at my nerve endings. *How dare he touch her? Last night he had his dick inside of her... but that was with my permission. And that was then. A moment in time which has now passed. This is now. When she's mine.*

I must make some noise, for Isaac raises his gaze to my face. "Look at him, Lena," he murmurs. "Look at JJ."

Lena turns toward me. She surveys my features and her brow furrows. "Why do you look like you're about to murder someone?"

"He's pissed at me," Isaac explains.

"Eh? And you were just saying the two of you understand each other better now."

"Oh, we do, thanks to you. And now, I understand that he can't bear the fact that I have my hand on you." Isaac pulls back his arm. The tension in my shoulders drains somewhat.

"This makes no sense." She pushes her mug of coffee aside, then locks her fingers together. "Last night, you didn't protest when I sat on his lap and called you over. Last night, you told him to show me how the Kane men could take care of me. Last night, you invited him to fuck me—"

"And that's the difference. I allowed it last night. It was at my behest that things happened the way they did. I approved of the two of us fucking you together. I let you take him into your body. I knew exactly what was going to happen and I let it, knowing it would heal the three of us. Make no mistake, Lena. It took place because I permitted it."

"Oh yeah?" Her voice turns casual. "It's because you gave me permission that I let him fuck me?"

"Of course."

She firms her lips. "It was your idea that the threesome take place?"

He hesitates. "You suggested it, you were up for it, but rest assured, I allowed it to happen. I gave it my blessing. I knew it was best for all of us."

Isaac clears his throat. "Umm, JJ, I don't think—"

Lena raises a hand. "No, no, let him get this off his chest." She turns to me. "You were saying?"

My heart thuds in my chest. My senses tingle. *What am I doing? Why am I trying to, once again, insist that I'm the one in control?* Things have gone far beyond that. Truthfully, nothing prepared me for what happened last night or how I feel in the aftermath. It's destroyed my composure, my balance, my sense of place in the world, even. The only thing I'm sure of is that she's mine. And I need to figure out how to convince her of that.

"All I'm saying is that it was a one-time thing. It's not going to happen again. You slept with him because I allowed it, and now we're moving on, all three of us."

She turns to Isaac. "Clearly, you're fine with this."

Why is she asking him that question? What does it matter what Isaac thinks anyway? Maybe it wasn't a pity fuck, but it was close. She didn't want him to feel left out. It's why she went over to him and sat on his lap in the sauna. It's what started the entire sequence of events. And no, I don't regret it. But I'm also not going to let it happen again.

Isaac meets my gaze, then nods. "I am."

She stares between us. "So, the two of you spoke and concluded that fucking the same woman helped to somehow heal whatever rift was between the two of you, is that it?"

"It wasn't any woman. It was you." I reach over to touch her, but she shrugs off my hand.

"I must have some magic pussy if your decades-old grouse with each other melted away after sex with me."

"Not just your pussy, but also your arse," I retort.

"Excuse me, what did you say?" She gasps.

"You heard me." I look between her eyes. "None of us regrets what happened. Indeed, it's helped us bury some ghosts from the past and move on."

"Maybe that's what the two of you decided, but what about me? What about what I think?"

"What is it you're thinking, Lena?" Isaac asks.

"Whatever it is you're going to say, let me just clarify that what happened last night is not going to happen again. Ever," I snap.

She shoves off the barstool. "And you're not even going to discuss why you've arrived at that conclusion?"

"Why should I?"

"See?" She stabs a finger in my chest. "This is the problem. You're way too autocratic. You make a decision and think everyone else has to fall in line. You're so set in your ways, it's infuriating."

"Not as much as you imply, considering I was an equal participant in what happened last night," I shoot back.

She huffs, "That's probably because you were curious about a three-some, is all."

"I've had threesomes before, and what we had was more than that. It changed things for me and Isaac, and it was all thanks to you."

"Will you stop saying that, please? I didn't do anything."

"You were generous and open with yourself. You saw how upset I was, and you couldn't just walk away." Isaac, too, slides off his stool. "You also wanted to show JJ how important he was to you. You wanted to be the bridge between the both of us."

"Literally," she mutters under her breath.

"We're very thankful for the role you played, but we don't need you to do it again." I reach for her again, and this time, she steps back.

"And what about me? What about what I want?"

I frown. "Are you saying you want to sleep with both of us? Is that why you're upset?"

"I'm upset because the two of you discussed things and came to a decision while I wasn't around. I'm upset because you think it was you who gave me permission to share my body with the both of you. I'm upset because" —she turns on Isaac— "once more, you're allowing someone else to make decisions for you."

"Only because JJ is right." Isaac drags his fingers through his hair. "What happened last night was a one-off. It can never happen again. You were never mine to begin with. And seeing how JJ is with you, how he looks at you like you're the only woman he's ever set eyes on, convinced me that I'm not the man for you."

"How big of you to say that." She folds her arms around her waist.

"What I don't get is what's gotten you so riled up. Don't you agree with our decision?" I growl.

"I... I don't know."

Isaac shuffles his feet.

I stiffen. My guts clench. *What is she trying to say? Surely not. It can't be.* "Are you disagreeing with us, Lena? Is that what this is about? Because I'm not letting that happen. You're mine, Lena. And I'm not going to share you again with anyone else."

51

Lena

Mine. Mine Mine. His words ricochet around in my head. My belly flutters. Why does this possessive streak in him turn me on so? And the fact that he not only allowed me to use my body to console his son, but also joined us? Why does that feel so forbidden, yet so erotic? And he doesn't want me to sleep with Isaac again. It's a one-time thing. That's good, right? I don't want to sleep with Isaac again, either. I only reached out to him because I felt sorry for him. It wasn't a pity fuck, though I did want him to feel included. Didn't want him to feel lonely. Wanted to, somehow, bridge the gap between him and his father, and JJ had caught onto that. He understood what I was trying to do even before I did. And then he got on board, to the point where he directed the proceedings. It's why he's decided that he's the one who allowed me to sleep with Isaac and him at the same time.

Only, I don't agree with that. He may have caught on quickly, but really, it was my choice to fuck both of them. And if I want to, I can do it again. *Do I want to fuck both of them at the same time again?* Not really. But the very fact he implied it was him in charge and he can tell me what to do is both exciting, and also frustrating, and so typically JJ. His dominance is what I love about him. His self-assuredness is also what I hate about him. It attracts me, yet threatens to overwhelm me.

I've always thought of myself as confident and knowing what I want. But meeting him has shown me there are depths to my personality I haven't yet plumbed. That deep inside, when it comes to sex, I want a man who can take charge, who will treat my body like it's his, who'll tell me what to do, and use my body, and fuck me so hard I see stars. Who'll demand things of me I've never dreamed of submitting to. Who I'll love to challenge, simply because I love the war of wills that follows, and the physical act of him making me submit to him is both an agony and a relief. A chance to finally give myself up, not think, not have to make choices. To allow myself to yield to him and let him have his way with me is such sweet sorrow and tingling joy. My toes curl. My scalp tingles. Pinpricks of electricity shoot through my veins. I'm aroused just thinking about it. I find myself leaning in close to him. Inhaling his scent. Drawing the heat from his body around me like a shield.

"Eat." JJ points at the still-full plate in front of me.

"And if I refuse?"

His eyes gleam. "I'll take great pleasure in feeding you, baby. You can count on it."

Isaac clears his throat. "I think I need to get going." He glances between us. "You're going to be fine, Lena."

We'll see.

"This is the right decision for all of us." He jerks his chin in JJ's direction. "I'll be out and about for the next few days, shooting. Then I'll hire a studio in Soho to develop the photographs, and decide which ones I'm going to use to inspire my next set of paintings." *It'll give you the privacy you need to figure things out.* He doesn't say that aloud, but he may as well have. Then he walks out the door.

The silence stretches. I don't sit down, don't eat, don't look at JJ. I really need to figure out what I want. It's not like I have feelings for Isaac. Despite the fact that I slept with him, I regard him more as a friend. As for JJ? What I feel for him is so much more complex. "I need a little time apart."

"Excuse me?" He seems taken aback, like he can't imagine anyone ever saying those words to him.

"I need to figure out my thoughts, JJ."

"It's Jack."

Blood rushes to my cheeks. Somehow calling him Jack feels very intimate. Like we're back in bed. Somehow, it feels right only in bed. "That's what I mean. You're constantly ordering me around, insisting it was your idea when I do certain things—"

"If you're alluding to the fact that we had a threesome with my son—"

I wince. When he puts it like that, it sounds so scandalous. Also, "That was *my* idea."

"It was my idea," he says at the same time.

I scowl.

He frowns.

"Not that it matters, I suppose. We were both a part of it, and we agree it was the right thing to do."

"And that's what I like about you." He reaches for my hand, and I let him take it. "Anyone else might have been scandalized by what happened. In fact, they'd probably never have taken a step in Isaac's direction in the sauna."

"I felt like I had to include him, you know?"

"I understand."

I shake my head. "And that's what's so annoying. You *do* get it. You get *me*… Mostly. It's just that your personality is too overpowering."

"It's what you find attractive."

"And I need to have my head examined for it. How can someone being such a jerkass be so—"

"Charismatic?"

"I was going to go for cringe-inducing," I mutter.

He reels me in toward him, and I should protest, but JJ in a black T-shirt and jeans is over-the-top-panty-melting. I manage to flatten my palms again his chest to stop his progress.

"JJ, stop."

"It's Jack."

"I can't call you Jack. You're my boss."

"And your lover."

I search his features. "Is that what we are?"

"Isn't that what we are?" he counters.

I draw in a breath and—mistake—it's JJ-scented. My ovaries seem to swell.

"Do you want kids?"

"What?" He stares.

"Children, JJ. You're what, fifty?"

"I'm forty-nine," he snaps.

"Do you want kids?"

He releases me. *Aha!* Apparently, I found something that puts him off. Typical male behavior. Talk about the real stuff, and they get all lily-livered.

"That phase of my life is behind me, girl."

"Oh, so now it's girl." I snort.

"You're my girl." His lips curl.

"Don't do that."

"Do what?"

"Smirk like an alphahole and go all possessive on me."

He opens his mouth, but I shoot up my hand.

"And yes, I find it hot and it turns me on, but it's not the solution."

"Told you, baby, sex is the solution to everything." His smirk deepens.

"It's sex that got me into this situation."

"What situation?"

"You know—being attracted to you, then actually sleeping with both of you—" I drag my fingers through my hair. "I don't regret it but, seriously, a threesome. With my boyfriend—"

"Your ex-boyfriend."

"Technically, he was still my boyfriend then. So, technically, I cheated on him with his father, then slept with both of them." I hunch my shoulders. "That really does sound bad."

"You don't have to feel bad. We did it because it was the only way for us to move forward. And things are so much better now."

"Maybe for you and Isaac, but I'm not sure where that leaves me. I don't regret doing it—"

"So you keep saying."

"But I also wonder what it says about me, you know? Am I so self-centered that I allowed my desires to overpower me?"

"You're being too harsh on yourself. Isaac himself says he understands why you did it. He holds no ill will toward you. If anything, he's grateful to you."

I wrap my arms around my waist. "Maybe so, but I need to figure things out for myself. I need to understand why I did what I did."

He blows out a breath. "I understand what you're saying."

"Do you?"

He nods. "No sex until you work things out for yourself."

"I think I need to move out—"

"No, absolutely not."

"It'd only be until I sort things through."

"I'm not letting you out of my sight," he growls.

"You're not my keeper, JJ. I can do whatever I want."

"Not in this instance. I've only just found you. I, too, am trying to figure out what I want to do about whatever it is between the two of us. I can't just let you walk away."

"I'm not walking away."

"You said you want time apart. I may not be a millennial—"

"I'm Gen Z, actually," I murmur.

"Thanks for pointing that out." His scowl deepens. "Either way, I'm not letting you leave. I need to see you every day."

"And I don't want to see you. At least, not outside of work. I need a chance to just be normal."

"Not happening." He folds his arms across his chest, mirroring my stance.

"If we want to go anywhere with whatever it is that's happening between us, then you need to learn to give a little."

"I'm too—" He firms his lips.

"You were saying."

"You can stay in a different room. You don't have to move into my bedroom," he says through gritted teeth.

I scoff. "And see you at every turn, and sneak peeks while you show off your sculpted physique while you swim every night?"

His eyebrows rise. "You spied on me swimming?"

"You know I did. So no, I can't stay here under your roof. It's too much."

"You mean you find me irresistible?" He smirks again.

"Oh, my god! Do you always need to have your ego stroked?"

A full-fledged smile lights up his face. He looks so much younger, so carefree, for just that moment. Is this how he'd come across if he were relaxed? More laid-back. More approachable. More fun?

"You do find me irresistible," he says in a satisfied tone.

"You know I do. And you know, even though it was you and Isaac fucking me, I couldn't take my eyes off you. Isaac was nothing more than an extension of you to me. You were the leader through and through when the three of us made love."

His gaze heats. Silver and gold flecks flash in the depths of his eyes. The heat from his body seems to dial up. The air between us heats.

"This is what I mean." I clear my throat. "We spend any length of time together, and invariably, things turn steamy."

"Nothing wrong with that."

"That's true, and it's exactly what I want to avoid right now."

"I can't let you leave, Lena." His tone turns serious. "I can't."

"You can, JJ."

He shakes his head.

"You have to, JJ. If you have any hope for the two of us getting together, then let me go."

52

JJ

"You let her go?" Isaac glances at me from across the pool table.

"She's in the city, just not in my house." I bend over the snooker table, position my cue, then let the ball fly. It cracks into the one halfway down the table, and both roll into the holes.

"So, you're keeping an eye on her?"

I stare at him.

"So, you *are* keeping an eye on her."

"I'm not the head of the Kane company anymore," I remind him.

"So, you killed the unreliable men in your syndicate, created a security company to absorb the rest, and now they take care of all of your security needs and perform errands for you, like this one."

"Huh." I straighten. "So, you have been paying attention."

"Just because I wasn't around doesn't mean I didn't have my own sources of information on you."

"Hmm." I scratch my jaw. "Your source couldn't possibly be my pretty Head of Human Relations who you seem to be spending a lot of time with, and who may have influenced your decision to accept the project of creating paintings for my offices."

His features pale. "You asshole, and just as I was thinking that perhaps we could have a relationship."

"Relax. Your friend is under my protection. She's been quite invaluable in helping to find jobs for my men within the Kane Corporation."

"You mean" —his brow furrows— "surely not. She's—"

"One of the good ones. The daughter of one of my most trusted men, who went to college and got a degree. I employed her legitimately. She was already aware of her father's role in my syndicate, and she wanted to help legalize the business."

"And you let her."

"It was helpful to have someone like her on my side."

He begins to protest, and I raise my hand. "I promise, she's in no harm. Quite the opposite. She's valuable to my business, and I take care of my assets."

"Like you're going to take care of *her*?"

I line up my shot again. "Perhaps." I keep my voice noncommittal.

"This is what I don't understand. You've always gone after what you wanted. As a child, I resented your being away, but as I grew up, some part of me also admired your single-minded focus."

I shoot him a sideways glance. "You had a funny way of showing it."

"Oh, don't get me wrong, I still resented you for being absent so much, but even I could tell you were successful. And some part of me knew you wanted to make amends. Why else would you install that state-of-the-art studio in the top floor of the house, eh?"

"You noticed?" I murmur.

"Of course, I noticed. I lived there, didn't I?"

"You never mentioned it."

"Didn't want you to think because I was grateful, I was forgiving you for everything."

I sink another two balls.

"I forgot how good you are at this," Isaac murmurs.

"I never forgot you and your sister. Even though I was away a lot, and I know it wasn't easy on your mother, I still remembered every birthday, every Christmas—"

"Sending presents didn't make up for your being away."

"I may not have been able to attend every PTA meeting, but I always tried to make it to the end-of-year school plays."

"You also missed it more often than not."

"The point is, I tried."

"The point is, it wasn't enough. Mom tried her best, but she was too busy with her social life. I mean, she was around, but not really."

"It's my fault. I should have incentivized her more so she felt compelled to be part of your lives. I should have made her more accountable."

"That's all you have to say?" Isaac bursts out. "She wasn't an employee."

"She was certainly better paid than my men, and more than many of my heads of departments."

"Taking care of a family is not like running a company."

"Thanks to you and Lena, I'm realizing that." I line up my next shot. "I'm not sorry about what happened between the three of us."

"Neither am I." Isaac replies.

"It's not going to happen again, though."

His lips quirk. "I heard you the first time and I wouldn't expect it to, either. I'll keep away from her, too, unless—" his gaze narrows "—she gets pissed off and decides to leave you."

"Not gonna happen." I tighten my grip on my cue.

He tilts his head. "She's not here."

"She needs her space to figure things out. I get it."

He straightens. "You do? I can't believe the man who decided the fastest way to take over a company was by shooting the CEO agreed to give her space."

"I was new to this entire corporate bullshit game. But I learned, didn't I?" I roll my shoulders. "And sometimes it's fine to play along with the other party's suggestion. Especially if that's the only way to win their trust."

"Hmm." He taps his fingers against his cue. "I have two questions for you."

I strike the ball, miss my shot. Damn. I straighten and level my gaze at him. "Shoot."

"One. Why did you decide to go legit? And two—" He walks over to the table and picks up a ball. "You're not really giving her space, are you?"

I allow my cue to slide down my palm until it rests on the floor. "It wasn't challenging anymore. I've made enough money that it's no longer a motivation. Also, I realized I've been lucky so far, and wanted to cash in and get out while I could."

"So, it's possible to leave a life of crime?'

"As long as you have enough money and power to influence your enemies, yes."

He nods slowly. "And my second question?"

I allow my lips to curve. "Of course, I'm giving her space."

"I don't believe you." He picks up two more balls and begins to juggle them.

"Believe me or not; it doesn't matter. She believes she has the space she wanted."

"You bastard," he says in a mild voice, then catches the balls in his hands. "Are you following her?"

"Of course not."

"Do you have your 'security team'" —he makes air quotes around the words *security team*— "following her?"

"What gives you that idea?"

"You're a canny motherfucker who'd never allow the woman you have feelings for to leave without keeping tabs on her."

The boy's clever and knows me better than I thought. "I am not like our friends from the *Cosa Nostra* who resort to such amateurish tactics."

"So, you have found a way to keep tabs on her?"

I raise a shoulder. "You can keep rephrasing your question, and my answer will still be the same."

"You're an asshole," he murmurs.

"I need to teach you more creative insults."

He laughs. "Fucking hell. At least you're not outright denying it."

I wipe the smile off of my face. "I'd never lie to you, Isaac. Not to you or your sister or, for that matter, your mother. Perhaps I was too upfront with her; it's why she left."

"You never loved her."

"And you tried to make up for it by taking her side." I squeeze my son's shoulder. "I'm not saying she was right, but you did the right thing."

"And you're doing the right thing by giving Lena space, even if it's only the illusion of doing so."

I search his features. "So, no hard feelings about the fact that your girlfriend chose me?"

His jaw tightens. "That's not a fair question."

"If the past has taught me anything, it's that it's better to talk things out than let them fester. It's not easy for me to have this conversation, either, but I need to know, Isaac."

"And if I say that I'll never forgive you for it?" He tips up his chin. "What then?"

"Then I'd say I deserve it."

His lips twist. He pulls away then runs his fingers through his hair. "I was pissed when she told me what she'd done. At first, my anger—and my pride—blinded me to the sense of relief I felt. Eventually, I realized I was glad she had because it gave me a reason to end the relationship. And I didn't have to worry about hurting her feelings or being the 'bad guy.'" He has the decency to look sheepish. I'm not sure if it's because he feels guilty or because he's comparing himself to me. He knows I don't pull my punches when it comes to doing the 'right' thing, even if someone else might get hurt in the process.

"She thinks she cheated on you."

"I cheated on her first."

"What?" I stiffen. "What the hell are you talking about?"

He reddens. "All the time I spent time away from the house—"

"You were having an affair?"

"I strayed… once."

"With the pretty HR manager?" I guess.

He rolls his shoulders. "It's complicated."

Something in my chest eases. Perhaps I felt I'd wronged him, too. After all, I ensured she was never too far away from me physically. I made sure we crossed paths in the office and at home, frequently. I felt her watching me as I swam in the pool in the evening, and I might have swam more often, just to show her what she was missing.

"You're relieved," he says flatly.

"I am," I say honestly. "I didn't think she was cheating on you. I knew the two of you weren't going to last."

"You mean, you wanted us to break up."

I hesitate. "Not going to lie. I didn't want her to be with you. And I might have urged things along faster in that direction. Even if I hadn't, it was only a matter of time before she left you. This way, I made sure she's still in the family."

His gaze narrows. "I don't know if I should be pissed with you or just envious that, once again, you went after what you wanted and got it."

"So can you, son."

He snaps his chin up.

Yeah, I've never called him that. I've never acknowledged our relationship so openly. I can't even say why, and that's my loss. I have a lot of time to make up for. And I intend to do things right by him this time.

"You're a brilliant artist."

He shakes his head, as if dazed. "You're kidding me, right?"

I laugh. "I should have told you that a long time ago. I confess, I don't always understand what you paint, but even to an untrained eye like mine, it's clear that your work is nothing short of genius."

His cheeks flush. "You really are making fun of me? Are you enjoying yourself at my expense?"

I shake my head. "I swear, it's the truth. I should have been more open with my feedback. I held off because I wanted you to run my company with me. I wanted you by my side, Isaac, and I was ready to do anything to get you there."

"I would have sucked at it. I never wanted to work with you, Dad. No offense."

A hot sensation twists my guts. He called me Dad. He stopped calling me that when he was five. And now, thanks to her, I have my son back.

I close the distance and hug him. He stiffens but doesn't pull away. In the way of most kids, he seems to suffer from my hug until I release him and step back.

"I know that now. I'm sorry I wasn't upfront about your talent earlier. I'm sorry for how bad I let things get between us."

He jerks his chin. "Can't say I've forgiven you completely."

"How can I make it up to you?"

He tilts his head as he studies me. "Are you serious about that?" he asks.

"You bet. I'll do anything. Anything to wipe the slate clean and rebuild our relationship from the ground up."

"Hmm…" He strokes his chin. "Now that you mention it, there is something…"

53

Lena

"Hey, Mom!"

"Hey, Dinky." My mother's sweet yet strong voice comes through the phone.

She still prefers to call instead of FaceTime, and thank God for that. I'm not sure I want to see her face when I confess the thing I've been meaning to tell her for so long. I've been putting it off, so much so, I haven't even gotten on the group chat since I moved out of JJ's place a week ago.

To be fair, I've been busy getting settled into my new place—which is in close proximity to Summer and Karma's place—while continuing to work at Kane Corporation. At least I haven't seen JJ since that day. He's only communicated with me through email and his personal assistant, which was good, even though I really don't enjoy interacting with Karen. Only, I miss him. More than I'd care to admit it. I've been trying to work out my feelings toward him, and I'm still unclear about what I'm going to do about it. I wasn't going to talk to my family in the midst of it. Also, what was I going to tell them? That I had a threesome with JJ and Isaac?

"I had a threesome, Ma." I squeeze my eyes shut. *No, no, no, I didn't just say that.* My ma's quite broadminded. She knows and accepts Isaac's bisexuality. She even asked me if I was in a three-way relationship with Isaac and Ben, and actually seemed disappointed when I said no.

She comes from a conservative Indian background, but her sensibilities are very much that of a hippie flower child of the sixties. Still, it's not every day you confess something like that to your family, especially in a telephone conversation. That's part of the reason why I haven't said anything in the group chat or called any of my family, knowing once I did, I wouldn't be able to stop the truth from coming out. And I can't even blame it on them. When it comes to my family, I just don't have a filter.

There's silence on the other end, then, "You know I'm not going to judge you for anything you do."

"Yeah." I blow out a breath. "I know that, and I should've told you something earlier, but I'm still trying to work things out in my head, you know?"

"Was it with Isaac and a friend?"

"It was with Isaac and his father." She can't see me, but if she could, she'd see me trying to hide from her gaze. Again, praise God for giving me a mother who refuses to use FaceTime.

"Oh."

Not much fazes my mom, but I think I succeeded this time.

I swallow. "Umm, Mom, you okay?"

"Are *you* okay?" Her tone is worried. "It's not something you got coerced into, is it?"

"You mean by Isaac?"

"By his father. He must be quite a bit older than you."

"He's twenty-six years older than me, Mom."

There's silence again... which seems to stretch at least a week.

Then, "You're old enough to know what you're doing." My mother's tone is soft. "I know your instincts must have told you it was okay to do so." She pauses. "And Isaac was fine with this, presumably?"

"Isaac and I are no longer together."

"Ah… I see."

There's a pause again.

"Me and JJ… uh, JJ, that's Isaac's father, and I—"

"You're with his father now?"

"Not really. I mean, I am, kinda, but not. I moved out of his house and am renting a place until I figure out my next move. But don't worry, Mom, I also have friends here. Friends who have proven to be a great support network. In fact, I was on my way to meet them when you called."

"So, you and JJ, are you going to get back together?"

"I'm not really sure, Mom," I say honestly.

"It's good you're taking your time to figure this out. Relationships are not easy, honey. God knows I've screwed up my fair share of them. And most of the time it's because I was impulsive, know what I mean? I allowed my heart to carry me away… Which, admittedly, in the moment, it wasn't too bad, and I still believe it was the right thing to do. I just wish I had the maturity to take things a bit slower." I sense her moving around. A door bangs in the distance then, "Mom?" Josh's voice reaches me, followed by more footsteps.

"Who are you talking to, Mom?"

"Your sister."

"Dinky? You're talking to Dinky?" I hear the sound of the phone being taken from Mom, then, "Dinky? It's you? Why haven't you been on the group chat? We were beginning to worry that you and Isaac were having trouble, and maybe that's why you'd gone all quiet."

"It's that, and more. I'm not with him anymore, but I am with someone else."

It's Josh's turn to go silent, then he chuckles. "O-k-a-y, well, that was fast. Either way, Isaac wasn't one-hundred percent into you, you know? He was always going on about his paintings and his art and finding his muse. You should've been his muse, Lena. Anyone could see you were too good for him."

"Ah, thanks, I guess. Josh, I gave Mom the lowdown. I'm sure she's going to share my news over family dinner."

"Right, well, gotta go. Mom's threatening to hold back her chicken curry if I don't hand the phone over to her. Bye, Dinky. Love you."

"Love you, too, Josh."

"Dinky?" My mom's voice again. "You do you, okay? Don't worry about what the world thinks of you. Don't worry about what we make of your man or your relationship. If he makes you happy—"

"I think he does, Mom."

"—then you need to figure out what you really want and go after it, ya?"

"Ya." I nod. Tears prick the backs of my eyes, and I lift my head toward the ceiling to keep them from spilling over. "I'm so sorry I didn't talk to you earlier."

"I understand the need for getting clarity on the status of your relationship in your head, but I also wouldn't have let more time go by without calling you."

"I know that." Maybe I counted on it. It's one of the things I love about my family, especially my ma. She knows exactly when to push and when to hold back. "Love you, Mom."

"Love you, honey. Now, I'd better go before your brother eats all of my vegetables before I can cook them."

I disconnect the phone, and it pings with a text from Summer. **You coming? Karma and I are waiting for you.**

"You sure he hasn't put cameras in your apartment, or bugged your phone, or has his security team following you?" Karma Sovrano cups her palms over her obviously pregnant stomach. She's staying at her sister Summer Sterling's townhouse in Primrose Hill. Karma and Michael came over from Sicily to attend Massimo and Olivia's wedding.

I've learned that Michael kidnapped Karma for a debt he thought her father owed his, but instead of exacting his revenge, he married and then fell in love with her. In that order. Karma had messaged Summer —or rather Michael had messaged Summer on behalf of Karma—to let her know she had a beau in Sicily, and that she should not worry. Karma stayed away nearly four months, during which time she'd gotten married and fallen pregnant. She probably would have stayed on in Sicily until the child was born, but Summer finally lost patience and told her she was hopping on the next flight to see her. At which point, Karma turned up with Michael in tow. Summer has refused to allow them to return to Sicily. She must have been very persuasive because both Karma and Michael have stayed. In fact, they managed to rent the townhouse next to the Sterling's. Because Michael had to return to Sicily for a few days for work, Karma has temporarily moved in with Summer. The sisters have had a wonderful time catching up.

I visited to hand over some important documents that JJ insisted I hand-deliver to Sinclair Sterling. Summer saw me and insisted I stay for dinner. Why the documents couldn't be emailed, like a normal person would have done, I don't know. Apparently, alphahole is old-fashioned when it comes to communication. He insisted they were so confidential he couldn't risk emailing them. He was also firm that it had to be me who delivered the documents in person. So here I am, after a delicious dinner that Summer whipped up for us.

She brings out big bowls of ice cream, and the three of us happily inhale the chocolate chip concoction. I place my spoon in my empty bowl with a sigh, and that's when Karma asks that question. Now I glance at her from under hooded eyelashes. "Um... JJ no longer runs an underground crime syndicate. So, he wouldn't resort to those tactics, would he?"

Karma and Summer exchange looks.

"What?" I glance between them. "What are you not telling me?"

"JJ's not blood-related to the Sovranos, or to Sinclair and his friends, but they are very similar in their approach to business. And toward their possessions," Karma finally offers.

"I'm not a possession," I protest.

"I say that in the most complimentary fashion," she adds.

"Is it complimentary to be seen as a man's possession?"

"His *most* valuable possession," Karma corrects me. "You already know my history with Michael. I've met JJ a few times since I married my husband, and I guarantee you, he's as much an apex predator as the Sovranos."

"He doesn't move in those circles anymore. In the time I've worked at Kane Enterprises, I can guarantee you the business is above-board. And I've worked closely with JJ. I have access to his correspondence. I've sat in on mergers and discussions. I know the cashflows, the projections, the P&L of that group of companies, and everything is above-board."

Karma raises a shoulder. "Doesn't mean anything. More than likely, he's hidden that side of himself so well, you just haven't spotted it yet."

I frown. "Maybe I have and it doesn't distress me?" I finally say.

Karma and Summer exchange another of those looks. They're talking to each other without words in the way close families can, or siblings who are on the same wavelength. Tears prick the backs of my eyes. Damn, I miss talking to my family. *And whose fault is that?* I'm the one who decided I couldn't tell them about the mess I've gotten myself into.

It's been a week since I moved out of JJ's place, and I'm no closer to resolving things in my head. Which is why, when JJ insisted I take the documents to Sinclair Sterling, I agreed. I hoped I'd run into Summer and have a chance to speak with her again. Also, I couldn't reasonably say no to JJ because the bungalow I moved into happens to be on the grounds between Summer's townhouse and Karma's temporary home. When JJ suggested it, I refused. I told him I could find a place of my own, but he put his foot down. He refused to budge on it, no matter how much I argued with him. Then, when I saw the place, it was so perfect, I couldn't refuse. I wanted to pay the rent, but again, JJ wouldn't hear of it. He was so persistent; I gave in and accepted his suggestion.

"I know we haven't known each other that long, but you can talk to us." Summer leans over and takes the empty bowl from my hands. Meanwhile, Karma hands over a tissue.

I dab at my eyes. "It's nothing. I'm just being emotional."

"You're from LA, aren't you? You must miss your family," Karma says gently.

"More so now that I split with my boyfriend."

"So, it's really over?" Summer tilts her head.

"It is."

"And JJ...?"

I shake my head. "I see him in the office, but it's strictly business." Of course, I asked for distance, only I didn't think JJ would accept my conditions and toe the line so willingly.

Karma has a curious expression on her face, but she doesn't probe about my link with JJ. Not that it's not evident, with what I said earlier. "It must not be easy, being on your own." She walks over and sits down next to me. "I'm glad you're so close to Summer."

Karma glances in Summer's direction. "I spent the last few months away from Summer, and I missed her every second." She winces, then rubs her chest.

"You okay?" I frown.

"Yeah, this pregnancy is giving me heartburn. It seems to have gotten a little worse lately, that's all."

"Are you taking your medication?" Summer leans forward in her seat. "It's one of the reasons I was so worried about you and tried to call you. I mean, I'm sure you wouldn't be that irresponsible. But I also know how stubborn you can be."

"Of course, I'm taking my medication." Karma rolls her eyes. "And we do have pharmacies in Sicily, you know? We're not completely cut off from the rest of the world."

"Considering you never returned my messages; you might as well have been." Summer scoffs.

"I did text you back, didn't I?"

"You were gone four months, Karma. Four. And I can count the number of times you messaged me on the fingers of one hand."

Karma has the grace to look sheepish. "I'm so sorry I wasn't exactly prolific in my communications. It's just that there was so much happening, I didn't have the time to return every single one of them."

"Every time I threatened to come over, you'd insist you were fine. If I hadn't pushed things, you'd have never visited." Summer scowls. "Of course, if you'd told me you were pregnant—" She glances down at Summer's bump, which is about the same size as her own bump, although, from what they've told me, Summer's further along. "— You'd have come at once."

Summer half smiles. "Maybe I should have, but it didn't feel right breaking the news to you by text message. Also, you had so much happening and you didn't hint about it to me, not once."

Karma glances away, then back at her. "Sorry, Summer. I know, I should have told you. My only excuse is there was a lot going on. Marrying the Don of the *Cosa Nostra* is not the simplest way to get inducted into the Mafia lifestyle, you know?"

Summer snorts. "You're quick-witted enough to deal with anything. Bet you had Michael and his brothers wrapped around your little finger in no time."

"How many brothers does Michael have?" I ask.

"There's seven including him. Xander, his youngest sibling, passed away in an accident a few months ago." Karma swallows. "It was a car bomb that didn't fully blow up. It caused enough damage that Xander was killed, and I miscarried my first pregnancy when I was thrown from the car."

"Oh, I'm so sorry for your loss." I touch Karma's shoulder.

She bites the inside of her cheek. "I was gutted when it happened, but I'm pregnant again now."

"To think you were the wild child between the two of us" — Summer shakes her head— "and now you're rushing headlong into having a family."

"I always thought you'd be the one to find a man and settle down and have lots of kids first." Karma gazes fondly at her sister.

"I did get married first. I honestly wasn't in a hurry to have kids, though. But then I got pregnant, and now I'm glad I did. This way, we can share our experiences." Summer beams back at Karma. "And with so many of the Seven becoming pregnant, we're going to be kept busy with baby showers for a while."

"These Seven are friends of Sinclair?" I heard about them, of course, but with so many new names and faces to keep track of, I'm still not entirely sure who's who.

"They're childhood friends. The seven of them run 7A together, and their wives have become good friends of mine. We've formed our own sisterhood, which is also my support network." Summer reaches for a glass of water. "You must meet them."

If I stick around that long.

"Are all seven of them based in London?" I tilt my head.

"All except Edward. He left after Ava and Baron's wedding and is, apparently, traveling the world at the moment."

"That sounds like fun."

Summer hesitates. "I suppose you could call it that."

I narrow my gaze. "That's not all of it, is it?"

Summer places her glass of water back on the table. "Ava first fell in love with Edward. He left her, asking Baron to keep an eye on her. Then she fell in love with Baron."

"Oh, wow." I straighten. "And she finally married Baron?"

"Not before the three of them slept together."

I open and shut my mouth. "So—"

Summer nods. "Exactly."

Karma glances between us. "Now I'm so curious." She looks at me with sparkling eyes. "I stopped myself from asking earlier, but is there some particularly tasty bit of gossip you're not sharing with me?"

I can't stop myself from chuckling. The sisters have such a great bond between them, and they're so easy to speak with. Not that my family isn't, but it had still been awkward talking to my mother and I'm still not sure how I'm going to explain JJ to the rest of my siblings. With Summer and Karma, it's different. They've seen their friend Ava go through an unconventional relationship, so I think they'll understand my point of view better. Besides, Karma is also married to the Don of the *Cosa Nostra*… So, if there's anyone I can confide in without being judged, it's probably these two. I place my glass of water on the table, then fold my fingers together. "Summer already knows this—" I turn to Karma. "I slept with my boyfriend's father."

54

Lena

Karma's gaze widens. She seems speechless for a second, then a smile curves her lips. "Older men, eh? There's something so appealing, so intriguing, so enticing about them, hmm?" She adjusts the pillow behind her back. "Michael is twenty years older than me. Did you know that?"

I shake my head. "I could tell he was in his late thirties or early forties, but no, I hadn't thought about the age gap between the two of you."

"Well, he is. Also, he kidnapped me."

I blink. "He what?"

She nods. "Kidnapped me. He pointed a gun at me, and I thought for sure he was going to shoot me—"

"But he didn't," I murmur.

"Instead, he pushed me into the boot of a car, then climbed in after me."

"He didn't." I shake my head. Michael Sovrano, that tall, massive Don climbed into the trunk after her? "It must've been a tight squeeze."

Her eyes gleam. "You have no idea."

"Then he married you?"

"To pay a debt our father owed him."

I glance in Summer's direction and find her features wearing a slightly stricken expression. "I'll never get used to you talking about this. After our father revealed who was after him, I should have insisted that you move in with me and Sinclair after we got married."

Karma snorts. "And be the third wheel? I don't think so. And Sinclair did have security on me. It's my fault that I gave them the slip and went on the run that day. I don't regret it, though. If I hadn't, I wouldn't have met Michael." Her eyes go all dewy. "I love him, Summer. I do. And it's not his fault I didn't come to visit, or update you on what was happening. That's completely on me."

Summer searches her features. "When I found out I was pregnant, you were the first person I wanted to tell. But you were gone. Thank God for the Sisterhood of the Seven, or else I'd have been so lonely."

"Sisterhood of the Seven?" I furrow my brow.

"That's our informal name for the wives and girlfriends of the Seven." Summer smiles, more than a touch of wickedness on her features. "Each of us is more than a match for our men. Put us in one room, and the Seven get worried."

With good cause, no doubt. I haven't met the rest of the Seven, nor their wives, but if the sisters are anything to go by… I have no doubt they're each a handful, and together have the kind of energy that could cause revolutions.

"You need to meet the wives of the other Sovranos, too. They've been my de facto family the last few months. They were my strength when I lost my child. Even Michael's brothers. And Xander, the youngest of the Sovranos who passed away… He was my best friend." She sniffles.

"Oh, honey." Summer joins us on the sofa. She wraps her arms around Karma. "I'm so sorry you had to go through that. I wish you'd called me. I'd have been there on the next flight."

"I knew you would, and maybe that's why I didn't call."

Summer leans back. "What do you mean?"

"It's just… It felt like I was too close to you. You knew me as your younger sister who you had to be responsible for while growing up. Whereas, I was now the wife of the Don. And with that, I had responsibilities." She coughs, then reaches over and sips from her glass of water. "My position was something I wasn't sure you'd comprehend."

That's something I understand. After all, it's a very similar reason that has me holding back from speaking with my family.

"Let me get this right," Summer says slowly. "You didn't call me because you thought I was too close to the situation?"

"I knew you'd want what was best for me, but I had to think about what was best for the family. The other women? They only know me as Michael's woman. The one who's responsible for the future of his family. They" —she places the glass of water back on the table— "they got why I did what I did…" She hunches her shoulders. "Or didn't do."

Summer searches her sister's features, then gasps. "You didn't tell him."

Karma rises to her feet and walks away.

Summer pushes up to standing, and follows her. "Oh, my god, Karma! You didn't tell Michael about your heart condition, did you?"

Heart condition. What heart condition?

Karma turns. She coughs again. Is her color paler than it was? Surely not.

"I couldn't." She wrings her fingers. "If I had, he'd have never allowed the pregnancy to proceed. He'd have told me that he didn't want children."

"And rightly so," Summer declares.

Karma places her palms on her swollen belly. "You don't understand. I want to give him children. I want children, a family of my own, Summer. Surely, you understand that?"

Summer's face softens. "I know we didn't have the best experience growing up, but we were lucky the foster family that took us in turned out to be all right."

"Sure, they provided us with all the material requirements—"

"And we were comfortable. We had each other. We didn't need anyone else," Summer says softly.

"We needed the love of a mother and a father." Karma's eyes shine. "I still miss them so much."

"You were too young to remember the details. It's why you think they were such ideal parents."

"Oh, but they were," Karma insists.

"That's why our father preferred to dump us into the system instead of finding a way to take care of us?" Summer scoffs.

"He tried his best. It's not his fault he got caught up in something bigger than him," Karma insists.

"What are you guys talking about?" I glance between them.

The sisters look at each other, then Summer blows out a breath. "You know how Michael's father was responsible for the kidnapping of Sinclair and the rest of the Seven when they were boys?"

I nod.

"He had an accomplice, Freddie Nielsen, who was killed in an encounter with the Sovranos." Summer locks her fingers together. "Our father was blackmailed by Michael's father into helping them. Only, he lost his courage and reported them. Then, he faked his death and fled to the US—"

"—leaving the two of you in foster care," I murmur.

"It's not as bad as it sounds." Summer leans forward on her feet. "Like I said, our foster parents were good to us. Not the warmest of people, but they were good to us. Compared to some of the other nightmarish stories one hears about, we were lucky."

"The two of you turned out well. And you have amazing husbands who love you, and you're both pregnant. You're going to have your own families, and you still have each other. That's pretty amazing, huh?"

Summer seems taken aback, then laughs. "It *is* pretty amazing. It all turned out okay."

"It did." Karma shoves the hair back from her face. "Is it hot in here?" she murmurs.

"Only problem is, Karma's heart condition means her pregnancy is high-risk, and she never told Michael so—"

Karma begins to slump forward.

"Karma!" I jump to my feet and rush toward them.

"Where is she?" Michael Sovrano bursts into the hospital waiting room. His hair is mussed. His tie is askew. The few times I've met him, he's been so impeccably well-dressed. Now his eyes are wild and his color is pale.

On his heels, Sinclair Sterling enters the room, followed by JJ.

Summer jumps up and rushes into Sinclair's arms. He wraps her close, tucks her head under his chin.

I rise to my feet. "She's inside with the doctor. They're examining her."

"Which doctor?" Michael turns to me. "Who's looking after her?"

"Umm." I take a step back. The man's sick with worry. I get it. But being the focus of those piercing black eyes of his is almost as nerve-racking as being the target of JJ's attention. Only difference is, I can read JJ's moods, including when he's angry. With Michael? All that worry bouncing off of him only adds an edge to his already threatening presence. "I think it was someone Summer called." I swallow.

Michael moves forward. My guts churn. Then suddenly, JJ's there. He plants his bulk between me and Michael, and shoves his hand into Michael's chest. "Back off, Sovrano."

Michael narrows his gaze on me. "Who's. The. Doctor?" His jaw tics. He runs his fingers through his hair. His fingers tremble. Damn, the man's beside himself with worry.

"Sovrano, get the fuck out of your head," JJ barks, and his voice is like a whiplash. I jump. Sinclair and Summer freeze. It must get through to Michael, for he blinks.

"Weston!" Summer pulls away from Sinclair. "Weston's with her."

"Weston?" Michael scowls.

"He's one of the leading heart surgeons in the city, and one of the Seven," Sinclair interjects. "She's in good hands."

"Why would she need a heart surgeon?" Without waiting for an answer, Michael pulls out his phone and begins to dial. "I need to call Aurora. She's Karma's doctor. She needs to be here."

"We do have good doctors in London. Weston is my childhood

friend. I'd trust him with my life. She can't do better than him," Sinclair assures him.

"I'm calling Aurora anyway." He spins around and walks out.

JJ turns to me. " You all right?"

The tension drains out of me, and I sink into the chair behind me.

"Hey." JJ walks over and sits down next to me. He doesn't touch me, though. "You okay?"

I nod.

"You don't look okay."

"It was so sudden. One moment we were all talking. The next, she'd collapsed. Luckily, the air ambulance was there in minutes."

"We have one on standby," Sinclair clarifies. He leads Summer over to take the chair across from me.

"She never told him. Karma didn't tell Michael." Summer chews on her lower lip. "How could she not tell him?" She wrings her fingers.

"Didn't tell Michael what?" JJ asks.

Footsteps sound behind us, then, "Didn't tell me what?"

55

JJ

Michael's already hard features seem to turn to granite. "What is it Karma didn't tell me?"

Summer pales further. She looks up at Sinclair for help.

Lena slides closer to me and my fingers tingle. I want to put my arm around her and pull her into my side. But this time… This time, it's up to her to make the next move. If she wants me, if she wants something more between us, then she needs to take the initiative. Oh, how I hate to admit that. But if I want to have any kind of a relationship with her, I need to respect her wishes. I've been in enough negotiations to know when it's time to fall back; but holding myself back from her is the most difficult thing I've done in my life.

Michael curls his fingers into fists. "Is someone going to tell me what my wife is supposedly hiding from me?"

Summer bites the inside of her cheek. She clutches at Sinclair's arm. She opens her mouth but no words come out. Sinclair places his hand on hers, and that seems to help her. "Karma, she—" Summer shakes her head. "She—"

"She what? What is it? What's wrong with her? Can somebody please tell me?"

Summer sways, and Sinclair pulls her closer.

"Anybody?" Michael turns to us. "Can *you* tell me what's happening?"

Lena glances at Summer to find she's buried her face in Sinclair's chest and is weeping silently. She pales, then tips up her chin. "Michael, Karma has a heart condition."

"Excuse me?" He stares as if he's not quite sure he heard right.

"It's true." Summer sniffles. She turns in Sinclair's arms. "She was born with a congenital heart defect that she has controlled with medication."

"I would have known if my wife had a heart condition, or if she were on any medication." Michael's scowl deepens.

"Karma hates talking about it to anybody. She doesn't want to be treated differently. It's why she didn't tell you about it."

His jaw tightens. "She doesn't hide anything from me."

"She did with this."

Silence descends. He takes in Summer's features, and must see the truth reflected there, for some of the color leaches from his features. "Is that why she's in there? I thought it was the baby, but it's her heart condition that's acting up?"

"It's both," Lena says softly.

Michael turns to her. "Explain," he says in a hard voice.

I don't know all of the details, but I've followed enough of the conversation to piece together what's happening. "If Karma's pregnant with a heart condition, it puts her life at risk."

Every muscle in Michael seems to coil in response. His shoulders bunch, and his chest rises and falls. He curls his fingers into fists, and takes a step forward. Lena shrinks back closer to me, when Michael sinks to his knees.

The lethal Mafia Don in his $7000 tailored suit digs his fingers into his hair and squeezes his eyes shut, while on his knees, on a floor covered with industrial carpeting.

"Oh, Beauty, why didn't you tell me?" His voice is anguished. My chest tightens. Not even I'm immune to the sound of a man's raw grief. Is this what love does to people? Does it reduce them to their knees, literally? While squeezing their insides like a car compactor?

Lena's breath hitches. I turn to find her watching me with a plea in her eyes.

Oh, no. No, no, no. I scowl at her. She glowers back at me.

I bunch my shoulders, and she digs her elbow into my side. "Go to him," she hisses.

"But you—"

"I'm fine. He needs you. He's your friend."

I hesitate

"You should go to him, Jack." She searches my features. "Please."

Maybe it's because she called me by my name or because she said please, or perhaps it's the genuine concern in her features, and I'm a sucker who can't say no to the plea in her eyes. Either way, I rise to my feet and stalk over to Michael, and grip his shoulders. "Buck up, ol' chap. She's in good hands. Weston's the best in the continent and he's with her. He'll do everything possible to save her."

Michael's big body sways, but he doesn't reply.

"Hold it together," I say sharply. "She needs you. Karma needs you, Michael. You can't lose your shit. She needs your strength to get through this."

Michael's throat moves as he swallows. When he opens his eyes, a tear leaks from the corner of one. He doesn't bother to wipe it away. He shrugs off my hold and rises to his feet.

"It's my fault. I should have paid more attention. What kind of a man doesn't know that his wife is suffering from a systemic condition?"

"It's not your fault," Lena says from behind me at the same time as Summer. She turns in Sinclair's arms and exchanges a glance with my woman—I mean, my employee... I mean, the one who is my life. If Lena were in the same position as Karma, I'd... I'd do anything to save her. I'd give my life to make sure she's okay. I'd... want to hurt myself for not figuring out she was hiding such an important thing from me.

"You know how adamant Karma is." Summer rubs her hand across her face. "If she didn't want you to know, there's no way you could have found out, Michael."

Michael rubs the back of his neck. "She wanted another child so quickly, and I agreed. I thought it would be the best way for her to get over the grief of losing our first. I should have told her to wait a little longer. I should have asked to look at her medical records closely. I thought—" His features grow thunderous. "Her doctor would have known. Aurora would have known, and she didn't tell me."

"Are you sure?" Summer sniffles. "She wouldn't have had access to her medical records from the UK. There's no reason for Aurora to have found out unless Karma told her, and she wouldn't have because she knew Aurora would tell you. She was adamant she wanted this child, Michael."

"*Cazzo!*" Michael's shoulders seem to swell. His biceps stretch his jacket sleeves. "If I had known how much danger she was in, I *never* would have allowed her to get pregnant."

"It's why she didn't tell you. She knew you'd have this reaction," Summer says softly.

"When she wanted to get pregnant so quickly after losing our first child, I agreed. I thought it was the best way for her to get over her grief. I never thought—" The tendons of his throat flex. "I never thought it would endanger her life. Never thought it would come to her fighting for her life. If something were to happen to her—"

"Nothing's going to happen to her," a new voice says from the doorway. "Not if I can help it."

Michael swivels to face the new arrival. All of our eyes are locked on the man who steps through the doorway. I recognize Dr. Weston Kincaid from my investigator's reports. Like I said, I'm thorough when it comes to researching who I'm working with.

Michael prowls over to him. "How is she? Is she okay?"

"She's fine. She had a bad scare, but she's resting now."

"Is she going to be okay?"

Weston hesitates. "For now."

"What do you mean, for now? Is she still in danger."

"Being pregnant with her heart condition means she is always going to be in some level of danger. This time, she was lucky, and hopefully, there won't be any further episodes until she gives birth."

"And if there are—?" Michael's voice trembles. "What if—"

"Let's not speculate, shall we?" Weston claps him on his shoulder. "For now, why don't you come back and take a look at your wife? And when you're done, why don't you come by my office and we can talk? We'll come up with a care plan for your wife to minimize the possibility of this happening again during her pregnancy."

"Thanks for seeing me home." Lena glances up at me from inside the doorway of the house she's currently occupying. A house I personally inspected to make sure it would be comfortable and secure for her. If I had security cameras installed around the perimeter, and I'm not saying I did, that's me watching out for her. That's all.

"Are you going to be okay?" I survey her features. There are dark circles under her eyes. Her cheekbones seem to stand out in relief. "When was the last time you ate?"

As if in response, her stomach grumbles. She laughs a little. "That wasn't embarrassing at all."

"Is there food at home? Should I order some for you? I—"

"I'm fine, JJ. Really. It wasn't me who almost lost my child again."

Karma and the baby were going to be fine. Summer also wanted to meet with Dr. Kincaid, so Sinclair had gone with her and Michael. Karma's brush with death had changed the dynamics of the relationship between Michael and Sinclair completely. Summer wanted to be there for her sister, and Sinclair wanted to support Summer. Lena and I waited outside Dr. Weston's office as the three of them met with him.

When they came out, Summer informed Lena that Karma would stay in the hospital under observation. Michael insisted on staying with her, and Summer and Sinclair were going to arrange to have clothes and food delivered to him. Also, once Karma was better, she was going to move back into their rental near Summer's place. Karma and Michael were going to stay in London until the baby was born so Karma could also be near Summer.

Summer and Lena hugged, with Lena promising Summer she'd be over to visit. Considering Lena stays in a bungalow on the grounds of their home, that's going to be sooner rather than later. Oh, and I told Michael I'd be there in his corner if he needs anything.

Michael held my gaze, then ignoring my proffered arm, he'd hugged me. Huh? Apparently even a Mafia Don needs people around him in times of crises. He told me his brothers were on their way to keep him company in the hospital, but he appreciated the offer. Then, he turned to Lena and thanked her for being there for Karma.

As I left with Lena, I ran into Luca and Adrian, who were on their way to stay with Michael. Adrian was on his phone issuing orders—to his team, no doubt—to block out the floor and have security posted around it. The right thing to do. The Sovranos might be turning legit, but their past would always dog their heels. I should know. I harbored the same concern. And when it comes to my woman, I'll stop at nothing to make sure she's safe.

"Do you want to come in?"

I blink, glance down at the features which are imprinted in my retinas, on my brain tissue, in my blood cells, in every fiber of my body. The face that haunts my dreams and stalks my every waking moment. Also, because I can't resist pulling up the security app on my phone and watching the live feeds of her to reassure myself she's safe.

Yeah, my comment earlier about not resorting to the amateur tactics of having eyes on her? Disregard that. Turns out, when it comes to her, I'll do anything to keep her safe. If it had been her in that hospital, if it had been her who'd had that scare, if it had been her who'd have to be monitored for every single second of her pregnancy to ensure that she made it through safely and after, to make certain that she was okay… To be honest, I'm not sure how I'd be able to survive. The constant fear that something could happen to her, something that's out of my control, something I could do nothing about except watch her keenly, keep her as close as possible, lavish as much attention on her as possible… And act as if every day, every minute, every second with her is a precious gift I'll never take for granted.

"JJ?" She frowns. "Did you hear what I said?"

I open my mouth to speak, but my throat is too dry. My brain cells seem to have all fused together. My guts clench. A shiver grips me, and all of the pores on my body pop.

I must make a sound, for her gaze widens. "JJ, you okay?"

I bend my knees, snatch her up, and throw her over my shoulder.

56

Lena

"What the— What are you doing?" The world tilts, and I'm faced with the sight of JJ's firm ass. And what an ass it is. I remember digging my fingers into it while he thrust into me. I remember the feel of it as I'd turned into his back while he was asleep and curled around him. I remember taking in its shape as he'd cut through the water in the swimming pool in his trunks, ogled at it as he strode away from me clad in his tailor-made suit in the office. I confess I've never seen it from this angle as I sprawl over his shoulder with my hair hanging down and brushing against his rear as he stalks forward.

The door slams behind us. The echo reverberates through the space, sinks into my cells, ricochets over my nerve endings. The pulse pounds at my temples, at my wrists, between my legs. *No, no, no, I'm angry at how he's treating me like I am a possession. At how turned on I am by how he handles me like I weigh nothing.* I'm not a tall person but I am also not that tiny, and I've never been flung over someone's shoulder like a sack of potatoes. Or his sex toy. A shudder grips me. *Oh no, no, no, not turning to mush just because he's using caveman tactics on me.* I struggle, try to loosen his grip on me. A sharp pain sears my backside. "What the hell? Let me go, JJ."

"No."

He marches through the living room and into the bedroom.

"I'm not going to sleep with you, you asshole." I pound my joined wrists into his back. His breathing doesn't even change. "What's gotten into you? You're acting crazy."

"I *am* crazy" —he throws me down on the bed, on my back— "for you."

I bounce once, shake the hair out of my face. "You said you'd give me space to figure things out. You said you'll let me leave so I can work things out."

"I'm tired of waiting." He rolls his shoulders, and my gaze is drawn to the breadth of his body. How big, how solid, how larger-than-life he is. The bedroom isn't small by any means, but JJ seems to take up all of the space in the room. I glance past him toward the open door, and he laughs. "Don't even think about it."

"Fuck you."

"That's the plan." He smirks.

"You're delusional if you think I'll still give us a chance after this."

"I'll take my chances." The buckle of his belt jangles, then he yanks it off. The swish of the leather against the fabric of his pants sparks goosebumps across my skin. My pussy clenches, and my thighs quiver. *Damn it, why am I so wet?* I jump up to my feet, and he peels back his lips. His incisors gleam, and for a second, he seems like a predator. A lion stalking its prey. A wolf pursuing its mate.

I definitely need to stop reading those smutty romance novels. Real life is nothing like the words between the pages. But being with JJ is the closest I've come to experiencing the kind of passion I thought was limited to fictional heroines. And he's so much sexier than any morally gray hero I've read about. He's my real-life Mafia guy, and I'm the woman he's going to bend over and fuck to within an inch of her life.

If I let him, that is. Which I'm definitely not going to. Stupid romance novels. It's their fault I've built up all those spicy scenarios in my head. I glance sideways to where the latest paperback I've ordered lies face down on the bedstand. Thank God for discreet covers. At least it doesn't give any hint of what's hidden between the sheets—of the book, that is, not of the bed. I'm not referring to the bedsheets. "Nope, n-a-a-h."

"Are you talking to yourself?" he asks with great interest.

"Of course not," I huff.

"Hmm." He glances toward the book.

Oh, no. No, no, no. I leap toward it, but he's already there. He snatches up the paperback. I yelp, try to reach for it, but he's so tall, even with my standing on the bed, he towers over me. I paw at his arm, and my fingertips slide off his muscled forearm. He switches the book to his other hand, using his free one to hold me at bay.

To my mortification, he begins to read aloud. "He tears off her panties. She whimpers. He ties the rope around her wrist and loops it around the headboard. Then he does the same to her other hand. Then he straddles her chest, squeezes her chin so she opens her mouth, and thrusts his cock down her—"

"Stop." My face is burning red. "Stop, stop, stop."

"No fucking way. This is what you like, girl? You want to be dominated by a man who ties you up?"

"Just because it's in the book doesn't mean I want it in real life."

He snorts. "Your annotations in this book suggest otherwise."

"That's just a compulsion. I like to underline—"

"The particularly horny passages of the book. Is this your kink, baby? You like to get yourself off while reading steamy books? This how you've been taking care of yourself while I haven't been around?"

I don't reply. I don't need to. I'm sure the expression on my face gives it all away.

He continues to read the rest of the page—a page I've read many times, a passage I'm intimately familiar with. I know exactly what happens next.

"You imagined us in this position?" He hands over the book. I pounce on it, then scramble to the other side of the bed and shove it inside the drawer there. When I turn, he's watching me with an intent look on his face.

"You know, you didn't need to get yourself off by reading books one-handed. All you had to do was call me and I'd have happily helped you recreate any scene of your choice. Or all of your scenes. Every night. Night after night."

I sink down onto the bed and cross my legs. "Can we talk about something else?"

"I'd rather talk about your favorite sexual fantasy."

My cheeks heat further. It feels like my entire body is on fire. My nipples pebble, and my toes curl. It's not like he's talking dirty, but the fact that he got a peek into the images in my head is beyond embarrassing.

I glance away.

He clicks his tongue.

"Don't hide from me, baby. I don't want any secrets between us."

I hunch my shoulders and try to draw even further into myself. Why am I feeling so defensive? It's not like we haven't fucked. Not like how we fucked is all that different from some of the scenes in my book. Still, he's stumbled upon what's a very private thing to me. A space where I'm completely true to myself. Where I can admit to just how much I want it like that… and with him. I do want it to be JJ. I do. I bite the inside of my cheek. "Fine, I admit it. I imagined you in place of the heroes I read in the books, okay?"

His eyes gleam. "Tell me more."

"Nothing more. They fuck. I imagine you fucking me."

"Do you come?"

I nod.

"How many times?"

"Many times." I clear my throat.

"How *many* times?" He lowers his voice to a hush, and a shiver coils down my back. The pulse between my thighs grows heavier, mirroring the rate of my heartbeat.

"Girl," he snaps. "How. Many. Times?"

"Three times," I burst out.

He glares at me, and I shiver.

"Okay, fine, I came three times when I read that scene, okay?"

His mouth curls. "And did you use your fingers to get yourself off?"

"And—" I stab my thumb in the direction of the bedstand drawer.

"Hmm." He strokes his chin. "Pussy or arse?"

"Excuse me?" I blink.

"You use them in your pussy or your arse?"

Heat flushes my skin. It's so filthy to hear him talk like that. So hot. So dirty. So much of a turn-on.

"Both, I take it?"

I nod.

"Lay back."

"What do you mean?"

He draws in a breath. "Lay back against the pillows, baby."

"Wh… why?"

His lips kick up and oh, god, that smile of his is not nice. So full of promise. So filled with confidence that I find myself doing just that.

He curls the belt around his other palm then stretches it out. He shakes it out, the sound like a whiplash. I jump.

57

JJ

"Let's see if I can't defeat your own personal record." I walk toward her, her eyes round. She slides up the pillows until her back is to the headboard.

I throw my leg over her waist, and without leaning my weight on her, I crowd her so she can't move further.

"J… JJ…" Her chin wobbles. "You… you don't scare me."

"Good. Raise your arms over your head."

Her pupils dilate. Her breaths come out in pants.

"Either you do it, or I'll do it for you."

She gulps, then raises her arms as directed.

"Good girl."

Her breath catches. Color stains her neck, then the tops of her breasts. Her nipples are peaked against the fabric of the dress she's wearing. I lean over, knot the belt around both of her slim wrists, then loop it around the headboard. I tighten it, and a shiver slinks down her body.

"JJ, please."

"It's Jack," I remind her.

"Jack," she breathes, and goddamn, the sound of my name from her lips thrums through my veins. The blood drains to my groin, and the crotch of my pants grows impossibly tight. I test the knot, making sure it's not too tight, then unknot the tie from around my neck.

Her jaw drops. "Wh-what is that for?"

"What do you think?" I place it over her eyes and her entire body jolts. It's as if I've buried myself inside of her, only I'm not yet touching her. Not really. "Relax, baby." I tie it around her eyes, then because I can't stop myself, I place my lips over hers, not touching her but breathing her air.

"I can sense you, JJ." She moans. "I know what you're up to."

"It's Jack, and I don't think you do." I lick her lips, and before the shudder can make its way down her body, I push off the bed. I pad away.

"Where are you going?" There's panic in her voice.

"I'll be right back, baby. I promise."

I walk into the bathroom, rummage around in the drawers until I find what I need, then I walk back and climb onto the bed. She tips up her chin, no doubt sensing my movements.

"Ready, girl?" I brush my lips over hers. When I pull back, she chases my touch. "So greedy." I chuckle.

She pouts. "You're such a tease. You—"

I hook the scissors in the neckline of the dress, then cut my way down the length.

"What are you doing?" She pants. "Are you cutting my dress? I love this dress."

"I'll get you a hundred more." I cut down the length of her torso, past her panties, until I reach the hem of the dress. Then I place the scissors on the bedstand.

I catch the two separate halves of the dress and tug them apart. Goosebumps rise on her skin. The honeyed curves of her breasts swell over the cups of her demi bra. Her nipples outlined against the fabric. Her waist is tapered and the slight swell of her belly dips down under the waistband of her panties. The dramatic flare of her hips calls to me.

I slide back to straddle her legs, then lower my head to the apex of her thighs. I sniff deeply, and a whine bleeds from her lips.

"Why do you do that?"

"Why, don't you like it?"

"I do, and that's the problem," she confesses. "Before I met you, I didn't think I could revel in the rawness of what sex could be between two people."

I draw her scent into my lungs and my cock throbs. "Jesus, baby, your scent is my downfall."

She half laughs. "I don't know why that turns me on."

"Because you feel the same way. I've caught you sniffing me, too."

"I don't." She scoffs.

"Sure you do. Nothing wrong with that. It's how animals recognize their mates."

She stills. "Is that what we are?" she asks in a small voice.

I glance up toward her face. "Aren't we?"

She swallows. "Jack, I—"

I grip the waistband of her lacy panties and tear them off.

She yelps. "Oh, my god." She squeezes her thighs together. Unbelievable. I haven't even touched her, and she's already so turned on.

"How aroused are you, baby, show me?"

She hesitates then parts her legs further. The pink-brown of her pussy lips glisten. A fat drop of cum slides along her inner thigh. I bend to lick it up. She gasps and her body jerks. She closes her bent knees, locking them around my neck. My face is smothered against her pussy but I'm not complaining. I grip her hips then swipe my tongue up her pussy lips. She groans, then thrusts her pelvis up and toward my mouth. I stab my tongue inside her wet slit, and her entire body jolts. Her back arches off the mattress and I begin to tongue fuck her in earnest.

I'd wanted to take my time with her, but the days without her, the yearning for her, the need to be with her—not just to hold her in my arms, but actually wanting to talk to her, to look into her eyes as she laughs, to hear her voice, pit my wits against her… I miss all of that. I miss her. The loss of her was a Lena-shaped hole in my life that nothing and no one else can fill. And then, there's her pussy. My favorite dessert in the entire world, which I'll never get enough of. I tilt my head and curl my tongue inside her melting core. She whines. I squeeze her butt cheeks, then swipe my tongue from rear hole to clit, then again. I curl my tongue around her swollen bud and she rears up.

"Jack, Jack, Jack, please," she yells.

I don't let up. I scoop up her cum and smear it between her arse cheeks, then slide my finger inside her. A jolt thuds through her. That's when I slide my other hand up, squeeze her nipple and bite down on her clit.

She screams as she shatters. Her entire body shudders. Moisture bathes my tongue, clings to my mouth and my chin. She loosens her thighs, and I crawl up and close my mouth over hers. She parts her lips and I kiss her deeply—tasting her essence, dancing my tongue over hers, dragging it across her teeth, the seams of her lips. She shudders, writhes under me and tugs on her restraints. I rise up to my knees between her legs, tear off my shirt and fling it aside. Then shove my pants down. My cock jumps out—large, throbbing, engorged with the need to be inside her.

"Jack," she moans, and my balls tighten. I squeeze the base of my shaft, then slide up until I'm poised over her face.

"Open your mouth, baby."

"Jack," she licks her lips. Then does as I ordered. I place the tip of my dick on the rim of her mouth, then bury my fingers in her hair.

"Suck me off, girl."

Before the words are out of my mouth, she rears up. My shaft slides across her tongue and hits the back of her throat. She gags but doesn't stop. She closes her mouth around my length, then hollows her cheeks. A line of fire detonates out from the point of contact.

"Fuck, fuck, fuck!" I tug on her hair.

She groans… moans… saliva drips down her chin. She pulls back, draws in a breath, and pants.

"Just like that, baby. Take another breath."

She does. That's when I feed her my cock again. This time, my shaft slips past her gag reflex. I wrap my fingers around the front of her throat and groan. "I can feel my length down your gullet."

Tears squeeze out from under the blindfold. I scoop them up and bring my fingers to my mouth. I suck on my fingers and the salty-sweet taste of Lena fills me. Something shifts in my chest. My heart begins to race. My pulse pounds behind my eyes. "I'm going to fuck your mouth, baby."

58

Lena

Fuck me. Take me. Own me. Possess me. The words seem to boil up from somewhere deep inside. I tug on my hands, but of course, they're restrained. I try to peer from under my blindfold, but there's no space. The scent of him envelops me, though. The taste of him is heavy in my mouth. The heat of his body pushes down on my chest, holding me captive. He fists my hair and my scalp tingles. I moan and his cock jerks down my throat. It seems to swell further, pushing up and into the walls of my mouth. He pulls out until he's once again positioned at the seam of my lips, then slides down my throat. I gag again, then swallow. A groan rumbles from him. He repeats the movement, and again, and again. Each time he fills my mouth he feels bigger, harder, more urgent. My core swells, the pulse between my legs so loud it seems to pound through my blood. I squeeze my legs together, try to clamp down on the yawning emptiness in my core.

His movements speed up. His balls slap against my chin. I feel the tension radiate off of him, sense his muscles tense. The very air around us seems to grow heavier with the impending release. The hair on my forearms rises. Static electricity seems to lick across my nerve endings. The ball of heat in my core tightens, curls in on itself. My entire body shudders. My toes curl. He speeds up even more, then growls, "I'm coming, baby. Fuck!"

He begins to pull out, but I close my lips around him and suck.

"Ah, fuck, Lena!" His voice seems stretched in a way I've never heard it before. The heat in the space grows even more intense. His body seems to shudder and then, with a low growl, he shoots his load down my throat. He stays there for a second longer, his cock pulsing. *Oh hell, I'm going to gag.* Before I do, he pulls out. He cups my cheek, and the next second, he's kissing me, absorbing my breath, swallowing the whine that wells up from deep inside. Then my restraints are gone, my blindfold falls away, and his dark gaze burns into me.

He searches my eyes with his probing, piercing ones, holding me suspended in time—in his arms, under him, with the scent of his cum on my breath. The next second he rolls, taking me with him, so I'm straddling him. His length pulses against my melting center. He grips my hips and raises me enough that I'm positioned exactly over his still erect cock.

"You didn't take one of those little blue pills, did you?" I murmur.

His brows slash down over his nose.

"It shouldn't be a completely unexpected question. You just came, and you're already ready to go, and considering your almost senior citizen status—"

He pistons his hips up and impales me with his hard, throbbing cock.

I gasp, try to speak, but I swear I can feel him in my throat. I thought that was an exaggeration made up by romance authors, but trust me—when you do, you know. I swallow, hold onto his wrists, and gasp.

"You were saying?" he growls in that dark voice that sends shivers of delight rolling up my spine. My thighs clench. I squeeze down on that hard column between my legs, and the muscles of his stomach jump. At least he's not unaffected by me, either. I should be confident of that by now. But looking at his beautiful features, those carved cheekbones, the hooked nose, that generous lower lip, not to mention the firm jaw, I feel I'm in a dream conjured up by my fevered imagination.

"Less thinking; more fucking," he snaps.

I can't stop the laugh that bubbles up. "Good to know your priorities are in the right place."

"You're my priority, baby. Always. Never forget that." His cock stretches me and his gaze holds me. His fingers massage the curves of my hips. He holds me in place, skewered on that monster cock of his, and I feel so engulfed by him, so overcome with emotion, that a sob wells up. I try to swallow it but he notices it.

"Lena, what's wrong?" He begins to pull away, but I squeeze my inner walls around him, and grip the outside of his thighs.

"Don't you dare stop now; you hear me?" I swipe at my cheeks. "I'm a woman. Sex is emotional for me. I'm allowed to cry."

He firms his lips, but to my relief, doesn't push it. He flips me over again, without slipping out of me—how the hell did he manage that? —then urges me to raise my legs over his shoulders so I'm bent almost in half under him. He sinks in farther, and at this angle, I can feel every ridge of his dick as he bottoms out inside of me. He brushes up against my pelvic walls and it's so intense, a fresh flood of tears squeezes out from the corners of my eyes.

"Ah, baby." He bends and licks up the moisture, then pushes his forehead into mine. "I love you, my girl. You know that, right?"

I nod. What else can I do? Of course, I've known it. But to hear him say it, with emotions crackling deep inside those dark eyes, and while he's still inside me… This is my personal fantasy, nirvana, a ten in every way, the perfect scene come to life from one of the spicy books I've read, a corporate merger executed with such style, with so much panache and heat and… Oh, my god, my thoughts are all over the place.

"Baby?" he whispers. "You okay?"

I shake my head.

"Tell me what you need."

I try to speak, but no words seem to form. My brain cells have all fused into a mass of yearning, a hunger that gnaws at my center. He searches my features, then cups my cheek. He rubs his thumb across my lower lip, before easing it into my mouth. I suck on it, and his gaze intensifies. I bite down, and his cock jumps inside my channel. I can't stop my lips from curling.

His eyes gleam. He curls his fingers around my throat, applying just enough pressure to hold me in place. Then pulls his other hand from my mouth and slides it down to twine his fingers with mine.

He twists my hand up and over my head, and without taking his gaze off of mine, he begins to thrust up and into me. Long, smooth strokes that jolt my body and move me farther up the bed. The headboard slams into the wall repeatedly. He picks up speed, grunting with the effort as he impales me again. His chest planes shift in a tectonic move that makes my mouth water. Sweat gleams across his shoulders. He grits his teeth, and the tendons on his neck stand out in relief. Color flushes his cheeks. He's the most alive man I've ever met. The most vital. The sternest. The most alpha. Most intense. Most… sexy. Most… tender, in his own way. And for the record, no one has ever fucked me with such focus before.

A thousand fires detonate across my skin, and my belly trembles. Sparks gather, whizzing into a tight ball of need in my center. He pulls out, then with a final plunge, he buries himself to the hilt inside of me. My entire body shudders. I squeeze down on his fingers.

"Come with me, Lena. Right now."

59

JJ

I watch her sleep sprawled on her front, her glorious mane curling around her shoulders and flowing down her back. I wind a thick, silky strand around my fingers, then bend my head and sniff it.

"You're obsessed with how I smell." She yawns.

"Strawberries and passionfruit and a hint of something spicy. I can never place what it is. Every time I think I know what it is, it eludes me."

"Cloves," she murmurs.

"Cloves?"

"It's in my shampoo. A special concoction that nourishes my hair. It's so thick, I need something more tailor-made to tame the bulk."

"I love your hair." I bury my fingers in it and tug.

She shivers.

I drag my fingers through her scalp, and she moans.

I follow the curve of her skull to the base where it meets her neck and scratch gently.

"Oh, god." A quiver grips her. "That spot... How did you find it?"

"I know everything about you, baby."

"I hope not. A relationship without any secrets would be so boring."

I still. "As long as it's not the kind of secret that involves life and death."

Her forehead furrows, then she crawls onto my chest. I hook an arm around her waist and hold her close. "I don't envy Michael right now. If it had been you in her place—" I shake my head. "I'm not sure how I would have dealt with it."

"She wanted his child. I understand why she did it."

"She should have told him. He deserved to know how much danger she was putting herself in."

She cups my cheek. "She wanted to be a mother. It's something only a woman would understand."

I turn my head and kiss her palm. "If something were to happen to you, I'm not sure I'd be able to bear it."

"Nothing's going to happen to me," she murmurs.

Something in her voice makes me glance toward her. "What?" I growl.

"What?" she says in an innocent voice.

"Oh no you don't. I know when you're overanalyzing something. Out with it, girl."

"So, it's girl when you're trying to steamroll me into toeing the line, hmm?" She traces a line down my jaw.

"Do you think I can steamroll you into anything? Also, I'm not going to let you distract me." I twine my fingers through hers, then place a kiss on each of them. "Now tell me, what's on your mind."

She hesitates.

"You can ask me anything, you know." I search her features. "You do know that, right?"

"I was wondering about the turtle in your bedroom."

"Solomon."

"Eh?"

"His name is Solomon. I rescued him when I was fifteen. And he's been my only constant companion—" I bend and kiss her lips "—until now."

I pull back, and she chases my lips with her own. Another long, drugging kiss later, I search her eyes. "Now tell me what your real question is."

Her gaze widens, then she snorts. "It's annoying how you always read my mind."

"L-e-n-a," I warn, and she rolls her eyes. A gesture I'll tolerate, but only from her.

"I'm waiting," I remind her.

She searches my features and whatever she sees there must reassure her for she finally says, "It's about children."

"What about them?"

"Do you want them?"

"Do *you* want them?"

She chews on the inside of her cheek. "Not right away, but at some point. I want your children, Jack."

I stare at her. Kids. Doing it all over again with her. With a woman who gets me better than anyone else. With someone who is my partner. With whom I can finally take off the mask I've worn for so long, a persona I've perfected over the years but which has felt so constraining of late. Now I know why.

I want more. I want life… as I had once hoped it would be. A future I'd thought would never be mine. A place I can call home, with someone who *is* home. A unit. A family that belongs to me, and to whom I belong.

"I thought I was too old to start again." I lean in and brush my lips over hers. "But when I'm with you, everything seems possible. When I'm with you, I'm greedy, Lena. Greedy for you, for us. For what we are together. For the shared experiences that will be ours. For the hopes and dreams and laughs and tears and happiness and sadness and grief and joy… All of those highs and lows I've shied away from for so long. All of those emotions I could never share with Isaac and Tally" —I swallow— "that I want to open up and invite you to be part of."

"And our children," she murmurs.

"And our children," I agree.

"And Isaac and Tally, too?"

"And them. And their families" —I lower my chin— "on one condition…"

She looks wary. "Which is?" she finally asks.

"You move your books into the library."

She laughs. "You do realize they're spicy romance books, which may not exactly fit in with your classics?"

"Oh, they're better than classics, considering I plan to enact each and every scene from these books in real life, with you."

She draws in a breath. Her golden-brown eyes shine. "That's the most romantic thing anyone has ever said to me."

"And I'm just getting started."

She sniffs.

"No more tears, baby." I kiss first one eyelid then the other. "No more wanting space, either. I want you in my corner. I want to be your backup. Without you, my days were long and lonely, but you burst into my life like a shooting star—all sparkly, and bright, and with so much to give. You dazzled me… You still dazzle me, Lena. You're what turns my dreams of tomorrow into a reality I can't wait to discover with you. Be mine, Lena. Stay with me, in my house, in my bed, in my heart, my soul. In every single fiber of my being. Be the mother of my children. Be my North Star… and my south, and my west, and my east. Be mine, Lena."

Her chin wobbles. She leans up and kisses me with so much passion, so much depth, so much emotion that my chest hurts. My heart stutters. My stomach seems to bottom out. My head spins. I kiss her back with everything I'm not able to put into words. I press her into the bed and she opens her arms, her legs, her heart, and welcomes me home. *Thud-thud-thud* my heart slams into my chest, echoing the beat of hers.

Thud-thud-thud. "JJ, Lena, you guys in there?"

"There's someone at the door," she whispers against my mouth.

All at once, my phone vibrates, as does hers.

I freeze. We stare at each other, then pull apart at the same time. "Karma!"

"You scared us." My girl takes Karma's hand in hers.

"That makes two of us," Summer says from the other side of Karma's bed. Sinclair stands next to Summer, one hand on the back of his wife's chair.

"I swear, when I saw you collapse, my heart almost jumped out of my chest." Lena claps her hand over her mouth. "Oops, sorry, didn't mean to say it like that."

Summer's lips twitch.

Karma chuckles, then coughs.

"Sorry, didn't mean to make you laugh, either." Lena looks stricken.

Karma rolls her eyes. "I'm not gonna die any time soon."

Michael makes a low noise at the back of his throat. Karma glances at her husband who's seated in the corner of the room. His gaze is focused on his phone, but his attention is on his wife. And rightly so. Karma looks pale; there are hollows below her cheekbones and purple patches under her eyes. Her eyes, though, gleam with humor. She's in good spirits, which is not something that can be said about her husband. Michael hasn't said a word since Lena and I walked in here.

After knocking on the door of Lena's house, Summer told us they were on their way to the hospital as Karma was awake. We'd followed them in my car. By the time we reached Karma's room, Summer and Sinclair were already there.

The entire time that Summer and Lena visit with Karma, Michael stays silent. Except for the occasional flicks of his gaze toward his wife to make sure that she is okay, he's been focused on his phone.

Luca and Adrian are positioned outside the room, with Christian, Axel, and Massimo at strategic points throughout the floor. Their wives have also been in and out, Karma told us. Seems the Sovrano clan has taken up temporary residence in the hospital. They managed to clear out the entire floor and occupy the nearby rooms so they could keep Karma company, and also act as emotional support for Michael. Not surprising, considering how tightly knit the Sovranos are.

Lena tugs on my sleeve. I glance down to find her glancing at Michael, then back at me.

"What?" I frown.

She rises to her feet, then circles her arms around my neck. I automatically wind my arm around her waist to hold her steady. "Why don't you take Michael out, so he can get a breath of fresh air?"

"Why would I do that?"

She pats my cheek. "Because you're his friend, and that's what friends do."

I may be older in years and experience, but I still have a lot to learn from her.

"Right." I glance at Michael. "Take him out."

"Why don't you go with them?" Summer places her hand on Sinclair's hip in an affectionate gesture.

"Why would I do that?" Sinclair's features wear an expression of confusion, which echoes my sentiments.

"Because we girls want time alone to catch up," Summer says patiently.

"Oh, right." Sinclair's brow clears. He looks toward me as if to say he'd prefer I take the lead in this. I blow out a breath. Considering the two of them were about ready to shoot each other until a few days ago, it's probably in everyone's best interest if I do.

I haul my girl up to her tiptoes, then bend my head and kiss her thoroughly. By the time I finish, she's flushed and her pupils are dilated.

"Hold that thought." I press another kiss to her forehead, then head in Michael's direction.

60

Lena

"Sooo, you and JJ?" Karma bursts out as soon as the door has shut behind the men.

"OMG, you guys are so cute together," Summer chirps.

My head is still reeling from that kiss. To think, it's just a meeting of lips, but JJ turns it into an erotic art form. I could probably come from just his kisses. An experiment I can't wait to try. In fact, I have come from just his kisses—to my lower lips.

"Lena?" Karma's voice cuts through my thoughts. "Earth to Lena, hello!"

"I'm here." I brush my hair back from my forehead. "Gosh, is the air conditioner working in this room or what?"

Karma and Summer look at each other, then they burst out laughing.

"What?" I stare between them. "What did I say?"

"There's nothing wrong with the temperature in here. It's you who's all heated up," Karma chortles. At least she didn't cough after laughing this time, which is an improvement, right?

"Oh." My cheeks heat further.

"So, you guys made up then?" Summer asks through her wide grin.

"It would seem that way, yes," I say slowly.

"You moving in with him?" Karma sits up, and Summer slides pillows behind her, while I pat down the sheet around her.

"I'm fine, you guys. I'm not an invalid, really," Karma protests.

"You shouldn't be exerting yourself. Doctor's orders," Summer points out.

"Sitting up in bed is not exerting myself."

"Umm, sorry, but you don't get a say in this. Not after what you've pulled on all of us." Summer scowls at her sister.

"So, you're going to be okay?" I turn to Karma. "You and the baby are fine?"

"We're fine, and hopefully, will be fine throughout the pregnancy." She tips up her chin.

"It's still a high-risk pregnancy, and things could flare up again," Summer points out.

"As could happen in any pregnancy." Karma scoffs.

"It's not in every pregnancy that the mother's health is in so much danger." Summer's chin wobbles. "Why did you do this, Karma? I mean, I know why you did, but still—" She places her palms on her bump. "I know how much you want this child, but I don't want to lose you."

Karma holds out her hand and Summer takes it.

"I know I'm being selfish, and putting all of you through so much worry, but I really want this baby, Summer. When he or she is finally here, everything will be worth it." Karma says in a soft voice.

"You're so brave, Karma." I reach for her shoulder and squeeze it.

She releases Summer's hand and settles into the pillows. "As are you, for pursuing what you want."

"You mean JJ?"

She nods.

"Don't know if I'm being brave or foolish. We're such different people. We come from different backgrounds, and of course, the age gap—"

"Doesn't seem to be a problem for either of you," Summer chimes in.

"You're right; it's not."

"Does Isaac have an issue with it?" Karma cups her chin in her hand.

"Nope, he thinks JJ and I are better suited to each other."

"There you go." Summer claps her hands. "Things couldn't have worked out better. And this means you'll be part of the Sisterhood of the Seven."

"Technically, JJ isn't one of the Seven, or one of the Sovranos," I point out.

"He's the bridge between the two." Summer drums her fingers on her bump. "He's the man both sets of seven respect. They trust him. It's why Sinclair didn't throw Michael out when he turned up at our place with JJ for Ava and Baron's wedding. Of course, the fact that Karma was with him may have helped." Summer laughs.

"JJ does have the kind of gravitas that allows him to hold his own against both Michael and Sinclair's larger-than-life personalities." I place the tips of my fingers together.

"Put the three of them in a room, and no opponent has a chance," Karma agrees.

"So, you going to marry him?" Summer asks.

I laugh. "Hold on, you guys are going too fast. We haven't had a chance to discuss all of that yet."

"Guess you were too busy making up for lost time, eh?" Karma cackles.

"Something like that." I fold one leg over the other. "Also, I'm not in a hurry to get married. I'm happy to take each day as it comes. We need to get to know each other a lot better first."

"He's crazy about you. He can't take his gaze off of you when you're together. And I bet he watches out for you even when you guys aren't together."

I tilt my head. Can't refute that. JJ's possessive protectiveness is like

page 362 at top

a warm blanket. I have to admit, it makes me feel cherished and wanted. Reinforces the fact that I belong to him. I should find it cloistering, but strangely, I don't. Somehow, it's reassuring.

"He gave me space when I asked for it," I finally say.

The sisters exchange another glance.

"What? Out with it, you guys."

Karma snickers. "You do know he maneuvered things so you'd move into the house set between both of ours."

"It's still my own place."

"And it's adjacent to two of the most secure locations in all of the city."

"Right." I lower my chin to my chest. *"Right!"* I sit up straight. "This way, he ensured I was protected."

Summer nods. "Security for our place is set up by Karina Beauchamp, who works with Axel, Michael's brother, who also has his own security firm, and who looked after the security arrangements for Karma and Michael's home."

"And those arrangements extend to my current place, so I was doubly protected," I exclaim.

"Yep," Summer agrees.

"Smooth move, if you ask me. You can't fault him at all on this," Karma offers.

"Wait. It wasn't JJ who suggested this place, though, it was you," I turn to Summer.

"And who convinced you to accept the offer?" Summer tilts her head.

I drag my fingers through my hair. "Isaac. You don't think JJ suggested to him that he should?" I glance between Summer and Karma. "He did tell Isaac." I firm my lips.

"You can't blame JJ for doing everything by the book and still getting his way."

I laugh. I can't help myself. "He's one smart alphahole."

"They all are." Summer chuckles.

"Alphaholes. Every last one of them," Karma agrees.

"Talking about us, ladies?" JJ's voice sounds from the doorway.

Footsteps approach me, and before I can turn, JJ's warmth surrounds the chair I'm sitting in. He squeezes my shoulder. "You okay?"

I glance up at him. "Never been better."

The skin around his eyes crinkles. Something passes between us, and our gazes heat. A pulse licks to life in my lower belly. His grip on my shoulder tightens. I lick my lips, and his gaze drops to my mouth. His nostrils flare.

Someone clears their throat. I tear my gaze from JJ's to find both Summer and Karma staring at us with knowing looks in their eyes.

"Ah—" I clear my throat. "Guess we should leave and let you all catch up as a family."

"Family?" Both Michael and Sinclair ask at the same time, twin expressions of consternation on both of their faces.

"You guys are bros-in-law. Did you forget?" JJ drawls.

"Trying my best not to dwell on that, ol' chap," Sinclair finally says.

"Do you have to keep reminding us of it?" Michael scowls.

I sense the mirth roll off of JJ, and it's such a refreshing change. I like seeing him like this—more relaxed than he's ever been before. Of course, it could also be due to the sex we had recently. I squeeze my thighs together, and his grip on my shoulder tightens.

"We'd best be off." There's an urgency to his tone, and I know he's thinking of how we left things earlier in my bed. Truthfully, I can't wait to be alone with him, either.

"Take care of yourself, Karma." I lean over and kiss Karma's cheek.

"I'm here to make sure she does," Summer says grimly.

I glance in Michael's direction to find his gaze fixed on Karma's features. There's so much love, mixed with a tinge of anger, but also, helplessness. Gosh, he knows he doesn't have a choice but to bend to Karma's will in this regard. Is that what happens to alphaholes when they meet the right woman? Do they fall so completely that they become helpless in front of their other half's resolve? Is that how JJ will be?

We drive in silence, JJ at the wheel. Come to think of it, he also drove from the hospital to my place during the earlier trip.

"Where's your chauffeur?"

"I told him I'd call him when I need him."

I frown. "Thought you preferred it if he drove the car?"

"I prefer to be alone with you."

"We had privacy with the window pulled up between the front and back compartments of the car."

"I wanted to drive you."

"Oh." Not sure what I should say to that. Maybe best to be silent? I glance out the window. When we turn toward Hyde Park, I realize we're headed to his place. He didn't tell me he was taking me there. He didn't ask me if I'd prefer to go to his place over the house I've been staying in for the last week. Admittedly, I prefer his place; it feels more like home. As we take the road that skirts around the park and turn into his driveway, a calmness envelops me. How weird. I take in the tree line on either side, the rows of wildflowers which crowd the center of the slope on one side, the duck pond on the other. He drives around the fountain and we come to a stop in front of the three-story Victorian building. He switches off the engine, and we sit there in silence.

I glance out the window on my side at the turrets on the south side. That's where Isaac has his studio.

"He's moved out," JJ murmurs as if he's read my mind. I wouldn't be surprised if he could. The man has an uncanny way of always knowing what I'm thinking. "Got a place of his own in one of those hipster-ish new areas, which I'm not sure even qualifies as London."

"If you mean Dalston, it very much *is* in London." I glance at him sideways. "Your age is showing."

He narrows his gaze on me. "In this case, I don't mind. I'd love to have him stay longer with us, but I'm not unhappy that he moved out."

"No?" I tilt my head.

"I want to have time with you, to get to know you. To make you laugh. To find out what you like to do. To cook your favorite dishes. Play your favorite music. Take you to the movies on a date."

"You mean, you'll take me to an actual movie in a cinema instead of watching it in that big-ass cinema room you have in the basement?" I tease.

He winces. "That's the only civilized way to watch a movie, but I thought you'd appreciate a real date."

"And you'll take me to Mickey D's for dinner?"

His expression morphs into one of horror, before he composes his features. "If that's what you want."

I burst out laughing. "Relax, I'm not cruel enough to put you through that. Besides, we don't have to do every single activity together, do we?"

"For you, I'll go to a McDonald's, or better still, have a chef come home and prepare you the exact same burgers using the same recipe."

I blink. "Isn't their recipe a secret?"

He stares at me.

"Right, do I even want to know how you'll swing that?"

"It's all legal, if that's what you're asking."

"I have no doubt it is," I say, and I mean it. JJ has a past that makes him morally gray, but when it comes to me, he'll never risk putting me in danger.

His features soften. "I know you'd have preferred for me to ask you if you'd move in with me, but I'm not giving you a choice about it."

I can't stop the surprised laughter that bubbles up out of me. "If you'd asked me instead of bringing me here, I'd have thought you'd been kidnapped and replaced by an alien."

He arches an eyebrow. "That some kind of pop culture reference?" His Brit accent deepens.

"Something like that." My grin stretches wider. "You're kinda cute when you go all hoity-toity on me."

"You're always cute, and sexy, and gorgeous, and beautiful. You're the most intriguing woman in the world. The most fascinating, the most beguiling."

My cheeks grow fiery.

"Hear my soul speak. Of the very instant that I saw you, Did my heart fly at your service." He glances between my eyes.

"The Tempest," I say softly.

"It's true. I'm not a romantic. I wasn't looking for love or for an emotional connection. Then you swept into my life, and it's as if my past finally let go of me. You made it possible for me to dream, to hope, to open my eyes to possibilities. By just being who you are, you changed me. And it was sudden, but it was also so real, so natural. So much a part of me. I saw you and realized my life as I knew it was over, and for the better. I met you and knew I belonged with you. That we were going to be together. Doesn't mean I accepted it. I fought it with everything in me, even as my instincts confirmed it was my last bastion. My last attempt to hold onto my individuality, myself, my identity, for soon it would no longer be mine."

"JJ..." I swallow. "I—"

He leans over and presses his fingers to my lips. "There's something else you should know. Something that I've been meaning to tell you but haven't found the courage to, until now."

My heart begins to race. My throat closes. "What is it?" I swallow. "You can tell me anything."

He takes my fingers in his. "Promise me you won't hate me."

"Nothing you do could make me hate you." I turn my palm up and interlink our fingers. "Now, tell me already."

"You know when you thought it was Isaac in your room making love to you while you were sleeping?"

"It was Isaac, and how do you—" I stare at him. "JJ, you didn't..."

He nods. "It was me. I crept into your room, and you were there, and I couldn't stop myself. I slipped into bed and finger-fucked you."

I pull my hand from his.

"And the time you slept in my office when we were working on the presentation? I said I wouldn't make a move on you—"

"But you did."

I don't need to see the look of contrition on his face to know, of course, he had.

I shove the car door open and step out.

The door on JJ's side slams, and he rounds the car toward me.

"I thought we couldn't be together, and if that was the only way I could have you, then I wasn't going to deny either of us."

I begin to pace. Back-forth-back.

The silence stretches.

"Lena, say something."

I turn to him and link my fingers together. "I knew it was you."

He blinks. "You did?"

"That time in my bed? I suspected it. It was how you held me. The confidence in your actions. How you maneuvered my body, how you knew what to do to make me come and—"

He looks at me expectantly.

"I never climaxed with Isaac, before that night."

His lips curl in a satisfied smirk. "But you came when I made love to you."

"I did. And then there was your scent." I close the distance between us, lower my face to his chest and sniff. "Sherry oak and cinnamon, with a dash of dark chocolate. It had to be you."

"You never mentioned it."

I raise a shoulder. "My subconscious insisted it was you. But my rational mind insisted it couldn't have been. And yet... I knew."

"And you guessed I'd made you come in my office?" He tilts his chin.

"I woke up feeling so relaxed, despite the fact that I'd spent the night on your couch. And that morning, you were acting more grouchy than normal, so I made a calculated guess."

He notches his knuckles under my chin so I have no choice but to look up into his face.

"Do you forgive me for what I did?" He searches my features.

"Do you feel sorry for what you did?"

He hesitates, then squares his shoulders. "No. I'd do it all over again."

My lips twitch. "That's what I expected you to say."

"So, you do forgive me?"

I search his features. "This morally gray space you occupy, that's your appeal. If you were any different, you wouldn't be you."

His eyebrows draw down. "You haven't answered my question."

I hold his gaze. "There's nothing to forgive."

Tension drains from his features. "I am what I am, Lena. But I promise I'll always take care of you. I'll protect you. I'll ensure you're always happy. That you never fall short of orgasms."

My smile widens.

"That you look forward to each day with a smile. That I'll do my best to make all your dreams come true. That you'll always feel secure. I'll never do anything to hurt you, I—"

"I love you."

61

JJ

"Excuse me?"

"I love you, Jack." Her lips curve against my fingers. "I should have said it to you earlier. I don't know why I held back."

"That's not why I made that speech," I mutter.

Her smile widens. "And you were doing so well."

"Not bad for someone who has never been in love before, eh?"

Her eyes glisten. "This feels like a dream."

"Believe it, baby." I slide my hand down and curve my fingers around her neck. "With you, I feel invincible. Like I've been given a second chance, and this time, I'm not going to blow it."

"Isaac and Tally—"

"Did Isaac tell you about the affair he had with my HR manager?"

She blinks, then nods. "He did. And I was relieved. I told him about us as soon as we slept together, but considering we'd been eye-fucking each other for days before that, a part of me felt like I had been unjust to him. But now, I realize while Isaac and I tried to be in a relationship, neither one of us was ready to commit to the other. Oh, we tried to make it work, but we weren't right for each other."

"Are you sad about it?"

She shakes her head. "It's what led me to you, so I don't regret my actions."

I tighten my hold around her neck. "I'm going to make amends for the past. I'm going to try my best to be a good parent to Isaac and to Tally. It won't be easy, especially with Tally—I haven't spoken to her in years—but I'm going to do my best to be there for her, for both of them, from now on." I search her features. "You make me wish I'd been a better man in the past, but since I can't change that, I'm going to ensure you have no cause for complaint from me in the future, at least not when it comes to my children or the kids we're going to have in the future."

Her pupils dilate. "Who'd have thought Mr. Stuck-up-Alphahole would turn out to be such a hot, sexy wordsmith?"

"And who'd have thought the gorgeous, curvy, spirited girl who stared at me with her golden eyes would turn out to be my match."

"You already got in my pants, you don't need to flatter me," she murmurs.

"One thing you need to realize" —I pull her toward me— "I mean every single word I say to you."

"One thing you need to realize" —she leans in closer until our breaths mingle— "when I'm with you, I'm always horny."

Her phone vibrates. She ignores it, brushes her lips over mine, and it buzzes again.

"Do you need to get that?"

"It might be my family." She nibbles on my lower lip, and my cock twitches.

"You *need* to get it." Can't believe I said that, but if I am going to do this with her, I'm going to do it right. Which means, I need to meet her family, and her mother, and get her blessings for what I have in mind.

She pouts. "But—"

I curve my lips against hers. "No buts. I do want your butt, but right now, you need to take that call and introduce me to your family."

She blinks. "You sure? They're a handful."

"But they're a part of you. Ergo, I need to get to know them and introduce myself, since they're going to be seeing a lot of me in the future."

She blinks, then nods. "My mom's ten years older than you."

"Is that a problem for you?" I search her features.

"Is that a problem for you?"

I shake my head. "I'm proud of you, Dinky. Proud of what we are together. And I want your family to be part of our happiness. Is that okay?"

Her chin wobbles, but her smile is so wide it lights up her entire face. Her golden-brown eyes sparkle. "Here goes." She answers the FaceTime call, then holds it up so both of us are reflected on the screen.

"Hey, guys, I want you to meet JJ."

A week later

"A million dollars and I get first right of refusal on the new app." Liam Kincaid holds out his hand. We're in the main room of the 7A Club. *My* club, which counts amongst its members, the most influential people in the world, and where I'm witnessing the first big transaction I've brokered. An arrangement that's going to show the zeitgeist just how powerful this organization is going to be.

The man opposite Liam blinks. "That's it? You're going to invest in my start up?"

"You do come ratified by JJ here" —Liam jerks his chin in my direction— "and believe you me, that doesn't come easily. He's done the hard work of vetting your financial plans. If he says it's poised to multiply my money by a factor of ten, then I take him at his word." Liam bares his teeth. "Of course, if you don't deliver, then I sell your company and all your assets and you work your ass off to pay off your debts."

The start-up guy swallows noisily.

"That won't happen." Liam's grin widens. He seems more like the shark he'd have to be to get where he is than the suave, Saville Row-suited gentleman he resembles.

"It… it won't?" The man's voice shakes. He has the brains to invent revolutionary concepts that will change the way we communicate, but when it comes to business transactions, he's a novice. Ergo, my club is the perfect platform for talent like his. He gets the investment, and someone like Liam, who's hungry for his next big success, gets first dibs when it comes to being an angel investor.

"Nope, you're far too smart, too strategic, too brilliant to let that happen."

"I am?"

Liam leans over and adjusts the young man's tie. The poor guy dressed up in his Sunday best—an ill-fitting suit bought off the rack from the high street, no doubt—for this meeting.

"Indeed, you are. You can't afford to fail your investors. If you do, you're done for. Your reputation is shot. And while some people have come back from it, I'll make it my personal mission that you won't." Liam pats his shoulder.

Nervous tension leaps off the younger guy. "If that's the case, why… should I let you invest?"

Liam smirks. "Given only zero-point-zero-five percent of start-ups ever achieve funding, you're in that infinitesimally tiny range, one you can't afford to walk away from. So, you'll take the deal and you'll make this a success. Now go, before I change my mind."

The younger man hesitates.

Liam glares at him. "Now," he barks.

The other man jumps up to his feet. He makes a grab for his papers, then turns and leaves. One of the sheets escapes and floats to the ground in his wake.

I pick it up and place it on the table between us.

"A bit harsh, even for you, Kincaid."

Liam raises a shoulder. "He's an adult, he knows what he's doing."

"But do you?"

"The fuck you mean?" He picks up one of the cigars from the holder and lights it.

"Heard you're getting married?"

"Pot, kettle," he says mildly.

"I love Lena."

"I love my inheritance." He smirks.

I bark out a laugh. "I used to think like you. Thought money and power were what's important in life."

"Is there anything else? And don't insult my intelligence by talking about love and the like, and—"

"Be careful before you say anything else. You don't want to have to take back your words."

"I never take back what I say." He places the cigar between his lips.

I pick up my own, survey its unlit tip.

"He's that proud, it eats up himself: pride is his own glass, his own trumpet, his own chronicle."

He blinks. "Since when did you begin to quote Shakespeare?"

"I always have." I tap my forehead. "Difference is, I say it aloud now."

He surveys me closely. "You've changed, JJ."

"No shit." I smirk.

"No, really. You're a motherfucking bastard who I wouldn't trust with anything except for your business instinct and your judge of character—"

"—you do realize that's a backhanded compliment?" I drawl.

"—I still don't trust you. Difference is, you seem more carefree, more relaxed, more, dare I say, optimistic?"

"That's what—"

"Nope, not that." He waggles his finger at me. "If one more of you tells me it's what the love of a woman can do to you, then I'm going to have to find a new circle of friends. Preferably, those who think unicorns don't exist in the real world."

"Isn't that what you're looking for, though, a unicorn?"

"Am I?" He frowns.

"That's what led you to investing in that young man's start-up."

"Sure, like any angel investor, I'm looking for that zero-point-zero-five percent one that'll gross a billion dollars in valuation."

"You sure you're not looking for that in the real world, too?"

His lips curl. "Oh, a billion dollars is definitely real to me."

"And when you find the right woman—"

He cuts the air with his palm. "Et tu, Brute?"

"Touché." I laugh. "Okay, no more talk about finding the 'one,' which brings me back to the question, 'The fuck are you getting married for?'"

"To lock down my inheritance. Need to seal the deal before my next birthday in thirty days, or else, I forfeit it."

I whistle. "We're talking about all of Kincaid Industries, I take it?"

"And then some."

"Cutting it close, aren't you?"

He scowls. "Tried to find a way out of it, but unfortunately, my father, it seems, has an airtight will."

"Maybe he had your best interests at heart?" Y-e-e-p, that's how much I've changed. As a father, I understand how sometimes a parent's actions can be misinterpreted by his child, and most of us have the good of our children at heart, even if we don't always express it the right way.

Liam's lips firm. "Either way, I'm not handing over the control of my companies. I've worked too hard to get where I am. No way am I going to—"

His phone vibrates. He pulls it out of his pocket and looks at it. "The fuck—?" he growls.

"What's up, ol' chap?"

He shakes his head. "Fucking hell, this can't be happening."

"Bad news?"

"She broke it off."

"Who broke it off?"

"My fiancée broke off our engagement," he says in disbelief.

I light up my cigar.

He sets his jaw. "It's all her fault."

"Whose fault?"

"Isla's. She's the wedding planner who's been filling my fiancée's—"

"You mean now ex-fiancée."

"—ears with feminist crap." His nostrils flare.

I clamp the cigar between my lips and puff on it. Nothing like a *Cohiba* to enjoy the evening's entertainment.

"I take it this Isla is also ugly to look at?"

"Don't be daft." He frowns down at the screen. "She's tiny and curvy and has masses of gorgeous hair that flows to her waist. And her eyes…" He shakes his head. "She has these amazing eyes that I could drown in."

"So, you like her?"

"Of course not." He snorts. "Can't be in the same room as her without one of us picking a fight. She's aggravating, adamant, and can't stop running off that mouth of hers. You should have heard her when I refused to attend the first wedding rehearsal." I open my mouth and he holds up his hand. "This wedding is going to attract a lot of media attention so Isla insisted on three rehearsals to make sure everything is perfect."

"A wedding you're going to have to call off, since your fiancée walked out on you," I remind him.

His forehead crinkles. "There is that, but no matter, the nuptials have to take place… In fact, you should have heard her yell when I refused to attend the first two rehearsals. She almost took my ear off." His lips twitch.

"You mean your ex-fiancée?"

"Eh?" He frowns. "No, I mean Isla. She's a dragon when it comes to arrangements. And when she gets angry, the tip of her nose turns red, and this cute furrow develops between her eyebrows." He touches the space between his own.

"So, I take it you do like her."

He wipes the smile from his face. "Didn't you hear me, Kane? Isla's the most annoying person I've ever met. She puts my teeth on edge. Something about her makes me want to—"

"Kiss her?"

He stares at me like I've gone crazy, which I may have. Blame it on the fact that I'm a reformed person, happily in love with a woman who lights up my life every time I see her. You know that old adage about people who get married wanting to find a spouse for all their single friends? It's true, and it extends to business acquaintances, too.

"—shake her so I can knock some sense into her." His gaze narrows. "In fact, that's what I'm going to do right now."

He slides the phone into his pocket, places his cigar in the ashtray, and rises to his feet.

"Where are you going?"

His eyes gleam. "To make her pay for this."

To find out what happens next read Liam and Isla's story HERE

Read an excerpt from Liam and Isla's story

Liam

"Where is she?"

The receptionist gazes at me cow-eyed. Her lips move, but no words emerge. She clears her throat, glances sideways at the door to the side and behind her, then back at me.

"So, I take it she's in there?" I brush past her, and she jumps to her feet.

"Sir, y-y-you can't go in there."

"Watch me." I glare at her.

She stammers, then gulps. Sweat beads her forehead. She shuffles back, and I stalk past her.

Really, is there no one who can stand up to me? All of this scraping of chairs and fawning over me? It's enough to drive a man to boredom. I need a challenge. So, when my ex-wife-to-be texted me to say she was calling off our wedding, I was pissed. But when she let slip that her wedding planner was right—that she needs to marry for love, and not for some family obligation, rage gripped me. I squeezed my phone so hard the screen cracked. I almost hurled the device across the room. When I got a hold of myself, for the first time in a long time, a shiver of something like excitement had passed through me. *Finally, fuck.*

That familiar pulse of adrenaline pulses through my veins. It's a sensation I was familiar with in the early days of building my business.

After my father died and I took charge of the group of companies he'd run, I was filled with a sense of purpose; a one-directional focus to prove myself and nurturing his legacy. To make my group of companies the leader, in its own right. To make so much money and amass so much power, I'd be a force to be reckoned with.

I tackled each business meeting with a zeal that none of my opponents were able to withstand. But with each passing year—as I crossed the benchmarks I'd set myself, as my bottom line grew healthier, my cash reserves engorged, and the people working for me began treating me with the kind of respect normally reserved for larger-than-life icons —some of that enthusiasm waned. Oh, I still wake up ready to give my best to my job every day, but the zest that once fired me up faded, leaving a sense of purposelessness behind.

The one thing that has kept me going is to lock down my legacy. To ensure the business I've built will finally be transferred to my name. For which my father informed me I needed to marry. Which is why, after much research, I tracked down Priya Kumar, and wooed her and proposed to her. And then, her meddling wedding planner came along and turned all of my plans upside down.

Now, that same sense of purpose grips me. That laser focus I've been lacking envelops me, fills my being. All of my senses sharpen as I shove the door of her office open and stalk in.

The scent envelops me first. The lush notes of violets and peaches. Evocative and fruity. Complex, yet with a core of mystery that begs to be unraveled. Huh? I'm not the kind to be affected by the scent of a woman, but this... Her scent... It's always chafed at my nerve-endings. The hair on my forearms straightens.

My guts tie themselves up in knots, and my heart pounds in my chest. It's not comfortable. The kind of feeling I got the first time I went white-water rafting. A combination of nervousness and excitement as I'd faced my first rapids. A sensation that had since ebbed. One I'd been chasing ever since, pushing myself to take on extreme sports. One I hadn't thought I'd find in the office of a wedding planner.

My feet thud on the wooden floor, and I get a good look at the space which is one-fourth the size of my own office. In the far corner is a bookcase packed with books. On the opposite side is a comfortable settee packed with cushions women seem to like so much. There's a colorful patchwork quilt thrown over it, and behind that, a window which looks onto the back of the adjacent office building. On the coffee table in front of the settee is a bowl with crystal-like objects that reflect the light from the floor lamps. There are paintings on the wall that depict scenes from beaches. No doubt, the kind she'd point to and sell the idea of a honeymoon to gullible brides. I suppose the entire space would appeal to women. With its mood lighting and homey feel, the space invites you to kick back, relax and pour out your problems. A ruse I'm not going to fall for.

"You!" I stab my finger in the direction of the woman seated behind the antique desk straight ahead. "Call Priya, right now, and tell her she needs to go through with the wedding. Tell her she can't back out. Tell her I'm the right choice for her."

She peers up at me from behind large, black horn-rimmed glasses perched on her nose. "No."

I blink. "Excuse me?"

She leans back in her chair. "I'm not going to do that."

"Why the hell not?"

"Are you the right choice for her?

"Of course I am." I glare at her.

Some of the color fades from her cheeks. She taps her pen on the table, then juts out her chin. "What makes you think you're the right choice of husband for her?"

"What makes you think I'm not."

"Do you love her?"

"That's no one's problem except mine and hers."

"You don't love her."

"What does that have to do with anything?"

"Excuse me?" She takes off her glasses and places them on the table with great care. "Are you seriously asking what loving the woman you're going to marry has to do with actually marrying her?" Her voice pulses with fury.

"Yes, exactly. Why don't you explain it to me?" The sarcasm in my tone is impossible to miss.

She stares at me from behind those large glasses that should make her look owlish and studious, but only add an edge of what I can only describe as quirky-sexiness. The few times I've met her before, she's gotten on my nerves so much, I couldn't wait to get the hell away from her. Now, giving her the full benefit of my attention, I realize, she's actually quite striking. And the addition of those spectacles? Fuck me —I never thought I had a weakness for women wearing glasses. Maybe I was wrong. Or maybe it's specifically this woman wearing glasses… Preferably only glasses and nothing else.

Hmm. Interesting. This reaction to her. It's unwarranted and not something I planned for. I widen my stance, mainly to accommodate the thickness between my legs. An inconvenience… which perhaps I can use to my benefit? I drag my thumb under my lower lip.

Her gaze drops to my mouth, and if I'm not mistaken, her breath hitches. *Very interesting.* Has she always reacted to me like that in the past? Nope, I would've noticed. We've always tried to have as little as possible to do with each other. Like I said, interesting. And unusual.

"First," —she drums her fingers on the table— "are you going to answer my question?"

I tilt my head, the makings of an idea buzzing through my synapses. I need a little time to flesh things out though. It's the only reason I deign to answer her question which, let's face it, I have no obligation to respond to. But for the moment, it's in my interest to humor her and buy myself a little time.

"Priya and I are well-matched in every way. We come from good families—"

"You mean rich families?"

"That, too. Our families move in the same circles."

"Don't you mean boring country clubs?" she says in a voice that drips with distaste.

I frown. "Among other places. We have the pedigree, the blood line, our backgrounds are congruent, and we'd be able to fold into an arrangement of coexistence with the least amount of disruption on either side."

"Sounds like you're arranging a merger."

"A takeover, but what-fucking-ever." I raise a shoulder.

Her scowl deepens. "This is how you approached the upcoming wedding... And you wonder why Priya left you?"

"I gave her the biggest ring money could buy—"

"You didn't make an appearance at an engagement party."

"I signed off on all the costs related to the upcoming nuptials—"

"Your own engagement party. You didn't come to it. You left her alone to face her family and friends." Her tone rises. Her cheeks are flushed. You'd think she was talking about her own wedding, not that of her friend. In fact, it's more entertaining to talk to her than discuss business matters with my employees. *How interesting.*

"You also didn't show up for most of the rehearsals." She glowers.

"I did show up for the last one."

"Not that it made any difference. You were either checking your watch and indicating that it was time for you to leave, or you were glowering at the plans being discussed."

"I still agreed to that god-awful wedding cake, didn't I?

"On the other hand, it's probably good you didn't come for the previous rehearsals. If you had, Priya and I might have had this conversation earlier—"

"Aha!" I straighten. "So, you confess that it's because of you Priya walked away from this wedding."

She tips her head back. "Hardly. It's because of you."

"So you say, but your guilt is writ large on your face."

"Guilt?" Her features flush. The color brings out the dewy hue of her skin, and the blue of her eyes deepens until they remind me of forget-me-nots. No, more like the royal blue of the ink that spilled onto my paper the first time I attempted to write with a fountain pen.

"The only person here who should feel guilty is you, for attempting to coerce an innocent, young woman into an arrangement that would have trapped her for life."

Anger thuds at my temples. My pulse begins to race. "I never have to coerce women. And what you call being trapped is what most women call security. But clearly, you wouldn't know that, considering" —I wave my hand in the air— "you prefer to run your kitchen-table business which, no doubt, barely makes ends meet."

She loosens her grip on her pencil, and it falls to the table with a clatter. Sparks flash deep in her eyes.

You know what I said earlier about the royal blue? Strike that. There are flickers of silver hidden in the depths of her gaze. Flickers that blaze when she's upset. How would it be to push her over the edge? To be at the receiving end of all that passion, that fervor, that ardor… that absolute avidness of existence when she's one with the moment? How would it feel to rein in her spirit, to absorb it, drink from it, revel in it, and use it to spark color into my life?

"Kitchen-table business?" She makes a growling sound under her breath. "You dare come into my office and insult my enterprise? The company I have grown all by myself—"

"And outside of your assistant" —I nod toward the door I came through— "you're the sole employee, I take it?"

Her color deepens. "I work with a group of vendors—"

I scoff, "None of whom you could hold accountable when they don't deliver."

"—who have been carefully vetted to ensure that they always deliver." She says at the same time. "Anyway, why do you care, since you don't have a wedding to go to?"

"That's where you're wrong." I peel back my lips. "I'm not going to be labelled as the joke of the century. Not after all of the invites have gone out, and with guests already on their way to attend the 'wedding of the century.'" I make air-quotes with my fingers. Not that I care about what the media calls my upcoming nuptials. It was Priya's idea, no doubt, fueled by Ms. Incompetent here, to build it up and invite influencers from all walks of life to attend, most of whom I have no interest in meeting. The publicity, though, has been beneficial. And it's not like I'll ever tell her, but I have Isla to thank for that. Nothing like a wedding to have the most hard-nosed investors develop warm, fuzzy feelings. Which will help with the IPO I have planned for the most important company in my portfolio. "I have a lot riding on this wedding."

"Too bad you don't have a bride."

"Ah" —I smirk— "but I do."

She scowls. "No, you don't. Priya—"

"I'm not talking about her."

"Then who are you talking about?"

"You."

Isla

I stare, sure I haven't heard him correctly. "Eh? What are you talking about?" I shake my head, as if that might clear it. "If this is some kind of joke—"

"Not a joke." He slides his hand into the pocket of his tailor-made slacks. "There's no way I'm not going ahead with that wedding. And I do need a bride. Ergo—" He tilts his head as if his words are self-explanatory.

"I'm afraid you're making no sense."

His lips twist. "Oh, you definitely need to be afraid, but of the repercussions from turning me down."

I scowl. "This entire conversation is fascinating but as you can see" —I gesture to the computer in front of me— "I have *miles to go and promises to keep.*"

"Quoting Frost won't change the fact that you're going to be marrying me in" —he pulls back his coat sleeve, exposing a watch that I have no doubt cost more than the annual rent of my office, and which is nestled amidst a smattering of dark hair on his thick wrist— "exactly forty hours."

A shiver of something—excitement, apprehension, nervousness, disbelief... maybe all of the above—ripples under my skin.

"I think you'd better leave."

"I think *you'd* better start making preparations to make things up to me." Bastard's grin widens. He's enjoying himself at my expense, no doubt about it.

Anger bubbles up, and I tamp it down. I can't afford to lose my temper. Liam Stick-in-the-mud Kincaid may not be utilizing my services any longer, but he's one of the most powerful men on this continent—in the world, even—and the last thing I want is to make an enemy of him. I curl my fingers into fists, draw in a breath, then another. When I finally speak, my tone is even. "What things? I don't have anything to make up to you."

"Oh, but you do. It's because of you my bride decided to jilt me at the altar—"

"You didn't reach the altar," I point out.

"Semantics—"

"Are everything." I allow myself a small, tight smile. I'm not going to let this gazillionaire-McGrumpy walk all over me. I have a couple of weddings to plan right after this one. They are nowhere near as high profile as Priya's but they'll keep me busy for a while. All the more reason to get this twatwaffle out of here.

"Which is why I can't marry you."

His dark eyes further. "Sure you can."

"I can't, I'm already married."

He lowers his gaze to my left hand before I have a chance to cover it. *Shit, shit, shit.*

"So, you're not only a bad friend, you're also a bad liar."

I shoot up to my feet. "I'm not a bad friend. I'm a good friend. The kind who had the courage to tell Priya exactly what she needed to hear when no one else had the guts to tell her the truth."

"You ruined her life."

"I gave her a chance to live life on her own terms, and I'm not a liar."

He smirks. "You lied that you were married."

"I am married."

"You're not wearing a ring."

"Plenty of married women don't wear rings."

His smile grows broader, and it's not a nice one. The hair on the back of my neck rises. Why do I get the feeling that I've walked into a trap?

He leans forward on the balls of his feet. "Isla Wilson, twenty-five, university dropout. Mother and brother live in Lymington. You had a happy childhood, until your father died of a heart attack when you were eighteen. A fact that made you decide to drop out of college and travel the world."

"That's very presumptuous of you to think one was linked to the other."

"Doesn't take much to join the dots."

"Go on," I say slowly.

"You tried your hand at being a tie-dye designer—"

"I like colors."

"A diving instructor—"

"I like the colors of fishes underwater." I raise a shoulder.

"A beekeeper."

"I like the color of—"

"Bees?" He smirks.

"I was going to say honey, but yeah, sure, bees, too."

"A professional bridesmaid?" He arches an eyebrow.

"Weddings can be very colorful, you know? Also, you'll be surprised how lucrative a job it is. Also—" I frown. "How do you know all this?"

"It's on your bio on your website," he points out.

Of course, it is.

"I also had you investigated."

I gape at him. "You had me investigated?"

"You didn't think I'd allow you to plan my wedding without making sure your background was acceptable? Which also means, I know you're not married."

I plant my hands on my hips. "And I intend to stay that way. I'm focused on building my career and my company—"

"And there won't be much of that left, considering I'll personally make sure you never work in this country or on this continent—or in fact, organize any wedding anywhere in the world—again."

My heart flips up into my throat, and my pulse begins to race. "You wouldn't do that."

"Try me." He reaches over, picks up the pencil I was using earlier, then twirls it between his fingers.

I try to focus on the action, but the scene in front of my eyes blurs. I blink away the hot tears that have accumulated in my eyes, and set my jaw. "You're blackmailing me."

He raises his gaze skyward. "Finally, she gets it."

"So, if I don't marry you, you'll destroy my career and my reputation."

He lowers the pencil to the table. "You'll pose as my wife. Put up a united front with me to my family. Convince them and my friends how much you love me. Also, you need to produce an heir—"

What the—? I shake my head. "Whoa, whoa, whoa. Hold on. Back up. What do you mean, 'an heir'?" I make air quotes with my fingers.

"I need to be married and have a child before I can get ownership of my business."

"You talk like this is a stipulation of some kind..."

He shuffles his feet. For the first time since he prowled into my room, he seems less than confident. In fact, he looks downright pissed. "My father's will says, unless I marry and produce an heir by the time I'm forty, I won't inherit my company or get access to my trust-fund."

"I see." I lean back in my seat. "So, this is why you proposed to Priya and hustled her into marrying you."

"If by that you mean I courted her—"

"You used your charisma to unduly influence her."

"—I wooed her, took her on dates, to dinners, even the blasted opera, then bought her the biggest engagement ring I could lay my hands on."

"You mean that tasteless hunk of stone on her finger?" I cover my mouth and cough. "No wonder it was so easy to convince her to walk away from you."

His jaw tics. A nerve pops at his temple. He looks about ready to burst out his uber-fitted suit. Oh, goodie. At least I got a rise out of him. That has to count for something, eh?

"That tasteless hunk of stone cost close to a million dollars," he says through gritted teeth.

"Money isn't everything," I announce in a prim voice.

"You certainly weren't complaining when you chose the most expensive venue possible for the wedding."

I straighten my spine. "If you mean the All Villa in Bali, that was Priya's choice. She wanted to get married in Bali, you know."

"And, no doubt, you jumped at the idea, considering you get a fifteen percent commission on the entire cost of the wedding."

"Hey, you get what you pay for. I've been busting my ass for the past few months to get this event organized. Do you even know what an impossible task I've pulled off? I've managed to get all of the preparations completed in eight weeks. Eight bloody weeks. That's just forty-two days. It normally takes close to a year to organize a ceremony of this scale. And I pulled it off in less than one-fourth that time."

"Good, so it won't be a problem to flip things around to accommodate yourself as the bride, too."

"I never said I was going to marry you."

"Haven't you been listening to anything I've been saying?" His features grow even harder. Grays and greens shoot through the blue of his eyes, until the color resembles that of a gathering storm. "If it's custody of the child you're worried about, once you deliver the child, we will separate. There'll be a prenup, of course, but I'll make sure you're reimbursed for your time." He says all of this in a voice so casual, he might as well be asking about the weather. No, strike that. I've heard people speak with more emotion about the weather changes in London than he has about his entire crazy-ass idea.

I curl my fingers into fists and resist the urge to leap up screaming. *Won't do to lose it. Need to keep my cool. Need to make him see just how crazy this entire conversation is.* "Have you even heard yourself? We barely know each other, and now you're saying you want me to marry you—instead of the woman the world thinks you're going to marrying. Not only that, you want me to produce a child, and then you'll divorce me?"

"We'll co-parent and have equal rights to the child." He raises his arms in a conciliatory gesture. "I'm not the kind who'll keep a mother away from her child."

"Of course not," I scoff. "But you're the kind who'd force a woman to marry him."

"Fake marry."

"Doesn't seem fake when we're supposed to produce an heir," I protest.

"There are ways of doing it without my having to touch you. Unless" —he looks me up and down and a calculating look comes into his eyes— "unless you prefer it to be done the old-fashioned way. In which case, I might oblige you. If you ask me nicely, that is."

My head spins. My heart seems to have taken up permanent residence in my throat. My stomach feels like a twister has become entangled inside.

"You're not making any sense. You can't walk in and threaten me into marrying you, then announce you need me to produce a child for you, in the same breath."

His grin widens. "I just did."

"There's still time." I raise my hands. "Walk away now, and I'll forget any of this happened. In fact, I won't even go to the media with news of how you intimidated me."

"You're not going to do that."

"Oh, yeah?" I shove the hair back from my face. "And why is that?"

"Because when you marry me, even though the marriage is fake, no one else will know. To the outside world, you'll be the wife of Liam Kincaid, which means, doors will automatically open for you. Your past transgressions—"

"Transgressions?" I shout.

"Transgressions" —he firms his lips— "will be forgotten. Socialites and influencers will queue up to patronize your services. You'll run the most successful wedding planning outfit in this country, if not all of the continent."

I blink. Now that he mentions it… it's true. Once I hitch my star to the Liam Kincaid reputation, it'll be easy sailing. Everyone will want a piece of my wedding planning company. I'll have more projects than I can handle.

"Your showpieces will, of course, be your own wedding. You can give it any twist you like; make it the kind of wedding you've always imagined for yourself."

"For myself?"

"You must have thought about how you'd like to get married." He glances at his watch and straightens. "Well, this is your chance to execute it. Use it to show the world and all the headline seekers exactly how it should be done."

"S-o-o-o, I can do anything I want for my wedding ceremony?" I pluck at the rubber band around my wrist.

"Yes."

"The budget?"

"Unlimited. I'll need to sign off on the bills, but nothing is too good for my bride. Whatever you want, you can have it."

I squeeze my fingers together. Surely, I'm not considering this. I'm not actually thinking of going through with this insane proposal of his. On the other hand, if I do, I'll have everything I want. The wedding of my dreams, the chance to prove a point to all the naysayers who thought I'd never make it, and a resounding 'fuck you' to all my competition. Hell, there won't be competition. I'll wipe them off the map with this show-piece of a wedding. No one will ever question my competency again. And I'll have enough clients to keep me going for years. Even after I divorce him, it won't make a dent in my reputation.

"Well?" He scowls. "What's it gonna be?"

I pluck at the rubber band with more intensity. "So, I can transform it into the wedding of my dreams, the kind that'll make every media outlet, gossip magazine, and wedding blog sit up and take notice?"

"Do you not understand English? Or have you not been listening to me?"

I straighten in my seat. "I heard you the first time," I say in a low voice.

"Good, so what's your answer?"

To find out what happens next read *Liam and Isla's* story **HERE**

Read *Sinclair and Summer's* story **HERE**

Read *Michael and Karma's* story **HERE**

Want to read a deleted scene from *Mafia Lust* featuring *Lena and JJ*? Click **HERE**

Read an excerpt from *Mafia King – Michael and Karma's* story

Karma

"Morn came and went—and came, and brought no day…"

Tears prick the backs of my eyes. Goddamn Byron. His words creep up on me when I am at my weakest. Not that I am a poetry addict, by any measure, but words are my jam. The one consolation I have is that, when everything else in the world is wrong, I can turn to them, and they'll be there, friendly, steady, waiting with open arms.

And this particular poem had laced my blood, crawled into my gut when I'd first read it. Darkness had folded within me like an insidious snake, that raises its head when I least expect it. Like now, when I look out on the still sleeping city of London, from the grassy slope of Waterlow Park.

Somewhere out there, the Mafia is hunting me, apparently. It's why my sister Summer and her new husband Sinclair Sterling had insisted that I have my own security detail. I had agreed... only to appease them... then given my bodyguard the slip this morning. I had decided to come running here because it's not a place I'd normally go... Not so early in the morning, anyway. They won't think to look for me here. At least, not for a while longer.

I purse my lips, close my eyes. Silence. The rustle of the wind between the leaves. The faint tinkle of the water from the nearby spring.

I could be the last person on this planet, alone, unsung, bound for the grave.

Ugh! Stop. Right there. I drag the back of my hand across my nose. Try it again, focus, get the words out, one after the other, like the steps of my sorry life.

"Morn came and went—and came, and… and…" My voice breaks. "Bloody asinine hell." I dig my fingers into the grass and grab a handful and fling it out. Again. From the top.

"Morn came and went—and came, and—"

"…brought no day."

A gravelly voice completes my sentence.

I whip my head around. His silhouette fills my line of sight. He's sitting on the same knoll as me, yet I have to crane my neck back to see his profile. The sun is at his back, so I can't make out his features. Can't see his eyes... Can only take in his dark hair, combed back by a ruthless hand that brooked no measure.

My throat dries.

Thick dark hair, shot through with grey at the temples. He wears his age like a badge. I don't know why, but I know his years have not been easy. That he's seen more, indulged in more, reveled in the consequences of his actions, however extreme they might have been. He's not a normal, everyday person, this man. Not a nine-to-fiver, not someone who lives an average life. Definitely not a man who returns home to his wife and home at the end of the day. He is...different, unique, evil… Monstrous. Yes, he is a beast, one who sports the face of a man but who harbors the kind of darkness inside that speaks to me. I gulp.

His face boasts a hooked nose, a thin upper lip, a fleshy lower lip. One that hints at hidden desires, Heat. Lust. The sensuous scrape of that whiskered jaw over my innermost places. Across my inner thigh, reaching toward that core of me that throbs, clenches, melts to feel the stab of his tongue, the thrust of his hardness as he impales me, takes me, makes me his. Goosebumps pop on my skin.

I drag my gaze away from his mouth down to the scar that slashes across his throat. A cold sensation coils in my chest. What or who had hurt him in such a cruel fashion?

"Of this their desolation; and all hearts
Were chill'd into a selfish prayer for light…"

He continues in that rasping guttural tone. Is it the wound that caused that scar that makes his voice so… gravelly… So deep… so… so, hot?

Sweat beads my palms and the hairs on my nape rise. "Who are you?"

He stares ahead as his lips move,

"Forests were set on fire—but hour by hour
They fell and faded—and the crackling trunks
Extinguish'd with a crash—and all was black."

I swallow, moisture gathers in my core. How can I be wet by the mere cadence of this stranger's voice?

I spring up to my feet.

"Sit down," he commands.

His voice is unhurried, lazy even, his spine erect. The cut of his black jacket stretches across the width of his massive shoulders. His hair... I was mistaken—there are threads of dark gold woven between the darkness that pours down to brush the nape of his neck. A strand of hair falls over his brow. As I watch, he raises his hand and brushes it away. Somehow, the gesture lends an air of vulnerability to him. Something so at odds with the rest of his persona that, surely, I am mistaken?

My scalp itches. I take in a breath and my lungs burn. This man... He's sucked up all the oxygen in this open space as if he owns it, the master of all he surveys. The master of me. My death. My life. A shiver ladders along my spine. *Get away, get away now, while you still can.*

I angle my body, ready to spring away from him.

"I won't ask again."

Ask. Command. Force me to do as he wants. He'll have me on my back, bent over, on my side, on my knees, over him, under him. He'll surround me, overwhelm me, pin me down with the force of his personality. His charisma, his larger-than-life essence will crush everything else out of me and I... I'll love it.

"No."

"Yes."

A fact. A statement of intent, spoken aloud. So true. So real. Too real. Too much. Too fast. All of my nightmares... my dreams come to life. Everything I've wanted is here in front of me. I'll die a thousand deaths before he'll be done with me... And then? Will I be reborn? For him. For me. For myself.

I live, first and foremost, to be the woman I was... am meant to be.

"You want to run?"

No.

No.

I nod my head.

He turns his, and all the breath leaves my lungs. Blue eyes— cerulean, dark like the morning skies, deep like the nighttime...hidden corners, secrets that I don't dare uncover. He'll destroy me, have my heart, and break it so casually.

My throat burns and a boiling sensation squeezes my chest.

"Go then, my beauty, fly. You have until I count to five. If I catch you, you are mine."

"If you don't?"

"Then I'll come after you, stalk your every living moment, possess your nightmares, and steal you away in the dead of night, and then…"

I draw in a shuddering breath as liquid heat drips from between my legs. "Then?" I whisper.

"Then, I'll ensure you'll never belong to anyone else, you'll never see the light of day again, for your every breath, your every waking second, your thoughts, your actions… and all your words, every single last one, will belong to me." He peels back his lips, and his teeth glint in the first rays of the morning light. "Only me." He straightens to his feet and rises, and rises.

This man… He is massive. A monster who always gets his way. My guts churn. My toes curl. Something primeval inside of me insists I hold my own. I cannot give in to him. Cannot let him win whatever this is. I need to stake my ground, in some form. *Say something. Anything. Show him you're not afraid of this.*

"Why?" I tilt my head back, all the way back. "Why are you doing this?"

He tilts his head, his ears almost canine in the way they are silhouetted against his profile.

"Is it because you can? Is it a… a," I blink, "a debt of some kind?"

He stills.

"My father, this is about how he betrayed the Mafia, right? You're one of them?"

"Lucky guess." His lips twist, "It is about your father, and how he promised you to me. He reneged on his promise, and now, I am here to collect."

"No." I swallow… *No, no, no.*

"Yes." His jaw hardens.

All expression is wiped clean of his face, and I know then, that he speaks the truth. It's always about the past. My sorry shambles of a past… Why does it always catch up with me? *You can run, but you can never hide.*

"Tick-tock, Beauty." He angles his body and his shoulders shut out the sight of the sun, the dawn skies, the horizon, the city in the distance, the rustle of the grass, the trees, the rustle of the leaves. All of it fades and leaves just me and him. Us. *Run.*

"Five." He jerks his chin, straightens the cuffs of his sleeves.

My knees wobble.

"Four."

My pulse rate spikes. I should go. Leave. But my feet are planted in this earth. This piece of land where we first met. What am I, but a speck in the larger scheme of things? To be hurt. To be forgotten. To be taken without an ounce of retribution. To be punished... by him.

"Three." He thrusts out his chest, widens his stance, every muscle in his body relaxed. "Two."

I swallow. The pulse beats at my temples. My blood thrums.

"One."

Michael

"Go."

She pivots and races down the slope. Her dark hair streams behind her. Her scent, sexy femininity and silver moonflowers, clings to my nose, then recedes. It's so familiar, that scent.

I had smelled it before, had reveled in it. Had drawn in it into my lungs as she had peeked up at me from under her thick eyelashes. Her green gaze had fixed on mine, her lips parted as she welcomed my kiss. As she had wound her arms about my neck, pushed up those sweet breasts and flattened them against my chest. As she had parted her legs when I had planted my thigh between them. I had seen her before... in my dreams. I stiffen. She can't be the same girl, though, can she?

I reach forward, thrust out my chin and sniff the air, but there's only the damp scent of dawn, mixed with the foul tang of exhaust fumes, as she races away from me.

She stumbles and I jump forward, pause when she straightens. Wait. Wait. Give her a lead. Let her think she has almost escaped, that she's gotten the better of me... As if.

I clench my fists at my sides, force myself to relax. Wait. Wait. She reaches the bottom of the incline, turns. I surge forward. One foot in front of the other. My heels dig into the grassy surface and mud flies up, clings to the hem of my £4000 Italian pants. Like I care? Plenty more where that came from. An entire walk-in closet, full of clothes made to measure, to suit every occasion, with every possible accessory needed by a man in my position to impress…

Everything… Except the one thing that I had coveted from the moment I had laid eyes on her. Sitting there on the grassy slope, unshed tears in her eyes, and reciting… Byron? For hell's sake. Of all the poets in the world, she had to choose the Lord of Darkness.

I huff. All a ploy. Clearly, she knew I was sitting next to her… No, not possible. I had walked toward her and she hadn't stirred. Hadn't been aware. Yeah, I am that good. I've been known to slit a man's throat from ear-to-ear while he was awake and in his full senses. Alive one second, dead the next. That's how it is in my world. You want it, you take it. And I… I want her.

I increase my pace, eat up the distance between myself and the girl… That's all she is. A slip of a thing, a slim blur of motion. Beauty in hiding. A diamond, waiting for me to get my hands on her, polish her, show her what it means to be…

Dead. She is dead. That's why I am here.

A flash of skin, a creamy length of thigh. My groin hardens and my legs wobble. I lurch over a bump in the ground. The hell? I right myself, leap forward, inching closer, closer. She reaches a curve in the path, disappears out of sight.

My heart hammers in my chest. I will not lose her, will not. *Here, Beauty, come to Daddy.* The wind whistles past my ears. I pump my legs, lengthen my strides, turn the corner. There's no one there. Huh?

My heart hammers and the blood pounds at my wrists, my temples; adrenaline thrums in my veins. I slow down, come to a stop. Scan the clearing.

The hairs on my forearms prickle. She's here. Not far, but where? Where is she? I prowl across to the edge of the clearing, under the tree with its spreading branches.

When I get my hands on you, Beauty, I'll spread your legs like the pages of a poem. Dip into your honeyed sweetness, like a quill pen in ink. Drag my aching shaft across that melting, weeping entrance. My balls throb. My groin tightens. The crack of a branch above shivers across my stretched nerve endings. I swoop forward, hold out my arms, and close my grasp around the trembling, squirming mass of precious humanity. I cradle her close to my chest, heart beating thud-thud-thud, over-whelming any other thought.

Mine. All mine. The hell is wrong with me? She wriggles her little body, and her curves slide across my forearms. My shoulders bunch and my fingers tingle. She kicks out with her legs and arches her back, thrusting her breasts up so her nipples are outlined against the fabric of her sports bra. She dared to come out dressed like that? In that scrap of fabric that barely covers her luscious flesh?

"Let me go." She whips her head toward me and her hair flows around her shoulders, across her face. She blows it out of the way. "You monster, get away from me."

Anger drums at the backs of my eyes and desire tugs at my groin. The scent of her is sheer torture, something I had dreamed of in the wee hours of twilight when dusk turned into night.

She's not real. She's not the woman I think she is. She is my down-fall. My sweet poison. The bitter medicine I must partake of to cure the ills that plague my company.

"Fine." I lower my arms and she tumbles to the grass, hits the ground butt first.

"How dare you." She huffs out a breath, her hair messily arranged across her face.

I shove my hands into the pockets of my fitted pants, knees slightly bent, legs apart. Tip my chin down and watch her as she sprawls at my feet.

"You… dropped me?" She makes a sound deep in her throat.

So damn adorable.

"Your wish is my command." I quirk my lips.

"You don't mean it."

"You're right." I lean my weight forward on the balls of my feet and she flinches.

"What… what do you want?"

"You."

She pales. "You want to… to rob me? I have nothing of consequence.

"Oh, but you do, Beauty."

I lean in and every muscle in her body tenses. Good. She's wary. She should be. She should have been alert enough to have run as soon as she sensed my presence. But she hadn't.

I should spare her because she's the woman from my dreams… but I won't. She's a debt I intend to collect. She owes me, and I've delayed what was meant to happen long enough.

I pull the gun from my holster, point it at her.

Her gaze widens and her breath hitches. I expect her to plead with me for her life, but she doesn't. She stares back at me with her huge dilated pupils. She licks her lips and the blood drains to my groin. *Che cazzo!* Why does her lack of fear turn me on so?

"Your phone," I murmur, "take out your phone."

She draws in a breath, then reaches into her pocket and pulls out her phone.

"Call your sister."

"What?"

"Dial your sister, Beauty. Tell her you are going away on a long trip to Sicily with your new male friend."

"What?"

"You heard me." I curl my lips. "Do it, now!'

She blinks, looks like she is about to protest, then her fingers fly over the phone.

Damn, and I had been looking forward to coaxing her into doing my bidding.

She holds her phone to her ear. I can hear the phone ring on the other side, before it goes to voicemail. She glances at me and I jerk my chin. She looks away, takes a deep breath, then speaks in a cheerful voice, "Hi Summer, it's me, Karma. I, ah, have to go away for a bit. This new… ah, friend of mine… He has an extra ticket and he has invited me to Sicily to spend some time with him. I… ah, I don't know when, exactly, I'll be back, but I'll message you and let you know. Take care. Love ya sis, I—"

I snatch the phone from her, disconnect the call, then hold the gun to her temple, "Goodbye, Beauty."

To find out what happens next read Mafia King **HERE**

Read Summer & Sinclair Sterling's story **HERE** in The Billionaire's Fake Wife

Read an excerpt from Summer & Sinclair's story

Summer

"Slap, slap, kiss, kiss."

"Huh?" I stare up at the bartender.

"Aka, there's a thin line between love and hate." He shakes out the crimson liquid into my glass.

"Nah." I snort. "Why would she allow him to control her, and after he insulted her?"

"It's the chemistry between them." He lowers his head, "You have to admit that when the man is arrogant and the woman resists, it's a challenge to both of them, to see who blinks first, huh?"

"Why?" I wave my hand in the air, "Because they hate each other?"

"Because," he chuckles, "the girl in school whose braids I pulled and teased mercilessly, is the one who I—"

"Proposed to?" I huff.

His face lights up. "You get it now?"

Yeah. No. A headache begins to pound at my temples. This crash course in pop psychology is not why I came to my favorite bar in Islington, to meet my best friend, who is—I glance at the face of my phone—thirty minutes late.

I inhale the drink, and his eyebrows rise.

"What?" I glower up at the bartender. "I can barely taste the alcohol. Besides, it's free drinks at happy hour for women, right?"

"Which ends in precisely" he holds up five fingers, "minutes."

"Oh! Yay!" I mock fist pump. "Time enough for one more, at least."

A hiccough swells my throat and I swallow it back, nod.

One has to do what one has to do… when everything else in the world is going to shit.

A hot sensation stabs behind my eyes; my chest tightens. Is this what people call growing up?

The bartender tips his mixing flask, strains out a fresh batch of the ruby red liquid onto the glass in front of me.

"Salut." I nod my thanks, then toss it back. It hits my stomach and tendrils of fire crawl up my spine, I cough.

My head spins. Warmth sears my chest, spreads to my extremities. I can't feel my fingers or toes. Good. Almost there. "Top me up."

"You sure?"

"Yes." I square my shoulders and reach for the drink.

"No. She's had enough."

"What the—?" I pivot on the bar stool.

Indigo eyes bore into me.

Fathomless. Black at the bottom, the intensity in their depths grips me. He swoops out his arm, grabs the glass and holds it up. Thick fingers dwarf the glass. Tapered at the edges. The nails short and buff. *All the better to grab you with.* I gulp.

"Like what you see?"

I flush, peer up into his face.

Hard cheekbones, hollows under them, and a tiny scar that slashes at his left eyebrow. *How did he get that?* Not that I care. My gaze slides to his mouth. Thin upper lip, a lower lip that is full and cushioned. Pouty with a hint of bad boy. *Oh!* My toes curl. My thighs clench.

The corner of his mouth kicks up. *Asshole.*

Bet he thinks life is one big smug-fest. I glower, reach for my glass, and he holds it up and out of my reach.

I scowl. "Gimme that."

He shakes his head.

"That's my drink."

"Not anymore." He shoves my glass at the bartender. "Water for her. Get me a whiskey, neat."

I splutter, then reach for my drink again. The barstool tips in his direction. This is when I fall against him, and my breasts slam into his hard chest, sculpted planes with layers upon layers of muscle that ripple and writhe as he turns aside, flattens himself against the bar. The floor rises up to meet me.

What the actual hell?

I twist my torso at the last second and my butt connects with the surface. *Ow!*

The breath rushes out of me. My hair swirls around my face. I scramble for purchase, and my knee connects with his leg.

"Watch it." He steps around, stands in front of me.

"You stepped aside?" I splutter. "You let me fall?"

"Hmph."

I tilt my chin back, all the way back, look up the expanse of muscled thigh that stretches the silken material of his suit. *What is he wearing? Could any suit fit a man with such precision?* Hand crafted on Saville Row, no doubt. I glance at the bulge that tents the fabric between his legs. *Oh!* I blink.

Look away, look away. I hold out my arm. He'll help me up at least, won't he?

He glances at my palm, then turns away. *No, he didn't do that, no way.*

A glass of amber liquid appears in front of him. He lifts the tumbler to his sculpted mouth.

His throat moves, strong tendons flexing. He tilts his head back, and the column of his neck moves as he swallows. Dark hair covers his chin—it's a discordant chord in that clean-cut profile, I shiver. He would scrape that rough skin down my core. He'd mark my inner thighs, lick my core, thrust his tongue inside my melting channel and drink from my pussy. *Oh! God.* Goosebumps rise on my skin.

No one has the right to look this beautiful, this achingly gorgeous. Too magnificent for his own good. Anger coils in my chest.

"Arrogant wanker."

"I'll take that under advisement."

"You're a jerk, you know that?"

He presses his lips together. The grooves on either side of his mouth deepen. Jesus, clearly the man has never laughed a single day in his life. Bet that stick up his arse is uncomfortable. I chuckle.

He runs his gaze down my features, my chest, down to my toes, then yawns.

The hell! I will not let him provoke me. Will not. "Like what you see?" I jut out my chin.

"Sorry, you're not my type." He slides a hand into the pocket of those perfectly cut pants, stretching it across that heavy bulge.

Heat curls low in my belly.

Not fair, that he could afford a wardrobe that clearly shouts his status and what amounts to the economy of a small third-world country. A hot feeling stabs in my chest.

He reeks of privilege, of taking his status in life for granted.

While I've had to fight every inch of the way. Hell, I am still battling to hold onto the last of my equilibrium.

"Last chance—" I wiggle my fingers from where I am sprawled out on the floor at his feet, "—to redeem yourself…"

"You have me there." He places the glass on the counter, then bends and holds out his hand. The hint of discolored steel at his wrist catches my attention. Huh?

He wears a cheap-ass watch?

That's got to bring down the net worth of his presence by more than 1000% percent. Weird.

I reach up and he straightens.

I lurch back.

"Oops, I changed my mind." His lips curl.

A hot burning sensation claws at my stomach. I am not a violent person, honestly. But Smirky Pants here, he needs to be taught a lesson.

I swipe out my legs, kicking his out from under him.

Sinclair

My knees give way, and I hurtle toward the ground.

What the—? I twist around, thrust out my arms. My palms hit the floor. The impact jostles up my elbows. I firm my biceps and come to a halt planked above her.

A huffing sound fills my ear.

I turn to find my whippet, Max, panting with his mouth open. I scowl and he flattens his ears.

All of my businesses are dog-friendly. Before you draw conclusions about me being the caring sort or some such shit—it attracts footfall.

Max scrutinizes the girl, then glances at me. *Huh?* He hates women, but not her, apparently.

I straighten and my nose grazes hers.

My arms are on either side of her head. Her chest heaves. The fabric of her dress stretches across her gorgeous breasts. My fingers tingle; my palms ache to cup those tits, squeeze those hard nipples outlined against the—hold on, what is she wearing? A tunic shirt in a sparkly pink... and are those shoulder pads she has on?

I glance up, and a squeak escapes her lips.

Pink hair surrounds her face. *Pink? Who dyes their hair that color past the age of eighteen?*

I stare at her face. *How old is she?* Un-furrowed forehead, dark eyelashes that flutter against pale cheeks. Tiny nose, and that mouth—luscious, tempting. A whiff of her scent, cherries and caramel, assails my senses. My mouth waters. *What the hell?*

She opens her eyes and our eyelashes brush. Her gaze widens. Green, like the leaves of the evergreens, flickers of gold sparkling in their depths. "What?" She glowers. "You're demonstrating the plank position?"

"Actually," I lower my weight onto her, the ridge of my hardness thrusting into the softness between her legs, "I was thinking of something else, altogether."

She gulps and her pupils dilate. *Ah, so she feels it, too?*

I drop my head toward her, closer, closer.

Color floods the creamy expanse of her neck. Her eyelids flutter down. She tilts her chin up.

I push up and off of her.

"That… Sweetheart, is an emphatic 'no thank you' to whatever you are offering."

Her eyelids spring open and pink stains her cheeks. Adorable. Such a range of emotions across those gorgeous features in a few seconds. What else is hidden under that exquisite exterior of hers?

She scrambles up, eyes blazing.

Ah! The little bird is trying to spread her wings? My dick twitches. My groin hardens, *Why does her anger turn me on so, huh?*

She steps forward, thrusts a finger in my chest.

My heart begins to thud.

She peers up from under those hooded eyelashes. "Wake up and taste the wasabi, asshole."

"What does that even mean?"

She makes a sound deep in her throat. My dick twitches. My pulse speeds up.

She pivots, grabs a half-full beer mug sitting on the bar counter.

I growl, "Oh, no, you don't."

She turns, swings it at me. The smell of hops envelops the space.

I stare down at the beer-splattered shirt, the lapels of my camel colored jacket deepening to a dull brown. Anger squeezes my guts.

I fist my fingers at my side, broaden my stance.

She snickers.

I tip my chin up. "You're going to regret that."

The smile fades from her face. "Umm." She places the now empty mug on the bar.

I take a step forward and she skitters back. "It's only clothes." She gulps. "They'll wash."

I glare at her and she swallows, wiggles her fingers in the air. "I should have known that you wouldn't have a sense of humor."

I thrust out my jaw. "That's a ten-thousand-pound suit you destroyed."

She blanches, then straightens her shoulders. "Must have been some hot date you were trying to impress, huh?"

"Actually," I flick some of the offending liquid from my lapels, "it's you I was after."

"Me?" She frowns.

"We need to speak."

She glances toward the bartender who's on the other side of the bar. "I don't know you." She chews on her lower lip, biting off some of the hot pink. How would she look, with that pouty mouth fastened on my cock?

The blood rushes to my groin so quickly that my head spins. My pulse rate ratchets up. Focus, focus on the task you came here for.

"This will take only a few seconds." I take a step forward.

She moves aside.

I frown. "You want to hear this, I promise."

"Go to hell." She pivots and darts forward.

I let her go, a step, another, because... I can? Besides it's fun to create the illusion of freedom first; makes the hunt so much more entertaining, huh?

I swoop forward, loop an arm around her waist, and yank her toward me.

She yelps. "Release me."

Good thing the bar is not yet full. It's too early for the usual office-goers to stop by. And the staff...? Well they are well aware of who cuts their paychecks.

I spin her around and against the bar, then release her. "You will listen to me."

She swallows; she glances left to right.

Not letting you go yet, little Bird. I move into her space, crowd her.

She tips her chin up. "Whatever you're selling, I'm not interested."

I allow my lips to curl. "You don't fool me."

A flush steals up her throat, sears her cheeks. So tiny, so innocent. Such a good little liar. I narrow my gaze. "Every action has its consequences."

"Are you daft?" She blinks.

"This pretense of yours?" I thrust my face into hers, growling, "It's not working."

She blinks, then color suffuses her cheeks. "You're certifiably mad—"

"Getting tired of your insults."

"It's true, everything I said." She scrapes back the hair from her face. Her fingernails are painted... You guessed it, pink.

"And here's something else. You are a selfish, egotistical jackass."

I smirk. "You're beginning to repeat your insults and I haven't even kissed you yet."

"Don't you dare." She gulps.

I tilt my head. "Is that a challenge?"

"It's a..." she scans the crowded space, then turns to me. Her lips firm, "...a warning. You're delusional, you jackass." She inhales a deep breath before she speaks, "Your ego is bigger than the size of a black hole." She snickers. "Bet it's to compensate for your lack of balls."

A-n-d, that's it. I've had enough of her mouth that threatens to never stop spewing words. How many insults can one tiny woman hurl my way? Answer: too many to count.

"You—"

I lower my chin, touch my lips to hers.

Heat, sweetness, the honey of her essence explodes on my palate. My dick twitches. I tilt my head, deepen the kiss, reaching for that something more… more… of whatever scent she's wearing on her skin, infused with that breath of hers that crowds my senses, rushes down my spine. My groin hardens; my cock lengthens. I thrust my tongue between those infuriating lips.

She makes a sound deep in her throat and my heart begins to pound.

So innocent, yet so crafty. Beautiful and feisty. The kind of complication I don't need in my life.

I prefer the straight and narrow. Gray and black, that's how I choose to define my world. She, with her flashes of color—pink hair and lips that threaten to drive me to the edge of distraction—is exactly what I hate.

Give me a female who has her priorities set in life. To pleasure me, get me off, then walk away before her emotions engage. Yeah. That's what I prefer.

Not this… this bundle of craziness who flings her arms around my shoulders, thrusts her breasts up and into my chest, tips up her chin, opens her mouth, and invites me to take and take.

Does she have no self-preservation? Does she think I am going to fall for her wide-eyed appeal? She has another thing coming.

I tear my mouth away and she protests.

She twines her leg with mine, pushes up her hips, so that melting softness between her thighs cradles my aching hardness.

I glare into her face and she holds my gaze.

Trains her green eyes on me. Her cheeks flush a bright red. Her lips fall open and a moan bleeds into the air. The blood rushes to my dick, which instantly thickens. *Fuck.*

Time to put distance between myself and the situation.

It's how I prefer to manage things. Stay in control, always. Cut out anything that threatens to impinge on my equilibrium. Shut it down or buy them off. Reduce it to a transaction. That I understand.

The power of money, to be able to buy and sell—numbers, logic. That's what's worked for me so far.

"How much?"

Her forehead furrows.

"Whatever it is, I can afford it."

Her jaw slackens. "You think… you—"

"A million?"

"What?"

"Pounds, dollars… You name the currency, and it will be in your account."

Her jaw slackens. "You're offering me money?"

"For your time, and for you to fall in line with my plan."

She reddens. "You think I am for sale?"

"Everyone is."

"Not me."

Here we go again. "Is that a challenge?"

Color fades from her face. "Get away from me."

"Are you shy, is that what this is?" I frown. "You can write your price down on a piece of paper if you prefer." I glance up, notice the bartender watching us. I jerk my chin toward the napkins. He grabs one, then offers it to her.

She glowers at him. "Did you buy him, too?"

"What do you think?"

She glances around. "I think everyone here is ignoring us."

"It's what I'd expect."

"Why is that?"

I wave the tissue in front of her face. "Why do you think?"

"You own the place?"

"As I am going to own you."

She sets her jaw. "Let me leave and you won't regret this."

A chuckle bubbles up. I swallow it away. This is no laughing matter. I never smile during a transaction. Especially not when I am negotiating a new acquisition. And that's all she is. The final piece in the puzzle I am building.

"No one threatens me."

"You're right."

"Huh?"

"I'd rather act on my instinct."

Her lips twist, her gaze narrows. All of my senses scream a warning.

No, she wouldn't, no way—pain slices through my middle and sparks explode behind my eyes.

To find out what happens next read Summer & Sinclair Sterling's story HERE

Want to read a deleted scene from Mafia Lust featuring Lena and JJ? Click HERE

Want to be the first to find out when L. Steele's next book releases? Subscribe to her newsletter HERE

Read about the Seven in the Big Bad Billionaires series

US

UK

Other countries

Claim your FREE contemporary romance boxset HERE

Claim your FREE paranormal romance boxset HERE

Follow L. Steele on AMAZON

Follow L. Steele on BookBub

Follow L. Steele on Goodreads

Follow L. Steele on Facebook

Follow L. Steele on Instagram

Join L. Steele's secret Facebook Reader Group

For more books by L. Steele click HERE

FREE DELETED SCENE FROM MAFIA LUST

WANT TO READ A DELETED SCENE FROM MAFIA LUST FEATURING LENA AND JJ? CLICK HERE

FREE BOOKS

Claim your FREE copy of Mafia Heir the prequel to Mafia King

Claim your FREE billionaire romance boxset

More books by L. STEELE

Join L. Steele's Newsletter for news on her newest releases

Claim your FREE copy of Mafia Heir the prequel to Mafia King

Claim your FREE billionaire romance

Claim your free paranormal romance

Follow L. Steele on AMAZON

Follow L. Steele on BookBub

Follow L. Steele on Goodreads

Follow L. Steele on Facebook

Follow L. Steele on Instagram

Join L. Steele's secret Facebook Reader Group

More books by L. Steele HERE

Printed in Great Britain
by Amazon

10766893R00241